WHAT IF YOUR DEATH COULD BRING YOU LIFE?

SECOND
CHANCE

I0593601

KYM STREAT

Clover Life Publishing

Copyright © 2022 Kym Streat.

Cataloguing in Publication Data:
Title: Second Chance
ISBN: 978-0-6453179-0-9 (PB)
ISBN: 978-0-6453179-1-6 (EB)
Subjects: Christian fiction. | Suspense.

Design and layout by Clover Life Publishing.

For those who never got a chance to live…

FOREWORD

Dear Reader,

Coming home from work one evening in 2012, this story dropped into my soul. I even remember the exact set of traffic lights at which it happened. With excitement, I eagerly rushed home, wrote an outline and the first several chapters.... then got caught up in the busyness of 'doing life'. And there it sat on my hard drive...

for… quite… a… long… time.

But God's timing is always perfect.

I never expected that I would publish anything. 'The Lie' was my first novel, and it felt like God literally pushed me to finish it. But when it was complete, I knew that this one, 'Second Chance', was to be next on His list for me to accomplish.

I hope this story affects you—breaks your paradigms, opens your heart, and shows you truth, inspires you and encourages you to rise and make a difference. But mostly... draws you closer to God and His truth!

Kym

A voice is heard in Ramah,
mourning and great weeping,
Rachel weeping for her children
and refusing to be comforted,
because they are no more.

Jeremiah 31:15

CHAPTER ONE

"OH GOD, I CAN'T BREATHE. GOD, GOD—I CAN'T BREATHE. HELP ME... somebody." Jason gasped, sucking in searing hot air. "Where am I? Oh God, I can't see! I can't see... please... somebody turn on the lights... where am I?"

Jason took a small single step with his arms forward, waving and groping through the thick, dense darkness that engulfed him.

"Anybody?" he cried. "Somebody?" he yelled out in part frustration and panic. "Oh God, where am I? It's hot... hot... so damn hot. Where am I? Help me!" The panic rose in Jason's throat, gripping him like a vice around his trachea. The heat burned and snatched away every single breath he made.

"I can't breathe." He turned his head slowly, waiting for his eyes to adjust. "It's so... so hot in here, turn the air conditioning on... WHERE AM I?" he screamed, panic-stricken. His head reeling, trying to recall the events leading up to this moment...

Nothing!

His mind was blank, all but returning immense confusion. The darkness lay heavily upon him. Not a single flicker of light was detected. It was as though light no longer existed. The fear increased, like liquefied mercury it rose from the pit of his stomach.

"This is not normal," he said, turning around, trying to blink through the blackness. "Where the heck am I? Where are the lights… what's going on? TURN ON THE DAMN LIGHTS!" he screamed.

He placed his hand outward, all but an inch in front of his face… Nothing… absolutely nothing. "WHERE AM I?" his hysterical scream cried out into the sheer blackness that surrounded him. He lurched forward, arms flailing about, trying to touch something… anything that would give him some clarity of where he was… a wall, a bed, a lamp… anything.

He took a few steps sideways, arms outstretched, trying to grasp hold of an object, feeling his way and hoping to touch something solid. There was nothing. "Help me!" he cried. "Please, someone help me!" he continued fumbling, arms outstretched as he took small sliding steps forward. And then… he sensed it.

Abruptly he stopped, for it wasn't just darkness, but something worse. It was an immense evil like he had never experienced, and it encased him. It wrapped around him—his skin crawled with it.

"WHERE AM I?" he screamed frantically. "SOMEBODY HELP ME!"

Jason quickly scrambled around blindly. His chest was bursting, his heart in pain—aching, pounding, and racing with immense distress. He wanted to run. He stumbled forward in panic—he could feel the powerful pressure upon him, lurching and groping at him like a desperate and vicious entity, coating him in oppressive fear and blackness.

"I don't understand," he whispered, turning his head from side to side to look through the blackness. "What is going on? Where am I?" Involuntarily, gasps rose from his throat. Sobs of despair and grief bubbled uncontrollably from deep within. Confusion and hopelessness encompassed him. His tears trickled, stinging his hot, dry, burning cheeks. "Help me… somebody!" he pleaded.

"Shut up!" The guttural rasping voice spat with venom.

Jason jumped sideways, wincing in fear, and recoiled to his left. The terror he perceived grew, and the hairs on his arms and body stood upright, tingling and prickling his skin.

Something was beside him—he could feel it… he just couldn't see it. He smelled it though, like a rotting corpse that had the graying, bloated and shredded flesh hanging and peeling from its bones. His senses reeling with the memories of past autopsies of decaying bodies. But this was rank… it was foul, even worse than he had ever remembered.

What is it? He thought, as the fear gripped him. He stood petrified… immobile. Sensing the eyes upon him, boring deep and dangerous into his soul. He knew that whatever it was… it was just watching, waiting for him to speak or move.

He froze for what seemed like minutes until his body broke under the intensity. His stomach lurched and churned. The fear and the nausea were so strong that it burst up through his esophagus and he stumbled forward spewing out the contents into the darkness.

"Ha-ha-haha," guttural laughter erupted, right beside him, echoing in his ears as he continued to vomit. It was merciless and evil.

Where am I? he thought, his mind trying to recapture events. "I don't understand." he spoke aloud for the first time since this thing was beside him.

"You will soon," it said with definite hatred.

"Who… who are you?" Jason asked hesitantly, looking around, trying to study the blackness.

"I am your worst nightmare, Jason."

"What do you m-m-mean?" he stammered, looking into the deep darkness at the direction of the voice, his body shaking and convulsing with sheer terror.

"You'll see!" It spoke and paused. "GATE KEEPER!" Its piercing shout echoed through the darkness, fragmenting any potential hope.

Suddenly, the sounds of scraping iron grinding and grating against solid stone rang out. It vibrated and pierced through the very core of Jason as the screeching of iron hinges opened the giant, blackened, solid plates.

As the darkness gradually disappeared, a glimmer, a dull orange glow, allowed his vision again. The massive black gates slowly swung open, exposing a large tunnel entrance within the solid stone. But what lay before him was a horror he had never imagined or even believed. A being so enormous and grotesque, its body shielded by scales mixed with seeping, festering sores. The stench was putrid, of rancid, rotting flesh and puss. Its head was malformed, with bulges and lumps like that of proteus syndrome. It stood, what must have been at least 30 feet tall, and its yellow bloodshot eyes were sitting unevenly on its face, one of them slightly hanging, drooping from its socket. It had two large, thick, black horns going straight outward from its head like an ox. Its mouth had slimy flesh like cords that seemed to stitch both of its lips together, leaving large openings for its rancid breath to leak out. It stood strong, gripping a hefty black sickle by its side with its enormous clawed hand.

Jason recoiled and stumbled backward with sheer panic-stricken terror. He screamed uncontrollably. His lungs burning and blistering with the hot air as his voice was shrieking frenziedly. He cried again, shaking profusely whilst scrambling and floundering backwards.

"No further!" the first creature behind him spoke as he shoved him forward towards the gate.

"N-n-n, No-No, what do you mean? I don't want to go there." Jason backed away again from the iron gates and the gate keeper standing before him.

"Few of you do." It replied.

"W-what?" Jason stammered. "I don't understand?" he whipped around to face the original voice. Jason didn't think he had anything left in his stomach, but what he saw made him vomit even harder. It was horrid —words could not describe it. He couldn't believe this creature had been beside him all along, watching him and waiting in the darkness.

The beast looked half-wolf and half-lion and it utterly oozed evil. Its long, sharp canine teeth hung longer than its jaw as it stood grinning down at him. Four horns like a goat swept backward over its skull and then curled outward along its mane. Two smaller horns protruded from its forehead. Its eyes were orange like cats' eyes, its body robed in a gray wiry fur, and its claws were shiny black and razor-sharp. Its large, jagged bat-like wings draped down its back like a hefty black cape.

"Haaa, haaaa, haaaaaaaa… Come on stupid, let's go home." It growled, baring its needle-like yellow fangs. It reached out and struck Jason across the head, its long black claws cutting deep into his flesh, ripping shreds of skin from his cheek.

The force spun Jason around to face the massive iron gates once again. He screamed and fell to his knees and clutched his face in agony, feeling the strips of cheek flesh coming off and hanging in his hands. The creature grabbed him and pitched him to his feet, then proceeded relentlessly to thrust him forward through the black gates. He had no choice—He had no power here… he had absolutely nothing.

"Welcome to HELL!" the gate keeper grinned, looking down at Jason as he walked past him through the massive black iron gates.

CHAPTER TWO

"WAKE ME UP! WAKE ME UP!" Jason screamed, "Wake me up!" he repeated over and over, "This isn't happening," he cried. He shouted and beat his chest, trying to wake himself up from this horrendous dream. *I must be sleeping*, he thought. He closed his eyes and screamed, "WAKE UP!" and slapped his own face hard to rip him from this terror nightmare.

The creature behind him kept him moving; it didn't stop shoving, pushing, taunting, and berating Jason. It continued relentlessly to beat him whilst directing him down through the massive stone tunnel.

"I'm dreaming." Jason said aloud. "This isn't happening. Wake me up…. WAKE UP JASON!" he screeched.

The creature burst into laughter once again. "Bahahaha! You dumb fool." it spat. "This is happening and you will never, *ever* leave here. This is where you belong. We *OWN* you," it snarled as it continued to shove Jason in his back, digging its long claws into his flesh at every chance.

Jason winced with pain. The open wounds on his back were throbbing as he reluctantly moved forward. Suddenly, a screech reverberated throughout the tunnel, blasting through Jason's core. He jumped in fright sideways as he looked at the gray face bulging outward from the stone— its arms started reaching for him. It looked part human and part demon. Its teeth were like hundreds of jagged stalactites angled backwards into its yawning, gaping mouth that was pitching toward him, snapping forward, attempting to clasp him in its vicious jaws. Jason halted, for out of the tunnel walls appeared hundreds of them, as if his very presence had awoken them from a deep slumber.

"Keep walking." The creature behind him rasped and shoved him forward.

As he walked onward, the wall demons were clawing and snapping at him, pushing outwards, bulging and bursting from the dark stone walls. They encased their torsos in the stone, but their faces, arms, and sharp claws were free to reach outward to clasp him.

With an ear-splitting scream, they were screeching his name. "Jason, Jason... Come here and be with us, Jason! Come join us!" Over and over, they were relentless. Jason in terror placed his hands tight over his ears, pushing hard to shut them out, walking faster whilst dodging their clasping claws.

The creature continued to march him forward, ignoring the wall demons until it came to the end of the tunnel. It reached forward and opened a large black iron door. The dull orange fiery glow emanated back up throughout the tunnel and the wall demons screamed in retreat, disappearing back into the stone. The creature grabbed hold of Jason and shunted him through the doorway before slamming it hard behind him.

Jason stood in horrific awe and looked upon the barren vastness. It opened up to a flat stone plain, spreading as far as his eyes could see. The cavernous rock formation that formed the ceiling high above was impenetrable. It was like a gigantic cave, and crawling with demons.

Within the stone plane were millions of fire pits smoldering and then igniting like tiny volcanos. As the demon pushed him down the stairs onto the flat rock bed, Jason fell to his knees and gasped in despair. A wave of intense, searing heat engulfed him. His lips instantly cracked and split from the suffocating dryness—his eyes squinted in pain from the scorching air that enclosed him. The stench was putrid, a mix of sulfur and rotting flesh emanating throughout the stifling atmosphere. Relentlessly, the creature picked him up and threw him forward onto his feet again.

"Keep walking," it demanded.

He could never have imagined this place. *The best movie producers could never portray this*, he thought in horrific awe. The sheer heat was unbearable. He felt his skin melt as he walked past each fiery pit and the pain was so acute at every burn he cried out and crumbled to the brown dry stone.

And at every stumble, this creature beat him until he got back on his feet. *What is this place?* he thought despairingly.

He came near one of the fire pits and went to walk past, but this time the creature told him to look. Jason hesitated but decided that he would do what it asked. He peered down into the hole, and what he observed sickened him to the core. He reeled back, not believing what he had just seen. The demon grabbed the back of his neck, forcing him to stare back into the scorching pit.

Whatever was in there seemed human, and they made eye contact.

"Help me!" a meek female voice said with desperation and despair. "Help me please, get me out of here."

At first, Jason's reaction was to recoil away, but the creature held him tight. He looked at her with pity as she stood inside the pit. Her head was bald and her gray flesh was decaying and hanging off in strips; there were gaping holes, allowing him to see inside and right through her body cavity. Jason took a breath and reached outwards, intending to help her. The creature squeezed the back of his head tightly.

"Look, but don't touch," it growled.

"Please help me." She continued, as she sobbed. "I've been here so long." her eyes pleaded, looking up at Jason.

Frightened, but urgently needing to know, Jason spoke, "How long have you been here?"

"This is my 185th year in this place," she sobbed. "I'm sorry, please God, forgive me," she clasped her bony hands together in prayer.

At that moment, she ignited. Flames flickered around her feet, climbing upward and through her. "NO, NO, NO! Please—no more!" she screamed as flames burst through her skin, engulfing her, burning the putrefying flesh from her bones.

Jason tried to avert his eyes, but the demon held his head firm, forcing him to gaze in terror. Her screams rang through his being, vibrating against his chest with the pitch and depth of her pain. He watched her burn before him—his heart ached and his tears evaporated before they even formed. Within minutes the fire died down and she stood in the pit before him as a skeleton of charred gray bones, desperately weeping.

Again, a wave of terror flowed over him, and his body shuddered. He felt the creature's grip tighten on his neck and its black claws biting, piercing his flesh. And then… as he watched to his horror, her own ashen flesh reappeared over her bones. She let out a piercing, agonizing scream as the grayish cadaverous sinews and muscle fibers appeared rapidly, and her body took full form again. She had become human once more.

He reeled back in sickening shock at what he saw, but the creature held him tight. His eyes widened with an intense stare as he saw things moving through the woman's flesh, bulging and stirring under her corpse-like skin and then piercing through it, coming out and then back into her body, squirming throughout her flesh again. She clutched at them, scratching and tearing at her own skin to remove them from her body. She screamed with desperation and panic.

"W-What are they?" Jason murmured. "Oh God, they're worms!" he recoiled backward in revulsion, pushing hard back against the creature's tight grasp. Worms, with thousands of tiny needles for teeth, crawled throughout the woman's frame. They continued to devour her rotting flesh as they moved throughout her entire body.

"Help!" she screamed. "Please help me. I can't go on. Tell people of this place. No one believes it's true… I didn't. Escape and tell them, I beg you… please tell them… Oh God, I want to die. Kill me! I can't continue… God, I hate you; I HATE YOU!" she screamed frantically with rage and torment.

The demon grabbed hold of Jason again and forced him back onto his feet, pitching him forward. As he walked, dread and hopelessness struck him like a wind-knocking punch to his stomach. The gut-wrenching knowledge that there was no escape from here… and no death. He didn't know how he knew… he just did, and the depth of knowledge was overwhelming. The knowing engulfed him and left him utterly wretched with misery. This was death, repeated… again… and again. It was a place of torture where he could never leave. A living terror that words could never come close to describing. It was Hell… and he was here. A wave of overwhelming despair crawled over him like maggots— his knees buckled and he crumbled to the hard-stone ground. The creature squeezed Jason's neck tighter, picked him up, and roughly threw him forward to his feet once again.

"Keep walking," the guttural voice said.

CHAPTER THREE

As Jason walked forward between the pits, people screamed out, begging for mercy, reaching out towards him for help. Some tried to climb out, but demons grabbed them and threw them back into their hole. Swiftly he ducked as hot coals rained from above, hitting and searing into his flesh. He winced as he heard grotesque winged creatures laughing and throwing the coals over everyone below. The millions of screams intensified as the pits erupted in flames again.

He abruptly froze as a hound-like creature raced past him with fiery glowing eyes, large horns, and long sharp spikes covering its shoulders like a mane. He noticed hundreds of them scurrying about between the pits with their oversized jaws and teeth. They were grabbing and dragging out the humans, then fighting over them and tearing them apart. He watched as they ate the slimy graying flesh before throwing them back into the holes again for their bodies to reform.

In the distance, he glimpsed monstrous dragons, some with three or four heads, roaming the vast plain, breathing fire and scorching people, picking them up and throwing them. Other evil beings scuttled about, running around throwing the humans back into their pits again.

Jason screamed in agony as a rat like animal, with burning red eyes and oversized fangs clasped hold of his foot, slicing off his toes. He tried to pull the rat off, but it latched onto his hand, shearing off his thumb. He dropped to the ground and screamed in misery as it scurried away to its next victim.

"HA, HA, HA," the demonic creature laughed. "You'd better get used to the hell rats," he grinned. "Now get on your feet."

As Jason went to stand, he plummeted to the ground again, screaming in agony as his toes and thumb reformed. The pain was profound as he felt the growth of bones and sinew snapping and clicking into place. He groaned with the torturous sensation of the flesh and skin as it moved and stretched back over.

"Get up and keep walking," the demon said as he pitched Jason forward once again.

Jason took a step forward, but as he did, he observed people suspended in mid-air, bound in shackles, and stretched out. They were being tortured by demons doing unspeakable things to them. They pierced some with thousands of long needles, perforating through their whole body. He couldn't believe what he was witnessing. He wanted to vomit again, but there was nothing. He desperately wanted water but knew in his heart that there was none in this place.

"W-where are you taking me?" he stammered.

"You will meet the Master soon and he will decide where to place you."

As Jason stumbled forward, despondency overwhelmed him. The vast scorched rock plain with pits scattered throughout seemed endless, and each contained a human screaming and burning in torturous terror. The noise was deafening, the screeching, screaming, crying, and wailing were unrelenting. People calling out for mercy, saying they were sorry, then spewing out profanities against God. The hatred was so forceful, the raw emotions of fear and suffering were extreme. Jason could no longer think nor breathe; his quick gasps of hot searing air were keeping him exhausted, confused and in unfathomable pain.

Swiftly, Jason stopped astonished as he saw a thick black mass of demons swarming, spiraling upward through a gap in the rock ceiling. It was a gateway out of Hell, back to the surface of the earth.

"Jason, Jason," a voice screamed. "You fool, what are you doing here?"

Startled, he looked up and recoiled in disgust. He recognized him immediately. It was an old college friend suspended just above him. He had a large hook going through his body and around his spine and Jason could see the whiteness of the vertebrae being pulled through the torn, graying flesh of his back. He had another large hook through his eye socket, which skewed his head sideways.

"T-Ted?" Jason whispered with trepidation.

"Yes, you idiot! You should have known about this place. You were the smart one. Why did you come here? Go back and tell them it exists. Tell them it's not a fairy tale or stories. Tell them it's REAL!" he screamed with pain.

Jason looked away; his stomach lurched at the grotesque sight of his old friend.

"Look at me, LOOK AT ME!" Ted screamed. "I have a family, Jason. Get out of here and warn them. Warn my wife and children, my parents. Please, I beg you, don't let them come here. Please help me, Jason… please." He pleaded, "Tell them that God exists, tell them that Hell is real, it's not made up… please tell them that—AAAARGH!" A demon drove a hook through Ted's mouth so he couldn't talk. He screamed in agony, as the hook ripped his cheek flesh off the bone, exposing his upper and lower jawbones and teeth. The demon pulled on the hook in Ted's spine and flew off with him.

Jason again fell to his knees as he saw the demon fly away with Ted across the plain. "G-God, if you're real—please, please help me," he whispered.

"SHUT UP!" The large demon struck him in the side, knocking Jason over. Its long claws ripped into his back, breaking several ribs and piercing through his lungs. "Don't you EVER say that name again," it threatened.

CHAPTER FOUR

Jason was in agony. The ripped flesh on his back and ribs grew and reformed, but the demonic creature remained relentless and unmerciful as it continued to push him along the stone plane.

All of a sudden, the creature cringed as a thunderous rumble echoed throughout the realm. The stony ground shook like an earthquake, and debris and rocks fell downward from the cavernous roof. Jason saw many other demons and creatures kneeling and covering their ears, trembling. The ones in the air had fallen to the ground paralyzed, as though there was an unseen force driving them downward. Then, as suddenly as it started, it stopped, and he watched as the demons got up, enraged, as if something had provoked their anger. The demon behind Jason stood up and struck him—the claws ripped into his flesh and scalp as he fell over and screamed in anguish.

"Down here." the creature rasped as he clutched Jason, picked him up again and quickly turned him towards a stone stairway leading downward.

Jason walked down the stairs with apprehension, and when he landed at the bottom, there were rows upon rows of prison cells. More hideous beings were patrolling the aisles, others pushing and beating, torturing the humans held within their cells. The demon continued pushing and shoving, directing him down an aisle.

"Here." It thrust Jason into an open cell, slamming the iron gate behind him.

Jason stood in the middle of his prison cell… still. *How did I get here?* he thought. "Why am I here?" he moaned.

"It's no use." The voice in the cell beside him said.

Relieved to hear a human voice. Jason stepped closer to the edge of his cell and saw an elderly man sitting on the stone floor in the dim lighting.

"It is pointless. Once you're here, then that's where you will stay for eternity." The man said.

"How do you know this?" Jason responded.

"Because I believe in what the Bible tells me… and this is our lot."

"If you believed what the Bible said, then why the heck are you here?"

"Well," he chuckled, "that's the irony of it," he paused, then got up and walked closer. "I guess it doesn't matter, you're the last person I'll ever speak to before I am placed, so I'll be honest with you, kid. I was a well-known minister, and I preached God's word to a very large congregation… millions, in fact. I had my own TV show on many channels. But to be frank, I loved the money and the lifestyle, and I didn't live what I preached."

"What do you mean?"

"Well kid, it ain't enough to just turn up to church on Sundays, you know, and then live the rest of the week as you please. It doesn't work like that. You have to know, and follow Jesus wholeheartedly." he paused with regret. "Oh, I looked good on the outside. I preached up a storm. I could bring a crowd and entice people to give into the ministry. Other ministries would even hire me to get people to give and raise money for their own benefit. I could bring in the cash, persuade the people to pledge an amount… Oh, I was so good at it. But when I break it all down, I wasn't serving God. I was serving myself… and I lost my reverential fear of God."

He paused and took a deep breath, taking a moment to ponder before he continued. "I accepted Jesus as my Lord and Savior when I was just sixteen-years-old and I knew straight away what my calling was. I knew that I wanted to serve God and preach the gospel to the unsaved. The message burned within my heart like fiery hot coals and I just couldn't wait to get out of Bible college into the real world."

The mans face contorted with remorse and his hard etched facial lines furrowed deeper with the agony of remembrance. "I loved God with all my heart and soul. But as the years went by, people hurt me and let me down. Unforgiveness and offence crept in, and the fire slowly went out. Sadly, I lost my reverence for God." He looked at Jason. "If you can understand what I mean," he sighed, "I continued to preach, but only what they wanted to hear. For instance, I would never preach on Hell or demons as that would scare people away, and heaven forbid, I couldn't have that," he chuckled with sadness, "as fewer people meant less money. Heck, I even told them that Hell wasn't even real." He shook his head with despondence and shame. "*Oh God*, how I have misled people..."

He hesitated for a moment before he spoke again "I would preach on the grace of God, that a loving God would *never* send people to a place like this, and that once saved you were *always* saved. But that's not true either; If you don't continue to follow Christ, then you can't expect to go to Heaven. I-I...", he choked, "I saw some of my former congregation here... burning, screaming out to me, calling me all kinds of names under the sun for the lies I have spoken... the lies they believed... Oh God, I'm so, so sorry." He crumbled to the stone floor, whimpering.

Jason looked on at this wretched soul, curled up in a ball, begging for forgiveness. It was at least five minutes before the preacher sat up and spoke meekly.

"I was in it for my benefit, not God's. I didn't want to put the money back into God's Kingdom, but feather my nest. I owned real estate, cars, jets—you name it, I had it. I'd make charitable donations and create schools with my name stamped on them. But that was it... *my name*, not His." He paused again, pondering and shaking his head in revelation before he continued.

"The funny thing is kid, it's not money that is evil... it's the *love* of it. Money can be a blessing or a curse. If I had loved God like I used to, and given back into His Kingdom like I was supposed to, and not lived for myself... God *may* have blessed me and given me all those material things anyway... and maybe even more. The thing is, I know other ministers that are God-fearing, truth-telling teachers, who God has blessed with riches and they give generously back into the Kingdom, but me... I kept it all to myself, for my gain," he snickered. "And where did it get me? What can money buy here?" he swept his arms outwardly with expression.

"Man cannot serve two masters. Unfortunately, I was foolish and served the wrong one."

"So that's why you're here, because you loved money." Jason pondered. "So that must be why I'm here, too?"

"Kid, you're here because you didn't have a relationship with Jesus Christ and didn't put him first in your life, simple as that. God often gives His people wealth so they can bless others, and make a difference in this sad world... but if you love the money over God, then that's when it becomes dangerous. It's not just the love of money though—it's all kinds of sin. You love doing the sin, then this is your destiny. This is eternity. We will never, ever leave here... except when we are thrown into the lake of fire." The man cracked and moaned. "Oh God, I'm so, so sorry—if only I had listened to your warnings... But it's too late now." he cried.

"What warnings?"

The man wiped his face even though no tears were present. "Many approached me and told me to turn from my ways. They saw right through my pretense and knew I didn't have a genuine relationship with Christ. God had told them to come and warn me I was going to Hell if I didn't change. But I thought I had time. I thought I would repent and ask for Christ's forgiveness at the last minute... before I died."

"SHUT UP WITH THAT NAME, PREACHER." A hideous reptilian creature threatened from across the aisle.

"But..." the man continued carefully, looking around, "I told those people I heard from God too... and that they were all wrong. I belittled and embarrassed them, and sent them away saying they weren't hearing from God at all. I continued to live my life in the same way as, deep down, I didn't want to change. That was until, well... I had a heart attack on the way to a speaking engagement in Houston. I presume my staff have already landed and taken my body off my jet by now." He started to cry again.

"But-but... why? I still don't get why you would be here. I mean, you believe in God, right? I never did... I never thought about it. I believed in absolutely nothing—I thought we died, and that was it."

"You don't get it, do you?" he said, frustrated. "If you do not have a REAL relationship with Jesus Christ, then this is where you will end up."

"SHUT UP, SHUT UP... IF I HAVE TO COME IN THERE, I WILL TEAR YOU APART!" the demon screamed the warning. "Your body is now in the morgue, preacher. Hahaha..." It cackled as it continued walking by.

The preacher grimaced at that thought before he took a breath and continued. "Look, you're here because you didn't believe or follow... you know who," he whispered cautiously. "My life is over; OUR life is done! What we did on earth set us up for where we will spend eternity and... we're *finished*." He shook his head sadly. "This is where we will spend forever, eternity, *infinity*... there is no going back, there is no relief and this will be the last time I will speak with another human properly. The rumors of drinking, parties, sex and fun in Hell are all lies. You've just seen what we are in for... a never-ending torture, a fire that never goes out, constantly burning us, where the worms will eat our flesh, where we *never die*. Get it?" he snapped, with pain and frustration in his eyes, "The Bible tells us about this place. I wish I heeded those warnings. God is merciful, but we all have a choice and I ignored His cautions. I have no one else to blame but myself, and... unfortun—," he suddenly choked, "I will be worse off than anyone here because I preached the gospel." He looked at Jason with utter regret.

Jason stood silent, speechless for a moment before he spoke again. "So, the Bible talks of this place?"

"It sure does, kid. Jesus talked more about Hell than he did about Heaven. He was cautioning us about our fate if we did not believe and follow him. You see—"

Again, the booming rumble shook the realm and everyone, demonic and human, hit the ground in terror. Jason's eyes met the preachers' as they lay flat facing each other, looking through rusty steel bars between them.

"It's the praises of Christians," he whispered. "Hell shakes when God's people praise and worship Him. It paralyzes' the demons... if only I had known how effective it was when I was alive. I would have done things differently... I would have never stopped praising him." He wept.

The rumbling instantly stopped, and Jason and the preacher looked around and gradually sat up.

"I need to tell you something else, I—"

"You're up, preacher!" the cell snapped open.

The preacher looked at Jason with absolute fear and despair—his eyes expressed everything of the pure terror that he felt. A large demon with a mass of hair cascading down its back and a crudely distended jaw rushed in and grabbed the preacher around his neck, lifting him off the ground. He screamed in pain as Jason heard the neck bones crack.

The man cried out a muffled, "Jesus forgive me," which enraged the creature even more.

"Shut up," it hissed at him. "Don't say that name. DAMN YOU!" it snarled.

Jason recoiled backward to the other side of his cell and watched as the creature opened its massive jaws and took a bite out of the man's neck. Its long, spiky, gray fangs sinking into his flesh as the man writhed and gurgled in agony. But there was no blood, just gray strips of sinuous tissue hanging from the gaping wound. Jason could see the man's trachea dangling freely, hanging and torn away.

The creature threw the preacher outside the cell and demanded that he stand and walk forward. Jason buckled at the knees and collapsed to the hot stony floor in distress as he watched the man stand, making sucking and gasping noises, holding his neck as he stumbled away with the creature berating and beating him.

Jason trembled uncontrollably. His stomach heaved and lurched. His mouth was dry, and he felt the skin on his lips tear with deep slits. He wanted out. He didn't understand how he had died, but he knew in his being that this was it. He knew he was to spend eternity in this place… and it shook him to the very core.

CHAPTER FIVE

It seemed like hours, or days... time didn't seem to matter here. Jason sat on the hot, dry, stone floor and watched as other people were tortured and marched from their cells. He had spoken to several others that had since come and gone from the cells beside him. A famous movie star who he had idolized and met. A well-known Formula One driver, a famous singer, an old friend, and to his surprise... a witch. The demons laughed at her, tortured and taunted her even more so. She seemed shocked and angered, spewing profanities and stating that they had promised her she would reign with Him. Jason didn't know who 'Him' was, but it chilled him to the bone when she spoke it. She screamed at the many creatures that surrounded her, yelling curses at them, demanding that they obey her, stating that they were her friends, her 'spirit guides' on earth and who have since betrayed her.

All Jason could think when he watched her silently from his corner, is that how could anyone willingly choose this disgusting putrid place that was nothing but pain and suffering. *Why would anyone live their lives knowingly to come here?* he thought as he watched her being taken away in the same manner as all the others.

He trembled and panicked at the thought of being next. The screams all around him were deafening. There were thousands, probably millions, and he could hear them all tormented. He couldn't sleep, but his eyes were dry and heavy. He felt tired and weak. There was no escape from this place, no respite—just sheer despair, hopelessness, and pure unadulterated terror. The emptiness and hopelessness were indescribable. His soul ached and longed to return to the outside world, but he knew this was it for him. The fear and anguish grew inside of him as he pondered his eternal fate.

"Pssst." A young man urgently whispered to Jason from the cell across the aisle. "Why are you here?"

"I-I don't know. I guess I never believed in anything."

"I knew Jesus. I loved and followed Him," the man responded with desperation and despair.

"Then why are you here?"

"I gradually walked away from Him because I wanted to live life *my* way. I went back to my old life, got caught up in partying again, drinking, sleeping around... I wasn't really living for Him anymore and I became lukewarm. My friends and I got drunk on Wednesday night, and drove around. We had an accident and two of us died. I could see the medics trying to revive me... but it was too late. I was standing outside of my body and then demons appeared and dragged me here. That was four days ago... Now I'm just waiting for my fate." He said fearfully, looking around.

Jason shivered at the thought of that word... FATE.

"I've seen so many come through," the young man continued. "Even people I knew. There are so many here." He moaned deeply and fell to his knees in despair.

"SHUT UP YOU! You talk too much." A bat-like creature spat as he walked down the aisle.

The man went silent until it passed by out of earshot. "I've seen preachers and priests I once knew here, but it's too late for us now." The man retreated to the back of his cell and Jason could hear him quietly weeping with regret.

He watched a woman enter the cell beside him. She had a gigantic serpent wrapped around her neck and chest. It had long needles over its entire body and it was pressing them into her flesh. She was screaming as it was biting the back of her head and sinking its long fangs into her skull. Her hands were desperately trying to pry it off, but without success. The flesh and skin were slowly being ripped away from her vertebrae and ribs, exposing the raw bone as it worked its way, twisting around her body. She fell to her knees in writhing agony.

The serpent stopped, and the woman stood again as the ripped flesh on her body reformed. She looked over at Jason. "I trusted him as my friend," she stated, with a mix of anger and regret.

Jason looked at her blankly, not understanding what she meant.

"This was my spirit guide. I'm a medium… a psychic. I had many spirit guides helping me—although they didn't appear to me like this. They appeared as normal people and I thought they were my friends." She cried.

"Why would you choose this?" Jason looked at her, baffled.

"Do you think I knew this would happen? Do you think I *knew* that these were what they really were?" she spat with instant rage and hatred. "*I trusted them*; they didn't show themselves as these disgusting creatures, they tricked me. THEY TRICKED ME!" she screamed with frustration and resentment. "They told me they were my friends and helpers and never revealed their true identity. I thought they had given me a gift from God."

"So, they were your helpers?"

"Yes, I made a covenant with a spirit. He appeared to me as handsome and kind. I thought he was my soul mate. Now look," she paused with sorrow. "This is him—this is the one who guided me." The serpent spat and dug his fangs into her neck as she wailed in misery.

Jason watched her, not knowing what to say, but he had to know. "Why would you do that?"

She cried in shame. "I asked for guidance and help, and Thomas appeared to me one night." She winced as the serpent squeezed her again and she started screaming. "You tricked me! I hate you.… GET OFF ME!" she screamed. But the serpent just squeezed tighter.

Jason backed away into the corner of his cell. It frightened him that someone would play with the spiritual realm, knowingly or unknowingly.

He sat and held his hands over his ears but could not shut out the sounds of sheer anguish echoing throughout the realm. His soul was in torment; his heart was in terror at every resounding beat. Hopeless noises arose from his chest as he sobbed deeply again. There were no tears, just muffled sounds and heartfelt pain. He sat, recoiled tightly in a ball in the corner, hoping to remain unnoticed by the creatures that skulked and stalked the aisles. He knew his fate and with desolate realization he knew he had never known or even sought-after God. He had lived for himself. Jason placed his head in his hands and profoundly wept, knowing that his lot was sealed, and that Hell was now…

his eternity.

CHAPTER SIX

IT WAS THE LARGE BRIGHT FLASH THAT STARTLED JASON. HE LOOKED upward and saw it coming from the stone ceiling. A massive bright beam of light radiated downward, straight into his cell. It illuminated his very being, the warmth burning throughout his body.

Screeching was heard, but not human. The demonic creatures were running, screaming in terror, scrambling away from this incandescent beam of light that had suddenly appeared and burst through the oppressive dark hue.

He sat motionless, basking in its warmth, looking upward but not game to move a muscle in case it left him. Then... he saw the most magnificent being standing before him. It was ablaze with intense light. It was human like but with glorious wide wings stemming from its back.

Jason gasped as the being held out its hand and beckoned to him. It was looking directly at him, calling him to come, to step forward and take its hand.

"Take me, please take me. I beg you!" He could hear the people screaming from the other cells. "Please, I'm begging you, take me from this place!" They cried out towards the being.

But it beckoned to him only, looking straight into his eyes, gently calling him with its expression. He hesitated in fear, but was so enthralled and mesmerized by its beauty that he reached forward and grabbed hold.

As he did, the entity pulled him in close and he saw a soft, peaceful human face. Its wings instantly snapped outward in a wide expanse and they took flight upwards.

No roller coaster ride or even his very own GT3 Porsche could ever equate to the rush that Jason felt. G forces like he had never fathomed hit him as he was being pulled up at a rate that was unimaginable. It was like a thousand volts of electricity pulsing through his body as he saw the stony walls and demons of Hell flicker past. He burst through the ground feeling the rush of cool earth air on his face again. But he didn't stop there. At missile's pace, they continued upward into the clear blue skies that gradually dimmed until they were bursting outward through the earth's thermosphere. It was boundlessly dark but also light as the stars were brilliant and the space and its surroundings were crisp and clear. He could see the sun burning in the distance and as they fleeted past, he recognized and named each planet in the earth's solar system. They kept moving upward, seeing new planets, bursting through nebulas and super-novas, galaxies and stars that the human eye had never seen, and possibly never would. He was rocketing at an inconceivable speed. The feeling was exhilarating and Jason gasped at the sights that surrounded him, in awe of the sheer size of the universe.

The velocity and light that surrounded him were so intense, he weakened. His senses moved towards blacking out completely. The being beside him looked over and gently squeezed him with its hand, and instantly Jason felt a pulsating rush of strength throughout his body, his senses clear again. He gripped tighter to the being's hand, and it smiled a peaceful, warm beam back at him. For the first time, he felt safe. Whatever this thing was beside him, it radiated the feelings of love, peace and grace, and he felt like he didn't care where it was taking him as long as he could stay by its side.

Jason could see a light in the distance getting stronger and larger until it was so bright that he felt he could no longer open his eyes. He shivered and convulsed as the beams of light pulsated through his very essence. The being again squeezed Jason, and he instantly felt able to endure. As they came into the intense light, their speed slowed and arced into a descent. The being gently unfurled its immense wings and they softly but swiftly alighted on magnificent garden grounds.

Jason stood in absolute wonder at the surrounds. The being remained beside him and smiled warmly, watching him intently as Jason's excitement heightened. His heart skipped at the miles of vibrant, bright green flowing grass with a dappling of trees and flowers gently swaying. The view was magnificent, and it took his breath away. He had never seen anything as glorious as this.

He looked down and felt the lush, soft, green grass beneath his feet—it felt alive and pulsating with energy. As he surveyed the area, there were plants and flowers that he had never seen before. The flowers that spread out across the fields had kaleidoscopic colors that were so rich and alive. Each bloom felt as though it was smiling and looking right at him, and he was sure he could hear all of them singing songs in unison. He looked to his left and saw a beautiful pond 50 feet away. The mirror-like polished blue remained still and peaceful, wooing him to come and dip his feet and feel its freshness. There was nothing to compare it with—it was absolutely breath-taking. He looked to his right and saw the soft rolling hills and tall mountain tops with sprinkled glistening snow on their peaks. Everything was intensified—the colors of the landscape, the feelings he felt, the peace and love. That's when he paused, pondering what he felt. It was pure, unadulterated love—no fear or pain—just a saturation of love. As though every negative feeling or emotion, every doubt, hurt and fear had been stripped away, and all he felt was adoration for the One who created this world.

"Where am I?" he asked the being in awe, hoping that this moment wouldn't pass.

The being did not speak, but motioned for Jason to walk forward towards a patch of shorter grass up ahead. Jason obeyed and slowly took his steps, taking in the surrounds as he walked. To his amazement, he noticed that the grass and flowers sprung back up as if they had never walked on it. The flowers' faces glowed and followed his direction, and he let out a small giggle at the sight.

At 500 feet ahead, he noticed a fractured and distorted ball of light slowly drifting towards him across the grass. He hesitated and the being beside him kindly nodded to him with a smile, gently reassuring and directing him to keep walking forward.

As the ball of light came closer, it rapidly morphed into the figure of a massive white lion with four white, silver-tipped wings that perfectly folded over its back. Its long white and silver-lined mane softly cascaded down its shoulders, flowing and moving ever so slightly—glinting and radiating violet and turquoise tones as it ambled to a stop directly in front of Jason. Its eyes looked kind but authoritative, frequently changing from emerald, sapphire and pearl hues.

"Hello Jason," a deep, masculine voice sprang from the lion as he stopped in front of him. "Thank you, Aduri," he said to the being standing beside Jason.

Aduri beamed an enormous smile and bowed his head slightly at the Lion in respect. He then turned toward Jason, nodded farewell, and elegantly flew off.

Jason watched in amazement at Aduri taking flight and then looked back at the lion standing before him.

"Ah, hello." Jason smiled nervously.

"I am Tolman, a messenger sent to meet you here." He smiled, showing his massive iridescent pearl canines. "I am here to help you understand and see truth."

Jason anxiously awaited in silence.

"You can speak, Jason. I am not here to harm you, but to help you. What do you want to ask?"

Jason shifted his weight with uncertainty. He knew this creature knew his thoughts before he even spoke them. "Is this Heaven?" he asked meekly.

"No, this is not Heaven!" Tolman responded, plainly. "Sin cannot enter Heaven! This realm is on the outskirts, but you can see Heaven's gates from here."

Jason didn't grasp Tolman's response, but remained in awe. "Wow, but this is so—wonderful." Jason stated, still looking around taking in the brilliant surrounds. He paused for a moment, then asked, "So please tell me… was I in Hell?"

"Yes, you were… where you belong."

The answer surprised Jason . "Where I belong?"

"It is only for the sake of the Lord's praying servant that you are here. You, however, do not deserve to be here at all. You should have remained there—in Hell—for eternity."

"I don't understand." Jason replied, confused. "I am here now, aren't

I? What do you mean I don't deserve to be here?" he shook his head in bewilderment.

"You do, or rather should I say, did, not believe in our Lord at all. You're a murderer, a liar, a cheat, and a drunkard. You are a lover of money, are proud and conceited, selfish and crude, you have no wife but sleep with many women and much more that I do not have the time to explain." Tolman said, nonchalantly.

Jason just stood a-gasp at how this creature could be so disrespectful and rude—calling him all these things but still smiling at him with the utmost love. Jason decided to ignore Tolman's statement. "Do I get to meet God?"

"No!"

"Then why am I here?"

"You've been given a second chance, Jason. On the prayers of a young man, God is giving you back your life…that is, depending on your decision." He murmured before continuing. "Our Lord is a gracious God and has honored the faith of this young man. So here you stand, saved by the grace of our God. This is a rare opportunity, and few are offered this gift as once they are in Hell, that is where they stay. Come!" Tolman directed. "I have brought some friends here that I would like you to meet."

Jason looked up and saw thousands of children running towards him, all under 15 years of age. It was like a massive army skipping and giggling happily amongst each other, whilst merging into one mass to stand before him. They were all excited, lively and beaming brightly.

They all waited silently, standing in front of Jason 20 feet back, until Tolman motioned with a slight nod. Then, a small girl stepped towards Jason and spoke in a beautiful, soft voice.

"Hi Jason, I'm Shenzhen. I was going to be a famous ballerina." She curtsied gracefully, then stepped back again, blending into the mass of children before him.

A ten-year-old boy stepped forward towards him and also introduced himself. "Hi Jason, I'm Jonathan. I was going to be a teacher." Again, he stepped back, turned around, and disappeared into the crowd.

Then another boy advanced, "Hello Jason, I'm Benjamin. I was going to be the President of the United States of America, and bring prosperity to the country." He said proudly before melding back into the crowd.

A girl moved forward and stood in front of him. "Hi Jason, my name is Helen. My destiny was to be a gospel singer."

Again, another girl walked up and introduced herself. "Hello Jason, my name is Chelsea, and I was to be a scientist who won a Nobel prize."

And another, "Hi Jason, my name is Leah. I was to be a mother and bring up four children who would follow God, love Him and become ministers."

Another, "Hello Jason, my name is Noah, and my destiny was to be an architect and build a beautiful cathedral."

"Hi Jason, I'm Andrew. I was to be in an organization that helped the needy in the developing world and war-torn countries."

"Hello Jason, my name is Abdul. I would have helped turn Islamic followers to Yahweh."

... And so it continued, each child moving forward and speaking. "I was going to be a soldier." "I was to be a wife." "I was to be in a rock band." "I would have been a doctor... a cleaner... a musician... a baker... an inventor... an engineer... a therapist... a prime minister... a pastor... a fireman... a nurse... a solicitor... a policeman... a farmer... a saleswoman..." On and on it continued, and Jason's head was reeling with names, faces and professions, totally confused at what the meaning of all this was.

It seemed like hours had passed with thousands of children stepping forward and stating their would-be professions... and then, as suddenly as it began, it stopped. The last child stepped back and then all the children dissipated, leaving Jason standing dazed.

"W-what was that all about?" he stammered in confusion.

"Why," Tolman paused, "these are all the children you murdered."

CHAPTER SEVEN

"WHAT?" JASON BLURTED, STEPPING BACK IN SHOCK AND DISGUST. "I have murdered no one. I have never even seen these children before. What are you talking about? You have got the wrong person." he looked at Tolman with repugnance and fear of the accusation.

"Their blood is on your hands, Jason. God wanted all of them to let you know the plans He had for every one of them, but you stopped them from fulfilling their destinies."

"No, no, believe me." Jason pleaded and took a step back. "Trust me, I have never, ever seen these children." He held out his hands in an appeal.

"I know you haven't seen them Jason, not in this form, but you murdered every one of them—some directly and others indirectly."

"Tolman, please… I didn't. I haven't seen them before, please… I don't understand," he appealed.

"Again Jason, although you didn't see them in this form, you murdered them."

"No, no, I promise you," Jason implored. "I promise you I did not take their lives. You definitely have the wrong person," he begged.

"You are wrong, Jason; I have the right person! Tell me," Tolman paused. "How many clinics do you have now?" he asked, as if already knowing the answer.

"Well, I-I," Jason took a quick breath, thinking it a rather strange question, "I have 237." He stated.

"237... that is a very large number to own, isn't it?"

"Well, I guess."

"Jason, let me ask you a question." Tolman looked sternly at him. "When do you class an embryo as being a baby?"

"Ah... well. I believe it only becomes a baby when it is fully born. Otherwise, it is simply a mass of tissue or merely a fetus."

"Really!" Tolman exclaimed. "Merely tissue? And that is your full belief, is it?"

"Um... well, yes... it is. I have always believed this and was taught this as a medical practitioner."

"Interesting." He paced back and forth, making Jason even more nervous. "For a well-educated man, you are very misguided."

"How so?"

"No, please, I'd like you to continue as I'm curious to hear your beliefs." His lip furled and he let out a slight snarl. "I will show you the truth in due time. Carry on." He said as he nodded, ushering Jason to proceed.

"Well, the fetus cannot exist outside the womb, so it isn't a functioning human until it is born."

"Mmm... but you were functioning, you had a heartbeat at 22 days, and you were human... wouldn't you agree?"

"Yes, but only until I was outside my mother's womb. Having a heart beat means nothing if you can't survive outside of a womb."

"Really?" Tolman lifted his eyebrows. "Tell me more about your views."

Jason shifted uncomfortably, but continued at Tolman's request. "Well, because it is still only a fetus, there is no damage done if it is terminated at that stage. It's the woman's right to choose if they do not want a child or have the means to support a child, then they have a right to decide. The woman can live a normal life, choosing the right time to start a family. Further to this, if there has been a rape or incest pregnancy, then she can move on with her life without the reminder holding her back."

"So, you're saying it is the woman's right to take the life of the human growing inside her?"

"Yes! And the law says so as well. It's not murder, if that's what you're alluding to."

"Isn't it? Your laws may state it's not, but morally… do you really think it isn't?"

Jason didn't respond.

"Let's talk more about your belief around the child not being human whilst in the womb. I'm curious, because the fetus has its own DNA by day two from conception. This shows it is its own living organism, doesn't it? If a fetus is developing, doesn't that mean she is alive?" But Tolman didn't wait for Jason to respond. "By day fourteen, the embryo has its own nervous system and some countries mandate a law against experiments on the fetus by this day. Why would that be? Is it because it's a living human that can feel?"

"I just don't think we should inflict unnecessary pain upon anything."

"But you do… you have and if you were now still living… you would continue to do so. There are thousands of abortions performed weekly. These defenseless children can feel pain and have survived outside of the womb with medical help. You know yourself there have been premature babies saved at twenty-one weeks, but you kill with no regard to life. You tear them apart and lay out the body parts and limbs on the table and count them to ensure the child is void of the womb. You have laws that say it is legal to end the pregnancy for any reason up to twenty-two weeks. If you wanted a boy instead of a girl—just get rid of it. That up to birth, a child can be terminated by a consenting physician. Your laws are twisted. It is a crime if a child is accidentally killed in the womb, but if it's intentional—an abortion—then it's not classed as misconduct. Your thinking is warped—You have mixed up right and wrong and blended into gray. Your morals are so flippant; you do what benefits you and then change the laws to make it acceptable to your conscience."

He paused for a second. "You know your nurses have therapy because of seeing the tiny contorted faces, seeing them recoil from the cannula or watching the babies scream in pain. What about those who do not die straight away Jason, the ones who are delivered whole, still moving in the palm of your hand, or the ones that are left alone alive on the table, in a room overnight because the procedure didn't go to plan? What about those, Jason—isn't that murder? Your senators have even rejected a bill to protect those born alive after an abortion. They prefer to leave them to die screaming, with no medical help… or worse, secretly help them die. How evil and heartless!" He sneered in disgust. "Have your hearts become so hardened that you cannot even recognize the taking of life? Is life only deemed precious when it is planned? So how can you justify that it's not human until it's born, Jason? Tell me."

"I-I," Jason fumbled at the bombardment. "We don't have live abortions. Our methods and strict policies in my centers ensure it's quick and complete."

"That you know of Jason…but that still doesn't make it right," Tolman snapped. "You just met thousands of children you murdered, and every one of them had a solid future, a plan for their life." Tolman paused, watching Jason shake his head in disbelief.

"No, that wasn't, it couldn't be…" Jason stumbled backwards, "are you saying—W-what are you saying?"

"Each child you saw died at your hand, Jason. YOU killed them." Tolman narrowed his eyes and looked directly at him. They started flickering from the calm pearl and turquoise hues to flashes of red.

"N-No, but that wasn't m—" he faded. "How could that be? But it's what I believe to be right and fair… for the woman… and—and taught." He feebly whispered.

"Fair? You want to talk about fair? Was it fair for each one of those children you met to not have a fulfilling life, the one that God ordained for them? Was it fair that you snatched away their right to live? You talk about the woman's right, well what about the child's right to life? To have a life filled with experience and meaning, to change your world, to affect others? How is that fair Jason—tell me?" Tolman said angrily, his eyes turning a solid ruby red, his pearl canines showing from his snarl, his silver tipped tail swept aggressively from side to side.

"I-I don't know, I-I—." Jason stammered awkwardly, taking a step backward in trepidation at the change in Tolman's eyes, "I-I always thought it was the right of the mother to decide, I never thought about the child." he said with deep pondering.

"You're right, you *never* thought about the child! They classed it as an inconvenience, an embarrassment, a secret, not the right time, too expensive… whatever excuses you humans come up with to make you feel that it's acceptably right. But you NEVER thought about the child and its right to LIFE."

His voice raised. "You've fallen like fools for Satan's pervasive lies and become a selfish bunch of arrogant beings that constantly live for your-selves and ignore the impact of your decisions. What right do you have to call judgment on another's life? What right do you have to murder?"

Tolman's eyes immediately changed color. The ruby red amplified intensity, its brightness glowing with each measure of his increasing anger. Tolman started making a chuffing noise as he stared straight at Jason, baring his teeth.

Jason stepped back in fear.

The lion's extreme rage was now showing—the rumbling raw tone started deep within Tolman's belly, and he discharged a roar so powerful, with such intense control and force, that it shook the surrounding land. The flowers and grass immediately fell flat from the vibrations and strength of the penetrating sound moving across the land like a wave. It hit Jason with a blast that cut like a thousand knives right through his frame.

Again, Tolman took another deep breath and roared, over and over, wave after wave, the deep sound filled with a mixture of anger, pain and profound sorrow echoing throughout the realm. An ice-cold hurricane formed from the vapor of Tolman's breath and continued to intensify at his every roar. It rushed like a whirlwind around Jason, encasing him, shaking and whipping his face and body with enormous energy. He could feel his fear returning and intensifying at every rumble and roar from Tolman.

The fury was rapidly rising from the lion, and then, at the very last roar Jason felt his fingers grow icy cold. Quickly, he held out his hands in front of him and watched in terror as his fingers, hands, then arms crys-talized with an icy violet frosting. The painful throbbing feeling of both intense heat and ice crept upward, stiffening and freezing his limbs into sparkling purple and white crystal granules as it made its way rapidly throughout his entire body. The fear was overwhelming as he felt the sensation of solidification set in. He had become frozen… an icy tanzanite stone…

immovable.

CHAPTER EIGHT

AND THEN...

I'm floating... Jason thought. He felt weightless, almost without form. His eyes wouldn't open, but he could sense the light refracted red-pink hue that encased him. A feeling of buoyancy and lightness in a watery fluid surrounded him. He could hear his own small heartbeat, but also a louder, much slower heartbeat that reverberated through him yet soothed him at the same time.

As he moved his hand forward, he could feel a soft, velvety barrier that bounced back at his touch. He felt small, yet safe. Then immediately he heard muffled talking, and he concentrated and strained to hear what was being said.

"You must get rid of it, Jane." He could hear the male voice state angrily.

"I can't... and I won't."

"Don't be stupid. We are about the open the practice in two months. How the heck are you going to work while you're pregnant?"

"I'll manage. I'll figure it out."

"I don't know how. This is such bad timing." A loud slam resonated and Jason jumped. He desperately wanted to open his eyes, but he couldn't. He felt helpless and nervous at the angry tones.

"It will be quick; you won't even feel anything. I can get Terry to perform it." The male voice continued.

"No David, I will handle this. I'll be able to still see patients right until I give birth. I'll be fine."

"What about morning sickness and time off? I can't do this alone, Jane. This was our plan to open our own practice and establish ourselves before we thought about a family."

"I'm already ten weeks now. I have had little morning sickness."

"So, you knew? You've been keeping it from me?" The anger in his voice intensified.

"I didn't know until yesterday," she snapped. "I've been so stressed about getting this building ready, organizing the fit-out, ordering the medical equipment. I didn't notice, and when I did, I put it down to stress." She responded irritably.

"Gees, Jane, this isn't the right time. It's not in our plan."

"I know... well, sometimes things don't go to plan, David... okay?" She retorted angrily, then paused. Jason could feel her take a deep breath. "David, I don't want to abort this baby—I don't want to go through that again... I can't explain it—I just don't."

Jason heard her breath quicken and felt the loud pounding heartbeat increase, and then a soft sobbing sound.

"Hey, hey, come here. I'm sorry... so sorry... I didn't mean to upset you, it's just that I'm concerned for you... for us. We've put a lot into this. This is our dream."

"I know... but it will be fine. I can be a mother and also a doctor. Trust me... please. I don't want to have another abortion."

Then there was...

Silence.

The quietness and stillness were overwhelming. Jason couldn't hear anything; it was as if he was in limbo.

And then...

Jason could feel himself growing... rapidly increasing. His senses enhanced—he could feel more, smell more, hear more. He took a deep breath and felt the warm fluid rush into his lungs and then expel when he breathed outward. Straining his eyelids, he felt them spring open and he could see. His hands were tiny, soft, vascular and pink. He moved his fingers slowly, looking at them with awe. His legs were curled upward and forward as he gently flexed his foot and moved his toes. Tiny particles were floating around him in the fluid that surrounded him. He knew exactly where he was… he knew exactly *what* he was.

The feeling of love for the mother that carried him and also for the one who created him washed through him like a tepid liquid. He could hear a choir singing, as if from angels, and felt harmony flowing throughout his whole being. It was like a trance of peace and love, and he heard a soft humming sound. There was singing coming from his mother and he saw a shadow of her hand above him, on her stomach, affectionately caressing him. "My sweet little baby…." Her soft voice was crooning him and he felt the love emanating from her… He felt safe.

"I love you little one," she said. "I can't wait to meet you. We will have so much fun together." She soothed.

Jason heard her loving words and felt the excitement rise at what she was saying, his heart beating faster at the thought of his life that was just beginning.

And then… THUMP!.

He felt himself bounce against something solid. The pain shot through his skull and spine as it knocked him around, bumping, turning, and beating him from side to side. The fear increased. He was a helpless captive, not knowing what was going on. Confusion and pain overshadowed—his heart raced, and he recoiled into a ball to protect himself. He heard intense screaming coming from his mother, the vibrating shrill piercing his ears as he heard the sirens and people shouting… and then it went black…

Nothing.

Then, as swiftly as it fell silent, Jason was awake again. He could hear voices.

"I recommend you abort the baby. We have completed the MRI but cannot determine if there is brain damage." a male voice said.

"But I'm 26 weeks."

"Jane, you are very lucky." The male voice stated. "You've sustained a fractured hip and concussion. It's a wonder that SUV didn't kill you. But… I can't say the same for the baby. I can't say with confidence that he will be a normal child. There is a 70 percent chance of brain damage."

"Jane?" Jason could recognize his father's voice and the level of concern in his tone. "We have to think about this. If the baby has sustained brain trauma, then… that will jeopardize our future. Please, honey. We need to decide… and I think we should abort."

"I don't know… I understand what you are both saying, but this is *our* baby David… our little boy."

"You don't have to decide straight away," the male voice said. "We can talk more tomorrow, but it needs to happen soon."

"We will think about it," his mother replied gravely.

Jason swiftly felt fear creep over him—he understood precisely what they were saying. He had full cognizance of the statements. His mind was alert and knowledgeable, just physically he had become the unborn child. He could feel an overwhelming hopelessness and panic rise within him. In hysteria, he started lashing outward—he kicked and punched, hitting the uterine wall with force.

"Ah," he heard and felt his mother wince with pain. "David, I think he is trying to tell us something. Come over here and place your hand on my stomach."

Jason continued to kick and silently scream, his fear deepening at the possibility of losing his life. "Don't do it. I'm alive and healthy. I'll be okay. I won't cause you any problems. Please, please, please don't harm me. I beg you, let me live my life. I promise I'll be good. Don't kill me. Please, please, please don't kill me… let me live."

CHAPTER NINE

ABRUPTLY, JASON FELT HE WAS BACK IN HIS ADULT BODY WITH THE sensation of the icicles starting to liquify. The cold and hot melted away from his skin, the solidification was reversing until he watched the last of the violet crystals melt and fall from his fingertips. Jason fell to his knees in front of Tolman.

He stayed kneeling, trying to regain his senses of what had just happened. Confusion reigned as he could see his beliefs before him, for they were like shards of glass shattering and falling down around him, tinkling and bouncing onto the illuminating green grass. The realization of the sensations felt by a child, even at such a young stage, overwhelmed him so much that his eyes glazed over. "I-I," Jason fumbled, his head spinning with confusion. "I believed it all to be truth."

"Well, if you had cared to study the truth Jason, you would have known that God said to His servant in Jeremiah 1:5, 'Before I formed you in the womb I knew you, before you were born I set you apart; I appointed you as a prophet to the nations.' Before Jeremiah was born, Jason... God had a plan. Before he was formed in his mother's womb... God had a plan for his life."

At these words, the ground made thunderous sounds and trembled. It was as though Tolman's voice had transformed into the rumble of rushing wind and running water entwined into one. The flowers, grass and trees all turned in one accord toward him and listen to the words vocalized.

Jason's heart raced. He shook at the power and the sound from the phrases that Tolman uttered. It was as though these words blasted straight through him like an atomic wave and smashed him with its pure truth. *Before I formed you in the womb, I knew you*; the words repeated in his mind; *I knew you before you were born. Before I formed you... I knew you*. All he could hear were the words that Tolman had spoken. God's very own words. Jason trembled, staring blankly into nothing, the words in his mind continually repeating themselves.

Tolman didn't hold back. "King David said to God in Psalm 139:13-16...

'For you created my inmost being;
you knit me together in my mother's womb.
I praise you because I am fearfully and wonderfully made;
your works are wonderful,
I know that full well.
My frame was not hidden from you
when I was made in the secret place,
when I was woven together in the depths of the earth.
Your eyes saw my unformed body;
all the days ordained for me were written in your book
before one of them came to be.'"

Tolman didn't stop but continued, "And our Lord's servant, Paul, said in Galatians 1:15, 'But when God, who set me apart from my mother's womb and called me by his grace, was pleased.'" He paused. "And to his servant Zachariah in Luke 1:15, even before his wife, Elizabeth, was pregnant with John, '... he will be filled with the Holy Spirit even before he is born'. BEFORE he is born, Jason." Tolman sighed, "Tell me, were all these men wrong? Were they foolish to believe the very hand of God created them? That He had planned them before creation? That He had thought about every one of them in precise detail and depth before He even formed the earth?"

A wave of sickness swept over Jason's soul. He knew he was wrong... *So wrong*; he thought. The significance of all these children he had just met struck him, piercing right into his soul. The experience of extreme fear and terror that he had just felt as the baby all came at him in a rush. The pain was so intense he thought his heart was being ripped right out of his chest. It was now clear to him what he had done. Another wave of emotion rolled through him. It was like he was being crushed with the intensity of the realization, the guilt, the condemnation of his actions… As though a giant boulder had been dropped upon him, and the weight of it was too much to bear.

"So, Jason, what is your explanation of that pronouncement from God? The claim that God has plans for all His children before they are created?" Tolman waited briefly. "Come on Jason, speak up."

Jason shook uncontrollably, unable to utter a noise, let alone form a sentence to answer. He stared for a moment, then his mind raced with visions of babies and fetuses, tiny torn limbs and crushed, fragmented parts… faces of women, the nurses, surgical instruments, the sounds of suction, screams and cries. Like a runaway train, it was all flashing before his very eyes.

"You are not stupid, Jason, so what is your answer to my question?" Tolman stepped forward and looked down, the gentle breeze of his breath brushing against Jason's face.

Jason remained kneeling in front of Tolman—tears streamed down his cheeks. It didn't matter where he was—the realization of his actions left him feeling so ashamed, so unworthy, so utterly sick to the core of what his life had amounted to… and mostly at what he had become. A professional killer of the innocent… a murderer. A cry lodged in his throat until he could hold it no longer, and it burst out like a heavy lump of lava, sob after sob, wave after wave. He saw truth—he saw what he had done. He saw what God saw… and he saw how very wrong he had been.

Tolman remained standing, looking down upon this sorry soul, watching every tear fall upon the ground, watching every convulsion of regret wash over him like a tidal wave. He watched as the realization hit this poor creature and annihilated him.

"I-I," Jason choked.

Tolman stood calmly and asked again, "Jason, I wish for you to answer my question."

Jason looked up and tried "I-I… can't—" Jason gasped in anguish and held his head in his hands and wept. His body shuddered and shook at the heart-wrenching convulsions pulsating throughout his core. The pain in his heart was so intense he thought it would burst, piercing it like a million tiny steel skewers driving right through it. He was utterly ashamed, and the weight of his guilt was overpowering.

Tolman softened, looking down at this poor creature, knowing that Jason had finally seen the truth. He broke the silence and spoke kindly. "Jason… God is a redeemer. He is the giver of life, not the taker. He wants to restore what has been stolen from you. He wants to turn the misconceptions and the lies that the enemy has pervaded into your world and show you the truth. It grieves God to see what humans do, what they deem as being morally acceptable. Your world is so mixed up—save the whales and trees, but kill the children. You get excited to find bacteria on Mars and deem it to be life, yet believe the miracle of a baby is not."

He halted momentarily. "Every child conceived—God has pre-ordained. He sets out the plans and destiny for every one of them before He even forms them in their mother's womb. Before He created the earth, He planned every single life. But what humanity does steals that away. Instead, you've believed the lies and deception that Satan has woven, greedily accepting his illusion and falsehoods that have been pervading mankind throughout the ages, fooling you to believe its not really a life, and that it's your right to choose. Who are you to take the life of another? Who are you to decide what is right? In God's eyes it is still murder, whether you take them at conception or at 100 years of age."

Jason broke. "Please, Tolman, I'm so sorry." Jason was pleading. "I deserve to be in Hell."

Jason could see it so plainly now. He looked at his hands and saw a filthy, bloodied stain covering them, dripping a dark maroon liquid. He knew it was the blood that he had shed, the stain from killing the innocent. He desperately tried to wipe it away, to hide and erase his transgression, but it just smeared and reappeared, continuing to pool and drip relentlessly from his palms.

He trembled as he realized the sin that he had committed, that he could not undo what he had done. The understanding of where he actually belonged rang true, and it hit with ferocity.

He cried out, "I am everything disgusting to God," he convulsed, with floods of emotion pouring out of him. "Please God, forgive me. I'm so sorry for what I have done—please God forgive me." Jason sobbed in torment, his heart pounding with agony, looking skyward with tear-streaked cheeks and heartfelt cries—he raised his arms high, begging for forgiveness.

His earnest cries were heard throughout the realm. Beams of colorful lights rapidly smashed into his heart, shattering the hard-black outer casing into a million tiny shards. Jason shuddered as a spectral of rainbow auroras throbbed through his body, making it convulse under its immense force. He felt himself being lifted off the ground; his arms outstretched in abandoned surrender as the beams pulsated through him. Wave after wave it shattered his thinking, his beliefs and broke into the very nuclear of his soul... and as rapidly as it came, it ceased, and Jason fell facedown onto the soft grass... motionless.

CHAPTER TEN

TOLMAN STOOD GALLANTLY AND WAITED UNTIL JASON FINALLY STIRRED, regaining consciousness. He lay still for a moment, half dreaming as he was coming out of his catatonic state. He felt different. All the shame, tears, sorrow and pain were washed away, and only pure love and peace enveloped him, covering and wrapping him like a soft velvety blanket. All that he felt previously had completely vanished.

Tolman waited patiently until Jason lifted himself from the ground and stood once again before him... made whole.

"I know you are sorry," Tolman stated tenderly, his eyes now returned to the calm flickering of sapphire, emerald and pearl colors. "God had to show you, to make you see and understand. To feel the pain. Through your repentance, God has now forgiven you. That is why He is giving you another chance, Jason, to return and make a difference and change what you have done."

Jason looked at Tolman, confused for a moment, pondering his words. Standing silently, he focussed on his emotions, noticing that he felt different... but had not forgotten the magnitude of his actions. He remembered everything... what he had done, how it made him feel and the enormity and consequence of it all. Jason wiped the tears from his eyes and stared expressionlessly at Tolman.

"I want to show you more, Jason… through your new eyes. Will you allow me?" Tolman asked politely.

Jason hesitated, feeling very fragile. "Okay." He responded meekly.

Tolman stepped forward and breathed gently upon Jason's face. Again, the icy cold mixed with heat encompassed him, but this time only around his face. As Tolman continued to breathe, bright orange and yellow crystals formed like a mask across Jason's eyes, blocking all sight. He felt peaceful as he stood unmoving, the tingling sensation creeping over his face.

Unexpectedly, he was standing outside an office, watching a female health care assistant interviewing a woman in one of his clinics. The assistant was speaking, but something else was standing right beside her. At first, he couldn't make it out, but when his eyes adjusted, he recoiled with repugnance and stepped backwards.

Tolman reached out with his gigantic paw and placed it on his shoulder to steady him.

Jason grimaced as he looked at the being next to the assistant. It was a black-cloaked creature with a human skull for a face, but its teeth were not human. They were like a row of crooked pointed canines that were salivating and drooling a rich red plasma. Its whole body was constantly dripping fresh crimson blood, pooling around the bottom of its soaked black shroud.

As Jason looked closer, he could see an opening in the creature's cloak and saw that its torso was skeletal and contained hundreds of tiny skulls covered in blood within its rib cage. Jason recoiled at the sight and gagged abruptly.

Tolman squeezed his shoulder reassuringly.

Jason watched as the creature reached forward and touched the assistant's head with one long, thin, purple needle-like nail protruding from its finger. As it drilled into her cranium, he could see its mouth moving, speaking in a whispering tone.

"The fetus is not developed enough to feel pain. It's merely tissue and does not have any senses or feel any discomfort yet." It spoke.

"The fetus is not developed enough to feel pain. It's merely tissue and does not have any senses or feel any discomfort yet." The assistant repeated to the woman sitting in front of her.

Jason could see the woman asking something else.

"The vacuum aspiration procedure is a quick process, which will only take about ten minutes. Most women can go home a few hours afterwards as long as there have been no complications." The creature whispered into the assistant's mind.

The assistant repeated the words as she smiled at the woman.

"Can I see the ultrasound?" the woman asked.

The demon drove its nail hard into the assistant's mind, and she grimaced.

"No, we don't do that. Besides…" she looked genuinely into the woman's eyes, "there's really nothing to see but just a clump of cells."

The woman leaned over, satisfied, and signed the paperwork to proceed with the abortion. Jason watched as the woman thanked the assistant and walked out of the office and into the waiting room.

He could see the creature grinning maliciously. It made a turn and seemed to look straight at him. Its red, hallowed eyes emitted pure evil, sensing him standing there. Its sly mouth started to grin at him and he knew that it was staring right at him. He could see its exposed torso again, and he quivered at the sight. It made him sick, and he wanted it to stop. He gagged again when suddenly the image transformed and he was standing across the road in a treelined park opposite the clinic.

He saw a woman sitting on a park bench with her head in her hands, sobbing. Upon her shoulder sat a small lizard-shaped creature, with four bulging eyes, and long barbs for fingernails that had attached to her skull. Out of its hands glugged a black gelatinous substance that was slowly trickling and oozing down the woman's head and over her entire face. The dark gunk permeated her skin, seeping and staining every pore as it continued to slide down the rest of her body. She twitched a little, wiping her cheek as though she felt the moist sludge invade and saturate her.

The creature was whispering in her ear, and Jason could hear the woman's thoughts.

I shouldn't have done it, she thought.

"You had a right, it's *your* body." The creature spoke.

Jason could see its long fangs and breath nearly touching her ear.

It took one of its razor-sharp barbs and slit her skin just over her heart. The woman flinched, and Jason saw the pain etched in her face. She held her hand over the wound as her tears fell.

"I've made a mistake. I feel so empty, so void. Oh no, what have I done?" she let out a whisper of desperation.

The creature seized the girl's skull and drove the barbs in deep. "Don't be stupid," it spat with concern and fury, looking around agitated. "There is nothing wrong with this, you're not a bad person. You're entitled to make that decision—it's your life, *your* future. Besides, you're not breaking any law, it's legal… and you won't regret it. You can now continue with your career."

The woman seemed to lift and brighten at this thought, becoming confident in her decision.

But then the creature drove its nail into the fresh wound over her chest and injected the inky glug directly.

She buckled over, "What have I done?" the shame and remorse gushed through her once again, and she broke down and sobbed.

Jason watched on as the demon repeated the affirmations that she had done the right thing, but then caused her to feel the disgrace of her actions. It was a sickening, repetitive cycle of shame.

The vision suddenly changed, and he was looking at someone different—another girl sitting on the same bench talking with a man beside her.

"Look, it's for the best. I don't want you to have a baby. We're too young—we have our whole lives ahead of us," said the man.

She sat looking longingly into his eyes. "But I thought we could get married; we could move into a house and raise our child… be a family."

"No, Tina, that's not how it will be."

"But—"

"If you keep it… then I will leave you—I won't stay with you! Look, I've made the appointment. All you have to do is go in and get it done. It will be fine, like nothing ever happened. I'll be waiting here for you."

Jason felt an overwhelming sadness as he saw the woman's face crushed. He could see that she longed to keep the child, and he watched as she stood up weeping, and then trudged reluctantly towards the clinic.

The image changed, and his focus was now on the door of the clinic. Jason watched as another woman went inside, and the vision quickly fast forwarded to when the same woman came out.

He noticed that she had a dark purple bruise forming on her heart. He also could see that she had the small lizard creature clinging to her, drilling into her mind with its wretched barbs, pouring out the same black, oozing gel.

He watched on as each woman who went in came out with a bruised heart and a similar creature clinging to them, driving their talons into their skulls, clinging tightly. Jason instantly knew where those creatures stemmed from, as he had seen them before in that horrid place from where he had been rescued. Immediately, an overwhelming nausea overcame him again.

Tolman briefly spoke. "This demon is staining them with shame and guilt. If they don't come to know Christ, then it's an unending cycle. Initially, it was a lure to make them feel empowerment, that it's their right, their choice and it would bring them freedom. But once done, for most it's a never-ending regret. What they need is support, Jason— support for themselves and their child. That's how you can change the perceptions of the children who are deemed as being mistakes. Watch!" Tolman directed.

A teenage girl was sitting on the bench. She, too, had the demon on her shoulder, berating and staining her. But this time, an angel stood close by, watching the girl intently.

The demon shouted at the angel. "Stay away. Get back! She is mine now!" It spat, baring its teeth at the angelic being.

The girl buckled over, with deep sobs rising from the pit of her stomach.

Jason could see the ache in her chest. It was like a dark gray fog swirling and hovering over her soul. He could see her purple-bruised heart beating with anguish at every groan she made.

"Can't we help her?" Jason choked, a lump of sorrow caught tight in his throat.

"Watch!" Tolman urged.

As the girl wept, she whispered "Jesus, I am so sorry."

"No-No-No," the demon shrieked. "Don't be stupid, there's nothing to be sorry about."

The girl ignored the irate voice in her head. "Jesus, I am so, so sorry. Please forgive me for what I have done. Please help me live my life right. I-I was just so scared."

Jason was blinded momentarily with a flash of light, and when his eyes adjusted, he saw a figure with his hand gently resting on the girl's head.

Jason could only see the back of a man in a white flowing gown with light emanating all around him. But he knew in his heart that this was Jesus.

The girl looked up, closed her eyes, and smiled. The dark gray mist over her chest and her purple-bruised heart became a bright light and the black stain that oozed down her face turned into gold dust that sprinkled her cheeks like tiny glistening freckles.

Peace fell on her swiftly, and her face looked surreal as she basked in the warm glow of her Savior, the one who had made her clean, the one that had made her whole.

Jason glanced towards the angel, and she smiled warmly back at him. He noticed the demon had taken off — cursing, looking for another victim.

The vision stopped and quickly switched to somewhere else. He saw himself talking with his CEO, Ben Crothers, and one of the board members, Bruce Campbell, in the conference room.

"Business is picking up. We have now gained another research company to purchase parts for study." Jason said.

"Saves on disposal fees." Ben commented.

"That's for sure," Bruce stated. "At least we can say that we are helping with research. Last year, they spent 76 million on buying fetal tissue—"

"And we definitely want more of that pie." Ben chuckled.

"For sure!" Jason agreed. "So, what else have you got?"

"The Los Angeles clinic has had another complaint; Another incomplete termination has occurred. That's the fifth one in the last few months now." Ben stated as he looked at his notes.

"Gees… who's responsible for that one?" Jason said with frustration.

"Bentley." Ben responded, "… it's mainly Dr. Bentley."

"Well, fire him. Speak with HR and get rid of him. We've had nothing but complaints since he started. He's obviously not ensuring all tissue is removed, so get rid of him and hire someone who can do the job properly. He's affecting our stats. I know plenty of practitioners waiting to get into our clinics. So, find someone new." Jason snapped.

As Jason watched the vision of this conversation unfolding, he felt sickened to his core for he knew that this was a rerun—it was truth. This conversation actually occurred, and he remembered every sentence… every word. But seeing it from a different angle made him feel so ashamed. It disgusted and repulsed him now that he could see it for what it was—so callous. He felt an overpowering sorrow at what he had said.

The vision suddenly shifted again, and Jason was watching a different scene. It was as though he was standing on the outside looking up at a magnificent temple located in Heaven. He could see individual lights that formed the shape of birds coming out from the top of the temple. They were all different colors—some multicolored, shooting upward and rushing outward with rapid energy and excitement. He could see something else on these bird lights, but they were moving too fast for him to see what it was.

Tolman spread out two of his wings and suddenly one of the bird lights froze in time for a moment so Jason could capture what was on it. It amazed him to see symbols stamped in gold. Somehow, he knew that they were ancient writings and strangely… he completely understood them.

It fascinated him to see everything in such detail as the name, date and purpose written on the creature of light. It read:

Michael Lindell, 7 Nov, Police officer & Kingdom Builder.

But he could see much more detail. It was the story of Michael's entire life written in this light. Where he lived, who his parents were, who he would marry, and without asking, Jason knew exactly what this beam of light was. It was a child being sent out, and he understood at that very moment, Michael Lindell had been conceived somewhere on earth. This light was his spirit, with his whole life written, planned, and set out before him.

Jason heard Tolman speak, "In the book of James 2:26 it states, 'The body apart from the spirit is dead.' Each light that you see has God's detailed thoughts on the child that, at this very instant, has been conceived. Each one is a precious gift from our Lord, each one is initiated from God and each one is given a purpose… a life."

Tolman dropped his wings and the bird of light flew rapidly past them and into the outer realms. Jason's vision quickly extended out further and followed the light. He saw the light flying through space at incredible speed. Stars and planets flashed by and then he saw the earth just before the light landed. He watched in awe as he could see the instantaneous moment of when a human egg was fertilized, and at the same time, the bird light entered with a spark and Michael Lindell's human life on earth had just begun.

Jason stood silent, processing what he was witnessing. He knew that his whole belief system had just been flipped upside down. He felt an intense sorrow wash over him at the many children he had taken from God. The conversations he had so flippantly about this precious life. He had never deemed these babies to be a life, simply a substance. Tears started to form in Jason's eyes as he recounted countless conversations and procedures, all about taking these valuable, precious lives.

Tolman spoke and broke his thoughtful silence. "David wrote in Psalm 127:3, 'Behold, children are a gift of the LORD; the fruit of the womb is a reward.' You have now seen the full truth, Jason."

At that point, the orange and yellow crystals that formed the mask covering Jason's eyes broke away and melted. He felt the tingling sensation as the crystals evaporated, clearing his vision and leaving him standing speechless in front of Tolman.

CHAPTER ELEVEN

Tolman smiled satisfactorily. "There a few more people that I have brought here that God would like you to meet, Jason. We are not finished yet."

"Oh?"

"Come, walk with me, my friend!" Tolman smiled, flashing the iridescent pearl canines.

Tolman and Jason slowly meandered down a golden, silver, and bronze cobbled pathway. Every large stone was perfectly placed with a mix of rubies, pearls, emeralds, and other stones that flashed different colors set in between. As they walked, Jason noticed each stone lit up under their weight and vibrated with intense energy. He could feel the tingling sensation tickling and surging up through his legs. It felt incredible, and Jason laughed at the feeling of pulsating energy.

Tolman's large white body gently swayed at his gait beside Jason, his mane lightly shifting and dancing at his graceful movement, his immense folded wings making a soft swishing sound as they continued to move forward along the path. His massive snow-white paws made gentle pattering sounds with clicking from his huge silver claws. Jason looked tiny in comparison beside this creature and his mind quickly wondered if Tolman was a being of combat.

"I am!" the huge Lion stated as he smiled towards Jason. His eyes quickly flashing a ruby color before returning to a calming pearl.

As they came to a small rise, there was a park bench underneath a tree in full blossom, with glimmers of pink, purple, and silver flowers.

"Please, take a seat and wait," Tolman requested then slowly sauntered away, leaving Jason, what he thought, there on his own. Gently, he felt a soft hand alight on his shoulder.

"Hi Jason," a sweet voice said.

He turned to see a beautiful woman standing near him. Her long blonde hair cascaded down her shoulders. Her elegant smile was mesmerizing, and her dress reflected a mixture of blue, aqua, and violet shimmering colors.

"May I?" she motioned to take a seat.

"Of course," he said in awe.

"I am Suzannah. We have met before, but I doubt very much that you would remember me."

Jason braced himself. After what he had just been through, he waited for the onslaught.

Noticing his apprehension, Suzannah spoke. "It's okay, Jason. I'm not here to condemn you. You have been through more than enough. I just need to tell you my story."

Jason breathed a sigh of relief.

Suzannah continued, "I fell pregnant at an awkward time in my marriage. We were really struggling with our finances, barely getting by. It was such bad timing. But Dennis, my husband, was so excited about it. I, however, couldn't believe it, here we were both working full time, trying to pay the rent and put food on our table, scraping by each day to make ends meet and he was jumping out of his skin about having a baby.

"It created so many arguments... we fought and fought over the child, about how we would afford the rent, food and bills. I would have to cut down on my hours at work or completely give it up. He kept saying it didn't matter, that we would be all right, that we would get through it. But we continued to argue. It was horrible.

"Then one day I just had enough, and at 13 weeks into the pregnancy, I came to your clinic for an abortion." She paused and took a deep breath before continuing.

"The staff were so nice. They told me it wasn't really a baby yet, so it would not cause any pain to the child, and that I can always have another when were back on our feet financially. They made it all sound so simple, methodical and very detached—like it was just a throwaway item. I was apprehensive, but when I saw you coming out from an office, you told me that everything will be all right and I will walk out of there feeling as though nothing had ever happened. That I could even go straight back to work the next day if I wanted. You were very convincing and your words put me at ease." she sighed.

"Well… I wasn't all right. All I felt was the emptiness, both in my heart and in my eyes. I was numb as I returned home from the clinic. When I told Dennis, he was so furious and extremely hurt. He cried for days and wouldn't speak to me. He said I murdered our child."

Suzannah briefly pondered before she spoke again. "I had felt different ever since that day. I couldn't explain it. It felt as though I had a hole in my heart and soul… as though a massive piece was missing, that no one else understood. I felt worse around the date that the baby would have been born." She paused in silence for a moment before continuing.

"Dennis and I were constantly fighting, mostly over stupid things, but I knew he never forgave me about my decision and it killed me to know that. He kept asking me which clinic I went to, but I avoided telling him. I regretted my decision every day until one night the guilt of what I had done overwhelmed me… and I just couldn't take it anymore…

So, I jumped.

"It was a cool rush at first when I hit the water. The fall, the freshness and freedom felt good for a split second—but then I instantly knew that I had made a huge mistake. I started thrashing and gasping for air, but the ocean waves were so massive, they were battering me against the cliff face. Over and over I was tumbling and turning in the current—I didn't know which way was up.

"The fear was overwhelming and the relentless, powerful, foamy white wash continued to beat every bit of oxygen from my lungs… choking and knocking all strength out of me. The cool water soon turned icy cold, and I started to grow weak and my muscles began to cramp. My lungs started filling with the stinging sensation of salty water at every gasp for air.

"My mind swiftly fleeted back to a day at Sunday school, when I had heard about Jesus and learned the Lord's Prayer. Suddenly, images of those words started moving across my mind, 'Our Father, whom art in Heaven...' I saw the large bold words so clearly. When I saw the words 'forgive us our trespasses', all my iniquities came fleeting back to me and I felt an overwhelming sense of remorse. It crushed me. And in my terror... and with my final breath... I called out to God to save me, and forgive me for all that I had done.

"The words in that prayer guided me through a prayer of repentance and salvation." She paused. "It wasn't instant, but within seconds it seemed peaceful. I could hear the slowing final beats of my heart as I felt myself descending, weightlessly drifting... slowly sinking downward... as the churning, violent thrashing roar of the sea above was quickly fading...

I was dead.

"It was serene... I felt free of all my fear, free of the guilt, free of regret and anger... free of the sorrow that I had carried around for so long. I was calm as I slipped deeper into the dark blue waters. And then I became surrounded by a soft, faint glow, becoming brighter and brighter, and my ears filled with a gentle whooshing sound like the wings of angels. I could hear the sound becoming louder and louder... and then I saw him... Aduri." She smiled. "He took my hand and then I was in Heaven."

She paused for a moment. "I now know what would have happened if I hadn't cried out to God that night in my very last seconds of being alive. I know where I would have ended up. In Hell, where you were, Jason. I too would have been there if I didn't ask God to forgive me for all that I had done.

"I should never have taken my life... it was wrong, but I am so thankful to God for his mercy and grace, that he came to me at that very last moment before I died and gave me a chance to repent and be saved. I am thankful that I made it to Heaven, but if I had my time again, I wouldn't have gone through with the termination. I would have done everything that I could to bring up our child." She paused in reflection. "I wonder daily about my husband Dennis and wish that I could tell him we're okay and that I love him very much... and most of all, that God loves him." Suzannah then turned to her right. "Rosie," she softly called.

A little blonde, curly-haired girl appeared walking towards them. She was the most gorgeous child Jason had ever seen.

"Rosie, this is Jason." She paused and looked straight at him. "Jason, this is my daughter."

Jason smiled, not just at Rosie, but at the goodness of God. *All the children*, he thought, *all the children he had terminated were here, enveloped in God's love.* He smiled at the irony. *Tolman was right! Who was he to take life, to snatch the life of something that the Creator of the universe so lovingly knitted together?*

Suzannah slowly got up from the bench "Tolman told me you're to return. You are very privileged! I hope you make a difference," she smiled and then took Rosie's hand. "Goodbye Jason," she said as she walked away and disappeared in a turquoise swirl of mist.

Jason sat on the bench quietly. He pondered at all the children he had met and the differences they could have made to the world. Did he terminate another Nelson Mandela or another Mother Teresa? Maybe a Nobel Prize winner who would have found the cure for cancer, or even a talented teacher that could have influenced a generation. The questions arose at what may have been, and Jason felt sad about the damage that he had caused.

"You cannot change the past, Jason." Tolman spoke. "But you can use your mistakes to propel you into making a better future." He continued, "God removes our sins as far as the east is from the west, my friend, and you are now redeemed. Your cry out for forgiveness and mercy has saved you, Jason. If you hadn't done this, then you would return to the place Aduri plucked you from."

"So, God still loves me, even after all the pain I have caused Him?"

Tolman smiled. "God has always loved you—it is you that didn't love God."

"I guess when you put it that way... yes, you're right."

"It's all about choices," Tolman continued. "You humans love to blame God when a disaster or misfortune hits, but you never gave him a second thought before the event. The world has taken God out of most things—the courtroom, schools, Christmas, Easter... and more. Yet they expect God to save them when a crisis hits... even though they never knew him or even acknowledged him previously."

He continued. "It seems so strange that you call upon God only when a tragedy occurs. It is so two-faced, don't you think? Here we have a loving Father who created the universe and all creatures, but humans prefer to ignore Him and live their lives as they see fit, then blame Him when something bad happens. Crazy!" Tolman shook his head. His eyes flashed a deep purple and his mane slightly flared. "You are very fortunate, Jason. People only get one chance at life on earth and their choice determines their eternal destiny. To love and follow God, or live their own lives and ignore him. Once they pass away and reach their final destination, their fate is sealed forever."

"And I would be one of them," Jason whispered with realization.

"Yes, but God has a plan for you. He wants you to return and change what you have influenced. To make them all realize that they are babies right from conception, that they are a pure gift and God has planned every single child—even if you call them mistakes."

Jason sat still, intently looking at Tolman. He desperately wanted to please God, to make a difference and change what he had done. The feeling of strength and love surged through him, invigorating him in wanting to change the world's view. He had a complete renewing of his mind.

"There is someone else here who wants to talk with you." Tolman said as he turned and sauntered away, disappearing into the air.

"Jason," a soft female voice spoke.

Jason got up from the bench seat and turned around to see a woman. "Sally? WOW! You look great!"

"I am great." She smiled. "Tolman wanted me to come here and talk with you, before your return."

"It's so good to see you."

"You remember how I left?"

"Yes, I'm sorry. I now understand what you were saying. I was just so angry and frustrated with your choice."

"I know you were. You now understand that I couldn't continue with the thought of all the terminations we were doing once I knew the truth. The corporation meant nothing once I opened my eyes to the killing. I had to end it there and then."

"I missed you, but I hated you for what you did to me because I trusted you and when you left, I had to find another CEO. It's never been the same, and I hated you for that."

"I understand... but I do not regret leaving. I know that what we did and what you continued to do was wrong. When I found Jesus, everything changed and I just couldn't stay."

"I respect that now, Sally, and I'm so sorry for the hurtful and harsh words that I spoke to you. Will you please forgive me?"

"Oh, I did that years ago, Jason. Long before I came home," she smiled warmly.

"I'm sorry. I couldn't believe it when I heard you had passed as I didn't know you were struggling with cancer."

"Well, that didn't eventuate until many years after I left the corporation. It wasn't what I had planned for my future… But I made it to Heaven, and for that alone, I am so thankful to Jesus."

Tolman motioned to both of them to finish up.

"Well, Jason, I guess this is it. You're lucky enough to get a second chance, so make it count. Please go back and make a difference. Change people's minds to see the heart of God for all children. Convince them that all are so, so precious." She smiled as she leaned forward and gently kissed him on the cheek. "Goodbye Jason, I hope to see you again… but not too soon." She winked as she turned and walked away, disappearing into the atmosphere.

CHAPTER TWELVE

"THERE IS ONE MORE FRIEND I HAVE BROUGHT HERE FOR YOU TO SEE," Tolman said, nodding in the direction to look.

At first, he couldn't make out what it was, but it was coming at him *FAST*... like a rocket across the grass. He could hear its thoughts projecting with excitement.

It's Jase, it's Jase, it's Jase... it was repeatedly thinking.

Then, at 300 feet away, he could see that it was a brindle-colored dog. His heart leaped for joy when he realized who it was.

"ARDIE!" he called, "ARDIE... is that you, buddy?"

At full pace, Ardie soared into Jason's arms, knocking him completely backwards and onto the ground. *Oh Jase, oh Jase, oh Jase. I've missed you, I've missed you, I've missed you.*

Jason heard Ardie's thoughts as he was excitedly bounding around him.

"Oh, buddy—I have missed you too!" Jason laughed. Then continued to pat and hug his old friend, rolling around in the grass, both ecstatic to see each other again.

Jason laughed with joy. "Oh man, I didn't know animals would go to Heaven!" he exclaimed in astonishment.

"Yes, they are God's creatures, too. God loves all of His creation," Tolman smiled.

Jason sat on the grass and hugged Ardie. "I never got over you, bud. You were the best dog."

He watched Tolman wander off, leaving them to enjoy each other's company.

───────

THEY RAN AND PLAYED IN THE GRASS, CHASING EACH OTHER, RUMBLING and loving each other's company again. After twenty minutes, Jason saw Tolman sauntering towards them.

"It is time!" Tolman said, and Aduri rapidly appeared and stood beside Jason.

Jason looked at Ardie. "Okay buddy, I will see you again. You behave yourself up here!"

Wha? But you just got here? Why you leaving? Ardie thought, confused, then sat in the grass and watched Jason intently.

Jason patted him reassuringly. "It's okay, bud." Then he looked at Tolman with a touch of concern on his face. "But what if I can't do it... what if I fail and disappoint God?"

Tolman's eyes flashed amethyst and pearl as he spoke. "Have faith, my friend. God will be with you always—you are not alone. Yes, there will be times when you will want to give up, but remember this experience. Immerse your mind in God's Word and you will be strengthened and encouraged. If you let Him, and I adamantly suggest you do, He will lead and guide your path. Listen to His promptings and you will be fine."

Jason took a deep breath. "Okay," he paused. "So, what now?"

"Aduri will take you back."

Jason looked down at his friend Ardie and back at his surrounds, and breathed in the peace and love that he felt. "I'm unsure, I mean... can't I just stay and enter Heaven now? I don't want to go Tolman, it's so beautiful."

Tolman gradually unfurled and spread out his four wings. Jason instantly saw thousands of children's faces scattered across his perfect gleaming white and silver tipped feathers. "These are the ones that you will affect if you go back, Jason. These are the ones that you will save and each one of these children will impact your world. You *must* return, for the sake of these and countless others." He paused for a moment, "But don't

59

worry, I will see you again… that is… *IF* you stay faithful to our Lord." Tolman smiled, knowing the sense of loss Jason felt about leaving. "For now, you must fulfill what God has called you to do. Remember where you were plucked from, Jason. That should be enough to spur you on. Remind yourself that your return is a very rare gift indeed."

Jason nodded thoughtfully, "Thankyou Tolman, for showing me the truth… and for saving me."

Tolman smiled. "It is God who has saved you, not I. I am only one of the Lord's servants." he paused and looked knowingly into Jason's eyes. "We will all be praying for you, Jason." Then he nodded to Aduri.

Aduri smiled and gestured for Jason to take his hand. Everything inside of Jason wanted to stay, but he gently accepted Aduri's offer and he felt the rush once again surge inside of him. More love, peace and overwhelming compassion. He knew he had to return and speak God's message.

Gently, he felt his feet lift off, and he tightened his grip on Aduri's hand. The momentum became faster and faster until once again they were at lightning speed. Time, stars, planets, solar systems were flowing past them like shining reflectors on a freeway.

He tried to take in this moment as much as he could, not wanting to forget anything that he had seen or experienced. He looked ahead and he could see the earth—at first, just a tiny blue speck, then quickly growing larger and larger until they burst through its atmosphere into its crystal blue skies. As they ascended, their speed slowed dramatically.

Aduri looked directly into Jason's eyes and smiled the most beautiful, encouraging smile that Jason had ever seen. He knew then that he would be all right. As Aduri's large wings unfolded to slow their descent further, he felt his grip loosen. Jason looked at Aduri and he again reassuringly smiled, then gently released his hand.

Jason felt as though he was free falling. He knew it was only several feet, but it felt both incredible and frightening at the same time.

Then,

BANG!

Like a truck, it hit him.

The rush of intense pain, the numbness, the incredible heaviness and the agonizing ache of his own body…

He had returned home.

CHAPTER THIRTEEN

ONE WEEK LATER.

JASON COULD FEEL HIMSELF WAKING UP, AS THOUGH HE WAS CLIMBING UP from the deepest of sleep. His throat was on fire and felt raw, dry and scratchy, like he had just swallowed a sheet of sandpaper. His eyelids were lazy and heavy and far too difficult to open. He continued to keep his eyes closed, waiting until he was more alert to open them. He knew exactly where he was and he had not forgotten his experience.

Jason moved his head and tried to swallow to gain some relief from the dryness.

"Jason… Jason," he heard a soft female voice say his name.

He stirred again, trying to open his eyes, but they were still so heavy.

"Jason, it's Nurse Cambridge. You were in an induced coma, and what you're experiencing is the process of waking up. Your throat will be sore from the breathing tube, which has been removed. I'll go get Dr. Roberts." She said, as he heard her footsteps going out of the room.

Only a few minutes later, Jason heard others enter the room. "Jason, it's Daniel Roberts. Can you hear me?"

Jason's eyes were still too heavy, but he could motion with his fingers in recognition of hearing the man's voice.

"Great, great!" Dr. Roberts continued. "Jason, as Nurse Cambridge explained, you've been in an induced coma for a week as you received a severe TBI from the accident and had a brain edema. Therefore, I recommend you go back to sleep for now. It will take a while for you to come out anyway, so don't fight to wake up. You're in good hands." He said, as he patted Jason on the forearm. "Good to see you back," he smiled.

Jason needed no more encouragement. He happily slipped back into his slumber.

TWO DAYS LATER.

"WE THOUGHT WE'D LOST YOU," SAID MARG SHELTON, JASON'S PA.

The smartly dressed, plump, middle-aged woman with a blonde bob sat and watched Jason delicately take a sip of his orange juice with his lunch. "I've got to tell you Jase, you look rather terrible." She grimaced at him with pity, but thankful that he was alive.

"Well, let's just say that I don't feel like running the Boston Marathon right now." His attempt at humor met with a wince when he smiled as his bottom lip had ten stitches on the inside gum and his top had five smaller on the outside. His nose was swollen from the break, which made it difficult to breathe, and hues of red, blue and black surrounded both eyes. He had eight stitches across the corner of his eyebrow, five broken ribs, a punctured lung and a broken collarbone. Fortunately, he had only received a few minor bruises, cuts and scrapes on his legs.

"You're so lucky, Jase. I don't know how you're still alive... What do you remember?"

"U-hem," Jason cleared his throat. "I don't remember what happened or how I got here. I finished dinner, got into my car, and started it. A few emails had come through, so I sat for a bit and scanned through them. I focused on my cell and nothing else. Next thing, I'm here."

"So, no one has told you what happened?"

"Well, you're the only one I've seen outside of this hospital."

"But didn't a nurse tell you what happened?"

"No."

"Okay, well, you had an accident with a truck. The truck driver drove into your vehicle."

"Was he out of control?"

"Well, not precisely," she paused. "He was in control."

"What do you mean? Didn't he see me?"

"No... he... well, he saw you... he——" She shifted uneasily.

"So, was he distracted? On his phone then?"

"Mm... well... no, not quite." She was nervous, not meeting his eyes.

"Marg, you're not making sense," Jason said out of frustration. "So he wasn't out of control and he saw me, so why am I even here?"

"Um, Jason, I don't know how to say this... He purposely drove the truck over the top of your Beamer."

Jason looked at her, dumbfounded.

"Jase——" she gulped, "he tried to kill you!"

"What? Are you sure?" he exclaimed, aghast.

"Yes!"

"I mean, are you sure it wasn't a mistake?"

"No, it's no mistake. He definitely wanted you dead."

"Why?" Jason's face was a mixture of confusion.

"Oh, I don't know. The police are still investigating. But he could be one of those nut cases we see every day out the front of our buildings."

Jason was silent for a few seconds, staring at her, confused and saddened that someone hated him so much that they wanted to kill him. "Do I know this guy? I mean, is he one of the regular pro-lifers?"

"No, he isn't, at least... well, I've never seen him before."

"Oh."

"Yeah, Jase—heavy, huh? We all thought you were gone. I'm so glad that you're okay. The place has been chaos without you."

"Yeah." Jason responded, his mind elsewhere.

She continued, "The board had so many meetings, coming up with contingency plans if you didn't make it. I mean, we weren't sure what would happen... there was all this squabbling and backbiting. Oh, it would amaze you at what's been happening."

"Did any of them come and see me?"

"Sorry, what? Oh... mm... well, I'm not sure. I mean, well, no one mentioned anything, but everyone was very concerned about you." She looked at Jason, sorry she had told him the truth.

Jason didn't speak for a moment, a wave of realization rushing over him. "Thanks, Marg. I guess… I'm exhausted… Would you mind?"

"Sure Jase, I'll leave you to rest up. I'll come back in my lunch break tomorrow, okay?"

"Thanks," Jason said as he watched her gather her handbag and walk out of his hospital room.

As he sat staring, his thoughts started running through his mind. *It was deliberate? Someone tried to kill me?* "Why?" he whispered, unable to fathom a reason. His thoughts started spiraling downward. He recalled Marg saying that no one else visited him. *They only care about what they can get out of the business.* A wave of emotion rolled over him and tears welled up in his eyes at the sheer reality of what his life amounted to. Nothing… he had nothing.

He was wealthy, he reasoned, but it was all for nothing. It meant nothing—it was just stuff, meaningless material things that were useless. *I've no one in my life at all.* His thoughts were drumming with the awakening truth that was a far cry from his logic only ten days ago. No one to love him, to share his days or his dreams. "I've been a fool," he whispered. *I've focused on the wrong things,* he thought. *I'm forty, with no family, no one to love.* It surprised him to find hot tears gradually trickling down his cheeks. "I am alone," he whispered. He felt sorrow—deep sorrow, not just for himself, but for what he had done. He let his emotions spill over with the enormity of his experience and the realization that someone wanted him dead.

He reached over to grasp the glass water jug on the table beside his bed, and as he lifted it, he saw something that he hadn't noticed before, as the refraction of the glass had distorted it. It was a small, black, leather-bound Bible, something that he had never read or even held before.

He picked it up and read the cover. "New International Version," he said aloud. He flipped it open, and read where his eyes fell on Hebrews 13:5:

'Keep your lives free from the love of money and be content with what you have, because God has said, "Never will I leave you; never will I forsake you." '

Immediately, Jason sensed relief and peace drift over him. "I don't have anyone here on earth," he said aloud, "but I've got the Creator of the universe with me always." The words comforted Jason, until again his eyes fell heavy, and he slipped back to sleep.

"Good morning, Doctor Miller."

Jason gently awoke to the nurse's soft voice speaking to him.

"You need to take your medication." she smiled.

"Okay," he said drowsily, as he propped himself up with his pillows. "What time is it?"

"Six. Did you sleep well?"

"Not really, it's hard to sleep here," he replied as his mind drifted back to the nightmares that haunted him all night.

"Yes, especially when the staff are checking you every few hours," she smiled.

Then Jason remembered. "Do you know where this Bible came from?" Jason handed it to her.

The nurse looked at it carefully. "No, I'm not sure, but I can check the register of who has been visiting if you like?"

"Yes, thanks."

She continued to look at his chart and make notes. "I'll do that now for you." She smiled, then wandered off and returned within a few minutes. "Actually, I remember now. Apart from your aunt, there has been a young man coming here visiting you regularly, and his name from the register is Ryan Carter."

"Really? I don't know a Ryan."

"Well, he was always asking about you and sitting by your bedside at least every second day. He is a lovely young man. I figured he must have been a relative. A son, maybe?"

"No, I don't have any other family."

She went on checking his blood pressure. "Well, everything is looking good." she smiled. "Can I get you anything else?"

"No thanks. I'm fine at the moment."

Ryan? Jason thought. *I don't know any Ryans. I wonder who he is? I hope he is not the guy that ran me over... Gees, wouldn't that be just peachy—my attempted killer visiting my bedside to finish me.* He continued to ponder. *Weird! Who visits people in the hospital unless they want something? Maybe he's a pro-lifer just hoping to flick the switch and do me in once and for all.*

Jason's thoughts continued to take him on obscure paths, which were only interrupted when the breakfast cart rattled into his room. *Just as well… I'm starving.*

CHAPTER FOURTEEN

I⟶ was 4 p.m. and Jason became more and more bored. The better he felt, the more he wanted to get out of the hospital. He filled his time with reading the Bible and flicking through medical magazines. Marg would call in at lunchtime and give him updates on the clinics, but listening to her just made him feel sick at the empire he had created. He had been thinking, constructing, and planning what he could do to change what he had built. He just had to know how.

"Ahem."

Jason suddenly jumped, surprised at the interruption.

"Ah, sorry, I didn't mean to startle you," the young man said awkwardly.

"No, it's okay. I was deep in my own thoughts." Jason smiled at the medium-built, handsome, dark-haired man in his early twenties. "How can I help you? Are you looking for someone else as I'm the only one in this room?"

"No, well ah… sorry, I meant to introduce myself. My name is Ryan Carter, and I was at the accident scene."

"Oh, you're the one that's been visiting. The nurse told me earlier that you had been coming regularly… Is there a reason for your visits?" Jason asked, a little hesitant about the answer.

"No, well, I mean, I understand you were in a coma. So, I doubt you remember much. I just wanted to make sure you were okay… It was pretty bad."

Jason secretly breathed a sigh of relief that he was not someone who wanted to harm him. "I remember absolutely nothing about the accident. My PA told me how I got here. So, I suppose you know more details?"

"Well, yeah, I was there when it happened. I saw it happen, and it was shocking."

"You didn't get hurt, did you?" Jason asked.

"No, I'm fine. I was at a distance. It's just that… well… you know, when you see something like that… it really affects you."

"I can imagine," Jason said.

Ryan smiled. "Anyway, I just wanted to know that you're okay. I won't keep you any longer. I know how tired you must be," he said as he started to leave.

"Please stay, Ryan… that is, if you have time. I'd like to know the details of what happened."

"Sure, I've got time." Ryan seemed almost relieved at the request.

"Also, I have to ask you—is this your Bible?"

"No, it's yours. I thought you might like it. I hoped it may comfort you," he replied.

"Well, it has… I really appreciate it. So, do you have some time now to tell me about what you saw?"

"I do. I've been waiting for you to wake up." He smiled.

Jason smiled in return, relieved that he would have the answers he was waiting for.

Ryan pulled up a chair next to Jason's bed and recalled the story.

"It was nearly midnight, and I'd been out to dinner with friends. I was standing on the corner of Kent and McGuinness waiting to cross the road, when I noticed your BMW parked on the opposite side. It impressed me. I mean, I love cars, and I'd only seen the black M6 Coupe in the magazines. It was mesmerizing. I just had to stand and look for a while."

"Yeah, it is nice… well, it was." Jason smirked, remembering the leather seats and the sheer power of the engine.

"It's awesome. I just love those aerodynamically smooth lines and its impressive engineering. It's such a powerful-looking vehicle," Ryan reflected, side-tracked. "Anyway," he caught himself, "I saw you get into it, and was secretly wishing that it was me, when I heard a truck start up…

um… I don't know, it must have been about half-a-mile back. I noticed it because it was such a still night and the truck's engine broke through the calm.

"I wanted to hear the M6 start up, so I thought I'd wait until the truck passed so I could get a good listen to the M6's engine purr. Well, even though I was staring at your car, I noticed this truck was really hammering. I mean, it was moving so fast. I thought it was strange, you don't see trucks going that quick around these streets… if at all."

He paused momentarily. "Anyway, I got nervous, so I backed away from the curb because I didn't want to get blasted by the gust of wind that it would create when passing. Then… well, only seconds before… I noticed it was in the lane you had parked in. He was driving right along the curb and was coming up fast behind you. I tried to get your attention. I screamed out to you, but it was too late. He just hit the back of your car and drove straight over you and plowed into a brick building. I couldn't believe what I saw."

Ryan took a breath, tears welling up in his eyes. "I felt so helpless. How could I know that the truck would do that?" he paused. "But what got me was the driver. It really shook me, because moments before he hit, I saw he was smiling—like he'd done it deliberately. I couldn't understand it. I just didn't expect that somebody would do that intentionally. So, I thought I was seeing things."

"Was he hurt?"

"Yeah, he was pretty smashed up. He'd driven into a building and was encased in the metal and brick chaos, but all I could think of was you. I dialed emergency, and they came within five minutes. The place was crawling with medics and law enforcement, and the police sectioned the street off. I thought for sure you were dead—no one could survive that."

"So, what happened next?"

"Well, I was standing outside the barricade tape zone, answering all the police questions while the firefighters were cutting your beamer apart to create access for the medics. I honestly thought there was no way someone was getting out of that M6 alive. Next thing I saw was the medics covering you with a sheet and then they left you while they moved off to work on the driver trapped in the truck and building rubble."

"So, I was dead?"

"I presumed so when they put a sheet over you and left you alone. Didn't they tell you that?"

"No."

"Oh." Ryan paused, as if regretting that he was the one that had told Jason. "I'm sorry. Do you want me to continue?"

"Please!"

"Okay, well, by this time, forensics had arrived and were collecting evidence and photographing the incident scene. So I was just sitting on the pavement at a distance, watching everything going on and, well, you will think this a little strange, but I had a real urge to pray for you. I'm a Christian and I believe Jesus raised people from the dead. I had a strong feeling come over me to ask God to give you back your life. You probably think this is weird, huh?" Ryan said awkwardly.

"No, not after what I've just been through."

"Well, I thought 'here goes', and I prayed."

"So, what did you say?" Jason interrupted.

"I said heaps of stuff, but mainly asked God to spare your life, to bring you back and to save you."

"How did you know I wasn't already a Christian?"

Ryan swallowed. "Okay, another bit of weirdness… I just knew in my heart where you were headed… and it wasn't Heaven."

Jason stared at him for a moment in reflection, then said, "Please continue."

"I must have sat there for at least two hours. It sounds crazy, right? But it didn't feel like it was that long, because I was just in the moment praying. There was an overwhelming power of God with me and I knew that something amazing was happening." Ryan chuckled. "I think everyone thought I was a fruitcake. They were all still dealing with the incident, but I could see them occasionally glancing my way in wonder."

"So, tell me more of what you prayed."

"I kept asking God to give you back your life, to reach you in Hell and bring you back so you could be a witness for him. I know it seems far-fetched, but I truly believed it… and I knew God can do the impossible."

Jason's eyes welled up with tears at the thought of what this young man had done for him. "Please go on," he whispered.

"So, about another half hour went by and I was fading. I was hungry, cold and losing concentration. Even though I still felt the power of God, I was so tired. It was at that point, when I nearly gave up, that I suddenly heard God clearly say, *Ryan, he's alive!* Which instantly blew me away," he grinned. "And at that very instant, a responder heard you groan... and then suddenly a burst of activity occurred from the medics as they got you onto a stretcher and into the back of the ambulance... and now you're here alive. God is so amazing!" he shook his head.

"Yeah, amazing," Jason said. "Thank you so much, Ryan," tears welled up again. "Words cannot explain how grateful I am."

"I know He spared you for a reason."

"Yes, you're right, and I know that reason."

"Tell!" Ryan asked inquisitively.

"Well... do you have time to come back again, maybe tomorrow?" Jason asked. Ryan then realized how emotional and fatigued Jason was.

"Oh, sure—it has been a lot to comprehend."

"Yeah... I've had a lot to think about lately."

"Well, I'll come back same time tomorrow if you like?"

"Yes, thanks Ryan."

"I'll see you tomorrow then," Ryan smiled as he got up out of his chair and walked out of the room.

Jason lay in silence, processing the conversation until exhaustion overcame him. "Thank you, God," he whispered as he gradually drifted off to sleep.

CHAPTER FIFTEEN

THE NEXT AFTERNOON CAME SWIFTLY FOR JASON. HE HAD BEEN SLEEPING restlessly and feeling emotionally drained from reflecting on the information that Ryan had given him the day before. In between his waking moments, his dreams were not peaceful. He would return to the horror of that place and then awake to the relief that he wasn't there.

"Hi Jason," Ryan came through the door with a smile.

Jason grinned, relieved that he had come back again. "I'm glad you returned."

Ryan smiled. "I'm glad that you're still alive!"

"Us both then! How was your day?"

"Good, I've just finished work. We had a great day."

"What do you do?"

"I work as the student coordinator for a youth center. We help get kids off the street, assist in re-educating and get them jobs. I love it, it's rewarding. Especially when you see such transformations."

"Wow! You must feel good at the end of each day!"

"Yeah, most days. Like always, there are difficulties, but it's great to see the kids thrive. I know it's where I'm supposed to be right now and it's exciting."

"What do you mean, you know?"

"Well, I know God planted me at the center for a season. It may not be forever, but I'm here doing God's work, and it feels great to know that I'm doing what God has asked me to do."

"Okay," Jason paused. "Look, I have to be honest with you, Ryan. You speak foreign to me," he smiled sheepishly. "I have never been around Christians, never believed and never read a Bible before now. The only encounter that I've had with Christians hasn't been positive. So, forgive me if I don't understand all your God talk."

Ryan chuckled. "No problem. I understand. I'll cool down the Christianese for you."

"That would be good." Jason smiled.

"Okay… while we are being honest… I need to tell you something that has been plaguing me and it's not pleasant," Ryan stated.

Jason nodded.

"This will sound terrible, and I've really been struggling with these thoughts myself, but…" Ryan paused awkwardly.

"Look, whatever it is, you will not offend me. I've grown a thick skin."

"Well," he paused. "If I had known it was you that night in the accident, then I would have walked away. Now I know that sounds awful… and it is… and I keep asking God to forgive me for thinking this way, but I can't help how I feel." He took a deep breath and continued, "But I have to say it, Jason, what you do and who you are is against everything I stand for. If I had known that it was Doctor Jason Miller squashed in that car, I… sadly… would have been totally relieved. I know it's wrong to feel this way, but I have to let you know why I feel so strongly about what you do."

Jason said nothing, but listened.

"My mother was a victim of a gang rape. They classed it as one of the worst cases. Through it she fell pregnant with me and all she wanted was to have me terminated because of what I represented and how I made her feel. She wanted to forget about it and get on with her life. So, she went to the abortion clinic to have my life extinguished. The state had agreed to pay for all medical costs because of the hideous crime committed against her. Anyway, there were some pro-lifers out the front of the clinic. An old woman met her at the gate and spoke gently to her about placing the baby for adoption. My mother pushed her away as she was angry and wouldn't listen and continued into the clinic. But, while she was sitting in the waiting room, she kept thinking about what the old lady had said to her. Even though I wasn't planned, I was still a gift from God and I was meant to be. She got up and walked out of that clinic and straight into an adoption center and registered me. That old lady saved my life. If it wasn't for her, I wouldn't be here, and if I wasn't here… then where would you be, Jason?" Ryan stared at Jason coolly.

Jason didn't know how to respond.

Ryan semi-exploded. "How many people have you aborted that could have made a difference? What gives you the right to take the lives of innocent children? Do you realize God sees what you do as murder? I thank God every day for my life and what he has done for me. How many other children could have been saved and raised in homes of people who couldn't have children by birth? Do you ever think of that, Jason?" Ryan got emotional, tears welling up in his eyes. "Why is abortion deemed as the easy way out, when there are so many people wanting desperately to become parents? How can you live with yourself, Jason? And that is why I would have walked away that night. I would have been happy that you were dead, that these clinics that keep popping up everywhere would be no longer. I know I shouldn't be judging you, but I hate what you do, and so does God. Do you even get what I'm saying?" Ryan concluded.

"Fully!"

"Excuse me?"

"I fully understand what you're saying, Ryan."

"You do?" Ryan blurted, expecting a fierce rebuttal in defense.

"Yes, I do. Now let me tell you a story."

Jason told Ryan about that night, where he went when he died, the terror he witnessed and felt, how he ended up in a different realm, Aduri, Tolman, the children, Suzannah, and some of what he experienced.

The nurses walked past, reminding them that visiting hours were over. But he continued anyway. It was 11.30 p.m. by the time Jason had finished.

"WOW!" was all Ryan could say at the end. His emotions overtook him and tears streaked down his face. "What an amazing testimony." Ryan shook his head in disbelief. "That's… so… awesome." He said as he wiped his face and composed himself. His heart was bursting with mixed emotions of relief, excitement, and amazement at what God was doing. "So, what are you going to do now?"

"Well, that is my dilemma. I know I can't continue in this profession. I've been considering closing all the clinics down."

"Are you serious? This is amazing—I'm so excited. God is so awesome."

Jason just stared again at Ryan and his weirdness.

"Ah sorry, I'll try to calm down the God language," he smiled, "but this is such a turnaround."

"After what Tolman revealed, I now know that it is wrong and I have to change it. I'm not sure how yet. I think the best and quickest way is to close them."

"Okay… what about this? Have you considered not closing them down, but… mmm, I don't know, turning them into adoption centers?"

"No, actually… I hadn't thought along those lines." Jason pondered for a moment. "I was on the track of shutting them all down, just forgoing everything and becoming a family physician."

"Jason, God uses bad for good. He can turn everything around. This could be a wonderful opportunity to change the view of adoption. Why not?"

"You may be right. This could be the answer. Although…"

"Although what?" Ryan asked.

"I'm not sure the board will go with it."

"Oh, and you were sure that they'd go along with just shutting up shop as well?"

"Yes, you're right, it doesn't matter what I decide, they will not be happy with it."

"Can you do it, do you think?"

"I can do what I like with the clinics—I own them. But I will suffer opposition from the members who have shares in them."

"Could they stop you?"

"No, I have the majority shares and my final say goes, but they could make it very hard for me."

"This is so exciting, just think, the abortionist turned adoption advocate. How great is THAT?" Ryan could hardly contain himself.

Jason smiled. "Yeah," he chuckled. "It is pretty amazing."

CHAPTER SIXTEEN

"You're gonna WHAT?" Ben Crothers, a good looking, 5'8 stocky man who was the CEO of Miller Corporation, didn't respond kindly to what he was hearing.

Jason sat calmly in his black leather chair at the head of the conference table and coolly made his announcement to the members of the board.

"Have you lost your mind?" Ben yelled across the table in anger, slamming his fists on the table. "You can't do that, Jason. It's absurd."

"I can, Ben," Jason responded and remained calm in the room that was filled with an atmosphere of anger and confusion.

"You are crazy." Ben continued. "This won't fly, you will bankrupt us all. You can't do this, Jason, come on—*think*. Look... I know you've gone through a rough time, but think rationally. This is just stupid, Jase."

Jason said nothing, but just stood up and exited the room. He could still hear the loud, frustrated and panicked bickering amongst Ben and board members as he walked down the hallway towards his PA Marg.

"I'm out. I'll be back tomorrow." He said to Marg as he gingerly walked by, still aching and tired from his injuries. She looked in the board's direction with apprehension.

"God, what am I doing?" Jason whispered under his breath as he exited his building.

Marg got up from her desk and crept closer to the boardroom door. Eavesdropping was her specialty.

"I wish he hadn't come out of that hospital." Ben spat.

"Now Ben, that's enough," one of the older board members shut him down.

"Well, we have to do something. We can't all just sit here and let him do this to us, to everything that we have built." Ben responded.

She heard the board members packing up and moving to get up out of their seats. Marg scrambled back to the desk just in time to see them all walk out.

TWO DAYS LATER.

"Is it true, Dr. Miller? You are changing the clinics into adoption centers?" a reporter said as she shoved the microphone into Jason's face.

"Uh, I'm not sure where you got your information from, but yes, that is my intention."

The reporter continued, "And how does the board feel about this move, are they unanimous?"

"Well, that's irrelevant. I am the owner."

"Yes, but Doctor, without the support of your board, surely you can't go ahead with this decision. I mean, how will it affect the many communities who use the clinics? What about the freedom of choice? Have you considered this?"

"Yes, I have considered everything, and that is why I am doing it." he smiled.

"Sorry, you may have misunderstood my question, Doctor. What about the right for women to choose?"

"What about the right for the child to live?" he stated.

"When has that ever come into consideration?" the reporter stood aghast. "You yourself have stated that it isn't a child until it is born!"

"I was wrong. Excuse me, but I have to be somewhere." Jason politely squeezed past the news reporter and the myriad of crew and cameras as he heard her finish her report.

She turned back towards the camera. "Well, there you have it, folks. Doctor Jason Miller himself has done a double-take and is shutting down his empire of abortion clinics. What will the communities do now? Over to you, Chuck."

Jason made it to his car. Before he pressed the starter button, he took a breather and sat for a minute contemplating what had just happened and wondering how the media got hold of this information so quickly. "Ben!" he said with an air of contempt as hit the accelerator and roared off down the street.

THE NEXT DAY

Jason burst through the door into Ben's office. "What are you playing, Crothers?" he said furiously.

Ben stood calmly, looked at Jason and politely dismissed his PA. "You tell me, Jason?"

"You went to the media on this?"

"I had too."

"Why?"

"Because you will ruin this company," he yelled as he threw a file across his desk, scattering the papers onto the floor.

"No Ben, I am doing what I know is right."

"Are you kidding? No one agrees with you. We all think you're nuts, Jason. And the people have spoken—the shares have taken a massive dive," he threw the morning's stock market report down on his desk.

"Yes, and that was your doing." Jason spat back.

"No, Jason, YOUR DOING! YOUR DOING." Ben pointed his finger accusingly. "Remember, you started this!"

"Ben, this wasn't the way I wanted to announce it to the world. This was a stupid, stupid stunt. Why did you do it?"

"Because I wanted you to see what a HUGE mistake you're making. That's why."

"You're wrong—I'm not making a mistake. You're a fool Ben, you shouldn't have overridden me on this. It was the wrong thing to do."

"No, it wasn't, Jason. You have lost your mind, and someone needs to shake you out of whatever la-la coo-coo land you're living in," Ben waved his hands above his head in mockery. "What the heck happened to you, anyway? Did that brain of yours go missing in the accident or something? Did you take some goody-two-shoes pill and go on a love trip while you were in a coma?" Ben said furiously.

"You have no idea!" Jason gritted his teeth.

"Obviously not, and I don't want to know. All I want is that we get back on track the way things were before you hit your stupid head and came back as Mother Teresa."

"Is that all you really care about?"

"Yes, that IS all I care about. We were on a roll and you stopped it dead in its tracks. Remember Jason, five clinics to open per month nation-ally—that's where I want to be, and that's where we should be RIGHT NOW!" He yelled and slammed his fist on his desk.

"Gees, you're greedy, aren't you?" Jason spat and looked at him with contempt.

"Oh, you oughta talk. Have you forgotten who YOU are? Your whole life is stepping over people and making money, so don't you belittle ME when you are the king of greed!" Ben pointed in his face.

Jason stared furiously back at Ben, although he could not deny who he was, even though he had now changed. To Ben, he was exactly the same Jason as he was before the accident, and he wouldn't understand.

"You make me sick," Ben spat. "You're a turncoat and a fool. I can't believe you are doing this after everything we've been through, everything we have built."

"We… we? If I remember correctly, Ben, you were an unhap-py, whining physician heading up a few small medical centers, busting to get into a big enterprise until I came along. You had done *nothing*. I invited you to join me after my CEO left. I've built this and I will do with it what I please!" Jason said with his finger in Ben's face.

"You don't know what you're saying. You're freaking delusional right now, Miller."

"That's where you're wrong, Crothers. I haven't been so clear in my life."

"We will put a stop to this!"

"WE?"

"Yes, WE. The board will not go through with it. We will stop what you're doing."

"Oh really, and how do you presume to do that when I am the owner and I have the majority of shares? Huh? How?"

"We will find a way," Ben sneered.

"Just be careful what you say, Ben. I have the power to fire you."

Ben looked at Jason in silence, not knowing how to respond to that statement.

"Oh what, worried about the 18.3-million-dollar waterfront house you've just purchased, are you?" Jason said sarcastically.

"Oh yeah, and you're such a saint, aren't you? What have you got? Houses, penthouses, fast cars, different girls every night. So don't you look at me and say you could do without the money. You're a two-faced deserter."

"No, I'm not. I just don't want to do this anymore."

"What? You care? You, of all people!" he spat. "Huh, that's a joke. You play on the emotions of women. I've watched you. 'Oh, you won't even give it a second thought, you can even go straight back to work'," Ben said sarcastically.

"Shut up, Ben. I'm not that person anymore."

"Oh yeah, right, I forgot. You had an accident and came back with Gandhi's brain."

"You're a fool, Ben. If you would just listen and understand why I am doing this and where we can take this company, it will be far better."

"We won't be taking this company anywhere. Do you realize what you will do to it? How the heck are you going to make money with adoption centers?"

"We won't... Well, probably not as much, anyway."

"Stupid move."

"I don't think we have anything more to say here, Ben."

"Yes, we do Jason. It has only just started. If you think I will let you ruin this corporation, then you have another thing coming."

"I think you have just given it a big helping hand yourself with the stunt you've just pulled!" Jason smiled slyly.

"No, you're wrong. The media will highlight what stupid decision you're making. The shareholders will not stand for it. They will have you! You're gone, Miller."

"It doesn't matter what the shareholders think. I AM the owner, the founder."

Ben stood fuming, contemplating his next move. "You have no idea what you have done."

Jason turned to leave. "I'll see you tomorrow," he said as he walked out of Bens' office.

JASON ARRIVED BACK TO HIS CAR, GOT INTO THE DRIVER'S SEAT, AND TOOK a long moment to assess. His adrenaline was still pumping through his body. "What am I doing?" he said, with a surge of doubt pulsating over him. His thoughts shifted, and he wavered in his decision, starting to doubt everything that had happened.

THAT NIGHT, JASON RETURNED TO THAT PLACE IN HIS DREAMS. HE AWOKE screaming, crying, and in a lather of sweat.

The doubt went away.

CHAPTER SEVENTEEN

JASON WAS SITTING IN HIS LIVING ROOM MID-AFTERNOON WATCHING the TV.

"Stocks have taken a dive in the Miller Corporation. Never have we seen the prices so low." Jason's ears pricked as he heard the female reporter on the TV. "It seems there's trouble at the helm and the board wants to oust Dr. Miller from his ship, but can they do it? Over to you, Chuck." She concluded.

"I don't know, maybe they will." Jason mumbled. "Maybe I should just shut them all down." He shook his head in dismay when he heard his cell ringing. It was a number he didn't recognize, so he hesitated before accepting it. "Jason Miller," he answered.

"Hi Jason, it's Ryan."

Jason was relieved that it was a friend. "Hi Ryan, how have you been?"

"I'm great, but how are you holding up? I've been watching the news, and, well..." he paused. "Looks like it's been a bit of a rough ride!"

"That's an understatement."

"Well, I've finished work if you wanna have a sounding board?"

"Sure! Do you know where I live?"

"Nope!"

"It's 9001, Atlantic Ave, Seagate."

"Okay, I'll see you soon."

———

"WOW, THIS PLACE IS AMAZING." RYAN SAID AS JASON LET HIM IN through the front door.

"Yeah, it's nice."

"Nice? That's an understatement!" he said as he looked around at the sheer luxury of the house whilst walking through to the kitchen and sitting on a bar stool near the large white granite island.

"Do you want a coffee?" Jason asked as he turned on the De-Longhi coffee machine.

"Please," Ryan responded. "I've had a rough day. Some kids were acting up," he smiled.

"Must be tough seeing them in trouble like that."

"Yeah, it is… but what makes it worthwhile is seeing them turn their lives around, going from desolate and addicted to self-sufficient and functioning well in the community."

"That would be fulfilling."

"So, what about you, how are you holding up?"

"Not so good. I'm at war with my CEO and the board, but I'm the founder and my final say goes. I set up the company to have safeguards, I have the controlling interest and limit the number of shares an acquirer can purchase. However, Ben is very cunning and I think they are angling towards temporary insanity to override my decision because of my TBI."

"Your what?"

"Sorry, my Traumatic Brain Injury."

"Oh yeah, gotcha." Ryan smiled before he continued. "Okay, so does that mean that they can stop you?"

"That I can't answer. I'm seeking counsel for a way forward, but it could be lengthy. In the meantime, the centers still have to operate as normal and I cannot stop that until they accept my decision. So… I'm stuck! Caught with doing something I no longer condone whilst waiting for the outcome. But…" Jason winced. "I may have gone in hot-headed. Maybe I could have announced it better. I kind of just dropped a bombshell on them."

"Yeah, okay, not received well?"

"Ah, no." Jason grimaced. "My fault, as I have a tendency to go full steam ahead once I decide. So, I'll just have to do some research and pitch it to the board in a way that I can show we can still operate and turn a profit, otherwise they will not go for it. They want to make money as that's how it's always been."

"So, do you feel that way now?"

"What about? Money? No, I don't. If we have to cut centers, I will. My eternal wellbeing is far greater than earning millions. I want to make it to Heaven, Ryan. I do not want to spend another millisecond in Hell. But if I can show that we can still make money through changing the model, then that might make it easier for me to convince the board... and also Ben."

"Tough one. We need to pray about it. That God will make a way and it will turn around."

"See here you go again... pray?"

"Yeah, pray. Haven't you ever prayed?"

"Only recently, out of desperation."

"Well, you've got so much to learn, then. I go to a great church in East Flatbush—did you want to come? You need to learn God's ways." Ryan chuckled.

"Sure, I'll go, but I don't know how they'll receive me. I'm not exactly in the Christian good books."

"Trust me, my church accepts everyone. You won't need to worry." Ryan smiled.

"Just as well." Jason smirked.

THE NEXT MORNING, MARG WAS CASUALLY WALKING DOWN THE HALLWAY, but slowed down to eavesdrop at the door of Ben's office.

"Yeah, I think we can get him on that. I'll talk to Ed and the others about it. It can't fly. I don't care what he's got in place, there is always a loophole.... yep.... okay... you're right.... okay, I'll talk to you soon." Ben said as he hung up his office phone.

Marg kept walking towards her desk. She sat down and picked up the phone and buzzed Jason.

"Hey, Marg," Jason answered his office desk phone.

"Look Jase, you know I care for you and want to see you come out of this well. But they are conspiring against you."

"I know, there's not much I can do... But what have you heard, anyway?"

"I just know that they are looking for loopholes. I'm worried about you, Jase. You've gone through a lot and I don't want to see you get hurt."

"I know... I really appreciate your concerns."

"All right then, just thought I'd let you know."

"Thanks, Marg." Jason hung up. He felt the anger rise and had a mind to go down the hallway and beat the living daylights out of Ben... But he called Ryan instead.

"Wassup?"

Jason was amused by the youthful expression. "Just feeling angry. I mean, murderous angry, and I don't know how to deal with it. I know how I used to deal with it, but it's different now."

"You need to take some time out, buddy, and pray. Look up Psalm 37:8-9 and just reflect on those words. Read it repeatedly and ask God for help. It'll work... trust me."

"All right, thanks. Appreciate your advice."

"Cool, see you later."

Jason decided he better make that phone call before he opened his Bible.

"Good morning, Barnes Law Firm, Mary speaking," the receptionist answered.

"Hi Mary, it's Jason Miller."

"Hi Dr. Miller, what can we do for you today?"

"I would like an appointment with Clifford tomorrow, if possible."

"He is full up tomorrow, but... I'm sure he can make room for you, just hang on a minute." Jason waited patiently and listened to the on-hold music.

"Dr. Miller, thanks for waiting. Clifford will move a few things around to fit you in. He said that he can have lunch with you tomorrow, 12 noon at Cheswick's, if that suits you?"

"Yes, that will be great. Thanks, so much, Mary."

"No problem, Dr Miller. Glad to be of help. Have a nice day. Goodbye."

"Bye." Jason said, then hung up, relieved.

Jason did as Ryan suggested and opened his Bible to the verses and prayed. As his anger lifted, he pondered how this kid had affected him so greatly. Not only praying for God to redeem him from an eternity in Hell, but also helping him learn the ways of God.

Jason felt overwhelmed. He never had someone in his life like this before. They were always befriending him for their own gain—women for the money he could lavish on them, men who had some business venture or idea they wanted him to invest in. He had never met anyone like Ryan, and it was like a breath of fresh air.

———

THAT NIGHT, JASON WAS SITTING IN HIS LOUNGE, CASUALLY EATING Chinese takeout in front of the TV and watching the late-night news, when a breaking story came through.

"The well-known New York lawyer, Clifford Barnes, was found dead in his Manhattan apartment this evening by his wife, Sylvia Barnes. Sylvia found her husband, Clifford, lying on the floor of their living room. Medics have since confirmed that Mr. Barnes died of a stroke and deem that there is nothing suspicious about his death."

"Mr. Barnes graduated from Yale Law School, moved to Washington and gained a Clerkship position at the Solicitor General's office. His career then spanned several top law firms until he moved to New York and opened his own private practice 25 years ago. He appeared before the Supreme Court more than a dozen times, and in his vast career, was involved in over 80 Supreme Court cases."

"It's a tragic blow to the law society. Clifford was an upstanding member of the bar who many of us looked up to." A fellow lawyer stated.

The reporter continued, "Aged sixty-eight, Clifford Barnes will be greatly missed. Clifford leaves behind his wife, three children and five grandchildren."

Jason switched off the T.V. then threw the remote across the room in frustration. "You've got to be kidding." He grasped his head in his hands with desperation and sadness.

CHAPTER EIGHTEEN

JASON WAS NERVOUSLY ADJUSTING HIS DARK GRAY TIE IN THE MIRROR. HE had his best Zegna suit on, a slim-cut wool blend in gray with faint black pinstripes, and a dark burgundy Armani business shirt. It was Sunday morning, and he wanted to look his best.

He stepped out of his recently purchased M6 BMW Gran Coupe, San Marino blue this time, that he parked across the street from the church. He was nervous as he'd never been to church before and felt apprehensive about people's reactions to him.

Ryan saw him and met him on the street in front of the church grounds. "Wow, dude! Look at you, all dressed up." Ryan stood back and looked him over.

Jason looked at Ryan, who was wearing jeans and a neat t-shirt with a print design. "What do you think... it's too much?" he shuffled nervously.

Ryan laughed. "No way! You look awesome, man. I just should have mentioned there's no requirement to dress up—unless you want to... sorry, that's on me."

They both walked in the church doors and Jason felt a little embarrassed by being so overdressed.

The pastor of the church came quickly towards them. He looked younger than Jason, mid-30s, he thought.

"Hi, you must be Jason?" he smiled warmly and stuck out his hand.

"Yes, hello."

"I'm Trent Darrow. Welcome to City Life Church. I'm the senior pastor. Ryan's told me so much about you. It's a pleasure to have you here, Jason. Also, a miracle." He beamed warmly.

"Thanks Trent, or should I call you Pastor?"

"No please, I don't need formalities... well, actually," he caught himself, "should I be calling you Doctor?"

"No, no, I don't want that." Jason smiled, relieved that this was a relaxed, friendly environment.

"Okay, great, I'll catchup with you later. Please go find yourself a seat and make yourself comfortable." Trent smiled as he moved off to greet others coming through the door.

Before they sat down, Ryan introduced him to a few more of his friends. Some were his age, but others were older. It calmed him to find a mix of demographics in ages within the congregation.

They finished their small talk and Ryan motioned for him to go to their seats as the service was about to start.

The music started to play, and the worship team sang. Jason looked around at everyone standing up and clapping and singing along to a large screen at the front with the lyrics on it. He tried his best to look normal, but inside he was uncomfortable and feeling way out of his depth.

Relief showered him when the music stopped, and everyone sat down. Trent came up to the front and spoke, and Jason sat and listened, mesmerized—soaking in the message.

————

"WELL, WHAT DID YOU THINK?" RYAN ASKED AS HE WAS SIPPING HIS latte in a café after the church service had finished.

"It was different, but I didn't know what to expect, so it would always have been a surprise. I've never been to church, only seen it on TV." He shrugged. "I thought it would be more like... I don't know, people in white robes, lots of candles or something along those lines."

Ryan smiled. "There are different denominations, but that's not what we do at ours. Well, I hope we didn't scare you away."

"I don't think so," Jason smiled. "I could feel the peace in the atmosphere—it was nice. Although I'm not sure about the singing… I felt awkward. But the talk from Trent was great."

"That's good. I'm glad you gained something out of it. Trent and his wife Leisa are amazing. They really listen to God and the direction He wants for the church. It's rare that you get a leader like ours who has such a heart to follow Christ and speak truth."

"Have you been going to that church for long?"

"Yeah. I've been going there for the past seven years. My parents go to another church."

"Why wouldn't you all go to the same one?"

"Well, I felt God prompting me to move churches, and this is the one he led me to."

"Okay then… So, you can hear God talk to you?"

"Yeah, all the time. I mean, it's not audible like you and I talking. It's more of a small voice inside here." He patted his chest.

"So, what does He say?"

"Anything. Like, if I worry about something, I will hear His voice telling me to trust and that it will be alright and it will work out. It's comforting."

"I kind of understand what you're trying to say. I just haven't experienced that and I'm not sure how to go about it."

"It's about building a relationship with God. Reading His Word, talking to Him and then listening and waiting for a response. For some people, it's not instantaneous, but I know when I read the Bible and really listen, I will hear Him speak to me, guiding my steps. If you seek to spend time with the Creator, you will get to know Him, build a relationship and hear His voice… trust me." He smiled.

It was strange how at ease Jason felt with this young man, something that he had never felt his entire life. He'd let no one get close to him, but this seemed different. "You know an awful lot about God for a young guy."

Ryan smiled "Yeah, I've been so blessed. My adoptive parents are strong Christians, they just couldn't have biological children. They loved and followed God's ways and taught me everything they knew. I'm very fortunate. But I found my birth mother twelve years ago, and she also became a Christian through getting to know my parents. It's amazing when you think about it. What about you and your folks?"

Jason shifted, not wanting to share but feeling obligated. "My parents died in a car accident when I was six-years-old. My aunt raised me. She taught me to do well in my education, gain a good career and make a lot of money. That was her motto, and she pushed me to succeed."

"I'm sorry to hear about your parents."

"They are a very distant memory now; I remember little about them. I thought more of my aunt as my mother—even though she wasn't the motherly type." He smiled with a hint of sadness. "She was a physician and so were my parents. She taught me to follow in their footsteps, so I did, but I wanted to go further and achieve even more. Well, what I thought was an achievement." He averted his eyes downward, realizing that his success had meant the death of so many innocents. A wave of guilt flooded over him.

Ryan noticed the change. "God removes our sins as far as the east is from the west, Jason. Remember that!"

"Yeah, I know." he said with remorse. "Tolman said that too. I'm trying to change things but I'm so hamstrung at the moment with all the legalities."

"The best thing that we can do is pray. Trust me." He smiled. "So, do you have any significant other in your life?" he shifted to a lighter note.

Jason chuckled. "Ah, no. I don't have a significant other. I did away with serious relationships about ten years ago—it became easier if they were just casual. Besides, women are the last thing on my mind right now. I don't know…. It's like my focus has completely changed. I'm not interested in women, money or my career right now. Probably because I had a reality check and went to Hell." Jason chuckled. "I've been reading the Bible you gave me and trying to understand God's word. But I will not know everything all at once and it feels a little frustrating at the time it's taking. All I know is that I have a desire to be a different person than who I was prior to the accident. You know… I guess I have this yearning to do what's right. Does that make sense?"

"Definitely!" Ryan smiled. "It's normal that you have a desire to know Him and do His Will, so I understand what you're saying. You've also had a unique experience, Jason, one that you will never forget… and need to share with others when you're ready."

"Yeah, I know… but not right now. My CEO is trying to pin a mental disorder on me and if I go around espousing what really happened, then they will have a genuine cause to believe that I'm not fit to run the company and remove me."

"Oh yeah, I guess I didn't think about that at all. I see where you're coming from."

"I also lost my lawyer the other night. He died of a stroke. You know, Clifford Barnes?"

"Ah, no I haven't heard of him, but… I don't hang out in the same circles that you do." Ryan chuckled.

"Yeah, I guess. Anyway, that's also left me in a bind, as I now have to seek someone else. Clifford has done all the legal work for me. He helped me start the company." He sighed with sadness and frustration.

"It's a big city. I wouldn't think it would be too hard to find someone else… surely?"

"Probably not, but it's finding someone whom I can trust… and also as good as him. Clifford was the best."

"We will need to pray on that one too." Ryan responded.

Jason paused in thought as he took a sip of his coffee. "I want to ask you something though."

"Yeah?"

"I recognize that I have done wrong things. I've hurt many people and done a lot of awful stuff. Trent's message on forgiveness this morning really hit me. But how can God just forgive me just like that, after everything that I have done?"

"That's the beauty of Christ's sacrifice! His love surpasses all our transgressions. It says in Ephesians 1:7 'In him we have redemption through his blood, the forgiveness of sins, in accordance with the riches of God's grace.' So, when God sees us, he does not see our sin because of Christ's blood that was shed for us. We become blameless. It also says in Romans 3:23, 'for all have sinned and fall short of the glory of God'. We are born into sin because of the fall of Adam and Eve, it's only through our repentance and acceptance of Jesus that we are reconnected back to our Father, God."

"So," Jason pondered, "Jesus died for my sin so I can be saved and go to Heaven. To me, that sounds like a rough deal for him."

"It was… and we should never take it lightly. He was tortured and beaten. The Scriptures state that he was unrecognizable… Hang on, it's somewhere in Isaiah." Ryan looked up the verses on his cell. "Okay, here it is. Isaiah 52:14 'Just as there were many who were appalled at him his appearance was so disfigured beyond that of any human being and his form marred beyond human likeness—'. Now this was foretold before Jesus's death, they stated it in the prophecies. Look, I'm no scholar, but this was written around 700 years before the birth of Christ. These prophesies described the manner that he was to die and what it would mean to mankind. There are over 300 prophecies throughout the Bible that Christ fulfilled in his lifetime, from his birthplace, right through to his death. It sounds like a rough deal, but it was God's plan of redemption all along. He knew He had to send His son Jesus to atone for our sins. It had to be a blood offering, so that is why He sent his Son who was without sin to redeem us. His love for us and His longing to be with us far surpasses the suffering that he had to bear through the sacrifice of his son Jesus."

"Okay… so I repent and accept and follow Jesus. But what about those who I have hurt?"

"Like?"

"Like all those women who I've persuaded to terminate their babies, directly or indirectly. I deceived and manipulated them to—to kill their children. Ryan, I have killed thousands and thousands. How am I any different to Hitler and Stalin in the way I've dehumanized these babies and murdered them? I have so much blood on my hands with the abortions I've performed, let alone the clinics I own, where we have dismembered millions and sold their bodies for research." Jason choked, his eyes abruptly welled up with emotion.

"Jason, Isaiah 1:18 says, '"Come now, let us settle the matter," says the Lord. "Though your sins are like scarlet, they shall be as white as snow; though they are red as crimson, they shall be like wool."'

Ryan continued. "Listen to those words, Jason, because you are forgiven for everything you did, but you need to forgive yourself as well. That is another step you need to take. And with those women, everyone has the opportunity to know Jesus. If they repent and follow Christ, then they also will see the truth. Those women will be forgiven and washed clean of any wrongdoing if they ask God for forgiveness. I don't condemn them, or you—nor should any other person, but they need to seek forgiveness from God, for He is the judge, not us."

"But what if they don't come to know Jesus, I mean… did I have the opportunity to know Jesus before I died?"

"Yes. You cannot deny that there was a void, a longing in your heart that you needed to fulfill, a want for something more. God places that yearning in every one of us to seek after him, to find the truth. The Bible states in Romans 1:20, hang on I'll look it up… okay, it says, 'For since the creation of the world God's invisible qualities—his eternal power and divine nature—have been clearly seen, being understood from what has been made, so that people are without excuse.' God sets eternity in our hearts, like a knowing that there is a creator. Unfortunately, people ignore God's prompts, they seek the wrong things, they will go after false religions or put everything into gaining material possessions."

"Like me building my empire."

"Yeah exactly… but were you fulfilled?"

"No. I can see that now. I was always chasing the next big thing. Building more clinics, buying more cars or real estate. Chasing another woman."

"But, can you honestly say that you didn't know about Jesus?"

"I'd heard about Jesus, but I thought he was just a good man, or a prophet."

"So basically, you heard about Him but chose not to investigate further."

"You're right, I didn't. I was too busy doing what I wanted."

"So, you ignored His promptings?"

"Yes, when you put it that way."

"See, God uses us to spread His gospel. He has missionaries, charity workers, pastors and more, and He will also give people visions. I heard a story where Jesus appeared to a Muslim to show him the truth. So, God reveals himself to those who are searching."

"I guess I never gave Him a thought. But now, I just want to change what I created and complete what he tasked me to do. I have had a royal kick in the pants and all I care about right now is fulfilling what He told me to do."

"Yeah, I totally get that."

"So, did you know your purpose in life?" Jason changed the subject.

Ryan leaned back in his chair in reflection. "I didn't at first. I got the grades to become a veterinarian or a doctor myself. But I felt God drawing me to social work and psychology. So that's what I did."

"That's amazing, to have the grades but follow what God wanted."

"It's about God's calling on your life and pleasing Him. That's all my desire has ever been."

"Yes, that's how I feel too, especially after what I've done. But I'm sure all Christians are like that. I have known none personally before, though, so I don't have a large sample to go off." Jason smiled.

"No, unfortunately, some think they are Christians, but aren't. They are not abiding in Christ."

"I don't get what you're saying. I thought once you become a Christian, it all instantly changes?" Jason said curiously.

"Believing that God exists won't save you. God makes it very clear of how we are to live our lives. In John 15:5, Jesus says, 'If you do not remain in me, you are like a branch that is thrown away and withers; such branches are picked up, thrown into the fire and burned.' So it's saying that you need to continue to have a relationship with Christ. Not just say a sinner's prayer, then return to living your life the way you have done in the past. When you give your life to Jesus, you don't suddenly become this perfect Christian either—it's a journey. You have a heart change that desires to learn His ways and let go of the wordly things. These transformations can happen quickly... or it can take time, but the evidence of Christianity is that you long to abide in Him and be obedient to His Word. It's apparent that those who aren't abiding in Him are not changing and basically, if they stopped believing in Christ, then their lives wouldn't be noticeably different. That's what I'm saying. They say they are Christians, but there is no evidence, no behavioral change, and no fruit."

"Right, I understand now."

"But, unfortunately, some believe that if you pray a one time prayer to accept Jesus that you will definitely go to Heaven, and it doesn't matter what you do from that day forward, you will still go to Heaven. This is misleading people and dangerous, as it makes people think that they only have to pray that, and then they are headed to heaven no matter what. It's not correct, nor is it biblical. Some preachers even say 'once saved, always saved', or some call it the doctrine of 'eternal security'. But it's false teaching."

"That's what that preacher in Hell told me. He said that he taught people that."

"Well, the Bible doesn't say that at all, in fact it's very clear in... wait a minute, I'll look it up." Ryan paused, as he typed in the scripture reference into his phone. "Okay, this is what it says in Colossians 1:21-23,

'Once you were alienated from God and were enemies in your minds because of your evil behavior. But now he has reconciled you by Christ's physical body through death to present you holy in his sight, without blemish and free from accusation if you continue in your faith, established and firm, and do not move from the hope held out in the gospel…' It's where it states 'if you continue in your faith, established and firm,' this means that IF you continue to abide in Him… but people don't see that."

Ryan paused momentarily. "Oh, and also, this one," he typed into his phone, "okay, so 2 Peter 2:20-22 says, 'If they have escaped the corruption of the world by knowing our Lord and Savior Jesus Christ and are again entangled in it and are overcome, they are worse off at the end than they were at the beginning. It would have been better for them not to have known the way of righteousness, than to have known it and then to turn their backs on the sacred command that was passed on to them…'"

He continued. "Also, there is a passage in Revelation 3:5, which says 'The one who is victorious will, like them, be dressed in white. I will never blot out the name of that person from the book of life, but will acknowledge that name before my Father and his angels.' So, where it's saying that your name won't be blotted out, then this implies your name can be erased and that you can lose your salvation."

"Really?"

"Yeah, being a Christian is a lifestyle change. If Christ is in us, we will be convicted of any sin we are doing and really want to change our ways and continue to follow what God wants for us. We will want to abide in Him. And don't be concerned, Jason… you can't accidentally lose your salvation. It's a choice. Most Christians will make mistakes at some point—they may sin. This doesn't mean they instantly lose their salvation, however if gone unrepentant, then that sin could cause a hindrance in their life, or open a door to the demonic to oppress them, and may even entice them to walk away from Christ completely. Which would mean that by their *own* choice, they lost their salvation. Does that make sense?"

"I think so." Jason paused, reflecting for a moment.

"But I also think that if you purposely sin repeatedly, believing that God's grace will cover you and you're not *wanting* to change this pattern, then I would question your salvation, because again… you're not actually abiding in Christ."

"Yeah," Jason nodded thoughtfully. "I recall when I was in Hell, I spoke with a young man who had been in a car accident. He said he was a Christian but became… what was it he said… something like… lukewarm, and that is why he was there."

"Yes, lukewarm. There are so many people and also churches like that now. The Bible is very clear about being lukewarm. Jesus states in Revelation that he will spit you out, and that means that you would head straight to Hell."

"So lukewarm people are what… half believers?"

"Like I was saying, they claim to be Christians, to believe in Jesus, but aren't genuinely committed. Some may go to church, appear to be a follower, say the right things when prompted, but they don't truly know or live for Christ. The Bible states it is far worse to be lukewarm than to be a complete non-believer. Jesus clarifies he will reject you if you're lukewarm."

Jason shuddered at the thought. "Yeah!" His stomach did a small churn.

"It's so interesting you got to speak with people there."

"Only before they placed us. We were in holding cells waiting for our fate. It was horrific what I saw and experienced. I watched so many people being tormented."

"Wow! Frightening."

"It was! I spoke with a preacher who apparently was famous."

"Really? Did you get his name?"

"No, not that kind of conversation," he smirked, "but he said he'd died having a heart attack on his jet."

"NO WAY…. Are you sure that's what he said? Because Pastor Tanner Morris, who was huge in the Christian world, died on his jet only —actually, it was when you died," Ryan looked astonished. "And I'm sure they said he had a heart attack."

"Well then, that was probably him. He told me he regretted not fully following God and ignoring all the warnings he received."

"Wow!" Ryan was dumbfounded. "I would never have picked it. He was so convincing, I thought he was the real deal man."

"Apparently not."

AT 9.30 P.M. JASON SAT ON HIS SOFT BROWN LEATHER LOUNGE, RELAXING after his dinner with a glass of red wine whilst responding to emails on his laptop.

"You're mine!"

Jason jumped up. His laptop fell forward and knocked over his glass of wine. The scarlet liquid splashed outward across the plush white rug. He reeled around—his skin prickled at the guttural, inhuman-like sound he had just heard only inches behind him.

"Who's there?" he said boldly. There was nothing visible, but he could feel something, a dark presence like he had felt in that horrible place.

His mind was whirling with the fear of his return there. He waited a minute, scanning the room. He relaxed slightly as his fear subsided a little.

Maybe I'm hearing things, he thought... *Maybe it's just the wine.*

CHAPTER NINETEEN

"Any messages, Marg?" Jason said as he walked into the reception area just before his office.

"Yes. Charles Declan called, wanting to set up a meeting with you regarding his shares. Amanda Dwight from Business Today wants to do an interview, and Dr. Creswick wants to see if you're available for lunch. Oh… and that medical report came through. I've put it on your desk."

"Okay… I'll call Charles myself. Say no to the Business Today journalist and tell Dr. Creswick I can't meet for lunch today, but I'm available tomorrow. Thanks Marg, you're a champ."

"Will get right on it," she beamed.

Jason continued into his office and shut the door. He sat at his desk and read through the medical report for his mother that he had requested weeks ago, and stopped at the written paragraph.

```
Patient sustained head trauma from a vehicular col-
lision on the left temporal bone, was in a concussed
state and had disturbance of vision and equilibrium on
arrival.
X-ray has concluded that the patient has an Iliac
wing fracture on the left side. Patient is 26 weeks
```

pregnant; MRI is inconclusive of brain stability/ab-
normalities of the fetus. Termination recommended.

Jason placed the report down and held his face in his hands. "God, this really happened?" He took a few minutes, his emotions reeling with the enormity of what he had read, but also the grace and forgiveness of God upon his life. Jason wept at the realization that he himself nearly didn't exist, that he too was almost a victim of an abortion.

He took a deep breath, wiped his face and collected himself, then continued to gather the data on adoption he needed to pitch to the board. He had decided that he should take a different tack and show the board how beneficial the change would be.

Ben stuck his head around the door. "We have set the date to do the Holmesville clinic opening."

"Right."

"We are still pushing ahead with our plans, Jason. We are not stopping everything just because you had a prick of conscience."

"You just don't get it do you? It's not a prick of conscience, Ben. It's a change that I want."

"You're the only one."

"That may be so, but if you haven't forgotten, I am the *owner*, the *founder*... remember?"

"Sure Jason, we'll see how that goes for you, shall we? Anyway, I just thought I'd let you know as you are to attend all new clinic openings." Ben said smugly, then disappeared back to his office before Jason could respond.

"Arrogant schmuck," Jason said under his breath. His cell suddenly beeped with a text message, startling him out of his emotional state.

Do you want to catch up for dinner tonight? Ryan.

Relieved at seeing this message, Jason responded. *Yes, I'll meet you at Ambrosio's, 7.30, my treat.*

"I'M TELLING YOU, BRUCE—WE HAVE TO STOP HIM." BEN SAID ADAMANTLY, pacing around in his office with agitation.

"Look, I agree. We need to nip this in the bud before it escalates."

Bruce responded. "Hopefully, it's just a passing phase. The bump on his head has sparked a conscience—it will go away in time."

"Well, we can't afford to have him force this on us."

"We'll come up with something. Be patient."

"A glass of mineral water please, and Ryan, you will have a—?" Jason asked.

"Just a Coke for me… thanks," Ryan responded.

The waiter nodded politely and walked away.

"Wow! We are from two different worlds, aren't we?" Ryan shook his head and smiled at Jason.

"Yes, I guess we are… is it strange?"

"Yes. I would have never imagined eating at a place like this—it's out of my league. I mean, one meal is probably my day's wage. Do you eat here often?"

Jason nodded. "At least once a week. I cook but I like to dine out too." He smiled. Looking at this young man reminded him of himself when he was in college, trying to earn a living while doing his degree. "Besides, I enjoy eating at nice places." He stated.

"Yeah, I can see why."

"Coke, sir." The waiter smiled as he placed the icy cold glass in front of Ryan and poured his drink.

"Nice, thanks." Ryan responded.

They both took a sip of their drinks and smiled.

"This is living," Ryan laughed.

"It certainly is… and I have you to thank that I can continue living," Jason smiled gratefully.

"So, how's things with you?"

"Hectic! The board won't budge. My CEO still wants me out, the shareholders are screaming blood, and I'm still having nightmares every night. Apart from that… doing great!" He smiled sarcastically.

"Gees, yeah, it would be tough. I don't know how it will turn out, but I know it will."

"How? It doesn't look that great from where I'm standing." Jason stated with frustration. "It's a mess and out of control. All I see is chaos, and I don't know what to do. I'm at a complete loss—I can't see where this is going."

For the first time, Jason let his guard down and let someone see his actual emotions. The hardness and the walls that he had built up over the years wavered, and he let Ryan have a glimpse of his vulnerability.

"It will be fine," Ryan stated. "God sent you back for a purpose. Nothing is coincidental with God… He is constantly in control. He's with you now—He's in your future and He's waiting at the end of your life. He knows how everything in your life will turn out, what choices you will make even before you've made them. When you will reject Him and the exact time that He can step in and save you, wrap his arms around you and welcome you into his fold. Nothing comes as a surprise for Him. But… I know it will work out. Anyway, God didn't say it would be easy, because it won't. However, he said that He will never leave you nor forsake you! And that should keep you going each day."

"I don't have your faith, Ryan. It's unchartered territory for me and I feel like I'm sinking."

"Are you still reading the Bible I gave you?"

"Every chance I get."

"That's great! Keep reading it—it will strengthen you and feed your spirit."

"What?"

Ryan chuckled. "The Bible is the Word of God. By reading His Word you are not only growing and feeding your spirit but also gaining wisdom and guidance on how to live your life. It's a must for Christians because you cannot be effective if you're not reading God's word. If you aren't reading his Word, it can leave you open to making wrong choices."

"Sounds like I've got a lot to learn."

"You do!"

"I have been reading it every night and also in the office when I can. It's helping me, but…" he sighed, "I still don't have a clear way forward. I'm blocked."

"God will unblock it. Just pray and be patient."

"How are your meals?" the waiter interjected.

"Amazing!" Ryan beamed.

"Thank you, sir. I will tell the chef," the waiter nodded, then walked away.

"Okay, where were we? Oh, I would like to ask you more about your experience in Hell," Ryan stated.

"Sure. What do you want to know?"

"You mentioned you spoke to people there. I was just curious about that."

"I saw lots of different people, even some I knew from TV and movies. There are millions of people there." Jason shuddered at the thought. "I don't know… it scares me as I knew nothing about that place. No one told me about it. I mean, no one really sat me down and informed me about God, Jesus, Heaven and Hell. My aunt doesn't believe in anything, so it became my belief too that nothing existed once we died. I was oblivious to my eternity, when that really matters the most, not all this material stuff." He waved his hand in a slight sweep. "It's meaningless compared to what I've experienced. And… it has scared me to death, Ryan. If it wasn't for your prayers and God's grace, then I would still be there. I narrowly escaped that place." He stopped short, tears welling in his eyes, his hand shaking. He took a quick sip of water to subdue his true emotions.

"Yeah man, I can't imagine what you went through. It would have been terrifying."

"It's beyond words… I could never describe to you the true nature of what it's like. I was in such immense pain. My flesh was being torn off at every attack from those creatures. The pain was beyond explanation, yet it hurt just as much when the flesh grew back."

"It grew back?" Ryan looked shocked.

"It's bizarre. You can be shredded from limb to limb by the creatures, or burned beyond recognition, yet your body reassembles itself. It makes itself whole again."

"I guess that would be where the Bible states that it's a never-ending suffering."

"Yeah, well, I lost my toes—bitten off by a Hell rat."

"A Hell rat?"

"Yes, it ran up and took off all my toes… and my thumb, however, it was just as painful when it grew back."

Ryan grimaced. "It's horrible to think that's your eternity… Well, until the final judgement and the Lake of fire, that is. It's a never-ending torture forever."

"Tell me about it. Try experiencing it." Jason's stomach churned, so he took another sip of mineral water to ease his nerves. "So are you saying there are two Hells?"

"You could say that the one you went to is a temporary place for humans. Once Judged, then those already in Hell, along with Satan and his demons, will then go into the burning lake of fire, which is the second Hell."

"Thank God I escaped that," he gulped.

"Yeah, it's scary."

"Unfortunately I saw an old friend there too."

"Oh man..."

"Yeah," Jason cringed. "He was being tormented in such terrible ways. He was yelling at me to escape and tell his family about Hell. But how could I? There's no escape. Once you're there, that's it. Eternity! I know it's only for the mercy of God that I am back here talking to you, and I am grateful for every second that I can breathe the cool air, or have a sip of water... or have a conversation. I will take nothing for granted again." His hands were trembling.

"So, you said you didn't believe in Heaven or Hell?"

"That's right."

"So, when did you understand where you were?"

"When the gate keeper welcomed me to Hell."

"Gees..." Ryan shook his head in astonishment.

"Yeah, it was daunting to face a demon that stood around thirty feet tall. The big iron gates swung open and the demon behind me pushed me forwards... I'm telling you Ryan, it is not a place that anyone wants to go to. Although—"

"Although what?"

"Well, actually there were some who went there by choice."

"Mm, I'm thinking I know what you will say next."

"What?"

"That they were witches... or warlocks or... Satanists—or something of that nature."

"Yeah, how did you know that? Do you know some?"

Ryan chuckled, "Ah no, but some of them don't understand and think they just have a gift from God or are fooled into believing they will have some power in Hell, so they choose Satan over God."

"Why would they? I mean, they treated them just as bad, if not worse, than everyone else."

"Satan is the ultimate deceiver. He promises them great things, but when they get there, they are worse off," Ryan said pitifully. "Also, there are secret societies that help people in life to become rich or famous. They form a contract, but it's a contract with Satan, and it's only a pact with death. The Bible says in John 10:10, 'The thief comes only to steal and kill and destroy; I have come that they may have life and have it to the full.'"

"Well, I can see why now." Jason smirked. "I couldn't understand why someone would aspire to go there."

"Nor I, but unfortunately they're deceived into believing that it will be good."

"Can I get you another drink?" the waiter asked.

"No thanks, I'm good." Ryan responded politely.

"Thank you, we're fine," said Jason. "Well, it's getting late and I still have some work at home to finish."

"Thanks for dinner."

"No problems. It was nice to talk to someone about my experience. You are the only one that I can share it with. Oh yeah, I haven't told you, but God also showed me I was nearly aborted myself."

"GET OUT! Are you serious?"

Jason relayed the entire experience of becoming a fetus and then reading his mother's medical report, proving that it wasn't fictitious.

"That is an amazing story. You have to write a book on this."

"Ah, not yet. They may put me in a padded cell if I spoke about it right now." Jason laughed.

———

Jason was back in his house, unpacking the dishwasher.

"You belong with me, you murderer." The hot-breathed whisper spoke directly behind him.

The voice, the breath, the smell was so clear and strong. Jason reeled around towards the intruder… but there was nothing visible.

His hair stood on end. He knew that this time he wasn't imagining things. It scared him.

Have my nightmares become real? He thought. *Did something follow me back?* That brought sheer panic into his heart. He could feel the beats rapidly increasing. *I need to get out of here.*

Jason raced upstairs, put on his jogging gear, and then sprinted out onto the streets to shake the feeling. His mind recalling the research on the effects of post brain trauma, and as he jogged, he rationalized the event and put it down to post TBI.

I've got to keep this quiet, he reasoned, as he rounded the bend and headed for home.

CHAPTER TWENTY

"Jase, you're looking awful." Marg commented as she handed him his morning coffee at the office.

"I haven't been sleeping much."

"Well, maybe you should take something for it because it will not help your case." She nodded sideways. "They're waiting for you... good luck!"

Jason walked down the hallway and entered the large conference room. Six sets of eyes were upon him. He could feel them assessing and scrutinizing his every action and movement. Ben and the board members Mal Dickson, Fiona Sampson, Ed Dwight, Bruce Campbell and Miriam Green all sat in silence as Jason strode over to his chair and arranged his notes on the large oak conference table.

"Good morning everyone," Jason opened the meeting. "Thanks for being here on time. Has everyone got a copy of the agenda?"

They all nodded.

"Great, let's get started then. Can I draw your attention to item number one, the Miller Corporation model change proposal? Whereby I will present the proposed change. I think from our last meeting I went in guns blazing... which may have put a few of you off. It wasn't my intention and I apologize. But it is a subject that I have become very passionate about." He paused as he clicked the first slide, showing statistics. "So first, I would like to start with data that reflects current trends." He paused. "In the US, there are roughly 135,000 adoptions per year. These adoptions range anywhere from 2,000 to 50,000 dollars." Jason hadn't finished speaking when Ben interjected.

"As opposed to over 850,000 abortions per year being conducted, costing on average 700 dollars," Ben scoffed.

Jason responded with frustration. "Sure Ben, I get it. I never said that we would make more money than we do now. I understand we may even take a loss initially, but if you patiently wait and listen to what I would like to pitch, I think we could still grow and turn a profit."

"How do you propose to change our paradigm, Jason?" Bruce asked.

"I propose we gain some help from outside—bring in some change agents that can help shift us to where we want to be."

"Where *you* want to be." Ben said snidely.

Jason ignored the remark and continued, "By doing this, I feel it will transition much smoother. In the meantime, Marg is investigating government funding and potential private or sponsor donations to help kick off this transformation."

Jason clicked to the next slide before continuing. "Child welfare services and the adoption agency industry have an annual revenue of 14 billion dollars, which grew at a rate of nearly ten percent last year. They expect this industry will increase at 2.2 percent over the next five years."

Jason paused before clicking onto the next slide. "So, statistics show that there are 36,000 adoption agencies and child welfare services across the nation. The speculated profit in this industry is around 375 million dollars. There is no dominant player, unlike in our industry. So, I feel that if we change our model with the number of centers we have across the nation, we could become *the* leading performer in this industry."

Ben shook his head and rolled his eyes, but said nothing.

"As you can see, we can gain federal funding, which we cannot get with our current services. But if you use the example from Violet Adoption Agencies annual report, you can see that they have received over 15 million dollars in federal grants, 12 million from private sponsors and 20 million from the fees of adoptive parents."

"That's still only a drop in the water compared to what we do now, Jason." Bruce stated.

"Yes, it is, but we can grow it. I mean seriously guys, how much money do we *really* need… or want?"

Jason stared as a few board members scoffed.

"Wow, you hit your head hard," Ben mocked.

"Come on, Ben. You received a nice income of over four million last year with bonuses. How much more do you need to be happy?"

Ben ignored the statement.

"It's a big call, Jase," Miriam stated. "I just don't see how this could work. The Miller branding has always portrayed the ultramodern pro-choice planning centers. How do you expect to do a double take when this is the way we do business, and that's the way the community across the nation expects us to *continue* to do business?"

"Corporations flex and change all the time," Jason responded.

"But not to this extent. This isn't just a flex, it is a complete turnabout. You can hardly compare this to any other corporation paradigm change." Ed stated.

"Yes, I get that Ed, I truly understand. But I believe we can pull it off. And Miriam, we can change the community's expectations. I mean, how would it feel if we were the ones to help influence the way people think about babies?"

"They're not babies." Ben stated.

"They are babies, Ben. What we do takes life away. I want to change that and give life back." Jason answered flatly.

"WOW! Who has stolen Dr. Jason Miller and replaced him with Dr. pro-lifer?" Ben belittled him.

"I guess you could call me that." Jason responded frankly.

"Look, this is ludicrous." Ben slammed his fist on the table and stated with venom. "We are 130 clinics away from matching our major competitor. They have 40 percent of the market. We sit around 31 percent and we are growing with the plans that both Jason and myself put in place before his accident." Ben glanced at Jason with contempt. "We are on track to be there in less than three years. Their domination is purely because they are also a health provider that can provide abortion services. However, at present, they get the numbers in the door because they are an all-encompassing service provider, whereby we only focus on one niche. Compared to their abortion income and expenses, our overheads are lower and we turn a greater profit compared to the number of clinics and staff that they have. As you're aware, we netted just over 170 million last year across our clinics. Per clinic, we earn more in abortions compared to them."

"You're right Ben, I agree. Their advantage is that they provide other health services to women. That's why I'm also proposing this." Jason said as he clicked to the next slide showing the new design of the clinics. "Looking at our competitors' last financial report, they pulled in over 560 million dollars in government funding for services such as birth control, breast and cervical cancer screening and treatment for STIs..." Jason continued. "360 million dollars from public payments for their services and over 400 million dollars from private donations and sponsors. Now that far surpasses what we make. Therefore, what I'm proposing is that we take on a similar model. However, instead of padding our bottom line with abortion services like they are, we change it to adoption services instead."

Mal interrupted. "We've spoken about expanding our services before, but everyone was adamant to focus on this one niche and be the best at it."

Ben interjected. "So, why don't we just change our current model and expand into these services right now, anyway? Don't change what we have, but expand on it? You've shown Jason, we will make far more money in doing this." Ben smirked as though he was a genius.

"Well, no... that's not what I'm getting at." Jason quickly responded. "The whole reason we are having this discussion is that I don't want to continue in the abortion industry, period."

"You don't want to continue, but everyone else does. It makes little sense to change the model we have. Our reputation is that we are the best in the field, and we might become the dominant player if we stick with our plan." Ben stated as he looked around to gain other's approval.

"He's right," Bruce stated, "I don't see why the sudden need to change the model, nor the plans we have in place for expansion just because you hit your head Jason and have come back with an overexcited conscience."

Ben and Bruce both chuckled.

"Hang on," Fiona spoke, looking straight at Bruce. "In Jason's defense, I think he is quite within his right to put forward this proposal. After all, he built the company. So, I don't have a problem with him presenting this to the board. Jason, I appreciate the fact that you have re-examined, however, this is business and I think it would be very difficult to change the paradigm so late in the game. Maybe five or six years ago we could have done it... but I can't see us being able to do that now. I think you will have to put forward a very convincing case. Give us real solid facts and illustrate how we could sustain the new model."

"I agree," Ed said. "I appreciate the thought you've put into this and your strong desire to change what you have created, Jason, but I cannot see how we could survive such a dramatic change and yield the profits we need for Miller Corporation's longevity."

Jason stood in silence for a moment, thinking before speaking. "Okay, I believe we can. So please consider this. What if I gather more information and show how we can transition to where I want to be, then show the potential income that we can gain?"

"I'll go with that," Miriam stated.

"Yep, I think that is a reasonable request, Jason." Ed responded.

Fiona and Mal nodded in agreement.

"Ben, Bruce?" Jason asked, waiting for their response.

"Sure, Jason, if that's what you want to waste your time doing. I still can't say that it will convince me." Bruce responded.

Ben said nothing, but crossed his arms and looked at Jason.

"All right, how about you give me eight weeks to conduct more research, gain federal information, put a business plan together and come up with a way forward that I can present?"

They all nodded except for Ben.

"Great, thanks for hearing me out." Jason said positively. "All right, let's move on to agenda item number two, which is consumables supplier change."

You're useless! It whispered into the tall, fair-haired, solidly built man's mind.

"Shut up, shut up. Leave me alone!" the man whispered, taking short panicked breaths, trying to control himself, pushing down the fear rising inside.

You didn't finish it, it said. *You can't finish anything.*

"Shut up! Shut up!" the man bellowed.

You're pathetic! A failure… the voice inside his head continued.

"Stop it! Stop it! Shut up!" the man screamed as he started slapping his own face in frustration, panic, and terror. "Go away, leave me alone." He yelled out, echoing across the concrete and iron halls.

"Hey, Talbot. Will you shut the heck up? Or I'll come in there and bust you up, man." The prison guard yelled at him through the iron bars. "One more peep outta you and I'll haul your butt down to isolation for the night. You understand?"

The man sat on the edge of his plain gray single bed; his head braced by his hands, loudly sobbing.

"Good… now keep it down." The guard said, then walked away.

CHAPTER TWENTY-ONE

It was Sunday morning and Jason and Ryan had just attended the church service. Jason had been wearing more casual clothes since his first day.

"How did it go with the board?" Ryan asked as he sipped his latte in a downtown café.

"Not well. They will be hard to win over." Jason responded.

"But you will change it to your model, right?"

"Well, yes, I can force it, but I'd like the board to be in favor and work with me. I don't really want to lose any of them."

"Sometimes you have to make hard choices."

"If it means removing people to do what God wants me to do, then yes, that will happen."

"Did you find another law firm?"

"Yes, I've made an appointment for tomorrow. Hopefully, I will gain some legal counsel in navigating through this mess." Jason rubbed his hand through his hair with some frustration.

"Sounds like a plan then."

"So," Jason changed the subject. "I've been reading the Word, and I was thinking about—" Jason pulled out a piece of paper from his jacket pocket. "Well, this scripture from Matthew 6:14-15." He read, "'For if you forgive other people when they sin against you, your heavenly Father will also forgive you. But if you do not forgive others their sins, your Father will not forgive your sins.' So, is this saying... that if I don't forgive someone, then God will not forgive me?"

Ryan nodded. "That's exactly what it's saying."

"But if God doesn't forgive me, then... I would go to Hell... is that right?"

"Yes, God is very clear that if we hold unforgiveness against anyone, then he will not forgive us. Jesus tells a story in Matthew 18:21-35 about a servant who had an enormous debt and begged his master to give him time to repay. His master took pity on him and canceled the total debt. But then that same servant went to another man who owed him money and threw that man into prison because he couldn't repay him. Anyway, the master found out and handed him to the jailors to be tortured. So basically, what this is saying is that if God forgives us for our sins, we *must* forgive others... else God will not forgive us."

"How do you forgive? If someone has hurt you greatly... then how?"

"Through an act of your will. It's difficult, as it goes against our human nature. We desire to get even, vindicate, and bring justice. Forgiveness is a supernatural act through the work of God in our lives. It takes time. I've had to say 'I forgive you' repeatedly and read scripture aloud even though I still felt the anger and resentment towards that person. Eventually something breaks, and all the hate, wanting to get even, or proven to be right, disappears. You're left with a sense that God will deal with it, and it doesn't matter anymore. It is purely an act of faith. In Mark 11:25, it says, 'And when you stand praying, if you hold anything against anyone, forgive them, so that your Father in heaven may forgive you your sins.'"

"Sounds difficult, because if I don't forgive, then I *won't* be forgiven."

"It's probably one of the most difficult things as a Christian to do. Because everything in your being just screams out for justice, it consumes your thoughts and you become bitter... but by hanging on to unforgiveness, it achieves nothing. But just to be clear, God never said to condone or make an excuse for what they did to you, or forget and trust that person again. He just wants us to stop holding resentment *towards* that person, as He is the judge, not us. Deleting a memory is very difficult, but when you choose to forgive, the sting goes and the enemy has no more power over you."

Ryan continued. "Unforgiveness is a huge stumbling block that Satan tries to use against us. He knows that if you continually refuse to embrace forgiveness, it means you haven't really recognized and accepted God's forgiveness for yourself. And someone who isn't forgiven by God, ends up in Hell. Unforgiveness also makes you physically sick."

"Really?"

"It does. Statistics show that 62 percent of cancer patients held unforgiveness. It can manifest itself physically, like poison in our system. The Bible also talks about rotting bones... Hang on, I'll look it up..."

"What? You don't know that verse off by heart?" Jason chided.

"Hey buddy, I memorize a lot of scripture, but I don't know *everything*." Ryan chuckled as he tapped away on his cell, looking for the passage. "Here... in Proverbs 14:30, 'A heart at peace gives life to the body, but envy rots the bones.'"

"Yeah, okay, I can see that when someone becomes bitter or angry, it affects them physically."

"Totally. That's why God says don't let the sun go down on your anger, because he knows how it can fester and harm us."

"Does this apply to forgiving yourself, I mean, for past mistakes?"

"It sure does. If you harbor unforgiveness against yourself, it can hold you back from progressing forward into God's fullness."

"Okay, well I'm trying to move forward but I'm weighed down by the guilt of what I have done." Jason suddenly welled up with tears and took a gulp before continuing. "Ryan, the children that spoke to me in that realm, all the potential that I took away. It crushes me to think I did that. Indirectly or directly, I killed them and stopped them from coming into existence. My actions went against everything that God created. I disappointed Him and I can't get over that fact." He took a sip of water, his hand shaking. "I don't harbor unforgiveness towards anyone else but myself. I am to blame for all those children being murdered." He paused and smirked, "I thought I was helping women, giving them choice and freedom—but I wasn't considering the choice of the child, or God... I don't know if I can ever get over that. When I was in that peaceful realm, I thought all the guilt was gone. But—" Jason stopped, his emotions catching him.

Ryan interjected. "It *was* gone! But God says that the devil roams around like a lion seeking whom to devour. He accuses God's children, bringing to memory your past, your failures, your mistakes. He tries to stop you from moving forward into the fullness and love that God has for you, keeping your focus on those mistakes. God doesn't want his children hindered and held back by the weight of guilt and past sin. That's why Jesus died on the cross to take all that away. But by holding onto that, all you're doing is disregarding what Jesus did for you... for us. Whether you were the one who murdered those children, or you're the woman who made the choice to have an abortion—Jesus died on the cross for those sins. If you earnestly repent, then you will be forgiven. You have repented, Jason, so don't let the devil keep putting thoughts in your head and reminding you of what you have done. If you keep hanging on to that, then you will prevent what God has for you... you'll block what He is trying to do in your life. Don't let this hold you back. You need forgive yourself."

"How?"

"Just talk to Him, tell Him how you feel... like you are with me. He knows what you're going through, anyway. Don't bottle it up and shut Him out or distance yourself, otherwise you are doing exactly what Satan wants you to do—furthering yourself away from God. You need to draw closer to Him."

Jason pondered in deep thought. "Well... thanks Ryan. I guess tonight I'll be doing some self-forgiving." Jason smiled gingerly.

THE CELL WAS COLD THIS MORNING, THE BLOND-HAIRED MAN THOUGHT. His single bed was uncomfortable, and it was hard to sleep with the noises in the night. He lay still, hoping that the voice in his head wouldn't start. He wanted a moment's peace, to fall back into slumber... to forget.

Useless! It started... Sooner than he had hoped.

"No, leave me alone." He whispered, burying his head under the covers.

Never! It responded.

JASON STIRRED IN HIS DEEP SLEEP. IT WAS 4.50 A.M. AND THE SUN WAS JUST about to shimmer. Peaking its golden hues over the ocean's surface, breaking through the darkness of the night. A sea breeze gently wafted through his open window and brushed lightly against his face. Jason groaned, moving his head from side to side, then pounding the bed with his arm.

"No, no, no. Mmm… No!" He started uttering in his slumberous state.

"You can't undo what you've done. You're a murderer. You're GUILTY AND YOU BELONG WITH ME!" the demon screamed at him.

He had returned to his nightmare. "Please… please, no. Get me out. P-p-please… NO!" he yelled, ripping himself out of his sleep.

As his eyes adjusted, he saw a dark shadow slowly move away from his bedside. He thought he heard footsteps and then the squeak of the loose board on the stairs. He jolted and sat up straight, looking around, rubbing his eyes. Jason squinted through the hue of the twilight darkness, trying to make out the image that had now disappeared.

He sat for a while, staring at the spot where he thought he had seen it. "I'm just dreaming again," he said as he fobbed it off as another hallucination, then went downstairs to make himself a very strong coffee.

CHAPTER TWENTY-TWO

Jason walked into a sleek white oak and chrome reception. The room was clean and minimalist, with a white leather lounge and coffee table.

"Good morning. How may I help you?" the receptionist greeted.

"Hi, I'm Jason Miller. I have an appointment with Olivia Chadwick."

"Sure, Mr. Miller. Please take a seat. Olivia's with a client. She won't be too much longer."

Jason sat on the lounge and started flicking through a magazine aimlessly, his thoughts distracted.

Only a few minutes later, the office door opened and an attractive, slim, fit-looking woman around five-foot ten stepped out talking to a male client. She wore a gray wool pencil skirt, pascal green top, gray heels and thin-framed glasses. Her long, dark soft curls were pulled back in a low loose pony tail.

The woman farewelled the male patron and swiftly walked over and held out her hand to greet Jason.

"You must be Jason?"

"Yes, hi."

"I'm Olivia. Pleased to meet you. Come in." She greeted warmly before motioning him towards the office door.

Jason followed her.

"Pease, take a seat."

Jason sat in a leather chair opposite Olivia.

"I was very sad to hear about Clifford. He was a great lawyer." Olivia stated.

"Did you know him well?"

"I didn't. We crossed paths occasionally, but I had heard admirable things about him. Such a shame, he was one of the good ones." She smiled. "How long were you with his firm?"

"Since I started the business."

"Wow, I've got some serious work to do then," she smiled kindly. "So, I have done some prelim work in understanding your organization. I guess I'll leave it to you to explain how you think I can assist."

Jason spent the next 45 minutes explaining what he would like to do with the corporation and how he would like to change it. Olivia asked various questions and jotted them in a notebook.

"Look, I think what you're proposing is relatively straightforward. It's not such a deviation as it's still within the medical industry. It would be different if you... say... wanted to become a telco." She smiled. "The tough part is gaining the agreement from your CEO and board members—that can be the tricky bit. I think if you pitch it right and have strategies in place to show the profits, benefits and a logical plan for how to move forward, it will transition smoother. It would be better to have them onside rather than turning it into a bun fight." She smiled. "I know it's a difficult time for you with losing Clifford—he would have been all over this, but please give me some time to go over the paperwork... I think I could do something for you." She smiled warmly.

"Great!" Jason said, relieved.

"So, if you're happy to work with me, I'll start getting the paperwork drawn up and we will go from there."

"Sounds good. Thanks for your time, Olivia." he said as he stood and reached over and shook her hand.

"Thanks Jason, I'll be in touch."

"I'VE ORGANIZED A MEETING FOR YOU WITH THE DEPARTMENT OF HEALTH Services on Wednesday and an appointment on Thursday with Violet

Adoption Agencies." Marg rattled off from her list as Jason arrived in the office.

"Perfect... you are a champ." Jason smiled.

"I've also been getting statistics from other adoption agencies. They have been helpful with information."

"That's good to hear... so they are happy to assist?"

"Yeah, they are. One lady said the more adoption agencies, the better."

"Wow, such a different mindset to where we are, isn't it?"

"You mean competitive?"

"Yeah, you know what it's like. Everyone keeps it all to themselves and makes a grab for more market share."

"Yes, it's different with these agencies. I've spoken to both profit and non-profit, and they want to assist. It's all about the children."

"Well, that's good to hear. Anyway, keep getting what you can. I'll start on the business case this morning."

"Oh, also I nearly forgot. I've made an appointment with Reeves Change Agents for you. I've done some research, and they are the best in the industry. They've done a few big corporations so they have some cred."

"Marg, you're brilliant." Jason smiled.

"I know!" she giggled.

"He's got to go, Bruce. I'm telling you, he will be our downfall if he doesn't." Ben said maliciously.

"What are you proposing?" Bruce asked.

"I don't know. I could dig up some dirt on him. Maybe speak with the female staff and see if there is any harassment. Or just focus on the TBI and try to get him declared as being unfit to practice or run the corporation. I'm sure I can get something on him."

"Big call. I hope you know what you're doing, Ben, because if you fail, then it will be your downfall, not his."

"I know, I know... I'll get something on him... it's just about finding the right thing."

. . .

"TALBOT! YOU HAVE A VISITOR." THE PRISON GUARD STATED THROUGH the iron bars.

"What? Who?"

"Dunno, some guy. Come on." The guard said as he escorted the blond man down through the corridors to the visiting room.

He sat in the plastic chair in a small booth with a glass partition and glared at the man sitting on the other side. "What do *you* want?" he asked gruffly. "What the heck are you doing here? I don't want to *ever* see you again."

"Look, I just want to say—"

"What? What *can* you say, Miller?"

"I wanted to say I'm sorry for what I've done in the past… and that I forgive you for what you did — for trying to kill me."

"You *forgive* me? Well, ain't that just dandy. Well, let me say this, Miller —I don't *forgive* you. I will never forgive you," he spat. "And I wish I killed you that night, and that you were rotting in Hell. So, don't you ever, *ever* come back and see me again, you—"

"Dennis, listen. I have something to tell you. I think I met—"

"Shut up. I said I *never* want to see you again," he hissed, then walked over to the guard and asked to return to his cell.

CHAPTER TWENTY-THREE

Later that night, Jason was sitting at Ryan's kitchen table sipping on a Coke.

"It didn't go well at all. He just gave me a piece of his mind and walked out." Jason stated.

"So… what… he didn't even hear you out?"

"Nope. He said that he wished I was rotting in Hell. Wasn't too far from the truth, really." Jason smirked.

"Gees," Ryan exclaimed, shaking his head.

"I know… it was bad. I feel like… I don't know, that it's not resolved, that I didn't get to tell him the story."

"Well, you're right, it's not resolved. He needs to know. I mean… are you sure that it was her?"

"I am. I can't explain it, but it's like… I just *know*."

"Yeah, I get it. I know that feeling. It's usually God speaking to you."

"Really? Do you think it is?"

"Sounds like!"

"Well, that's neat," Jason smiled, relieved. "I mean, to have God communicating with me."

"That will increase." Ryan smiled, enjoying seeing this new Christian grow. "The more you spend time with God, his voice becomes clearer. At present, it may be an impression or a feeling like you have now. But then it gets stronger and you can hear His voice speaking to you, guiding you with decisions, encouraging you."

"That would be good. I really need that."

"Well, every Christian needs that. It's like having a compass out in a forest—you're less likely to get lost and put in danger."

"I like that analogy," Jason smiled. "So, without God's voice, you're like a boat out at sea without a rudder."

"Nice one," Ryan laughed. "Have you got any more?"

"Nah, I'm done," Jason smiled.

"So… what's going on with Chance?" Jason grinned.

Ryan blushed. "Yeah, she's nice. I think she could be *the* one. I'm just waiting to get confirmation from God."

"Hey, no offence—but that sounds so weird to me, Ryan. So, you ask Him?"

"For sure! This is a major decision and I don't want to stuff it up. If I marry the wrong person, then it can hinder the calling on my life. So, I have always mandated that God would be the one to choose my partner for me."

Jason just shook his head. "Wow! We come from two different worlds."

"Yeah, we do." Ryan shrugged.

"I've never known people to live the way you do. To seek God for everything," Jason pondered. "I've always strived to get ahead, maintain total control and decide based on facts. This to me… well, it seems so foreign."

"Yet to me it's natural, and how I have always lived. It says in Proverbs 3:5-6 'Trust in the Lord with all your heart and lean not on your own understanding in all your ways submit to him, and he will make your paths straight.' I would rather live by that, then get into trouble with bad choices."

"Okay… interesting. So, like with Chance—do you just ask God about her?"

"Yeah well, I don't hear an audible voice saying 'she's the one,'" Ryan laughed, "but I've known her for about two years now, and it's only recently that it feels different between us. Let's just wait and see." Ryan smiled.

Jason stood up and stretched. "Who are these?" looking at the photos on Ryan's fridge.

"These are my kids," he smiled.

"What?"

Ryan snorted. "They're my *sponsor* kids."

"Oh, wow—you sponsor three?"

"Yeah—one from World Vision, one from Compassion and another from a local school program."

"That's a nice idea." Jason said, as he read each child's brief story underneath their photo.

"Yeah, I write to them once a month and receive letters back. It's cool to see how I can change their lives just by paying around ten dollars a week per child. I mean, I spend more than that on coffees." Ryan laughed. "Chance has a couple as well and most people in our church sponsor at least one child."

"Okay, I like the sound of that."

"Good! I wish all Christians thought that way."

"They don't?"

"Not all… no. There are over 700 million people in poverty, living on less than $1.90 a day. And 17,000 children under the age of five that die every single day from preventable causes—like access to clean water, malaria prevention, nutritious food… just basic things needed to survive. That's over six million preventable deaths per year. Yet there are 2.19 billion Christians worldwide. Now, you do the math. We may eliminate poverty if each Christian sponsored one child or supported a charity that helped those in need."

"Gees, I never thought of it that way."

"It's true. God commands us to look after the poor. I get frustrated because people just make lame excuses about not helping. There is no reason not to help others in need, whatever way you can. These charities ensure the kids get clean water, healthcare and education. They also help entire communities build wells, schools, health clinics. There is so much they do—they even work with political leaders and local governments to change policies and laws to help their people."

Ryan continued, his passion showing. "I mean, some stories of kids that have grown up in these programs are so amazing, they're changing countries. Some become teachers or doctors in their home community, but there are also some that have joined the UN and helped change laws in their own country. It's fantastic!" he beamed.

"Okay, well, you've inspired me. Where can I sign?"

"I know, I know." Ryan shook his head. "You shouldn't have got me started." Ryan laughed. "I'm just passionate about this stuff."

"I can tell, and it's great. No, seriously, I will definitely sign up to these charities."

"Good. Now, do you want another Coke?"

"Yes."

Ryan tossed Jason another drink from the fridge.

"So, back to Dennis," said Jason. "Do you think I should visit him again?"

"Look, I think you should pray about it, but… maybe writing him a letter would be better, so he can read it slowly and let it sink in. I mean Jase, really, it will be hard for him to take when you tell him you think you met his wife in that realm."

"Yeah, I just have this strong feeling that I *must* tell him."

"Well, if you have that feeling, then it's most likely God prompting you. You don't know how it will pan out, only God does. So, let's continue to pray about it and if He says to write a letter, then be obedient and do it."

"Okay, I will."

———

DENNIS TALBOT PACED ABOUT IN HIS CELL, AGITATED AT JASON'S VISIT.

The voice in his head started at him again. *Forgive? Forgive? Who does he think he is? You should have killed him.*

"Shut up!" Dennis said as he smacked his head with his palm. "Stop it."

You're hopeless, nothing but a loser. You can't do anything right. He should have died in that accident.

"Enough… stop… just stop." Dennis begged, tears welling as he continued to pace.

You would have been a hopeless father anyway, the voice said stingingly.

"LEAVE ME ALONE!" Dennis screamed. Those words cutting him to the bone. He broke down and wept.

NEVER! the voice shrieked back.

CHAPTER TWENTY-FOUR

At 7 p.m. later that week, Olivia drove into Jason's driveway, stepped out of her blue Audi, and rang the doorbell.

Jason opened the door, dressed in his running gear and still sweating. "Oh, hi—I wasn't expecting you." He glanced down at his wet tank top. "I was about to take a shower."

"Sorry, I was in the area," she grimaced, "and thought I would drop off some papers for you to sign. Do you want me to leave them with you? You can drop them by later?"

"Hey, no… do you want to come inside?" he motioned. "I can make a coffee if you like and sign them."

"Sure!"

"What would you like? Do you want a flat white, cap… latte?" he said as he walked through to his kitchen.

"I'll take a cappuccino." She smiled as she sat at the kitchen island.

"Okay, but… could you please excuse me for a moment? I'll be right back." Jason hurried upstairs and quickly changed out of his sweaty clothes and sprayed on deodorant.

His cell beeped with a message—it was Ryan. *Heading your way, see you in five.*

Jason dashed downstairs into the kitchen, pressed the DeLonghi button, and after a moment, handed Olivia her coffee.

126

She passed him the paperwork and Jason started reading through the contract.

"Nice place you have!" Olivia said as she glanced around.

"Thanks."

"Have you been here long?"

"About six years," he said as he continued to read the agreement.

"It's nice to hear the ocean so close."

"Yeah, that's what I love about living here—the sound of the surf. It makes you feel alive."

"It does!"

"Okay, so that seems good," he said as he signed the bottom of the agreement and slid the papers back across the kitchen bench towards her.

"Great, I look forward to working with you."

The doorbell chimed, "Excuse me," Jason hurried to the entrance to let Ryan in.

"Hey dude," Ryan said.

"Hey… Coke?"

"Yep!" he said as he followed Jason through to the kitchen.

"Olivia, this is Ryan," Jason introduced them.

"Hi Olivia," Ryan greeted.

"Hello Ryan, pleased to meet you," she said as she held out her hand and shook it warmly.

Jason handed Ryan a Coke. "Ryan works down at the youth center."

"Really? That's great. I spent a lot of time there… a long time ago." She smiled tenderly.

"Really?" Ryan said curiously.

"Yes. In short, I was in foster care, ran away, lived on the streets for a while until I came to the center. Sister Marguerite took me under her wing and helped me study and get a scholarship to Yale."

"Wow, Yale. That's impressive."

Olivia blushed. "I'd have been thankful to get into *any* university."

"Sister Marguerite still works there, although she is not as agile as she once was." Ryan smiled.

"She is such a precious soul. I meet with her for coffee once a month."

"That's great! Yeah, she really connects with the kids. I enjoy working with her."

"Rewarding work!" she stated.

"It sure is—it's the best."

Olivia took the last sip of her coffee and looked at Jason. "Anyway, I'd better get going. Thanks for signing these for me."

"No problems," Jason smiled.

"I'll be in touch, Jason. Nice meeting you Ryan."

"Sure, you too." Ryan responded.

Jason walked with Olivia out the front door to her car, said goodbye, and came back inside.

"She seems a nice lady." Ryan winked playfully.

"What?" Jason said as his mind had already wandered back to work.

"Are you serious? Olivia!"

"Oh, yeah… I guess."

Ryan laughed. "Well… anyway, are you making any headway with the changes?"

"Yes, Olivia is giving me advice on how I should go about it."

"Well, that's positive."

"Yeah, it is. I've had to get this business case written to convince the board. I really don't want a fight."

"I've asked around and there's nothing on the harassment side." Ben stated.

"So, he's clean. I hope you were discrete to not raise concerns amongst the staff?" Bruce asked.

"I was. They didn't know what I was doing. I said I was taking a random survey on management."

"You better hope so because if it gets back to Jason, you might be in strife."

"It's good, Bruce. Trust me. But… I heard something though."

"What?"

"It was to do with the accident. Apparently, someone overheard Jason saying to a friend in the hospital that he went to somewhere, like Heaven."

"No way, seriously?"

"Seriously. He thinks he went on a trip." Ben chuckled.

"You may just have something here."

"I think so. If we can couple the TBI and the hallucinations about his trip to Heaven, then we may just be able to convince the others he is not fit to run the company… or that this is driving the sudden change in his behavior."

"Yes, that may work."

"We know what head trauma can do. I'm meeting with a neurosurgeon to gain an understanding of the affects it has on a person's behavior. If I can put together a convincing argument, we may just be able to persuade the board to remove him."

"Good work." Bruce nodded in agreement.

"WOULD YOU LIKE SOME WATER?" JASON ASKED AS HE POURED THE mineral water into a glass for Olivia at the café.

"Thank you! So, I had a look at Ben's employment agreement. He's obligated to keep the proprietary information of the business whilst in employment and thereafter confidential. You could disqualify him for unfitness for when he breached his contract and went to the press." Olivia stated.

"I could, but what's the point? It's already out now." Jason replied.

"Well, he has a legal obligation to which he broke. Anyway, keep that up your sleeve in case we need to use it against him."

"I'd like to keep Ben. He is an excellent operator. I guess… that is, if I can harness him for good… and not evil." He laughed.

Olivia grinned. "Okay, I get it. But he sounds so disrespectful."

Jason sighed. "Ben and I have a unique relationship. We have always been frank with each other and spoken our minds. It's worked well in the past as it brings a balance, because I can be doggedly in my decisions, and besides, I've never enjoyed working with anyone who will just roll over easily. I chose him for that very reason. But… things have changed—I have changed, and now it's not working so well."

"I can imagine." She paused thoughtfully. "So… can I ask you for an honest answer?"

"Sure."

"Why the change? I mean, you're such a successful corporation— you're progressive, making money. I don't get it."

"Well, it will probably sound a bit cliché, but… I had an accident and was clinically dead. When I came back to life… I guess you could say that I had a new perspective."

"Okay, but it takes more than a new perspective. You seem driven, adamant to change things urgently, like you know something."

"I am, and I do."

"Okay, so you said you had an experience. I'm curious… can you share it with me?"

"I'm not sure you would believe me."

"Try me."

"I'm trying to eliminate the possibility of the board deeming me to be insane, or unfit, so I'm not sure it would be a good thing to talk about right now."

"Jason, I have your back. You've signed on with me, so it's fine, but I get it if you don't feel comfortable talking with me about it. I wanted to understand why the immediate change of heart. It may help give me some perspective."

Jason sighed. "How long have you got?"

Olivia looked at her watch. "Well, I've a meeting at 2.30, so you have an hour fifteen," she smiled.

Over lunch, Jason shared a very abbreviated version of his experience of dying, going to Hell and the other realm, as well as the reason he had decided to change his corporation.

"Wow! What an experience." Olivia said, amazed.

"Do you believe me?"

"Absolutely. Why wouldn't I?"

"Because… it sounds crazy." He grimaced.

"Okay," she laughed, "I get it, you're right. Don't speak of this before we get this sorted, otherwise they will have grounds to deem you as unstable. I'm not sure if they would take it that far… but keep it under wraps until this is over."

"I will."

"One thing Sister Marguerite taught me was that our life is eternal—that what we see isn't everything, that there is a supernatural realm around us."

"She is right."

"I know… she's been right about most things."

"Sounds like a good friend to have."

"She's the best. I feel like she's the mother I never had. I'm so thankful for what she did and for the love she showed me."

"So, let me ask you a question. Do you believe in Jesus?"

"Absolutely!"

"That's a relief. I wasn't sure."

"One thing I loved about the youth center is that they gave you a choice—they forced nothing on you. When I was there a few months, I could see the difference between the kids that followed Jesus and the ones that didn't. It didn't take me long to want what they had." She paused and looked directly at Jason. "It will not be easy, but I will do my best to help you change everything. I understand and I am on your side, okay?"

"Thanks, I appreciate it."

———

9 P.M.

"You can't reverse what you've done!" a voice whispered.

Jason stopped abruptly—mid-stride as he was going through the kitchen. He turned around in confusion—attentively listening—waiting.

Nothing!

"I need another scan," he muttered, then continued into the lounge room.

CHAPTER TWENTY-FIVE

"I wrote him a letter," Jason said to Ryan as they sipped their coffees in a café after church.

"Great! So, you felt like doing that?"

"Yeah, I prayed and had that feeling again. You're right, if he can read it in his own time, it may be better."

"I'd like to be a fly on that wall." Ryan responded, a little apprehensive.

"Mm, I'm not sure of the response it will get, but at least I know that it's what God wants me to do."

"And that's the key—obedience to what God wants, no matter what we feel."

"Well, looks like that's the only thing that I'm obedient to. I can't believe it's been nearly seven months since my accident, yet I have made no progress on the changes. It's so frustrating that the machine is still running and I can't do a thing to stop it. It's like watching a horror movie play out, and I'm a captive audience that can't leave."

"God understands… it's not for lack of trying, Jason."

"I know that, but it's just so discouraging. You would think something that I created, something that I own—I could stop in an instant, a flick of a switch. But no, I have to jump through all this political malarkey to satisfy everyone before they decide. It's so annoying."

"I can imagine."

"Yeah, sometimes it would be nice to just walk away. Maybe I should have shut them all down completely."

"You would still fight the same battle with the board. They wouldn't let you shut them. And there would probably be even more community uproar. So, what difference does it make?"

"I guess!"

"Least this way, you're adding value, you're introducing more services, along with providing education on adoption and helping families and children. That's a far better outcome than shutting down the centers."

"Again, Ryan… you are right." Jason shook his head. "How did you get so smart at such a young age?" Jason chuckled.

"It's the wisdom of the Lord." Ryan smiled cheekily.

"Yeah well, I'm needing some of that wisdom, I assure you."

They both laughed.

"So, what's the update on Chance?"

"Okay, I'll fess up. She is the one." Ryan smiled.

"So, are we going to have a wedding this year?"

"Highly likely," Ryan beamed.

"That's great buddy, congrats." Jason patted him on the shoulder.

"What about you?"

"Me? You've got to be seeing someone to get married, Ryan, and if you haven't noticed… I'm not seeing anyone."

"What about Olivia?"

"No! We have a professional relationship. My focus is purely on doing what God has asked me to do. I don't want to end up where I was. I need to change this and I will live the rest of my days trying to achieve that… and that's all I want." Jason paused for a second. "There is one thing I've been wanting to ask you."

"Yep, shoot." Ryan said as he took another sip of his latte.

"If God is such a loving and kind God, then why did he make Hell?"

"Ah yes," Ryan smiled, "the age-old question."

"So, it's not just me?"

"No, many people ask that question, but it is simple to explain."

"I'm all ears… go ahead." Jason waved.

"Okay, well, when Lucifer became rebellious and deceived a third of the angels into trying to supplant God, they were all thrown out of

Heaven. So that's why God created Hell as their punishment for rejecting Him. Hell was a place meant only for Satan, formally Lucifer, and the demons. Then God created man, to which he also gave free will. Man can either accept and acknowledge God or reject Him."

Ryan took a breath before continuing. "We are eternal beings and when we die, we have to go somewhere. But please get this… God does not want anyone to go to Hell. He doesn't want anyone to perish. The passage says in 1 Timothy 2:4 'who wants all people to be saved and to come to a knowledge of the truth'. But God is a loving God and provides free choice. If a man wants nothing to do with God whilst on earth, then He allows the man to have that freedom of choice… to be apart from Him."

"Why couldn't we all go to Heaven then?"

"There's two reasons that I see. First, is that you're forcing people to do something that they didn't want—they wanted nothing to do with God on earth, therefore you're giving them 'no choice' but to be with Him. And second—well, Heaven is perfection, therefore, God cannot allow corruption into a perfect place. Hell is ultimately where sin and evil reside, so evil must stay in Hell for Heaven to remain pure."

Jason looked at Ryan blankly.

"It's like this." Ryan slid an empty glass in front of Jason and filled it with mineral water. "Would you drink this water?"

"Yes." Jason shrugged.

"Why?"

"It's clean, refreshing… and I like mineral water," he smiled.

"Okay, what if I place a drop of poison into the glass?" he dropped a bread crumb from his plate to demonstrate. "Now will you drink it?"

"No."

"Why not?"

"Because it's polluted with poison and it may harm or… kill me."

"Ah really?"

"I see what you're getting at now." Jason smiled, nodding his head. "It will pollute Heaven."

Ryan smiled. "Exactly. God will not allow someone who doesn't even acknowledge Him or want to be with Him into Heaven. Why should he? Therefore, if a man rejects the only way to Heaven, then the only place for him is Hell. It's their choice!"

Ryan paused and typed into his cell. "Okay, so… Jesus is talking about this in Matthew 25:41, when he is telling a parable about separating the sheep from the goats. It goes like this. 'Then the King will say to those on his right, 'Come, you who are blessed by my Father; take your inheritance, the kingdom prepared for you since the creation of the world.' So, here he is talking about those who are his followers and have accepted Him as their Lord and Savior. However, later on he states in Matthew 25:41, 'Then he will say to those on his left, 'Depart from me, you who are cursed, into the eternal fire prepared for the devil and his angels.'"

Ryan took a quick breath. "This is where he is talking to those who have rejected Him. Can you now see that Hell was created for the devil and the demons? We were never meant to go there, but through our rebellion, sin and rejection of Jesus Christ, then there is no other place for those who do not believe in Him, or want to be with Him."

Ryan proceeded. "Revelation 21:27 says this about Heaven, 'Nothing impure will ever enter it, nor will anyone who does what is shameful or deceitful, but only those whose names are written in the Lamb's book of life.'"

"It still doesn't seem fair, though." Jason responded thoughtfully.

"Mercy without justice is careless. God is love, and therefore, true love must care enough to demand fair and equal punishment. So, if he treated everyone the same and let all go unpunished… like, say he treated Hitler and Mother Teresa alike, then he would be an unjust God, yet if he punished all of humanity regardless, then he would be a merciless God. Genesis 18:25 says, 'Far be it from you to do such a thing—to kill the righteous with the wicked, treating the righteous and the wicked alike. Far be it from you! Will not the Judge of all the earth do right?'"

"So it's simply our choice to go to Hell!"

"Yes! Anyone who does not want to be in God's presence must be allowed to exercise their free will and separate themselves from God. But God makes it very clear that the consequence of rejecting Him is death. Revelation 21:8 states, 'But the cowardly, the unbelieving, the vile, the murderers, the sexually immoral, those who practice magic arts, the idolaters and all liars—they will be consigned to the fiery lake of burning sulfur. This is the second death.'"

"I see," Jason paused. "So, I guess all Christians believe this?"

"No, unfortunately not. Some don't believe in Hell, even though Jesus not only spoke of it, but described it in vast detail. He spoke about Hell more than he did about Heaven, because he doesn't want anyone to go there. As a Christian, if you don't believe in Hell, then you're not accepting the Bible as truth, and God's Word, but only choosing to accept portions of it."

"You're right! Actually, you know that preacher I met in Hell that I told you about?"

"Yeah."

"Well, he said that he told his congregation that Hell didn't exist, and that he regretted it because it was a lie."

"I've heard there are preachers who believe and teach that, even though it's not biblical."

"It's misleading… to lie to people about their eternity."

"It sure is, I'd say some are misguided and haven't researched the Bible themselves, or others don't want to tackle the tough subjects in fear of people leaving their church."

"That's exactly what that preacher in Hell said," Jason recalled. "He didn't want to lose his congregation, so he told them Hell didn't exist."

"Well, I would hate to be the one standing before God explaining that some of my congregation went to Hell because I told them it wasn't real."

"Yeah, that would be scary."

"So, are you going to write the book?"

"As soon as I've got Miller Corp sorted, and it's locked in with the changes, then I will start it."

"That's awesome. I want an advanced copy and I want it signed." Ryan smiled.

"Ha, you're optimistic. I'm not exactly a fast typist or an English literate. I'm a doctor… have you seen our writing?" he chuckled.

Ryan cracked up laughing. "Yeah, you doctors have terrible writing. I've seen those scripts, you can't read them," they both laughed.

It was 11.30 p.m. and Jason was back from a late-night run. He showered, made a hot chocolate, and sat on the lounge with his laptop to complete some work.

What? he thought and abruptly stopped typing at hearing a noise upstairs, then slowly rose, straining to listen. He heard it again… a knocking sound. He held his breath and listened.

Knock, knock, it sounded.

He crept closer to the bottom of the stairs and stopped… holding his breath.

Knock!

His back started tingling as he slowly climbed the stairs, one step at a time, listening intently.

Knock, knock.

He stopped, then slowly he moved again, upward until he entered the hallway.

KNOCK! KNOCK! KNOCK! Louder this time.

He paused; it was coming from his bedroom. The blood rush of his heart beating harder resounded a deafening thump in his skull. He took a swift silent breath and began to creep tactically towards his room.

Knock!

He halted and waited. His heart skipped a beat as its rhythm increased, drumming hard against his chest. The adrenaline intensified as he inched along the hallway towards his bedroom.

Knock, knock, knock.

His heart leaped as though it was about to burst free from his rib cage. Taking a small quick breath, he slowly peered around the door.

Nothing!

The room was empty.

There was no intruder.

Confused, Jason cautiously stepped into the room and gazed around. There was nothing… He released his breath and started to relax.

WHOOSH!

A powerful blast of wind hit against him hard, tipping him backwards and driving him to the floor. The forceful tempest swirled over him for a second and as it did, he caught the distinct whisper —*You belong with me*! as the gust abruptly left through the door.

BANG!

The door slammed shut—the lights went out.

In the blackness, Jason got up gradually and stood unmoving; He felt the tingling fear creep over his body as his skin prickled. The dreadful thought that he may not be alone crept into his mind.

CHAPTER TWENTY-SIX

Marg waited eagerly at her desk for Jason to arrive. She had started two hours early to ensure everything was ready for the presentation. Checking and double-checking that the computer, presentation, copies for the members and the projection screen were ready to go. She didn't miss a thing.

"Hey Marg, you're in early." Jason stated as he walked in. "I'm heading downstairs—do you want me to grab you a coffee?"

"Oh, yeah sure. That would be lovely," Marg responded gratefully. "I need a little wake-up." She smiled.

"Okay, I'll just put my laptop in the office. The usual?"

"Yes, thanks!"

"I'll be right back." He smiled.

"Hey, nutbag. I heard you talking to yourself again last night. I wish you would shut up—you're keeping everyone awake with your muttering," said a large, muscular man covered in tattoos from his neck downwards.

Dennis looked up from his breakfast tray but said nothing as the trepidation crept over him. He didn't want to start a fight with Benny. He was

139

the biggest, meanest and most respected con in the prison and he'd witnessed what happened when you got on his wrong side.

"You gonna answer me?"

"I'll keep it down." Dennis said sheepishly.

"Good." Benny walked off to another table to eat breakfast with his gang members.

"Okay, so it looks like we are all here," Jason said eagerly. He was keen to start his presentation and lay out the plans before the board members.

Marg hung around in the back corner, ensuring everyone had what they needed before she left and shut the boardroom door. She wasn't a believer, but she sat at her desk and whispered a quick prayer.

Ryan and Chance were having breakfast in the park. They purposely took an hour before work to pray for Jason, as they knew how important this day was. Whilst they sat on the park bench seat and sipped their coffees, they each prayed that God would help Jason and give him wisdom and strength.

"Marg has printed and also bound both the presentation and business case for each one of you, so you can make notes on the pages. I'm happy for you to fire questions at me during the presentation. We have all day if need be to look at this proposal."

He took a quick breath. "So, I'll get started. As you can see on page one, I have outlined the adoption statistics—these are the same ones that I discussed at our last meeting when I presented this concept to you, therefore I don't feel the need to reiterate those stats. I think the agreed focus here is the way forward for the new model and the indicative profits for Miller Corp."

Jason continued onto the next slide. "As you can see, our major competitor receives between 39 and 45 percent in federal funding for their health services—this equates to around 500 million dollars per annum.

These services cover a range of cancer screening, STI treatment, contraception, along with other women's health services."

"But what can *we* get?" Bruce asked impatiently.

"If you go to the next slide, it's on there. I have spoken with the Federal Health Services and there's a potential to gain grants to 80 million dollars initially. They advised that as we grow our business, then these grants will theoretically increase."

The members nodded their heads in approval, pleased at what they were seeing—all except one.

"Potentially?" Ben stated.

"Yes, Ben. We have to apply for the federal grants. It does not guarantee us funding, so I'm basing my plan on what the government agencies have communicated."

He continued. "The next slide shows the income that we can gain by public payments. As you can see, this far surpasses what we earn in our clinics now. If we use our competitor as a model, then you can see the profit that we could make. I'm not saying that we attempt to match them, but we could definitely take a chunk of that pie from them."

"You're really just pushing to expand our services. Which, I guess, is just going to pad the adoption side because that will not make much at all." Ben said sarcastically.

"I'm leading into that Ben—but thank you for your prompting, as the adoption information is on the next slide." He smiled graciously, but inwardly wanted to reach over and grab Ben by the throat. "Okay, as you can see, fees for adoption range from 20K to 50K. This depends on the services provided."

"Wow! That much?" Mal exclaimed.

"Yes, it's not cheap to adopt a child—however, there are government grants for families to help with the fees."

"So why so much?" Fiona asked.

"Legalities, birth mother fees including hospitalization and general health check-ups, counseling, home case studies and agency fees."

"So, people will pay that much for a child?" Ed asked.

"Yes. There are over 130,000 adoptions per year."

"Wow! We are definitely in the wrong business." Mal looked around and laughed.

"But there are alternatives, whereby there are little to no fees required." Jason stated. "If the child is in permanent foster care, then the carers can apply to adopt, which takes around 12 months. On the next slide, I have a list of agencies that we could partner with to allow this service so we could refer patients on to them. Marg has already done some legwork for me and gained a commitment from these agencies."

"Whoa!" Ben held up his hand. "So, we are now moving from abortions to adoptions and now to foster care? What the heck are you doing? Where is the money in that?"

"This is the reason I want to expand our services, Ben, to allow us to make it financially easier for people to adopt or take a child into permanent care. We will still receive the general medical fees and such, and also there will be people who will want to pay for adoption, so we are not losing out."

"I like it," Mal stated. "It's wholesome, there's something about it… it just feels good."

Ben rolled his eyes.

"Hey, Talbot. You've got mail." The guard said, as he handed Dennis the letter.

Dennis looked over the envelope and saw Jason's initials and business address on the back. He paused for a moment, contemplating binning it, but decided against it. He ripped the edge of the envelope, tore it open and pulled out a hand-written letter. It read:

Dennis,

I know that my recent visit wasn't received well, hence why I've written to you as I have something important that I need to tell you. At least this way you can read it and contemplate in your own time, or destroy it… whatever, I don't know.

On the night that you drove over my vehicle, you may not have known I died. I was clinically dead for nearly four hours and that started a journey I am now very grateful for.

I was taken to a place that I cannot even begin to explain, but it was a place of tortures and horror that mankind cannot fathom. In short, I went to Hell, where I saw friends and others that I recognized being tortured and burned in horrific manners. The time that I was there, I spoke to a few people and learned of their journeys and why they were there. They told me they were there because they did not follow and know Jesus Christ. I too didn't know Him, growing up not believing in anything, but it was the worst experience and I hope someday I can tell you, face to face... in detail.

However, I'm so grateful to be given a second chance at life. Someone was praying for me whilst I lay dead in the car, and while they were trying to free you from the truck wreckage.

His prayers worked, and I was taken to a different realm. A glorious and majestic place. It was there that I realized what I sinner I was. It was there that I saw I was a murderer, that I had killed thousands of innocent children. It was there that God showed me the blood that covered my hands... but it was also there that I fell to my knees in repentance, asking for God to forgive me... and He did.

God gave me a second chance, Dennis, to come back and change the world's views on abortion. To show that it is against God's will and that every child conceived is a precious gift from our Creator and should be cherished.

But there is something very important that I have to share with you. Something that I believe you need to know, and this is what I was trying to tell you when I visited.

God allowed me to speak with others whilst in that place, but one of them stood out. Her name was Suzannah.

Dennis instantly choked, a feeling of muddied clumps caught in his throat, scrambling to get out. His emotions rose inside as he wiped away the tears and continued to read on.

She told me her story... of your story. Of how you wanted to keep the baby, and that she didn't because of financial difficulties. She told me she came to my clinic and had the baby aborted at three months. She also told me of the destruction and breakdown that it caused to your marriage.

She spoke of depression and profound regret, of the immense heartache, of feeling isolated and alone. Of how the communication between you both disappeared, and she felt secluded within her own dark thoughts.

She told me about the night that she jumped, and the panic she felt when she had realized that she had done the wrong thing. That her only saving grace was that she cried out to God for forgiveness, before the waves and sea overtook her.

Dennis, I need to tell you that Suzannah is in Heaven; she is beautiful and made whole. She told me how much she loves you and hopes that you are okay.

Dennis clenched his teeth as he felt the pain in his heart start again. The feelings he fought so hard to suppress were resurfacing. Through the raw emotion and tear-blurred vision, he continued to read.

But more importantly, she showed me your daughter, your little girl Rosie. She is there, with Suzannah and she is so very precious, words cannot describe. You have a daughter, Dennis… in Heaven.

Dennis gasped. The painful anguish that balled up in his chest rose and burst outward as he sobbed with deep profound pain. He held his hand over his mouth in the attempt to muffle the heart-wrenching sounds.

I realize this is emotionally hard to perceive, and that it was probably best to write to you instead of visiting. But last, I want to ask for your forgiveness. For the part that I took in taking your baby away from you, for the hurt that I have caused you and Suzannah, for the pain of not holding your baby girl. For that, I am truly sorry.

I have come to follow Jesus and I am doing my best to change Miller Corporation into something other than what it is, a killing factory. I am deeply ashamed of what I have created, and through God, I am doing everything in my power to stop it and to change people's views on abortion.

I'm sorry, Dennis, and I hope that one day you will find it in your heart to forgive me. I also hope that you come to know Jesus as I have.
Regards
Jason Miller.

Dennis crumbled to the hard-concrete floor of his cell. He clenched the letter against his chest as the crude sorrow poured out of him in deep gasping, agonizing cries.

CHAPTER TWENTY-SEVEN

"So, this brings me to the *how* we will achieve what I have presented." Jason said, "I'm proposing to bring in change agents who can facilitate our transition and—."

"And how much will that cost?" Bruce butted in.

"It's not cheap, but it will ensure that we get it right and the change can go smoothly." Jason stated.

"How much?" Ben stared blankly.

"Around 290K."

"WHAAT?" Ben said, then put his head in his hands and rubbed his face. "Seriously Jason, do you think we need to pay people to do this?"

"If we want it done right, yes I do."

"But it's like we are throwing away nearly 300K… for what?" Ben sneered.

"It's not—if we do it right, then we will be better off. I met with Reeves Change Agents and they have personnel that have medical backgrounds and an understanding of our environment. We would get three agents over the course of 12 months that will lead and facilitate."

"Lead?" Ben exclaimed. "Isn't that my job?"

"Yes, Ben it is—but they will assist and guide you through the transition."

Ben shook his head, unimpressed.

Miriam spoke up. "Jason, I think what you have proposed sounds solid. You've shown us the why and have demonstrated the how. I like it."

"Me too," Fiona stated. "I think this model will be a better way to sustain Miller Corp in the future. Also, by diversifying our services, it doesn't pigeonhole us into one area like we are doing now."

"I concur. This new model will allow us to build a more robust company where it can withstand the ebbs and flows of the medical industry." Mal stated with a smile.

"Great," Jason beamed. "So, are there any further questions regarding what I've presented?"

Both Bruce and Ben sat in silence—their faces blank and arms crossed.

"Okay then, well, it's been a productive session. If you're satisfied that I have explained the new model adequately and there are no further questions... then I guess we can close the meeting with the view that it goes to vote in a week." Jason said as he looked around.

"Agreed." Mal stated, and everyone nodded.

"Okay then, thanks everyone for your time. I look forward to our next meeting." Jason smiled as he packed up.

Everyone got up out of their chairs and left the boardroom.

Marg couldn't wait to get in there and speak with Jason.

"So, how did it go?" she said excitedly.

"Marg," he sighed with relief, "I think it went really well. The work that we have done over the past few months has paid off."

"That's great news," she beamed, "so how did Ben take it?"

Jason rolled his eyes. "As expected, he and Bruce are the antagonists. But I only need the majority votes and the others seemed in favor of the new model."

"Fantastic!" Marg clapped her hands.

BRUCE AND BEN WERE HAVING A LATE LUNCH AT A RESTAURANT.

"That was a load of baloney." Ben smirked.

"Look, it was an excellent demonstration, and I can see that it can work, but —"

"I don't want it to. I want to continue with the model we have planned."

"If you let me finish… I was about to say I don't think it fits the Miller Corp ideology."

"Well, everyone else seemed to like it… and *that* puts us in a precarious position."

"Well, you've got all the research that you've been doing over the past few months… Maybe it's time that you called a meeting yourself— without Jason—and put forward the facts. Sooner rather than later… Like tonight, before they set their decisions in concrete."

"Good move," Ben raised his wineglass in salute.

THEY HELD THE SECRET MEETING AT A RESTAURANT IN A PRIVATE FUNCTION room. Miller Corporation board members all sat around the table and casually ate their meals and conversed before Ben started the meeting.

"Thanks for coming tonight on such short notice. I realize that we only met today, but I have my own concerns with the sudden need to change the model of Miller Corp and I wanted to give you my view without opposition from Jason."

He took a breath. "I've been conducting my own research over the past few months and have spoken with Dr. Franks, the neurosurgeon at St Peters, and Dr. Chandler, a neuroscientist at Main Medical Research. They provided some insight on the effects of TBI on both personality and decision-making ability."

Ben handed out a sheet of paper printed with a list of disorders. "If you look over this list, you'll see that I've compiled the effects that can stem from a TBI such as Jason's. I don't need to go through each one, as most are self-explanatory. But basically the condensed version is that damage to the amygdala, hippocampus and frontal and temporal lobes can leave a person with explosive emotions, verbal outbursts, physical hostility, memory impairment, executive dysfunction and anxiety, along with a myriad of other physical injuries such as blurred vision, slurred speech, paralysis. As you can see… it's an exhaustive list."

He paused. "Now, I realize that Jason doesn't present any of the physical injuries that we know of. He was lucky to escape these. However, it's his executive functioning skills that I want to hone in on, the sudden change in his personality and ability to make sound decisions."

He took a sip of water before continuing. "Jason presents the typical pattern of a TBI victim, whereby he is displaying executive dysfunction. These functions refer to the group of skills used to make decisions, plan, problem solve, make sound judgments, and generally get along with people. Now we know Jason's TBI occurred in the frontal lobe area, and this is where the executive functions are controlled in the brain—so it now makes sense why his behavior since his accident has become so contradictory. We all know that the Jason we see now is definitely not the Jason prior to the accident. He used to be in control, driven, a strategist that we could follow, who had the vision and the ability to make Miller Corporation the leader in its field. But it's clear that he is not the same person after his accident."

He paused and looked around the room. It was silent as everyone was intently listening. "Now the TBI alone is enough to raise concerns, but the fact that Jason was declared clinically dead at the accident scene… Now, that just compounds the behavioral change.

"I spoke with Dr. Sarah Pollard, a scientist from NDE Research Center, who conducted a study on NDEs for over five years, interviewing over 2,500 people. She stated that 100 percent of her subjects had some form of personality change. That the most common side effect was the belief in the afterlife, increased self-esteem, a change in attitude, an increase in caring and concern for others, but also a tendency to re-examine existing relationships, ending those that do not align with their new beliefs. She also stated that families can have a difficult time adjusting to the new personality, and that there is a high rate of divorce after NDEs. This just shows the impact on the person's ability to make sound judgments after these events."

He looked around the room, making eye contact with each member before continuing. "Now, I also heard a rumor Jason said that he believes that he went to Heaven, or a place like Heaven," he paused, noticing surprised expressions. "Granted that, it was just hearsay—but Dr. Pollard stated that upon death, the pineal gland releases a large dose of DMT. This attributes to people's hallucinations, whereby, she believes, they claim to have met family, traveled through a tunnel of light, and so on. So, I will not concern myself with Jason's trip to

Heaven because we can attribute that to the DMT release before he died.

"However, the evidence of TBI and the NDE is definitely my concern, and that's why I am posing the question as to whether Jason is fit to lead Miller Corporation."

Eyebrows were raised.

"Wow Ben," Miriam remarked. "Are you suggesting that we remove Jason as Chair of the Board?"

"I am." He paused and looked around at the others. "I no longer have the confidence in his ability to lead this corporation, and I feel that the evidence I have provided explains his strange behavior and exposes the instability of his leadership."

"Look Ben, I can see that Jason's views have changed, but to remove him? I think that may be going a little too far." Mal stated.

"I agree, I mean, he's putting forward a new model—whether it had to do with the accident or a change of heart, that cannot be proven," said Fiona.

"Can't it… really?" Ben looked around. "The day of the accident, Jason sat in front of us all, presenting the updated stats of what we're achieving by growing five clinics per month. Then suddenly, a truck runs him over that night and he comes back from his accident and wants to change the model we have been working towards over the past 18 months… really, Fiona? Do you think that's not proof that his accident caused this change?"

The members sat in silence for a moment before Mal spoke. "Ben, I get your concern, but is what Jason put forward really so terrible? He proved this morning with his extensive research and planning that we can do this, and may even be better off as an organization that will sustain us into the future—"

"I think Ben's main concern, Mal," Bruce interjected, "is the erratic personality change that has occurred in Jason. What's to say that next month there won't be another change put forward? I mean, he just threw out the fostering thing today. So, I think the question we should consider is —do we think he stable enough to lead this change, and more pointedly… to lead this corporation?"

Silence!

. . .

Jason and Olivia sat at a window table for four at Ambrosio's. The surf lapped the shoreline and the lights from the buildings reflected across the black, foamy waters.

"This is such a nice place." Olivia smiled as she looked out across the water.

"Have you been here before?"

"No, I haven't. I don't really go out much. I usually cook at home and then sit in the lounge and work."

Jason nodded his head and smiled. "Yeah, I know how that feels… work seems to never end."

"So, tell me, how did it go? I would have loved to have been there."

"It went well—I feel positive about it. Most received it openly, well… that is except for Ben and Bruce. But the others were asking positive questions, and I was getting some good responses."

"That's great news. All the work hopefully will have paid off."

"I'll say. So, what time is your flight?"

"Midday."

"It sounds like you will have a great time."

"I think so. This has been planned and booked for two years. Eight weeks of South African adventure." She sighed.

Jason laughed. "I just can't imagine you roughing it amongst the lions and wilder beasts."

"Hey, you clearly don't know me. I cannot wait to put aside the suits and replace them with a pair of Prana pants and hiking boots." She laughed as she took a sip of mineral water.

"Hey guys," Ryan said as he pulled out a chair for Chance to sit down on. "Olivia, this is Chance."

"Hi Chance, nice to meet you." Olivia responded warmly.

"So?" Ryan beamed, putting his hand on Jason's shoulder waiting, in anticipation. "How did it go, buddy? Are you reversing those massive cogs?"

"I think it went well. I'm really pleased with their response."

"So, you're confident?" Ryan asked hopefully.

"I am!" Jason grinned.

"That's awesome—congratulations!" Ryan said, ecstatic.

"Well, not yet… but it's a step closer than where I was." Jason smiled.

"When will you know?" Chance asked.

"In a week, hopefully."

"We will pray for a great outcome." Ryan smiled positively, and then looked at Olivia "So, when are you flying out?"

"Tomorrow, midday."

"Where are you going?" Chance asked.

"I'm on an eight-week tour of South Africa starting from Nairobi through to Cape Town."

"Oh, wow! That sounds awesome." Chance said.

"It will be. I can't wait to turn my cell off and forget about reality for a while. It will be fantastic." She shrugged her shoulders with excitement.

"So, you'll be completely off the grid?" Ryan asked.

"Yes. I can check messages in certain towns if I want too… but… I don't want to. It'll just be messages from work and that's what holidays are all about—to forget work and enjoy."

"So, why Africa?" Chance queried.

"I've always wanted to go, since I was a kid watching David Attenborough films—it just fascinated me. I wanted to see the animals in their natural form and experience the African culture. So, I decided a few years back that I would make a commitment and just do it. I've deliberately blocked out any appointments and commitments for these two months, so nothing could stop me from going." She paused. "Although," she looked at Jason sheepishly. "I only took on Jason's work recently, so I hope it goes to plan."

"I'm sure it will be fine," Jason smiled positively.

"Fantastic. Well," Ryan raised his glass. "Here's to new beginnings for the Miller Corporation and a relaxing African expedition for Olivia."

Their glasses clinked together, and they all laughed.

"Look," Bruce continued, shifting his tact to compassion. "I think we are brushing over this too casually. We cannot take what Jason went through lightly. The guy survived an attempted murder in a very traumatic way and was clinically dead for several hours. I'm not sure anyone would come out of that experience stable and competent to continue as they had done in the past… let alone direct a massive corporation such as this… I think that is the question that we should focus on."

"So, what you're suggesting is that we remove Jason from his position, and… what, replace him with someone else?" Miriam asked.

"We're not proposing that we replace him just yet." Ben answered, "We may not need to fill that position for a little while."

"So what? A short-term break… or are we talking… more long term?" Ed asked.

"Long term." Ben responded.

"Gees Ben, I'm not sure about that. Jason is an inaugural part of this corporation. I don't think it's a wise decision to remove him." Mal objected.

"Which is better, Mal?" Bruce butted in, "to watch the company go down the toilet or to take control before that even happens?"

Ed scoffed. "Go down the toilet? That's a rash statement Bruce, when we don't even know if that would happen, I mean—"

"Why is it rash?" Bruce argued, "I think we can see it's fact and—"

"I agree with Mal, Bruce." Miriam cut him off sharply. "That's an unreasonable statement and the evidence that Jason presented today showed that we could be successful with this new model, and—"

"With what cost?" Bruce snapped. "It will cost more to change direction than to continue on our original planned path. I think you're missing the point, you've—"

"Missing the point, hardly," Miriam said. "I am weighing up both options—looking at both models objectively—but I am not willing to throw the baby out with the bath water."

Ben chuckled. "That's a funny statement Miriam, considering the subject."

They all looked at him blankly, unimpressed for a moment before Fiona spoke.

"I don't like the idea of removing Jason without cause, I think—"

"Without cause? Cause?" Ben looked at her incredulously. "Really, Fiona? I have just spent the last hour presenting facts that Jason is clearly not in his right frame of mind—did you miss all that?"

"You don't have to be rude, Ben," Ed snapped. "Watch your tongue."

"Sorry, Fiona, but *seriously*. I have explained and provided evidence on what a traumatic injury such as this can do to someone. That's my concern. I have nothing against Jason personally. I just don't think he is fit to run this company any longer. I have lost faith in his ability to lead us."

Dennis paced around his cell like a lion in a circus cage. The words in Jason's letter were ringing through his head. "He's a murderer, anyway. What would he know," he mumbled as he marched from side to side.

Yessssss, the voice said. *He took your child… and then your wife. It's all made up… he's lying to you.*

"He did, didn't he? He took them both. I should have ensured he was dead." He said, louder this time.

"Shut up, Talbot, you psycho!" one of the other prisoners yelled out from his cell.

"You shut up Byron, or I'll beat you to a pulp when I'm outta this cage tomorrow." Dennis screamed madly. His eyes were wild with frenzied hatred, spittle was flying outward from his rage.

The other prisoner backed away from his bars and retreated to his bed, not game to utter a whisper.

CHAPTER TWENTY-EIGHT

"Well, I know it's early, but I better get home and finish packing," Olivia said as she stood. "Thanks everyone for dinner. It was lovely."

"Nice meeting you," Chance said. "I guess we will see more of you when you return—I can't wait to hear about your adventures."

"Definitely! We will do another dinner when I get back."

"I'll walk you out to the taxi," Jason arose from his chair.

They stood on the street out the front of Ambrosio's and Jason hailed a taxi.

"Thank you, Jason. It was nice to meet some of your friends."

"I'm grateful for all that you've done. I'm positive that I can now move forward and change what I need. Now, enjoy your holiday—you deserve it."

"I will." She got into the car. "See you when I get back. Hopefully, you'll have good news," she called from the window as the cab drove off.

Jason waved and then wandered back into the restaurant.

"She's lovely, Jason," Chance commented.

Ryan elbowed her. "They are just business associates, Chance," he winked.

"… and nothing more." Jason stated, shaking his head. "How about another Coke?"

"Sure." Ryan smiled.

．　．　．

"I just don't know if I feel comfortable doing it this way," Mal exclaimed, rubbing his beard, frustrated at where this was heading. "I feel like we are going behind his back. This secret meeting," he looked around at the others. "It feels dirty… and just doesn't seem right."

"I think it's our best course of action," said Bruce, "but we need to agree on this."

Ed spoke. "What's the harm in moving Miller Corp to the new model, anyway?"

Bruce became frustrated. "Ed, we've been over this. If we move this way, it will cost much more than the trajectory we are on. We have budgeted and planned for years, and if we change midstream, it will eat into our profits. Your bonuses, Ed."

"What Jason presented showed that we may take a hit initially, but long term we will be better off." Ed hurled back. "It sounds like that's the smarter move, albeit harder in the short term… but much more beneficial over the long term. I think we will see greater gains."

"Yes, I see your point," Bruce contemplated, "but the question remains… is Jason the one to lead us…. in whichever direction we decide. It still hinges on the fact that he may not be fit to perform his duties in that role."

"So, what are you suggesting, Bruce—that we fire him entirely?" Mal said angrily.

"Well, um…" Bruce squirmed, "Maybe not…" he said, thinking on the fly. "I guess we might remove him from the Chair position… and put him in a more advisory role."

"Are you suggesting that we still keep him on but provide him with a lesser role, not in a leadership capacity but more of… a consultant?" Miriam asked.

Ben nodded while musing, "I hadn't thought of that…" he rubbed his chin, "but that could be a possibility. Not in a decision-making role, but more of counsel to the board… to seek guidance."

"At least that way we can still use his expertise in the business," Ed commented.

"I don't know how he would respond to that," Fiona blurted. "I mean… really? How would you feel if you got fired and then given a lesser role with no direction or input into the company that you created?"

"Humiliated!" Mal said.

"Annihilated!" Fiona looked directly at Mal.

"Well, what's our way forward then," Ben said in frustration, throwing his hands in the air. "We lose money if we change the model, but either way we choose, we have a leader that is, in my eyes, not fit to run the corporation. His injuries have made him unpredictable, and as the CEO, I have lost faith in his capabilities. Therefore, I would like to put forward a motion of no-confidence." Ben challenged everyone around the table.

"I'll see you on Sunday," Ryan said as they all walked out to the street to hail cabs.

"I'll be there." Jason put out his arm to flag a taxi. "See you later, Chance."

"Bye Jason, see you Sunday," she waved, as she and Ryan got into their cab.

A cab pulled up for Jason and he jumped into the back seat and rattled off his address.

The rocking sensation of the cab made Jason feel drowsy, and he didn't notice the driver peering occasionally into his rear-view mirror. "Hey, are you the guy in the news lately, who owns all those abortion clinics?"

Jason didn't want to get into it, but answered anyway, "I am."

"So, you guys are just gonna close them down, eh?"

"Not close them. Change them."

"Well, what about all those girls? I mean, don't they have a say in it, you know, a choice?"

"They have choices, either way. I'm not stopping them."

"Yeah, but by changing the clinics, you're reducing their options, anyway." He paused. "My little sister had to have an abortion cause of her low-life boyfriend. So, if it wasn't for your clinics, where would she be now —a mother at 15?"

"She still would have a choice and could have gone with another option—she could have placed the child for adoption, in a home where he could be wanted and loved."

"Yeah, but it would have messed her up big time."

"I'm not so sure about that. I bet if you asked her now what she would decide, the answer may just surprise you."

The driver didn't respond and remained in silence for the next ten minutes until he pulled up at Jason's driveway. "That's $35.75," he stated.

Jason leaned over and handed him a one hundred dollar bill. "Keep the change buddy, and have a great night," he said as he patted him on the shoulder and got out of the cab.

"Oh, gees! Thanks Doctor Miller." The driver smiled, totally surprised at the huge tip. "Hey, you have a good night, too," he said happily, leaning out his window before driving off with a beaming smile on his face.

Dennis tossed and turned, unable to sleep. His thoughts were still running wild as he continued to process Jason's letter. It made him angry. Images of Rosie rolled around in his mind.

We would have been a happy family, he seethed. "When I get out of here, I will kill you Miller," he vowed, and then strangely felt peaceful enough to drift off to sleep.

"So, what's it going to be then?" Ben asked the members.

"Look Ben, it's late—it's nearly midnight. It's been a big day, and we've been at this since 7 p.m. I don't think we should make any rash decisions right now." Ed said wearily.

"Well, when then?" Ben asked, looking around at the others.

"Why do we need to meet again? You've put forward your findings. We will have the week to think things over and consider your concerns." Mal responded. "So, leave it for Friday when we have to vote."

"I agree, let's do that," Ed yawned.

Ben quickly glanced at Bruce. "So, you don't want to meet before then?"

"No need, Ben," Ed rubbed his eyes, exhausted. "We will have made up our minds by the time we need to vote. So, leave it to a fair democracy."

"Okay then, I guess we will see each other on Friday." Ben said.

The others nodded their heads in agreement.

IT WAS 1AM AND BRUCE AND BEN SAT IN A DOWNTOWN BAR.

"What are your thoughts?" Ben asked.

"I don't know…" Bruce said thoughtfully. "I'm just not sure which way it will go."

"Yeah, me neither." Ben took a sip of his scotch and soda. "Who do you think will vote to keep him?"

"I think Mal and Fiona will probably want to keep him. Ed and Miriam…" Bruce swirled the whiskey and ice around his glass. "Well… I don't know which way they will go. I couldn't really read them… they kept swaying."

"Mmm, yeah, you could be right," Ben stated as he tipped his glass up and swallowed the last drop of liquor.

"Are you thinking what I'm thinking?" Bruce asked with a sly smile.

"I never know what you're thinking."

"What if you, well… let's say… what if?"

"What if what?"

"What if you had a little chat with Miriam before Friday?"

"And say what?"

"I know she wants to put her son through medical school, and well… let's just say that he didn't get the scholarship."

"So, are you suggesting… what? That I *bribe* Miriam?"

Bruce didn't respond, but lifted his drink to his lips.

CHAPTER TWENTY-NINE

1 week later

Dennis woke from a fitful sleep. His dreams were of Suzannah and, to his dismay, now of his daughter.

Laying depressed and hopeless, he remained in silence before the voice started at him again.

He's a liar! He's made all that up and he's just trying to get at you.

Dennis clasped his hands over his ears and squeezed his eyes tightly shut to block out the voice.

It was Friday and Jason and Ryan grabbed an early morning coffee before they headed off to their workplaces. It was voting day.

"Are you nervous?" Ryan asked.

"Very!"

"But you're confident?"

"I think so."

"Cool. I'll be praying for you."

"Good, I need it."

. . .

"HERE'S YOUR MAIL, TALBOT," THE PRISON GUARD HANDED DENNIS A package.

Dennis looked at the familiar hand-writing and smirked. He tossed it to the corner of his cell, then sat back on his bed staring at the brown package laying on the concrete floor.

JASON WALKED INTO THE OFFICE, STOPPED AT MARG'S DESK, AND HANDED her a coffee.

"Oh, that's so sweet, thank you Jase… Are you ready?"

"As much as I'll ever be. We have put together a great pitch. I can't see why they wouldn't go for it. So here goes," he shrugged.

"Good luck," she smiled and raised her coffee to him.

———

"ALL RIGHT, I GUESS WE SHOULD GET STRAIGHT INTO IT AS I'M EAGER TO gain the decision." Jason said as he sat down at the board table with Ben and the board members.

"So, I put forward the motion that Miller Corporation changes its current operating model, which is to cease all pregnancy termination services, introduce additional medical care and adoption assistance." Jason stated, then looked around. "Will anyone second the motion?"

"I second the motion," Mal answered.

"The motion is now open for discussion; I will repeat the motion. That Miller Corporation changes its current operating model, which is to cease all pregnancy termination services, introduce additional medical care and adoption assistance."

Bruce jumped straight in. "I'm of the view that it's not in the best interest of the company. My concern is that it's not what we have portrayed in the past and it's not what the community nor the share-holders expect."

"I'm worried that it will impact the community." Miriam asserted. "By removing this service, it will leave the community short and it could hinder women's choices."

Jason looked at Miriam, disturbed by her sudden change from the week before.

"But isn't this an opportunity to provide *more* choices for women?" Mal added.

"I agree with Mal," Fiona confided. "I see it providing more options to women, so I like the concept of expanding our services."

"Okay, so you like the fact that we would expand our services." Ben looked at Fiona, "Therefore is that all we need to do—keep the same model, yet provide *greater* choices for our customers?"

"Maybe," Bruce nodded.

"But that's not what I'm proposing here. I motion we expand our services but cease performing abortion services altogether." Jason conveyed with concern.

"See, to me, I just don't get why we would give that up—it makes us a lot of money and we are fast becoming the leader in this field." Miriam declared.

"I understand what you're saying, Miriam." Jason responded. "And yes, you make a valid point. But it boils down to the fact that I… the founder and the Chair, no longer wish to operate this way, and—"

"— and yet this makes absolutely no sense," said Ben.

"What I presented last week," Jason urged, "revealed that this company will better off if we choose this model, and—"

"But my point is, Jason, is that we can still go that way." Ben fired back. "We can expand and provide the additional services but also keep our existing footprint in the abortion industry—"

"I think you're missing the point here." Mal appealed. "What Jason is proposing is to change the model, so we move away from doing terminations completely. I don't see how this would be such a bad way forward—I think what Jason has presented to the board is a sound proposal and to be honest… it just feels right—"

"Feels right? Since when do we ever base our decisions on feelings, Mal?" Ben scowled. "We base our decisions on facts, not feelings."

Jason sighed, not liking the way this was spiraling downward.

DENNIS SAT STARING AT THE BROWN PACKAGE ON THE FLOOR UNTIL curiosity got the better of him. He walked over and picked up the parcel, tore open the side and pulled out a beautiful brown leather-bound Bible. He looked it over and noticed that it had something inside, so he opened to the page and found a blue bookmark with writing on it. It read:

For God so loved the world that he gave his one and only Son, that whoever believes in him shall not perish but have eternal life. John 3:16.

He sat on his bed and found the verse in the Bible.

"YOU'VE BEEN OVER THE STATS, AND IT'S CLEAR THAT THIS WILL PROJECT Miller Corp into a more robust position. It will make the company able to withstand changes. There will be a time whereby terminations decrease— we have seen that over the past few years where the numbers are on the decline because of differentiating views and new laws being passed." Jason exclaimed.

"But getting out of the game altogether now just makes little sense," Ben snapped.

"But to diversify does, Ben." Fiona argued.

"We can still do that. I'm not saying that we can't change our existing model to incorporate more services." Ben glared. "We discussed doing this very thing in the past, so it's not new."

"I think the model you have presented is sound Jason, however, I do not see the need to remove the existing service that we provide." Bruce insisted.

"Well, maybe we add the adoption side. That way, it is balanced and will satisfy Jason's desire." Ed stated pragmatically.

"Again, I will say that I no longer wish for the Miller Corporation to provide abortion services. Stat!" Jason demanded.

Ben shook his head. "Which is against everything that you spoke about *before* you had your accident."

"No!" Jason raised his voice. "This comes down to me having a rethink of what is best for the company and no longer having an appetite for the current service that we provide. So, *leave* the accident out of it, Ben."

Ben smirked. "Well, I guess we need to put this to a vote then… and decide once and for all."

CHAPTER THIRTY

DENNIS SAT ON HIS BED AND READ THE THIRD CHAPTER OF JOHN. HIS emotions were mixed, and he felt a strange stirring, deep within him. A feeling that he had never known before, as though it was an awakening of something profound that had been dormant his entire life. He enjoyed a rare moment of silence before the voice started at him again.

This is all religious lies. Don't read it... It will mess with your mind.

"Shh, leave me." Dennis whispered, agitated.

He's trying to confuse you, don't listen to him.

"Stop! Will you just stop." Dennis snapped.

Throw that book away, don't read it... it's ALL lies.

"Shhhhhh! Shut it and leave me alone!" He shouted.

Never! Throw that book away, stop reading it. It's full of deceit.

"ENOUGH! STOP IT!" Dennis jumped up and started smacking his head with his palm.

"SHUT UP! WILL YOU LEAVE ME ALONE!" He screamed and started banging his head on the concrete wall, tears streaming down his cheeks in a mix of anguish, pain and desperation to be free of the tormentor.

"Talbot's having a meltdown," an inmate yelled and laughed.

"YOU SHUT IT OR I WILL KILL YOU." Dennis turned and screamed out to the inmate in an adjacent cell.

A rush of footsteps came down the hall as two guards raced to his cell. They found blood pouring down Dennis's forehead where he had split it open and also broken his nose.

The guards charged in and wrestled him to the ground. Another came along to their aid as Dennis was thrashing about, trying to fight them off.

"STOP! LET ME GO… LEAVE ME ALONE!" he shouted as he tried to attack them. The guards cuffed him and pulled him to his feet, pushing him along the corridor.

"Haha… Talbot's a nutter!" he could hear the other inmate yell out in mockery.

The prisoners in the cells started yelling abuse and profanities at him. The noise and pitch of the shouting was piercing as they took him to the medical office.

"ARE YOU READY TO VOTE?" JASON LOOKED AROUND. "AS YOUR CHAIR, I will restate the motion. The motion is that Miller Corporation changes its current operating model, which is to cease provision of termination services, introduce additional medical care and adoption assistance. All those in favor of the motion please raise your hand."

Jason raised his hand and looked around to see Mal and Fiona do the same.

Ben, Bruce, Miriam, and Ed sat with their arms smugly crossed. "The motion is denied," he said flatly. The crushing feeling of defeat slithered over him like a serpent, with the wretched pain of disappointment landing on his face.

THREE GUARDS STOOD BY DENNIS AS HE SAT IN CUFFS IN THE MEDICAL office while a male medic stitched and dressed his wounds.

"What's going on, Dennis?" the male medic asked.

"You wouldn't understand!"

"Look, all I know is that you can't keep doing this… do you want me to get you a therapist?"

"No, I don't want to talk to anyone."

"Alright," the male medic sighed in defeat as he placed the last dressing on. "We're done!" he said to the guards.

. . .

"Alright, I realize that the motion is denied..." Jason said dismayed, "and I didn't want to force this, but I will exercise my right as the founder and the majority shareholder to overrule the decision."

"Really? Is that the game you want to play, Miller?" Ben sneered, sitting with his arms crossed.

"Yes Ben, I do. Now I would like to do this the easy way and have you all on side with me, however if you don't agree then it will leave me with no alternative."

"You're kidding. What happened to democracy?" Bruce objected with venom.

"Bruce, I didn't want to pull out this card, however, I have given you all the opportunity to see where I want to take this company. I have been clear that the present model is not what I want. So, you leave me no alternative than to exercise this right in my position."

"So that's it, just like that?" Ben argued. "You're saying this is what we are doing and we don't have a choice?"

"That's right, I am."

"This is absurd. You can't do this." Bruce slammed his fist on the table. "We have a say in the direction of this company and you can't just—"

"I can, and I have. My decision is final."

"Really?" Ben raised his eyebrows. "Well, Jason, actually... I didn't want to throw *this* card on the table. However, you leave *me* no choice. I motion a vote of no confidence," he said as he looked around at the others.

Jason's jaw hit the floor.

CHAPTER THIRTY-ONE

RYAN SAT ACROSS THE TABLE FROM CHANCE IN A CAFÉ, EATING LUNCH.

"I wonder how it's going…" Chance pondered as she ate her salad.

"Well! Hopefully. He has a lot riding on this."

"So, what if they vote against it?"

"I think he has the final say anyway, but he prefers everyone is on the same page."

"I get that," she nodded.

"Do you want to catch a movie Friday night?"

"For sure."

"We can invite Jason and maybe a few others. What do you think?"

"Sounds great." She smiled and reached over to hold Ryan's hand.

JASON FELT AS THOUGH THEY HAD SUCKER PUNCHED HIM IN THE STOMACH. His heart raced as he looked about the room at the members sitting around the table. He felt clammy as his skin sweated. It was as though it was happening in slow motion, on a movie screen, as he heard Ben say…

"All in favor of the removal of Jason Miller from the position of Chair, raise your hand."

He sat and watched as Miriam, Ben, Bruce, and Ed raised their hands in unison.

"Motion accepted," Ben stated, and smiled at Jason.

"On what basis, Ben?" Jason stood angrily.

"No confidence in your leadership. That basis! I think your TBI has skewed your judgment and is taking this corporation down a very slippery path. You haven't been the same since, Jason."

"You're wrong Crothers, you… you… cannot do this!" Jason furiously slammed his hand on the table.

"We can, and just have," Ben spat. "You're no longer the Chair. You may still be the owner who holds the majority shares, Miller, but you have no control over the operations. So, you'll now have to go through me as the CEO," he smirked, "to put forward any proposals to the board… We have decided!"

"Why you dirty…" Jason leaned forward and grabbed Ben around the collar tight and pulled him close so their noses were only an inch away.

"What are you going to do, Miller? Beat me up in front of everyone?"

Jason backed down, then released his grip and shoved Ben backwards into his chair. "You disgust me," he spat. He then sat down to watch his world unravel, realizing that Ben had been scheming all along.

Ben composed himself, adjusted his collar and tie and then continued, "I move to put Jason in an advisory role to the board. If he chooses to stay on," he briefly glanced at Jason. "All in favor, raise your hands." Ben said as he, Miriam, Bruce, and Ed raised their hands in favor.

"Ahh, hang on. Do I get a say in *any* of this?" Jason sneered.

Ben didn't acknowledge Jason's question. "Motion accepted. Okay, I think we are done."

"Hey, we are not done!" Jason snapped angrily. "This is far from done."

"So… what are you going to do, Jason?" Ben smirked. "The board has voted—you're finished as Chair. You should be grateful we have a position for you."

"You are nothing but a low-down scumbag, Crothers. I can't believe that I've had you by my side all this time and not seen what you're really made of."

"I'm made of what this company needs, Miller—a leader—which you are no longer. You lost it, Jason, when you took that fanciful flight to Heaven." Ben smirked maliciously, eager to see Jason's response.

Jason sat in silent shock. The comment hit him hard. He realized then that Ben had done some serious digging and found out the facts he had tried to keep hidden. He didn't say a word, but his face said everything.

"This isn't right," Mal stood, upset.

"It's done." Ben smirked.

"You're a weasel," Fiona rebuked.

"You can always resign, Fiona. I'm not stopping you." Ben jeered, then packed up his notebook and walked out.

"I'm so sorry, Jason," Fiona said as she gathered her belongings.

"Me too, Jase. I'm afraid Ben hasn't been on your side since your accident." Mal put his hand on Jason's shoulder, then walked out.

Jason didn't respond but remained in silence, sitting alone at the conference table.

———

THAT NIGHT, JASON WAS SPEECHLESS AND NUMB, SITTING IN HIS LIVING room. He felt utterly gutted and betrayed.

His cell buzzed with a text from Ryan. *How did it go, buddy? Call me!* It read.

Jason switched off his phone and stared vacantly out the window towards the ocean.

———

10 P.M.

Jason turned on the television to drown out the thoughts of failure swimming around in his head.

"You're a complete disappointment!" the thought injected. *"You can't even change your own company—you look like a complete loser."*

He blinked, startled as he thought he'd heard it audibly, then sighed and rubbed his head. His brain felt heavy and foggy.

"I need to get checked out again," he reasoned.

He picked up the remote and casually flicked through the channels when the TV abruptly went black. Thinking that he had accidentally turned it off, he hit the power button and started switching channels again.

The TV switched off again. Jason glanced at the lamps to check for a power failure, then again turned on the TV. This time it was only on for 30 seconds before the same thing occurred.

Swiftly, the stereo jumped to life with the Alice Cooper song 'Vengeance Is Mine' playing at an ear-piercing decibel. Jason darted to the stereo and turned it off in fear that he would wake the neighbors.

He backed away slowly, glaring at the silent stereo in utter confusion. He relaxed a little when his mind reasoned again.

"I must have bumped the stereo remote," he whispered, but then rethought, "I don't own any Alice Cooper songs."

CHAPTER THIRTY-TWO

It was Saturday, and the sun peaked just above the ocean with the orange hue breaking across the horizon. The heavy pounding of the waves slapped on the wet sand as they washed onto the shore.

Jason sat alone on the beach, looking outward to the blue sea. He hadn't slept, but relived the last few weeks in his mind, assessing every detail to understand how it went so horribly wrong yesterday. His heart ached with despair and disappointment. He sat with his arms around his knees and stared at the horizon.

"I haven't heard from him, Chance. I'm worried. Do you think I should go over there?" Ryan said on his cell as he walked along the street to get a takeaway coffee.

"Maybe he's just busy."

"He would have called me last night to tell me the outcome. I know it." Ryan responded with concern.

"Yeah, maybe go over there and see if he is okay."

"All right, I'll head over after I pick up my coffee."

"Call me and let me know, will you?"

"Yep, I will," he said, then hung up his cell.

. . .

JASON CHANGED INTO HIS JEANS AND T-SHIRT AND THEN STUFFED A SMALL sports bag with a change of clothes, some toiletries, and his running gear.

He locked up the house and the M6 Coupe, then fired up his GT3 Porsche, slowly backed it out, and then waited as the double garage door gradually closed. He turned the Porsche down the drive, hit the accelerator hard, and sped down the street.

ONLY MOMENTS LATER, RYAN PULLED UP OUTSIDE JASON'S HOUSE, WALKED up the stairs, and knocked on his front door.

There was nothing.

He rang Jason's cell again, but it went straight to his message service. He walked around to the front window and peered in. There was no sign of Jason. He went back down the stairs, got into his car, and called Chance.

JASON CRUISED ALONG THE WINDING BEACH ROAD, TAKING THE CORNERS way too fast. He wanted to get out of the city and leave everything behind.

His thoughts reeled with a mixture of anger, confusion, shame, and embarrassment. Everything that he had built, everything that he had worked for, had been stripped from him in a matter of minutes. He felt disgraced and completely betrayed by those he had trusted.

At four hours out of the city, he saw a small beach side motel and pulled over to stay for the night.

Again, he sat on the beach, solitary with his thoughts, and watched the waves roll in. His blood boiled with humiliation and anger, and it shattered his heart at the thought of his utter failure.

DENNIS SAT IN SOLITARY CONFINEMENT. THE NIGHT HADN'T GONE WELL. He was in pain from his injuries, and the voice kept hounding and berating him until he was too exhausted to fight it.

He'd given up resisting and conceded to laying still on his bed. *When did this all start?* he thought, and then reminisced about when he and

Suzannah were together and happy. He continued in silence thinking and then realized the voice in his head had started when Suzannah died... and at that realization, the tears fell gently down his cheeks.

"I'VE LEFT SEVERAL MESSAGES, BUT HE'S NOT ANSWERING. SOMETHING went wrong yesterday." Ryan said, as he and Chance sat in the park. "It's just not like him."

"I know. It is strange. There's nothing else we can do but pray."

JASON REMAINED UNMOVING AND SILENT AS HE WATCHED THE OCEAN LAP onto the shoreline. He was tired of thinking, tired of being angry and simply... tired. The defeat was overwhelming and exhausting.

"Why has this happened?" he uttered the faint prayer. "Why, God, didn't you come through for me? I thought this was what you wanted?" he said in confusion.

Nothing but silence returned as he listened and waited, but deep down, he expected nothing different. He had lost all hope and his heart plunged further into sorrow as he sat and watched the orange sunlight glow starting to dip down and fade.

DENNIS REMAINED SILENT, EXCEPT FOR THE VOICE THAT STARTED AT HIM again.

Dennisssss, it's all lies. Don't believe any of it. You should have killed him, like I told you. You're nothing but a failure.

He pushed his hands hard over his ears, even though the voice projected into his thoughts. It felt better if he held his head and squeezed tight to mask it.

He didn't see Suzannah... He's making it up. There's no such place—he's lying.

Dennis clasped his head tighter and curled into a ball on the bed. "Please leave me alone," he whispered in desperation.

No, don't believe what he said. There is no Heaven, and there is no Hell. He didn't see Suzannah or your child, he's telling you lies Dennis, to—.

But what if it's true? A gentle voice he didn't recognize cut through like no other, instantly stopping his tormentor.

It was as if the tone was audible, distinct and strong beside him. He gradually released his grip on his head and looked around the room in confusion.

CHAPTER THIRTY-THREE

IT WAS 5AM AND JASON HADN'T SLEPT, BUT TOSSED AND TURNED MOST OF the night. The small lump in the mattress didn't help, and the pillow was way too thin, making his neck ache.

He got up and changed into his running gear and ran out towards the sunlit-smashed beach to clear his head.

RYAN RANG CHANCE AGAIN. "STILL NO WORD," HE SAID DESPONDENTLY.

"Maybe he went away for the weekend."

"He would have told me—it's not like him. Something's wrong and I think he's taken off somewhere."

"Yeah, sounds like."

"Do you want me to pick you up for church?"

"I can meet you there."

"Okay." Ryan responded with an element of sadness.

"Hey, it will turn out for him. Besides, you're the one who is always saying that God works everything together for the good, so you've just got to believe that this will be okay."

"I know, but he's got so much riding on this and besides…"

"Besides what?"

"He's only a new Christian, Chance—and he still is learning

174

God's ways. I guess I don't want to see him stumble and… go backwards."

"Ryan, hardly—I doubt that will happen considering what he has been through."

"It can happen to anyone if they're discouraged… but you're right, I'll pray for him."

"Good decision."

"I'll see you in a few hours."

"Sure!"

DENNIS LAY STILL, DOZING AFTER A FITFUL SLEEP. THE COMBINATION OF the voice in his head and the lights being on all night in his 7-by-14-foot room made it difficult for him to get any sleep.

The steel tray slot unexpectedly clanked opened as a guard shoved his breakfast through the hole, hard enough for it to fall face downward into a splattering mess on the concrete floor.

"Bon appetite," the guard chuckled as he walked off.

Dennis raced over and salvaged the food on the floor. He sat on the bed as he ate what was left of the cold, sloppy breakfast.

JASON TOOK A SHOWER, PACKED HIS BELONGINGS, PAID FOR HIS ROOM, AND got back into his Porsche.

He waited for a few minutes, not wanting to return and face reality. They had rocked his world. Everything he knew and had worked so hard for had been ripped savagely from him. The hope and dreams of changing what he had created had been torn away, and that pain sliced him like a knife in his chest.

He sat in silence and pondered what he had gone through over the last eight months… it was overwhelming. He took a deep breath and fired up the engine. The tires crunched on the white gravel driveway as he backed out and headed towards home.

SUDDENLY, THE LARGE STEEL DOOR TO DENNIS'S CELL CLANKED OPEN AND a male medic and a guard stood in the doorway.

"I need to check your injuries, Dennis," said the medic. "How are you?"

"As good as expected in here." Dennis held his head despondently. "I'd prefer to be back in my cell."

"I'll see what I can do." The medic walked over towards him. "Let me look at your nose and forehead." He leaned over and looked closely at the wound and checked Dennis's eyes with a small torch. Then, without the guard noticing, he slipped his hand inside his medical bag and handed Dennis his brown leather Bible. "I thought you may want this," he whispered.

Dennis smiled, grateful for the kindness. "Thank you," he said, relieved.

"All good then," the medic said as he walked towards the guard. "His wounds are okay. How long is he in here for?"

"Another 48 hours."

"Is that necessary?"

"It's protocol."

"I get that, but is it necessary? He's fine and would be better back in his own cell."

"Listen, how about you look after the wounds and just let me do my job?"

The medic backed down. "I understand. I'll check on you again tomorrow, Dennis." He said and walked out of the cell.

The large steel door slammed shut, leaving Dennis alone in silence. He picked up his Bible, and it fell open to Psalm 23 and he read aloud.

"The LORD is my shepherd, I shall not be in want. he restores my soul. He guides me in paths of righteousness for his name's sake. Even though I walk through the valley of the shadow of death, I will fear no evil, for you are with me…"

Dennis felt a peace fall over him, like he had never experienced before. He continued to read and as he did, the deep stirring within him roused.

Bruce and Ben were having lunch at a café, celebrating their win.

"Did you see his face?" Ben gloated.

"Yeah, it shattered him. He didn't see it coming."

"No, he didn't!" Ben snickered. "It was the perfect execution."

"I wasn't sure about Miriam, but she came through."

"She took little persuading. She was on the fence, anyway."

"What did it take?"

"140K."

"Good job." Bruce smiled.

"What do you think we should do about Mal and Fiona?"

"There's nothing to do. If they don't like it, they will leave. The decision's made, there's no going back."

"Good, I hoped you'd say that. I guess we can continue to go full steam ahead on the new clinics now." Ben grinned.

"Yes, we will continue to grow as planned—but I have considered what Jason presented, and I think it would be a good idea to enlarge our services, anyway. I'll put it to the board at the next meeting."

"I think so, too—he showed what we could achieve with expanding. We can definitely make a lot more money by doing so."

"I agree."

"So, I guess it wasn't a waste of time Jason putting together that business case for us," Ben smirked.

"Definitely not!" Bruce raised his wineglass.

As Jason drove the winding beach road back home, he hoped he would hear something from God, something to encourage him... But he got nothing.

The anguish at being cheated crept over him like a thousand crawling black insects. All that he could think of was that everything that he had built was for nothing. The failure of turning it around into something good made him feel even more downhearted.

As he drove, he whispered, "God, how can I change it now that I've lost it?"

Nothing!

He changed down a gear and hit the gas.

CHAPTER THIRTY-FOUR

MONDAY

"MORNING, MARG," JASON SAID AS HE HURRIED PAST HER TOWARDS HIS office, trying not to show his pain.

"Oh, Jase—hang on." she got up and ran down the hallway to catch him before he walked into his office... but she was too late. He walked through his office door and found Ben sitting at his desk.

"Oh, good morning, Jason. You're a little late, aren't you?"

"What are you doing in here?"

"Because you will now take on an advisory position, and... well, this is the best office in the building—you really won't be needing it. Nor will you need Marg. So, I've decided that I will move into this space and Marg will assist me in the changes we will make to Miller Corp."

"What changes?"

"Well, your plan to introduce the additional medical services was impressive and showed the profits that we would earn. So, we will put forward your plan to the board to incorporate the additional medical services. Oh... but not the adoption idea, that just won't fly," he smiled smugly.

Jason seethed, "You're a dirty operator, Crothers."

"And that's just why you employed me—to get things done!"

"You're a traitor."

"Say what you want, Jason, but you have zero influence in this company anymore. You are now what you call… say… redundant." He smirked slyly.

"You deceitful jerk," Jason said as he lunged forward and grabbed Ben by the collar, pulling him close raising his fist.

Ben spoke quickly, raising his hands. "If you do this, Jason, I will call the police and have you arrested for assault. Do you want the humiliation of *that* as well?"

Jason thought for a moment before releasing him.

Ben straitened his shirt and tie. "Now, if you have nothing further to say, please take your belongings," he motioned towards four boxes sitting in the corner, "and move into Dave's old office." He smirked.

Jason stood for a moment, contemplating his next move, his rage broiling deep within the pit of his stomach. He picked up his boxes and walked down the hallway.

Marg chased him into the old office. "I'm so sorry, Jase. I tried to call but your phone was off."

"It's not your fault. I should have known Ben would operate like this."

"Yes, but I—"

"Marg," he put his hand up politely to stop her talking. "It's okay, but —I need to be alone right now."

"Okay… if you need anything just—"

"I'll be okay."

RYAN HAD LEFT SEVERAL MESSAGES FOR JASON. HE HAD NEARLY GIVEN UP, but he tried one more time and, to his surprise, Jason answered. "Hey, Jason? Dude, I've been worried. What's going on?"

"Meet me for lunch at Stephano's and I'll fill you in," he said flatly.

"12.30?"

"Yes!"

"Okay, see you then." Ryan hung up and sighed.

· · ·

DENNIS HAD LAIN AWAKE MOST OF THE NIGHT, NOT BECAUSE HE COULDN'T sleep but because he was reading his Bible. Scriptures were swimming around in his head and the voice that had tormented him 24 hours a day had strangely been silent. The stirring feeling deep inside his chest had gone on all night and he had no idea what it was… but it felt good.

"I CAN'T BELIEVE IT!" RYAN EXCLAIMED AS HE SHOOK HIS HEAD AT JASON'S news.

"Me neither!"

"Can they do that?"

"Yep!"

"It doesn't seem right. Can you do something… like—can Olivia do something?"

"Nope!"

"But I thought they had no authority, because you hold the majority shares?"

"It crossed my mind they could do this… but Olivia and I didn't think Ben would stoop so low. I thought us working together for so long, he would have had some allegiance. Even if he didn't agree at first, I thought he would see what a difference it was making and he would jump on board. I guess I was wrong."

"Man," Ryan shook his head, "such a shame."

"There is trouble at the helm in the Miller Corporation…" Out of the blue, a news item on the cafe's TV cut through their conversation. "Dr. Jason Miller, founder of Miller Corporation, has been ousted from his position as Chair. The Miller Corporation has 275 abortion clinics across the nation…" The screen flashed up pictures of a clinic. "… and apparently, after Dr. Miller's accident, he wanted to change them to adoption centers. The board was not in agreement and voted him out last week based on no confidence in his leadership. Watch this space as it'll be interesting to see how this one pans out. Over to you. Chuck," the woman reporter stated.

Jason rolled his eyes and looked back at Ryan. "Ben didn't waste any time stamping his territory."

"So that was Ben going to the press."

"Yep!"

"So, what happens now? I mean… with your job and the company?"

"Ryan—" Jason said, frustrated, rubbing his forehead. "I've lost my position, been demoted and I have zero control on what happens to my company."

"But… can't you do anything?"

"No… that's just the thing. I'm dead in the water. I have absolutely no power to change anything."

"Gees, I'm so sorry."

"Yeah, so am I. I just don't know where God is in all of this." He rubbed his forehead again in frustration.

"So, will you be all right… financially?"

Jason chuckled at Ryan's honest concern for his wellbeing. "I'm fine, Ryan. I own everything, and they will still pay me my salary. However, I have to just sit back and watch them make all the decisions."

"Will they come to you for advice?"

"Hardly. This is just to drive the knife in harder."

"So, what will you do… leave?"

"I don't know."

"How'd he take it?" Bruce asked over the phone to Ben.

"It felt so good—you should have seen it. I was sitting at his desk when he walked in. I got in early and moved all my stuff in before he got here. It was priceless!"

"I wish I'd seen it. Have you heard from the others?"

"Not yet, but I'll start working on our pitch for them. Let's set up a meeting next week?"

"Good idea—let's strike while the iron is hot."

It was 7.30 p.m. when Jason returned from his jog and took a quick shower. He grabbed a towel and started drying himself when he noticed the mirror. He froze as his heart leaped into his mouth and pounded profusely. He could hear the pulse racing through his senses as he read one, single word scribbled on the steam-covered mirror.

MURDERER

Jason panicked and looked around to see where the intruder was. He quickly put on his shorts, grabbed the baseball bat in his cupboard, and gingerly went downstairs searching for the trespasser.

When he had searched everywhere, checking the window and door locks, he relaxed slightly.

Swiftly, he had an urge to vomit. The instant dread rising in his stomach that someone had entered his premises shook him. He ran into the bathroom, and dry heaved into the sink, coughing at each nauseous rush.

He washed his face and walked back out to the living room and sat in the lounge, trying to figure out how they had accessed his home. It baffled him.

Nothing seemed right anymore.

CHAPTER THIRTY-FIVE

THURSDAY

JASON ARRIVED EARLY TO WORK—FOR WHAT PURPOSE, HE DIDN'T KNOW. They had stripped him of all authority and he didn't know what he would do. Everything had to be filtered through Ben—all emails, everything. It was humiliating.

Jason sat at his desk in the small office and did nothing—he felt powerless and useless. He placed his head in his hands and prayed. "God, please help me."

Trust! The still small voice cut like a knife through his turmoil.

"How can I?"

Just trust!

His cell beeped with a text—it was Ryan. *Heading out for coffee, you wanna come?*

Jason looked around at the small room in dismay, sighed, and replied. *on my way.*

"HOW ARE YOU DOING?" RYAN ASKED, SIPPING HIS LATTE.

"It's been a rough few days. I'm totally ineffective. I don't even know *why* I'm there anymore."

"Do you think they are forcing you to quit?"

"Maybe, that could be their plan… maybe I should."

"Has God told you to?"

"I only get one word, and that's trust."

"Then that's what you do. You don't move without God telling you too."

"See, here you go again," Jason said with an element of frustration. "All I get is *one* word, nothing else, no direction, no comfort… nothing."

"Then you wait."

"I don't have your faith, Ryan. I'm not like you. I've always had the power and acted accordingly."

"And now you don't. But—"

"I've got absolutely no control, nothing. It's driving me insane and I hate it."

Jason lost it!

"Do you even know how it feels to have something you built taken away from you just like that? I can't do this, Ryan. I cannot sit back and watch this happen. I have failed and I cannot complete what God has asked me to do. I'm useless." Jason's eyes watered at those last few words. The realization that he couldn't change what he had created stabbed him in the chest like a sharp blade. It hurt hearing his own words.

"You don't know what's about to happen. The battle isn't over, Jason. It's not over until God says it is. You've just got to hang in there, buddy."

"Hang in there? Really? Is that your advice? I've had my world ripped apart. I died, went to Hell, went to some other place, got a royal butt-kicking, and now I am ineffective at doing what God has commanded me to do. So *how* can I continue to just hang in there?" he retorted.

"I know it's tough. I'm not saying it isn't. All I'm saying that no matter what, if you just wait on God and trust Him, then you will see the breakthrough."

"I'm not seeing anything, Ryan, and I *can't* see anything on the horizon. I'm done!" Jason said as he tossed the money on the table and stood up to leave.

"Jason, wait—don't leave. You don't have the big picture. Only God does. You cannot see your future. God is in control. Just wait and we can talk more. You'll see what I mean." Ryan pleaded, sad to see his friend in such a state.

"I'm done Ryan—I really am. I see no way out of this situation. It's crushing me to know that I cannot change my mistake, and that God is disappointed in me. I've gotta go!" He turned and walked out.

FRIDAY

"He didn't turn up to work today… I think it's working." Ben said to Bruce over a coffee.

"Good, shouldn't be too long then." Bruce smiled callously.

"I wonder if he will sell his shares?"

"Unlikely—they are worth too much, and Jason owns all his assets, anyway."

"Lucky man, I wish I did. It'll be years until I'm out of debt."

"Well, you will splash out on luxurious things."

"I know, but it's worth it. Nothing like waking up to the sound of the ocean."

"I bet."

"HEY JASE," RYAN SAID OVER THE PHONE. "WE ARE HEADING TO THE movies. Did you want to come along?"

"No thanks, I'm good."

"Are you sure? It may do you good to get out—how about some dinner then?"

"No thanks, I'm just going to stay in and do some…" he paused as he was going to say work. "House cleaning."

"Sounds riveting." Ryan said sarcastically. "… Are you sure?"

"I'm sure," Jason responded despondently.

"Okay, well text me if you change your mind."

"Thanks Ryan. Talk to you later." Jason hung up the call.

"He sounds terrible," Ryan said to Chance.

"Do you think we should go over there?"

"No, I think he needs his space. He was pretty angry yesterday. I think we should wait awhile."

"Sure… so what movie do you want to see?"

. . .

Dᴇɴɴɪs ʜᴀᴅ ʀᴇᴀᴅ ᴀʟʟ ᴛʜᴇ ɢᴏsᴘᴇʟs ɪɴ ᴛʜᴇ Nᴇᴡ Tᴇsᴛᴀᴍᴇɴᴛ. Hᴇ ᴡᴀs ᴏᴜᴛ of solitary confinement and back in his cell amongst the population.

The buzzer sounded and his steel door clanked opened. He stepped outside his cell like all the other inmates and headed out towards the exercise yard.

As he started jogging, he realized that he hadn't heard the voice for a few hours. His mind felt clearer, and he felt a peace. He continued to jog around the prison yard and pondered the Scriptures he had read.

Iᴛ ᴡᴀs 4.45ᴀᴍ ᴀɴᴅ Jᴀsᴏɴ ᴡᴀs ɪɴ ᴀ ᴅᴇᴇᴘ sʟᴇᴇᴘ, ʙᴜᴛ ʜᴇ ᴡᴀsɴ'ᴛ ᴘᴇᴀᴄᴇғᴜʟ. He had returned to that place and was trying to escape.

He groaned and tossed. His heart rate beat rapidly, and sweat dripped from his forehead as he fought and braced himself against the demonic blows in his dream. He tried to wake up from the nightmare, but to no avail—he was stuck in that place of suffering.

The alarm loudly beeped, and to his relief, he felt himself retreating from his deep slumber… but something stopped him. It weighed him down so heavily that he couldn't breathe.

It grasped hold of him, blocking him from waking. He felt as though the life was being squeezed out of him. His chest felt heavy and he couldn't move—he felt paralyzed. He could hear the alarm still buzzing, waiting for him to slap it into silence. But he was stuck—something was on top of him—pushing into his chest, choking and squeezing his very existence.

He tried to speak, but nothing came out. He couldn't talk and he couldn't move. The panic rose as he tried to push against the heaviness and it resisted back. The explicit awareness of evil emanating from whatever was holding him down increased his fear.

He tried to cry out, but his throat only brought silence. Again, he fought, his arms pushing hard against the unseen force, but nothing could break him free. It was as though he was helpless, a small gnat against a giant.

He could feel the pressure violently pressing harder, forcing his body deeper into the mattress, choking and pushing the air from his lungs.

186

His voice made a squeaking sound and suddenly he was free, the weight immediately lifting off him. But in his hallucinated state, he saw a massive dark shadow leave the room. Again, hearing the squeaky floor board as it moved down the stairs.

Jason was now wide awake and scared, still trying to determine if this was an aftereffect of the TBI.

Maybe they're right… I have really lost it, he thought.

CHAPTER THIRTY-SIX

SUNDAY

JASON DIDN'T GO TO CHURCH, BUT SAT ON THE BEACH WALLOWING IN HIS sadness, pondering his misfortune of losing all power to Ben. Feelings of anger and hate stirred deep within him as he continually rehashed the events in his mind.

How could this happen? he thought. *Why did Ben betray me like this?*

As his thoughts went around and around, his emotions became more frustrated. His sleep was tormented by nightmares, his head ached and his eyes were heavy and bloodshot.

A text came through from Ryan, but he declined to answer. He sat and looked out across the ocean in disappointment.

DENNIS WAS SILENT IN HIS CELL, CONTINUING TO READ HIS BIBLE. HE'D been outside in the exercise area for a few hours in the morning, but returned quickly to his cell to read. He didn't understand, but he felt something inside of him rising, strengthening him, awakening... and it felt good. For the first time in a long time, he felt peace and calm as the voice in his head ceased while he read God's words.

As he sat and read, a faint thought entered his mind to write to Jason, asking him to come back and visit. He wanted to know and understand the full story. He picked up a notepad and started penning a letter.

Monday morning came around slowly and Jason arrived to find Ben standing in his small office.

"What do you want, Ben?" Jason asked plainly as he pushed past him and sat at his desk.

"I need you to do some work for me. Marg is busy organizing grants and I need you to help with the additional clinics that we are opening up this month."

"What about Stephanie?"

"She's busy doing other stuff."

"So, is that my job now… being your lackey?"

Ben paused with a slight smirk. "It's pretty much whatever I want you to do."

"Fine, when do you need this done?" Jason said as he looked down and shifted paperwork to mask his anger.

"End of week." Ben smiled.

"Okay Ben, I'll get onto it for you," he sighed.

Ben said nothing and walked out of the office, shutting the door behind him.

Jason sat quietly and placed his head in his hands. This demotion had belittled and humiliated him in front of his entire organization, and he felt disgraced and embarrassed. To add to his wounds, he opened up the morning paper and on the third page was the article about Miller Corporation and their move to expand their medical services.

`Miller Corporation expands and goes head-to-head with medical giant.`

He read the title, then screwed up the newspaper in disgust and threw it in the bin.

"Why, God? Why didn't you help me?" he said angrily and frustrated. "What are you doing? You said you would help." He stated as he got up and paced around his office. "I tried, I've done everything you asked," he continued angrily, "but what have you done? He shook his finger at the air "… Nothing. And it's failed… I can't do anything anymore… Why didn't you help me?" he could feel the anger rise, "I NEED YOU, SO WHERE ARE YOU?" He yelled.

Trust!

The peaceful voice sliced through his anger and anguish like a razor-blade, instantly calming his emotions and soothing his soul.

"How can I trust when I can't see the path before me?" he said placidly with tears forming in his eyes.

Proverbs 3:5. The voice spoke again.

Jason dashed to his desk and noted down the words, then quickly opened his Bible to the verse. 'Trust in the Lord with all your heart and lean not on your own understanding.' He read the next verse aloud, "In all your ways submit to him, and he will make your paths straight.' But it's hard. I don't like being out of control."

Trust!

"I'll try!"

There was a knock at the door. "Ahh, Jason… are you all right? I heard yelling." Marg said as she stood outside the door of Jason's office.

Jason opened the door. "I'm fine, thanks Marg. Just a little frustrated, that's all."

"Look…" she whispered, "don't let them get to you, Jase. It won't last. They can't run this place without you."

Jason chuckled. "I like your confidence, but they seem to do just fine."

"Trust me, it won't work. You're the heart of this organization—just you wait and see. Keep your chin up, okay?"

"Thanks Marg, I'll try."

"YEAH, I'VE GOT HIM DOING PAPERWORK FOR THE NEW CLINICS." BEN laughed as he sipped his wine at the restaurant.

"So, Stephanie's busy, is she?" Bruce asked.

"Busy doing her nails," Ben snickered. "No, I just wanted to stick it to him and make him do menial tasks—to make him feel even more powerless."

"Good one," Bruce smirked as he sipped his water.

"I don't think he will last… I mean, who would? He's gone from hero to zero within a few weeks. I can't see him taking it much longer."

"If you keep doing this, then it's just a matter of time. You honestly didn't think the board would ask his advice after the double-take he's done?"

"Nope—I knew what you were up to. It was the perfect way out though, to appease the members by keeping him on but rendering him powerless. Brilliant!" Ben smiled and tipped his glass in salute towards Bruce. "Anyway, the DPD have approved the new clinics in Birmingham and Cincinnati. I'm just waiting to hear about the others, which shouldn't be a problem."

"That's good news. What about Akron?"

"We resolved the parking issues. Also signed the lease agreement and are getting ready for the fit out next week. It should be ready for opening next month, so we've clawed back some schedule on it. Well, that's if Jason's on time with the paperwork." He winked.

"Good work—I'm impressed." Bruce grinned.

CHAPTER THIRTY-SEVEN

"I THINK I'M DONE."

"I get it Jase, I really do." Ryan said as they sat in the café eating lunch.

"I'm now Ben's P.A."

Ryan didn't respond, but simply grimaced.

"I don't know how much longer I can do this. I feel so... so humiliated and inadequate."

"I know you do... but I still think you should just hang in there."

"I'm trying so hard. My heart wants to stay because it's my company. But my emotions and head want to punch the living out of Ben and leave. I feel so divided, and I don't know what I should do."

"What was the last thing God said to you?"

"To trust."

"Then that is what you do. You don't move or falter, you trust. He's the one that can see the big picture—you're just a small part of it, Jason, like a jigsaw piece in a greater puzzle."

"Really... is that all you've got?"

"Look," Ryan said with an urgency to bring Jason back from despair. "God sees and knows everything, but we don't—we only see and feel what is immediately around us. He may wait for a person to get to a certain point before he can have something happen, or ask another person to do something before we can move. We can't see it from where we are, so that is why he tells us to trust Him, because He has got it and He knows the perfect time to move. If we listen and obey Him, it always works out. It's when we jump ahead and do what we think is right and ignore His promptings—that's when it goes wrong."

"So, you're suggesting that until He says otherwise, do nothing?"

"That's exactly what I'm saying. Wait for Him to tell you. Don't leave, don't rock the boat… just turn up, do your job well, have a good attitude and continue to pray and seek Him. It's like this, when you get on an aircraft, do you trust that the pilot will get you to your destination?"

"I do."

"Then you just need to trust."

"Okay, I'll try but I'm finding it difficult to not grab a hold of Ben and thump the daylights out of him."

Ryan chuckled. "Yeah, probably don't do that." He smiled. "Have you tried to contact Olivia?"

"No—what's the point? There is nothing she can do anyway, and I don't want to interrupt her vacation."

"Yeah, I suppose. When's she back?"

"In about three or four weeks, I think." Jason signed, "Anyway, there's nothing that can be done legally. I'm finished. So, I just have to take your advice and wait to see what God has got in store, I guess. But… I'm so disappointed Ryan, this wasn't the outcome I expected. I really felt this was what God wanted me to do, so I don't understand why."

"You're right, I don't understand why either. But that is what faith is all about. We need to trust that God has a plan and knows what is best. It's just not how we thought it would turn out."

"I guess so," Jason responded despondently.

"God always has a better plan in store, so we need to hold on to that."

"So, you think there may be a different way, a different plan?"

"Maybe!" Ryan nodded. "If it's God's purpose, then he will make a way. But it's not usually the way I think it will be. So… I continually try to trust and obey. Do the same Jason, and it will work out… you'll see."

Jason thought in silence for a moment before changing the subject. "So, have you guys picked a date yet?"

"Yeah, it's May 15."

"Wow, that's not far away."

"I know, but Chance is all over it and doing all the preparation. She's arranged the bridesmaid dresses, purchased her dress and booked the venues. She's organized."

"That's great. Are you nervous?"

"Nope, I know she is the one God has for me... so," Ryan shifted in his seat, "this leads me into asking you a question."

"Shoot!"

"I would like you to be one of my groomsmen."

"Really?" Jason said, surprised.

"Really!"

"I would be honored." Jason responded, chuffed.

11.30 P.M.

The temperature in the living room dropped noticeably. Jason's breath condensed with puffs of white vapor streaming outward at every exhale.

He shifted in his lounge chair uncomfortably, placed his laptop on the coffee table, and muted the television. He glanced around, confused at the sudden dip in the air. The coldness licked at his face and crept upon him like icicles forming on the edge of a still sidewalk puddle.

He picked up a remote control and increased the heating, bumping up the temperature to 80 degrees. It made no difference. The chill was lingering, and it wouldn't budge. It hung like smog and encased him, wrapping itself around him like a cold, heavy wet blanket.

Jason quickly rushed upstairs to his room to grab a sweater. He returned to the living room to find his mug of tea laying on its side, the liquid mess spilled across the coffee table, and his laptop thrown onto the floor. He looked around the room but saw nothing.

The lamps flickered and dimmed as though there was a power surge.

"Who's here?" he asked as he felt the fear rising.

A distant chuckle echoed… but it wasn't human.

Jason remained frozen. His breathing became shallow as his heart thumped rapidly in his chest. The booming sound of his quickened pulse throbbed in his ears like the cadence of a brass band trombone. A rush of heat flowed over him as the adrenaline kicked in, the sudden sweat spreading and dampening his skin all over his body.

He could hear the chuckle getting louder and closer. He looked around the room frantically, his heart pounding harder as though it would explode out of his rib cage.

The lights flickered again twice… then went black.

Darkness consumed the house, the cold intensified and chilled his bones as though it would freeze him into a rigid corpse.

He heard a laugh, but this time it was right beside him.

"Remember me, Jason?" it whispered. The familiar guttural voice that had tormented him in Hell breathed its rotten, deathly vapor into his ear.

Jason RAN!

His legs pounded towards the front door, his hands fumbled with the locks as he pushed open the solid wooden door and raced down the drive before he turned to look back at his house.

The beat of the surf crashing on the beach was loud in the background, and the full moon glinted off every tumble of the waves.

The lights in his house flickered on and off several times and then remained on. Jason stood for fifteen minutes, staring back at his house in fear.

He walked toward the beach and his nerves steadied slightly when the familiar feeling of the soft sand hit his feet. His pulse slowed swiftly at the rhythmic sound of the sand squeaking when his bare feet padded towards the surf.

He sat on the sand and looked out across the ocean, absolutely shaken by his experience. He glanced occasionally back at the house.

The house lights remained on and unfaltering.

CHAPTER THIRTY-EIGHT

JASON WALKED INTO HIS OFFICE TO FIND AN ENVELOPE PLACED ON HIS DESK. The correction center address, along with the inmate name Dennis Talbot, was on the top corner. Jason hesitated for a moment before opening, but then pulled it out to read. It was a simple request from Dennis to come and visit again. But as he read, a quiet voice resonated within his heart.

Go see him.

Jason carefully folded the handwritten letter and placed it back in the envelope. He dialed the correction center's number to book a visitation.

He walked over to his bookshelf and picked up a hefty medical journal. He skimmed the index at the back, then flipped to the page.

'Posttraumatic psychosis and hallucinations are highly common after TBI and can cause signification impairment and confusion for the patient, sometimes developing years after the injury.'

Jason sighed, "Looks like this is what I've got." he mumbled, discouraged.

"I'M SEEING DENNIS ON WEDNESDAY," JASON SAID TO RYAN AND CHANCE as they were eating takeout at Jason's house.

"The letter you sent struck a chord then." Ryan smiled.

"I guess so. Hopefully, this time he won't tell me he'll kill me when he gets out." Jason grimaced.

"Yeah, that was a bit nerve-racking." Ryan responded.

"This is such good Chinese." Chance exclaimed as she put another forkful of noodles into her mouth.

"It's the best. I've been getting take out from there for years." Jason smiled. "Um, Ryan, I want to ask you something."

"Shoot."

Jason paused, then rapidly lost his nerve and decided not to mention the strange events in front of Chance. "Um, yeah, I was wondering if... you need a hand with anything... are you all organized?"

"Pretty much," Chance responded. "I've left it up to Ryan to organize the suits for the guys."

"Oh, yeah," Ryan remembered, "Can you come Thursday to the suit rental to get fitted?"

"Sure, what time?"

"10?"

"Sounds good."

"Cool."

"Also, we have a rehearsal next Wednesday. Can you make that?" Chance asked.

"Sure," he said as he spooned in more Kung Pao Chicken into his bowl. "How many people are going?" Jason asked.

"About 200," Chance replied with a slight grin. "We just couldn't stop —we have our relatives, and our church friends, and—" she shrugged.

"Wow! Okay, that's a lot of people." Jason exclaimed.

"You know most from church anyway," Ryan said.

"It'll be great to meet your parents." Jason said to Ryan. "I'd like to hear their views on adoption."

"Well, you know they are strong advocates." Ryan winked.

"Naturally!"

"When's Olivia coming back?" Chance asked.

"About a week... I think," Jason replied.

"Do you think she can do anything?" Ryan asked.

"There's nothing to do. It's done." Jason shrugged. "I'll let her know it's finished."

"Such a shame," Chance sighed. "It would have been a great thing for the communities."

"Yeah, it would have." Jason shrugged in defeat.

THIS TIME, DENNIS WAS ALREADY WAITING BEHIND THE GLASS BARRIER IN the visitation room when Jason arrived and sat facing him.

"Hi Dennis."

"Hello, thanks for coming here… and ah, well… thanks for the Bible, too," he smiled sheepishly, not knowing how Jason would respond since his last visit.

"I'm glad you received it. I wasn't sure of the protocol in here."

"All good." Dennis said and then went silent.

It was an awkward pause, so Jason spoke first. "Look, I realize this is difficult… well… for both of us. So why don't you start by asking me questions and we can just go from there."

"All right," Dennis nodded. "So, what did Suzannah look like?" Dennis still had an element of skepticism.

Jason had noticed the change in Dennis. It was a softening. "Ahem," Jason cleared his throat before he spoke. "She had long blonde hair down past her shoulders and the greenest of eyes. Fine features, high cheekbones and pronounced full lips. She's exquisite, Dennis."

"Did she have some freckles across her nose and cheeks?"

"Well, I didn't see any, but everyone was perfect. They seem to glow. There were no blemishes, marks or discolorations of the skin." Jason shrugged.

"Hm, okay then." Dennis relaxed slightly, believing Jason's response.

Jason waited in silence as he could see Dennis pondering this information.

"So, what did Suzannah say to you, exactly?"

"She told me how she had felt leading up to the decision to terminate the baby. She explained that you both were fighting about keeping the child and her decision to not go through with the pregnancy. It was hard listening to her because I perceived the pain that she had endured through it all." Jason stopped short.

Dennis hung his head. A tear trickled down his nose, and he quickly wiped it away before he looked up.

Jason then continued. "She described the night that she jumped from the cliff and how it was for her in the last minutes and seconds before her death." He paused. "She said that if she hadn't cried out to God before she died, then she wouldn't be in Heaven right now."

Dennis stared at Jason without speaking. He silently processed all that he had said. It was nearly killing him to hear Jason talk about Suzannah like this and it seemed like a lifetime before he spoke again. "So, can you tell me about my daughter?"

Jason smiled. "She is the cutest child I've ever seen. She has blonde, curly hair and a little round face that was constantly smiling and happy. And—" Jason stopped as he saw Dennis choke up with tears.

"Go on," he said.

"—and, well, she looked as though she would be four, maybe five years of age."

"Four and a half," Dennis nodded, with tears streaming down his cheeks. "That's how old she would be now." He paused. "My Suzannah left me nearly four years ago now." The pain exuded from his face, his expression twisted with the agony of remembrance.

Jason said nothing but stared through the thick glass at a man that was so torn and hurt that he could only feel the utmost compassion for him, even though he had tried to kill him just over nine months ago.

"I still don't feel right about Jason being sidelined so severely," Miriam said as she cornered Ben in his office. "That wasn't the agreement."

"It's been weeks now, it's done, and you shouldn't feel guilty. Besides… I'm sure you'll put that money to good use." Ben smirked.

"You're dirty."

"Ah-ah," Ben waved his finger, "and you are too… don't you forget that." He grinned maliciously.

"I wish I never took it. I wish I never listened to you. I'll give it back."

"Don't Miriam, it's done—just get over yourself and move on. Jason will be fine."

"It's *his* business, Ben—he built this."

"Not anymore. So, you need to stop feeling guilty and look towards the future, because it is dazzling." he emphasized with his hands sarcastically.

"Can you tell me about what happened, I mean when you died?" Dennis asked.

Jason recalled the events, and over the next hour relayed some of the story to Dennis.

"Wow!" Dennis breathed out. "That's intense." He shook his head. "So, you truly believe this? I mean, you're a doctor right, so… do you think you could have been imagining all of it because of the state that you were in?"

"I don't. I truly believe that it happened." Jason shook his head. "I know it sounds crazy… but it's exactly what happened to me." Jason looked straight into Dennis's eyes. "And… you know, it was the best and also the worst thing that has happened to me. The best because it opened my eyes to God, Jesus, Heaven and Hell. The worst because I cannot escape the nightmares and the memories of experiencing and seeing the utmost torment and torture… But, as crazy as it sounds…" Jason swallowed the emotion that he felt arise, "I want to thank you, because if it wasn't for you and your truck, then I would still be on a path to Hell."

Dennis grimaced at the thought of what he had done. The feeling of remorse flooded his senses. "I-I, don't know what to say. I mean, I know what I did was wrong, and that I deserve to be in here. But what I did to you is unforgivable."

"Not through Jesus, it's not."

"I think we should put it to another vote," Miriam stated in anger as she moved around Ben's office.

"Why? It's done… he's out." Ben shrugged. "You cannot back out just because you're feeling a little guilty."

"A little? Ha, more like a lot… what I did went against all my morals, and you… you dangling money in front of me when I needed it just makes it all the worse. It makes me sick to think I accepted it and betrayed someone whom I think... and still think is competent and in his right mind." She snapped.

"He's not. I've proven it—you saw all the evidence. You cannot deny he hasn't changed."

"Yes, he's changed, but not like you and Bruce are making out. He's thought it through and reconsidered. People do that after an experience like he's had."

"I don't think you're seeing this clearly, Miriam."

"Oh, I am Ben. I see now that you and Bruce have been plotting against him. Even when he lay in the hospital, you vultures were scheming and talking about what we can do if he didn't come out. You make me sick," she spat.

"THROUGH JESUS." DENNIS WHISPERED THOUGHTFULLY BEFORE LOOKING back at Jason. "I-I've been reading the Bible you gave me. Particularly those guys, you know... John and Matthew, Luke and Mark."

"Yeah?"

"Well," Dennis reached to the side and picked up his Bible and opened it to the bookmark. "I keep reading this from Matthew 11:28-30." He read, "Come to me, all you who are weary and burdened, and I will give you rest. Take my yoke upon you and learn from me, for I am gentle and humble in heart, and you will find rest for your souls. For my yoke is easy and my burden is light." Dennis paused. "What do you think it means?"

"Ah, well... look Dennis." Jason shifted in his seat uncomfortably. "I'm not a preacher. I'm far from qualified, as I'm very new to this too. But I guess I can have a go at explaining, if you're willing to listen... I mean I could be wrong." He shrugged.

"No, go ahead... I want to hear."

At that moment, no one saw the large angel enter the room and place his hand on Jason's shoulder. The demon that had been tormenting Dennis recoiled in fear and backed away to the far corner of the room, huddling and shaking.

"Okay, so, I think it means that if you believe what Jesus claims, being that he is God's Son, and accept Him as your Savior, then he will give you peace and rest from your burdens."

"So just believe this?" he pointed to the Scripture.

"Yes, he is saying that you don't have to struggle and try to control your life, or do everything in your own strength. That you just need to come to Him and he will give you rest, guide you and make a way for you. But I have a friend named Ryan, he's all over this. I can ask him if you like?" Jason backpedaled.

"Okay! But what you've said sounds good. So——"

"Time's up, Talbot!" They heard the guard say.

"Uh, okay, then… I guess that's it… thanks for coming out and seeing me." Dennis said plainly.

"That's fine. I'm glad that I got to tell you my story. It didn't feel right not telling you."

"Well, would you come back again next week? That's if you want to. I'd like to ask more questions." Dennis asked sheepishly.

Jason looked surprised as he thought this would be the last time Dennis would ever want to talk with him. "Okay, sure. Same time?"

"Yeah, I'm not going anywhere—so whatever suits you."

"All right, I'll see you next week then."

Dennis nodded and smiled slightly as he stood up.

Jason watched as they escorted this broken man out of the room.

11.45 P.M.

Jason turned off the sports channel, picked up his laptop and sat comfortably back in his leather lounge, deciding to catchup on some emails… that Ben had screened.

"Jason!" He heard a whisper calling him.

Startled, he looked up from reading and glanced around, listening intently.

"Jason, come here!" the whisper said.

Jason slowly rose, thinking he was hearing things again.

"Down here!"

Jason looked over towards the basement door with curiosity and concern. "Who is it?" he said boldly.

"Jason, come here!" it whispered again, and the basement door clicked and slowly swung open with a creak.

Jason walked cautiously over towards the door. "Who's there? I'm calling the police!" he said, then waited silently for a response.

Nothing.

He glanced across the room to the open window and felt the soft breeze flowing. He shrugged and shut the door to the basement and walked back over to the lounge, shaking his head, deciding that he would see someone tomorrow about getting another scan.

"Jason!" It whispered louder. "Down here!" and the door to the basement clicked and gradually swung open again.

Jason turned around to see the door wide open. He carefully started moving towards the door... paused... and then grabbed the Yankees-signed baseball bat that hung on the wall nearby. He entered the doorway and put his foot on the first stair.

"Jason, down here," it called.

Jason raised his bat over his shoulder, ready to strike as he took the next step downward.

BANG!

The door slammed shut behind him with force.

Jason whipped around and grabbed the handle to open it, but it wouldn't budge—it was locked. He frantically pulled and pushed to open it, but it was jammed shut. He started barging it with his shoulder hard and charging it to break the lock. Fear and panic enveloped him as an intense rush of wind whipped around him.

"You belong with me!" a guttural whisper said amongst the rushing gale that had encircled him.

Jason panicked and swung the bat hard, but it didn't connect with anything. The whirlwind force was pushing hard around him, encasing him with the evilness that he had felt once before.

"You shouldn't have escaped!" it said with a growl.

In a terrified, fear-ridden frenzy, Jason turned and swung the bat hard to smash the lock. With all his strength, he barged the door, and it busted open with such force that Jason continued through the doorway, crashing facedown onto the floor back into the living room. He flipped onto his back and scrambled backwards with his bat armed ready, facing the door opening.

Nothing was there.

Just silence.

CHAPTER THIRTY-NINE

Jason awoke from a fitful sleep, tossing and turning most of the night. He had sat on the lounge with the bat staring at the door until 3am before getting the courage to go to bed. But he didn't sleep well—the overwhelming fear of what was in the basement, mixed with despair at what his life had become, shrouded his thoughts.

He was afraid! Afraid that he had lost his mind, afraid that he had disappointed God and terrified that he had somehow brought that demon back from Hell. The future without his company looked bleak, his promise made to God... unattainable.

His thoughts spiraled downwards as he lay in bed, tiredness and heavy-headed fog crept over him. He swayed his feet over the edge of the bed and sat for a moment with his head in his hands.

"God... what am I doing? This has all gone so wrong." He sighed.

He slowly stood up and walked over to his closet, put on his running gear, and went out for a jog to clear his head.

"You don't look so great." Ryan exclaimed, "Everything okay?"

"Not really. Ah—" Jason was about to tell Ryan about what was happening at home, but decided against it for fear of sounding irrational. He also didn't want to establish that he could be going insane. "I'm just not sleeping that great. Work is pitiful. I add no value and I've become Ben's gofer."

"Tough!" Ryan responded, as they sat and ate breakfast in a café.

"Yeah it is," Jason sighed. "I'm just sitting in my tiny office every day, seeing the changes happening around me to my corporation, which I have absolutely no control over. It makes me so angry. God is not doing *anything*."

"It looks that way, but God is always doing something in our favor. We just don't always see it."

"See…" Jason became frustrated. "How can you just say that? How do you know it will work out in my favor?"

"From experience, trials build our faith and character. Think of it like a muscle, it can be worked and become strong, or if left… it remains weak. If God handed everything to his people on a silver platter without letting them work at it, wait for it, grow and trust… Then we would be a bunch of weaklings, crying and throwing tantrums every time things didn't go our way."

"So, by me going through this, it will give me more faith and character —is that what you're saying?"

"It will, but it also depends on *how* you go through it. You've got a choice. You can either fall into a heap of despair, hating God, wallowing and feeling sorry for yourself… and I guarantee that attitude will not build your faith. It may even delay the outcome. Or, you can believe that God is in control and He will work this for good. Romans 8:28 says, 'And we know that in all things God works for the good of those who love him, who have been called according to his purpose.'" Ryan paused before continuing. "I bet when you first had your goal of starting your business, there was a process. It didn't just happen instantly for you?"

"No, it took a few years of planning, and there was a point when I nearly gave up as it was so difficult. But I persevered, and it grew to what it is today."

"And are you stronger for it?"

"Yeah, I am. I learned a great deal and I know everything there is to know about that business. I've been through a lot and I think nothing, well except for being removed from the captain's position, would phase me."

"And that's exactly how God builds his people's character and faith. If it's what God wants you to do, if you're on the path that God has set out for you… then God will work it in your favor. We just never know how, but we have to remain faithful and trust in Him."

"It's hard."

"Never said it was easy, dude."

Jason sighed before changing the subject. "So, you all set for the wedding?"

"Besides selecting the suits, there's nothing else for me to do than watch Chance walk down the aisle."

"Yeah, that will be nice to see." Jason smiled gratefully. "Thanks for letting me be a part of it." He suddenly felt a wave of sadness wash over him at the thought of not having any family.

"Hey, you all right?" Ryan picked up on the mood change.

"Yeah, I'm good."

"Look buddy, you are like family to me, okay? I can't wait for you to meet all the relatives," he smiled excitedly.

"Do you think they will accept me? I mean, knowing what I do for a living?"

"Hey, they aren't all saints either you know, but I still love them." Ryan quickly glanced at his watch. "You ready? We've got to get measured."

"Yep," Jason said as he downed the last of his mineral water. "Let's do this."

Dennis sat on his bed in his cell. He had pondered everything that Jason had said to him. His thoughts moved to the times he and Suzannah were together. He reminisced about the simple things that they shared. At this time of the morning, they both would read the paper, sip coffee, and occasionally hold hands across the table. A tear slowly edged down Dennis's cheek.

He killed her. It was his fault. The voice started.

"Be quiet," he whispered, desperately not wanting it to speak again.

You can't believe him, it's all liiieeeessss. It hissed into his mind. *There is no Heaven or Hell. He's just trying to torment you.*

"Shut it!" Dennis raised his voice louder, his anger peaking. "Be quiet!" he spat.

There was silence for a moment. The voice had ceased, and Dennis relaxed slightly.

You'll never hold your daughter because of him, it whispered again.

At those words, it was like a dagger had entered his heart, and Dennis's rage broke out like a tormented caged beast. The feelings of pain, anguish, hate and loss all came at him and slapped him in the face like a roaring hurricane.

He lost it!

He stood up and screamed at the top of his lungs. "I SAID SHUT UP! SHUT IT— SHUT UP—I HATE YOU! YOU HEAR ME?

LEAVE ME ALONE!

LEAVE…

ME…

ALONE!"

he roared, as he grabbed everything that wasn't tied down in his cell and started thrashing, smashing and throwing it around.

You'll never get rid of me, it hissed venomously.

Dennis snapped and started scratching, slapping and punching his face and head—trying to break free of his harasser. He ran at the concrete wall with his head, knocking himself backwards.

Lying on the cold, hard floor, he kept smacking his face. He could see no way out of his torment. The anguish and pain overtook him, and he felt death calling to him—its grip tightening itself around his soul like a steel vice.

Yessssss… the voice said… *death will set you free.*

"THE SUITS LOOK FANTASTIC." RYAN SAID AS HE, JASON, AND TWO other groomsmen met Chance and her bridesmaids in a café afterwards.

"Great! So, you guys are all sorted?" she said, relieved.

"Yep," Ryan smiled.

"Well. Ryan took a forever to decide which tie he should wear," one groomsman chuckled. "You would think he was the one picking out the wedding dress."

"Hey, don't give away my flaws," Ryan laughed. "I picked out the perfect one to complement the suit," he reassured Chance.

. . .

Overwhelmed with grief, Dennis could see no way out. His tormentor continued relentlessly, ravaging his mind and thoughts. Screaming into his psyche, berating him and pushing him further and further over the edge of his steep, anguished cliff.

Yessss, death. It's the only way to be free, it called persistently, pursuing and stalking him like a stealthy black jaguar.

As he lay on the floor, his only escape, he thought, was to die. He lifted his head and started smashing it against the solid concrete floor. With every blow, his distressed cries and painful sobs echoed down the corridors as he attempted to crack open his skull.

"Well, I've got to go." Jason said as he took the last sip of his latte.

"Oh, you're not staying for lunch?" Chance asked.

"No, I've got a few things that I need to catch up on, so I'll leave you to it," he smiled as he nodded goodbye to the others.

"Okay, buddy," Ryan said. "Chat later."

"Yep, I'll call you."

"GUARD, GUARD!" an inmate shrieked. "TALBOT'S LOST IT AGAIN!"

Two prison guards came running to Dennis's cell, finding him unconscious with his head lying in a pool of his own cherry red blood.

"Gees," one said, "Call the medics." He shook his head.

3.56 a.m.

Jason had returned to that place again in his dreams. He could hear the screams, feel the dry searing heat and the excruciating torment. He felt the demon strike him on his back and grab his arm.

"DIE, MURDERER!" it screeched at him. "You belong to me—You shouldn't have escaped."

He panicked, jerked his arm away and felt the intense pain of the claws penetrating deeply, ripping into his flesh. Another demon leaped

209

onto his back and bit hard into his neck, driving its claws into his cranium. Jason screamed in agony—the deep cuts in his arm opened up, revealing his muscle tissue.

He panicked as he fought the demons, trying to break free from the hell that encompassed him. He continued to thrash and scream, taking blows and bites from his tormentors, being dragged and cut. His heart was pounding and he could hear the loud booming sound of his pulse echoing in his ears.

"You're mine!" the demon screamed in his face. "You belong here with me!" it raged, its drool flying as it spat with fury. It lurched forward and grabbed Jason around his neck and squeezed hard.

Jason felt the life being taken from him as he gasped and took violent gulps to awaken from his slumberous coma.

"You will die… you're mine." the demon berated and grinned, revealing its sharp evil fangs.

Jason continued to gasp, reaching forward, clutching the wiry fur and brute muscles of the dark demonic arms that held him down so tightly. He tried with all his might to push against them, to remove the attacker. To save his life. He gulped and lurched forward under the weight of the demon and let out a slight squeak. "Jesus!"

The demon quickly weakened and released his grip slightly.

Jason screamed louder. "JESUS!" and abruptly lurched awake, his eyes popped wide open as he sat straight up in his bed.

His body was dripping with sweat. His breath was fast and panicked as he tried to calm himself and untangle himself from the twisted sheets.

He reached for his bedside lamp, and when he did, he saw the large gashes down his arm and the blood trickling along his smooth, tanned skin. He stared at the four bloodied claw marks that went downward towards his hand.

At that moment, Jason realized his dreams were real, that he wasn't delusional, and it wasn't a result of his head injury. He *had* brought something back, and it was right here with him…

NOW!

CHAPTER FORTY

5 A.M.

"RYAN, I GOTTA TALK TO YOU. CAN YOU MEET ME AT THE CAFÉ?" Jason spoke into his cell in a breathless panic, standing outside his own house.

"Sure buddy." Ryan squinted sleepily, blinking at the clock on the bedside table. "Wassup?"

"I can't explain it over the phone—it's too weird!"

"Okay, what time?"

"Now?"

"Sure, I'll see you soon." He yawned.

Jason lifted his sleeve and stared at the raw bloodied marks that streaked along his arm.

"GEES, ARE YOU OKAY? YOU LOOK PALE." RYAN LOOKED AT JASON WITH concern.

"No! I'm not."

"Are you sick? You look like you've seen a ghost."

"I'm not sure that I haven't." He felt as though he would vomit.

"What do you mean?"

"Look," Jason said as he lifted his long sleeve to reveal his arm.

"Woah! What did you do? Pick up a wildcat or something crazy?"

"No, I wish it was that simple."

"So, what happened?"

"I was dreaming, having another nightmare that I was in Hell and when I awoke, these were on my arm."

"Mmm, okay… this could be serious."

"You think? I can't even sleep anymore as I'm so freaked out about what's been happening at my house," Jason responded in a panicked tone.

"Hang on… what are you telling me… that there's been other stuff?"

"Yeah, there has."

"Like what?"

"Writing appearing on the mirror, hearing whispers and voices, things being moved around, lights flickering, music playing—that I don't even have in my collection, mind you… knocking and banging noises… I've also been seeing things too. It's been terrible."

"So, why didn't you tell me this before?" Ryan said, astonished at hearing this.

"At first it was subtle. I thought it was just me. Thinking my brain was still healing from the TBI and it was the side effects… you know? It happens—brain injuries can do weird things. So I put it down to that. I also thought I was just having flashbacks, hallucinations and memories of my time in Hell… so I kind of pushed it aside and kept thinking it would eventually go away in time. I even thought about getting another head scan done, but I was afraid that it would get back to Ben. You know… people talk, and I couldn't afford any suspicion that I was having some issues. But I guess that doesn't matter now, does it? They got rid of me, anyway." He sighed despondently.

"So, this has been going on for… what? Since you had the accident?"

"Yeah, pretty much. It didn't start right away, but it's been gradually getting worse."

"Dude! You should have told me. I can't believe you didn't." Ryan said, upset.

"I-I thought I would sound so stupid if I said anything."

"Oh, man… people suffer through lack of knowledge." Ryan shook his head.

"What?"

"It sounds like something followed you back to torment you."

"I suspected that… Oh man, what do I do?" Jason freaked out.

"Look, don't worry—it's fine. We will just get rid of it." Ryan reassured.

"What? You can do it… just like that?"

"Of course. Greater is the One in you, than the one in the world."

"I don't get it."

"That's paraphrased from 1 John 4:4, but basically, Jesus defeated Satan at the cross. The devil and his demons cannot withstand the power of Jesus. That power lives in you, Jason," he pointed. "You have the power to tell this demon to get out of your house and leave. Luke 10:19 states, 'I have given you authority to trample on snakes and scorpions and to overcome all the power of the enemy; nothing will harm you.' Simple!" Ryan smiled.

"Really, just like that?"

"Yes. And you could have done this at the very first instance as it has no power unless you give it power."

"Meaning?"

"It plays on your fear and lack of knowledge, and will get worse if you allow it… like you have. Anyway, we can remove it."

"Have you done this before?"

"Yep, a few times now."

"No way!" Jason said, shocked.

"Yeah way," Ryan chuckled.

"Wow! Sounds like you're a regular demon slayer."

"Hardly!" Ryan laughed.

"So when—where?"

"Okay, so an old friend who I hadn't heard from for about four years moved into a house. It wasn't an old house, probably only about three years old. But the previous tenants must have done séances there… and man, there was some activity in that place. But my friend couldn't break his lease so he stupidly asked a medium to remove the evil spirits, and when that didn't work he paid two hundred dollars to get a specialist cleanser in." Ryan chuckled. "So, this lady came in and walked around and burned sage and did what they call smudging. However, this just made everything worse. It was as though she just stirred them up and the spirits became furious. He was getting pushed around, things were getting thrown at him, his bed was shaking, kitchen cupboards were slamming in the night, you name it… it was happening. He knew I was a Christian, so he called, desperate for me to come and see what I could do. So, I came over and when I walked in, I felt it instantly. The hair on the back of my neck stood right on end and my arms prickled like goose skin."

"Have you felt that at my house?"

"I haven't… no."

"Well, it doesn't happen all the time, it's sporadic."

"Mmm okay."

"Anyway, so, what happened?"

"I prayed."

"Saying what?"

"Well, from memory I said something like… that I claim the blood of Jesus over every aspect of this house, and said in the name of Jesus, I take authority over every demonic power and unclean spirit in this house and told them to leave… and they did."

"That simple?"

"That simple!" Ryan beamed.

"And… so what happened to your friend?"

"He became a Christian there and then," Ryan smiled. "He heads up Youth at our church."

"No way… that's Max?"

"Yep, Max." Ryan grinned. "I think God has such a cool sense of humor." He laughed. "What a way to come to know Jesus, hey?"

Jason pondered for a moment. "So why would people go to mediums instead of Christians?"

"Lack of knowledge. They don't understand that mediums, psychics or spiritualists hold no power at all—in fact they can get themselves, and the person who hired them, in more trouble if the spirits are malicious. Which they are… they are demons—and there are no good spirits." Ryan motioned quotation marks with his fingers. "It's foolish to think these things are harmless, or to partake in certain events… like Halloween."

"Bad?"

"That night is where the witches, or advocates of Wicca, warlocks or satanists summon spirits. It's their celebration and a night where the veil between the two realms is the thinnest and spirits can circulate with the living easily. So these occultists cast spells or curses and conduct sacrifices, in aim of harming, creating havoc or seducing people into Satan's darkness. It's the devil's holiday. They look forward to it as we look forward to celebrating Christmas. But any participation—like handing out treats, dressing up or putting out those pumpkins is an invitation for these spirits to enter your household. It's saying that Satan has a right to own you and it opens doors to demons and puts curses on your family. You only have to research it. So it shocks me to see Christians celebrate it, thinking it's harmless. They are so naïve and don't realize what they have opened themselves up to. It's a pagan celebration and God says in 1 Corinthians 10:21 'You cannot drink the cup of the Lord and the cup of demons too; you cannot have a part in both the Lord's table and the table of demons.' Even the founder of a Satanist church said that he was glad that Christians worship the devil one night a year. So what's that telling us?"

"But movies make out that Halloween is just fun, and that there are good spirits... like good ghosts."

"That's Hollywood, but that's not reality... did you meet any good spirits in Hell?"

"Heck, no!"

"Well, that's where they stem from—people are easily fooled. Some churches even try to do their own celebration, labeling it anything but Halloween, so they don't feel like they are missing out, slapping the name of Jesus on it, wrapping candy in some scripture. It would be better if it was an intentional gathering of Christians praying and worshipping Jesus to combat the enemy and try to take back this night, or inviting the unsaved inside for a meal or movie, but having no association with Halloween at all. Unfortunately, what these churches do is pretty much Halloween without the creepy aspects thinking they're safe. But seeing the damage demons cause people, why would you even want to partake in that celebration? I've even heard people justify it by saying, but Jesus ate with sinners. Yeah, He did, but He never partook in a pagan ritual or *did* their sin. He showed them truth."

"I never thought about it this way."

"The Bible says that Satan prowls around like a lion looking to whom to devour. The goal with Satan is to get as many souls by any means possible. That means deceiving, tricking people into thinking something is harmless and using subtle influences that steer you away from knowing

God. Or if you're already a Christian, trying to distance you away from God so you become lukewarm or cold, or hindering you in ways to make you struggle. The Bible is clear in telling us to avoid stuff like this. It talks about it in Deuteronomy… Hang on, it's easier if I look it up…"

Ryan paused and pulled out his phone. "It's in chapter 18, verses 10-13… I won't read it all but… okay—yeah, so it goes like '… who practices divination or sorcery, interprets omens, engages in witchcraft, or casts spells, or who is a medium or spiritist or who consults the dead. Anyone who does these things is detestable to the Lord…'."

"Right, so it's like those people I saw in Hell who had those spirit guides when they were alive?"

"Totally! They think they have a gift from God, but it's not—it's from Satan and it's evil. If you are not a born-again Christian, then you hold absolutely no power over the devil. It says in James 2:19, 'You believe that there is one God. Good! Even the demons believe that—and shudder.' Demons cannot withstand His power, and as Christians, we have the authority and can command them to leave." Ryan shook his head, "There were even some guys in the Bible who tried to cast out demons using Jesus's name—but they did not know Jesus, they were not born again. They were just using his name, and the demons beat them up. So, you can't go mucking around with this stuff, it's serious."

"I'll say." Jason looked at his arm.

"Look, it's not what the movies make out! You cannot communicate with the spirit of the dead. The mediums are talking with demons, they just don't realize it. There is an example in Luke 16:19-31 when a rich man is in Hell and calls out to Abraham asking him to send Lazarus, who was in Heaven, to warn his family about Hell."

Ryan looked up the scripture on his cell. "So Abraham responded, 'They have Moses and the Prophets; let them listen to them.'

'No, father Abraham,' he said, 'but if someone from the dead goes to them, they will repent.'

'He said to him, 'if they do not listen to Moses and the Prophets, they will not be convinced even if someone rises from the dead.' So, you see… it doesn't happen. The only place in the Bible where it looks like someone may have communicated with the dead was Saul when he spoke with Samuel in 1 Samuel 28:12-13. But there is controversy around that passage—some believe it was God allowing it one time, as he can do anything, others believe it was a demon because the prediction turned out to be false in the way Saul died. So, I cannot answer that one."

Jason pondered for a moment. "So, can people have demons? Like—you know… all those movies?"

"Sure can!"

"Even a Christian?"

"Yes, because though your spirit is saved, your flesh isn't. Even though you became a Christian, you still can be under the power of demons and it's important that you get prayer and go for deliverance to be free. In Matt 10:5-8, Jesus told the disciples to go among the believers, not the gentiles, and cast out demons. In Acts 8, Philip preached the gospel, *then* cast out demons amongst those who had received the message. Luke 22:3 says that Satan entered Judas, who was one of Jesus' disciples. There is no verse in the Bible that says that once you're born again, you are automatically delivered or immune from having demons. This is why we see so many Christians battling issues, because they haven't been delivered and are still living under the power of demons and have demonic strongholds over them."

Jason looked confused.

"So, take Sarah at church. Now she has been open about how she overcame her drug addiction, right?"

"Right."

"Remember that she said that she became born again, but the pull to do drugs was still there? She tried again and again to overcome it, but she kept succumbing to the urge and going back to her dealer?"

"Yes."

"Well, that's a demon dragging her back to do the things she is trying to stop. Do you remember what she said about how she got free?"

"She said that she went for deliverance?"

"Correct!"

"Then she said that afterwards, the urge had completely disappeared, and she was free."

"Exactly! She was being influenced and pulled away to keep doing the sin. That's what the demonic does, even if you become a Christian. There are still things in your past that can be a door to let the demonic have a right to torment you. Like Sarah and her drug use—she was forgiven, however the pull was still there... the demonic still had a right... you know?"

"Mmm, not really. I thought it was different when you accepted Jesus."

"Okay... well, let's look at it this way," Ryan pondered for a minute. "You've got an impressive house!"

"Yeah!"

"Say you rent out a room. So legally you're in contract with another person to rent that space and use your facilities. They come and go as they please, but they also play loud music, start leaving rubbish around and defiling your property. You can't keep your house clean or in order because you have this person in it that is spoiling it. They even may influence you into doing the same. But you cannot remove this person unless it's done legally, as you have given them a right to be there, you signed a contract with them. Well, it's the same with the demonic. When you sin, it gives a legal right for Satan to be in your life. The only way to remove that right is to acknowledge the sin and repent of it. Then it breaks that power and you can cast it out."

"So how do I know that I have a demonic stronghold?"

"They can be obvious... like being drawn to look at pornography, or stealing... or as subtle as a behavioral pattern like lying, compulsive eating, anger, being overly anxious, or you can have terrible thoughts, doubts or feelings about yourself... or be having suicidal thoughts... these are all a clear giveaway of the demonic in your life. I had a friend tell me that every time she saw a large tree while driving, she had a thought enter her mind to drive straight into it. Now that's a demon! ... Anyway, these patterns can be stubborn and seem impossible to break, and it's like a repetitive cycle that's difficult to overcome through your own strength. This is a regular tactic that Satan uses to trap us and hinder our spiritual growth and make us feel defeated. It's a way he can hold us back or even stop us from receiving a blessing."

Ryan paused and took a sip of water. "2 Corinthians 10:4 says 'The weapons we fight with are not the weapons of the world. On the contrary, they have divine power to demolish strongholds.' So, you need to recognize your sin or behavior and repent, otherwise you may never change and you will live contaminated and continue to struggle in that area. You need to pray and sometimes even fast. Or, like Sarah, go seek a good

Christian counseling and deliverance service. To be honest, I think all Christians should go for deliverance."

"Have you been to a Christian counselor?"

"I have, and also return when I feel the need."

Jason sat and took in what Ryan was saying. He felt overwhelmed, and Ryan could see it.

"Look bud, everyone goes through this. No one is without challenges. It's a process and I know that when I get a bad thought or a feeling, I ask God to reveal the sin that allowed it to enter. Then I pray for forgiveness and tell that demon to leave in the name of Jesus, and if it still doesn't leave, I take it to Gods Court room. Or I seek help from Trent, or another godly person whom I can trust."

"Court room?"

"Yeah, the spiritual realm operates in a legal system. I'll lend you a book about court room prayers. They are so powerful for breaking the legal rights of the enemy off you and your generation."

"Sounds so hard," Jason said, feeling despondent.

"Hey, I didn't mean to bring you down, man. You just need to hear the truth. Many people live out their Christian walk hindered and suppressed, not understanding that these are the things holding them back in their faith and lives. They continue to contaminate their relationships and churches with undealt with sin or behavior. But if they simply sought godly help or guidance, or used their authority in Christ to cast out demons, it could save them so much trouble… Look, I'm just being honest and saving you a world of hurt." He put his hand on Jason's shoulder to reassure him.

"No, it's good Ryan. I appreciate it. I just feel like I have so much to learn."

"You're learning—trust me." He smiled.

"So, you were saying before that you have had more experiences of getting rid of demons?"

"Oh yeah, we digressed, didn't we?" he laughed. "Sure—so another time, one of my Christian friends purchased an old desk at an antique store. It seemed nice, and she really liked how it suited her house. But she didn't realize there was a demon that came along with it."

"What? In the desk?"

"Yeah, it was attached to the desk. Evil spirits can tie themselves to objects. So, I pray over things that I've purchased."

"Really?"

"Yep. You just don't know where it's been, or who has had it before you, or if it's had a curse placed on it."

"This just seems too far out for me."

"Satan uses every opportunity to bring us down. Was going to Hell too far out?"

"You're right… I didn't believe that would ever happen… So anyway, what happened with the desk?"

"Well, over the next few months, she became downhearted and depressed. There wasn't anything noticeably triggering it, but then suddenly she lost her job, got in a car accident, her cat died and weird things started happening—"

"So, you're saying that it started from the desk?"

"I am, and it did. By introducing that into her life, it influenced and affected her mentally and physically—she just didn't know it. Like renting out a room to someone in your house." he smiled.

"Good one," Jason laughed. "So, what happened?"

"It just so happened that she invited me and five other friends for dinner. Throughout the night, I kept looking at that desk in the corner—I sensed something was wrong with it. So eventually after we washed and packed up the dishes and were sitting in the living room having coffee, I asked her about it."

"And?"

"Well, I told her straight up that something was wrong with it, that it didn't feel right. Everyone agreed, as they all had the same impression. She got defensive and told us how much she loved it and how it suited the house. So, we decided to pray over it and anoint it with oil so we could get rid of whatever it was… thinking she could keep her desk."

"Did it work?"

"Well, the funny thing was that as soon as we all started praying, we heard this massive cracking sound. It was loud and unnatural. We all jumped back in fright—it was freaky—but we kept on praying. What we discovered afterward was that the desk had cracked right through the middle. We hadn't even touched it, we just started praying over it."

"Wow!"

"Yeah, my friend was shocked but extremely grateful not to have that demon in the house any longer. Anyway, she hasn't looked back since. She got a better job, insurance came through with the car, and she feels much better."

"Okay, so what do we do for me?"

"We go into your house right now and kick some demonic butt, that's what we do." Ryan grinned.

CHAPTER FORTY-ONE

"So how do we start?" Jason stood in his living room.

"We pray!"

"Okay," Jason responded, apprehensively.

"Right, then." Ryan said as he looked around. "Are you ready?"

"Yeah… why, is something going to happen?" Jason said edgy.

Ryan shrugged. "Dunno… maybe. Okay—here goes!" Ryan smiled and prayed, "Lord, I ask for protection over Jason and myself. I ask that you bring angels here to help us as we pray over this house." He looked at Jason, who had his eyes clamped tightly shut, waiting nervously.

Ryan smiled, then continued, "In the name of Jesus Christ, I command every demonic spirit in this house to leave, and—"

Jason suddenly jumped and looked around. "Do you hear that?"

"Hear what?"

"That growling sound," Jason said, his face ashen.

"Can you still hear it?"

"Yes, it's loud."

"Where is it coming from?"

Jason looked over toward the corner of the living room. "That direction," he pointed nervously, his finger shaking slightly.

Ryan turned towards that direction and continued. "I take authority over you, demon, and command you to depart this house in the name of Jesus." he stated with authority.

Jason clamped his hands over his ears while Ryan looked at him. Jason could hear the growling growing louder and louder, then turning into a howl.

"What's happening now?" Ryan looked at Jason.

"It's howling and also making scratching and scraping sounds."

Unexpectantly, a lamp flew directly at them. Both Ryan and Jason jumped sideways to avoid the impact and watched as it smashed onto the hard-wooden floor.

"Demon!" Ryan shouted. "We are children of the most-high God. You have no authority over us or this house. I command you to leave in the mighty name of Jesus Christ."

It was a scream that neither Ryan nor Jason would ever forget. It was deep and primal, piercing their ears as they both clasped their hands tightly over them to shut out the resonating sound. The tone roared right through them and then a powerful rush of wind, like a tornado, smashed against them, blowing chaotically around, thrusting a newspaper into the twister.

Ryan looked over at Jason. He saw terror in his eyes and the blood drain from his face.

Jason's heart thudded in his chest and he froze at the sight. It was here —it was him—the demon that tormented him in Hell was standing right in front of him, tangible and in a full rage. Teeth bearing, drool cascading from its frothing jowls—it reached out towards him, its long talons stretching out to clasp around his throat.

"You're mine! You should have NEVER got away!" it seethed. Its rage was clear and its desire to bring him back to Hell was strong.

THE BEEPING AND WIRING OF MACHINES GRADUALLY BROUGHT DENNIS OUT of his deep sleep. As he gained consciousness, the intense pain and throbbing of his head injuries felt like a dull sledgehammer against his skull. He slowly opened his eyes.

"Hey Dennis," the familiar male medic came over. "How are you feeling?"

Dennis said nothing, just looked at the medic's name tag for the first time through the haze. *Malcolm.*

"You have sustained head trauma, so you will be in here for a while longer. I've brought some of your things." He said and patted the brown leather Bible sitting on the bedside table. "Now use the buzzer if you need anything. We are just outside at the desks."

"What happened?"

"You don't remember?"

"It's fuzzy."

"Right, well, I think we need to get you some counseling and some medication, okay, buddy? You tried to self-harm, and you did a great job of it too," he smirked. "So, this time, its mandatory therapy. Now I've got two other patients that I need to see, so I'll be back in half an hour." He left the room.

Uselessssss. The familiar voice had returned.

Dennis's emotions overtook him and he cried desperate, wound-stinging tears of defeat and despair.

You can't even kill yourself.

Ryan could see Jason's fear-riddled stare and shouted at him. "COMMAND IT TO GO, JASON!"

But Jason froze, his gaze focused on the demon reaching for him.

The demon lunged forward and grabbed Jason around his neck.

He fell to the floor, fighting against his assailant. It wrapped its claws around Jason's throat and squeezed tightly. Jason gasped and jolted for air. He fought and gulped against the demon's hands. No breath, no air was entering his lungs—the demonic clasp blocked it. The surge of panic intensified as he strained and rolled to break free of its grip.

Ryan jumped into action and yelled at the top of his lungs, pointing at Jason. "I COMMAND YOU DEMON TO GO IN THE NAME OF JESUS!" he screamed with both boldness and fury.

The demon jolted hard, sparks of bright burnishing light flew against it, hitting it directly in its chest and sending it toppling backwards. Jason gasped and felt the burning sensation sting as the fresh air poured into his lungs. He jumped straight to his feet and yelled, "You don't own me, demon. With the power of Jesus, I break all authority you have over me and command you to leave. NOW!" he wheezed.

The demon flapped and beat its large black bat-like wings in panic. The rushing sound was so strong as the violent rotation of twisting air thrashed around them both.

DENNIS'S SOBS INTENSIFIED AS THE VOICE CONTINUED TO BERATE HIM. It wouldn't stop.

You're a failure. No one cares about you—you have no one. You wait until you get back into the population—you're gonna get knifed. Everyone hates you, Dennis...

Out of frustration, he clawed at the drip in his arm, forcefully yanking the IV cannula out. Unrestrained, he leaped up out of the bed. With both anger and fear, he started for the door just as Malcolm came out of an adjacent room.

"Dennis! Stop!" Malcolm yelled and held up his hands. "STOP RIGHT THERE!" he demanded.

Dennis didn't stop. He continued to rush towards Malcolm and shoved him forcefully to get passed.

"GUARDS!" another male medic screamed and hit the panic button as Dennis pounded and barged against the large security door that locked both patients and medics inside the infirmary.

"You can't leave Dennis, so don't do anything stupid." Malcolm yelled as other medical staff and security guards hurried around.

Dennis realized he was trapped and instantly gave up. With overwhelming despair, he leaned his back against the door and slowly slid to the floor in defeat.

The guards rushed forward, restraining him, while another male nurse injected a sedative.

THE DEMON LET OUT ANOTHER EAR-PIERCING SHRIEK AS JASON SAW TWO angels step forward, their swords drawn and pointed towards it.

Ryan again clasped his ears tightly at the sound of the blood-curdling scream.

Jason watched as the demon scrambled and fumbled backwards to avoid the angelic blades. With one strong blow, a blade struck it and it fell to his hulking knees. Another sword came down, slicing it in two, its body falling face forward onto the floor.

Jason watched in awe as the body of the demon slowly faded into a swirling mist of gray smoke and disappeared. He looked up at the two angels and smiled graciously.

"What's happening now, Jason?" Ryan said as he gradually unclasped his ears, and sensed the peace.

"Angels… I-I see Angels." Jason beamed. His legs suddenly felt weak, and he sat on the floor in amazement, staring.

Ryan swiftly dropped to his knees and prayed. "Thank you, Lord, that we have the authority in Jesus Christ over the enemy. Thank you! We put the blood of Jesus over this house so that nothing evil can enter." He then looked over at Jason. "You okay?"

"I am now!" he said in awe as the angels nodded, smiled, then with a flash disappeared.

"It'll be all right now."

"I'm glad," he said, relieved. "Do we need to do anything more?"

"No, it's done. Just ensure you keep being obedient to God and don't give the enemy a door to enter." He placed his hand on Jason's shoulder.

"Okay," Jason said, still shaken.

"WOW! Now, that was cool. I think we should do this more regularly." Ryan laughed and then stood up, reaching his hand forward to help Jason to his feet.

"You have a weird sense of fun." Jason checked himself over, rubbing his neck.

"Come on, Jase. You gotta admit that was a totally awesome experience."

"For who? You're not even scared?"

"No way. There's no reason to be."

"But it tried to kill me!"

"It wouldn't have. We have the authority. You just needed to speak out sooner. You'll learn!" he smiled and patted him on the back. "Come on, make me a coffee?" Ryan beamed.

Jason shook his head and walked over to the Delonghi. "You know I have about a thousand questions about what just happened."

"I know." Ryan smiled. "We've got plenty of time."

CHAPTER FORTY-TWO

"Hey Jason, I'm back." Olivia stated over the phone.

"Hi Olivia, how was your vacation?"

"Fantastic, I had a great time. But more to the point, how is your new business venture going?"

"Yeah, well, it's probably best that I catch up with you in person. Do you have time to meet up for lunch today?"

"Um, let me just check," there was silence as Olivia checked her diary, "Yes... I should be fine, how about 1 o'clock at Saffron's?"

"Sounds good, I'll see you then." Jason hung up.

Jason sat nervously at a table set for two at Saffron's, a high-class restaurant. He had gotten there fifteen minutes early and ordered mineral water whilst he waited for Olivia to arrive.

"Hi Jason," Olivia beamed as she walked in.

Jason immediately got up and helped her into her chair. "Great to see you. You look well rested... and very tanned." He said, noticing her glow.

"Yes, I got a little sun and fresh air. It was great! So, tell me what's been happening?"

"No—you first. I'd like to hear about your break."

"Ahh, where do I start? Well, I mostly stayed in camps—and they exceeded my expectations. The people and the atmosphere were friendly and the food—oh! Well, it was just awesome. I think I've put on a few pounds," she laughed. "Oh! and I got to see the wilder beast migration. It was so amazing," she continued excitedly, telling Jason all about her holiday while he listened intently.

"Okay, enough about me," Olivia said. "I can fill you in more later. What I really want to know is how it's going with your modifications at Miller Corp. Have you changed the clinics yet?"

"Well, actually…" Jason shifted slightly in his chair. "It didn't get accepted."

"What? But you were so sure they would go for it—we were so sure…. what happened?"

"Well, it gets worse." Jason paused and took a quick sip of mineral water. "They have removed me from the chair position."

Olivia's face said it all. A look of incredulous shock stared back at Jason. "They didn't?"

"They did!"

"Oh, Jason… how?"

"Ben put forward the no confidence motion, and I'm afraid, the majority ruled in favor."

"Why that…" she seethed.

"Yeah, my thoughts too. It's clear that he had been doing some digging in the background because he had researched my TBI. He knew what he was doing."

"Jason, I am so sorry. I didn't see this coming. I mean, we both knew it *could* happen if they suspected… but I didn't think they would." She shook her head in dismay.

"Me neither. I guess I was too trusting."

"So, what are you doing at the moment?"

"They have me as an advisory to the board, but they never use me. Ben thinks I'm his PA, so I spend my days doing odd jobs for him."

"Oh, no… that's terrible," she paused. "I don't know what to say… I feel that maybe I should have done something—"

"There's nothing you could have done—a vote of no confidence is resolute."

"Unfortunately, yes, it is," she sighed. "Are any of the board members' term limits coming up?"

"No." Jason raked his fingers through his hair in frustration. "I'm pretty much dead in the water."

"Yeah… So… what is your next move?"

"That, I don't know. I feel humiliated and embarrassed to show up each day, and it's taking everything in me not to tell Ben to shove it where the sun doesn't shine, but—"

"And that's putting it politely."

"I feel that I have to stay right now. I don't know for how long but I'm doing it… no matter how hard it is."

"It must be tough!"

"It is, trust me… it is."

———

3 P.M.

"I'd like an appointment to see one of your inmates. His name is Dennis Talbot." Jason said over the phone to the prison receptionist.

"I'll just check for you. Who is speaking?" she asked in a dry Texan drawl.

"My name is Jason Miller."

"One moment." The woman said and placed him on hold for a minute before returning. "Sorry Mr. Miller, Dennis can't take any visitors as he is in the infirmary."

"Oh, is he all right?" he said, concerned.

"I can't give you any details because of privacy, Mr. Miller, but I can give him a message for you."

"Right, okay then. Can I leave him my phone number?"

"You can! I can give him a message to call you sir."

"Yes, could you please?" and Jason gave her the number.

"Thank you, sir. I will pass that through to him."

"Thank you for your time." Jason hung up the call, then dialed Ryan.

"Wassup?" Ryan answered.

"I just rang the prison and Dennis is sick or something. He is in the infirmary."

"Is he all right?"

"She wouldn't say, so I gave my number for him to call."

"I hope he is okay—I mean, you've just connected with the guy."

"Yeah, but you know how dangerous prisons can be, anything can happen."

"True, I'll be praying that he's okay and that you can still see him. Hey, did you want to grab a bite tonight? Chance and some friends are heading out for pizza."

"Thanks, but not tonight. I've got a few things I need to do."

"No worries, talk soon Jase."

"Yep, see you."

"Barnes Law Firm, Mary speaking."

"Hi Mary, it's Olivia Chadwick."

"Oh, hi Olivia. How have you been?"

"I'm great. How are things there?"

"We're getting there. The firm changed ownership, but… everyone really misses Clifford. It's just not the same without him."

"I can imagine, he was a significant loss. They kept his business name then?"

"Yes, they kept the name because it's so well known. Poor Clifford, so much more to give." she sighed. "Anyway, I'm sure you didn't ring to chat. How can I help you?"

"I was hoping to come over and gain copies of Miller Corporation's financial documents, contracts, agreements, and basically all historical records. I obtained the most recent ones before I went on holidays, but I would like to get a copy of all the remaining files."

"Sure, I don't see that being an issue. Clifford always had a soft spot for Jason."

"Would you mind if I came over now?"

"That will be fine. Do you want me to start the process?"

"Yes please, that would be great. Thanks Mary."

Jason's cell buzzed with an unknown number showing on the caller ID. He answered hesitantly.

"Hello?"

"Hi Jason, it's… um, Dennis Talbot."

"Dennis, how are you?"

"I'm um... well, I'm not doing so good. I got myself a little messed up."

"Oh?"

"Yeah, just got some head injuries that will heal, but I'm in the infirmary for another four days so it's probably best to see me after I'm out of here." Dennis was hoping to heal more before he saw Jason. "I should be out by Monday afternoon, so what about Tuesday?"

"I can't do Tuesday. How about Wednesday?"

"Okay, I'll let them know."

"See you then," Jason said, then heard the phone line click silent. He didn't know what God was doing, but he sensed something. He could feel a stirring within. His revelation about forgiveness and God's grace brought him to a place of seeing beyond the norm. To now see Dennis through God's eyes and not his own.

He sat for a moment and prayed, thanking God for bringing him to this place of restoration and allowing these friendships to form. For the first time in a long time, he realized he hadn't felt alone.

THAT NIGHT, OLIVIA SAT AT HER DINING TABLE WITH ALL THE MILLER Corporation files piled high. She sat and ate her Chinese takeout while meticulously reading old contracts, agreements, and every piece of legal material that existed for Miller Corporation.

JASON SLEPT THROUGH THE NIGHT PEACEFULLY, SOMETHING THAT HE hadn't done since his accident. There were no noises, no attacks, no weirdness, and no menacing voices. He now felt peace in his house. His nightmares had ceased, and he hadn't dreamed of Hell since Ryan got rid of the demon.

At 5am the alarm buzzed to life, and the radio kicked in. Jason got up, stretched, changed into his running gear and headed out into the cool morning, sucking in the fresh salty air as he ran.

6.12am

"Jason, it's Olivia." She spoke hastily on her cell phone.

"Hey, are you okay? It's early, and you sound flustered." Jason asked, concerned, as he walked into his kitchen from his morning jog.

"No, I'm fine… I think I've got it." she said excitedly. "I haven't slept because I stayed up reading all night… and I've found it." she blurted, fueled on a coffee high.

"Got what?" he said as he made his protein shake.

"I've found a way. Listen, I'll fill you in when I get there, but I want you to call a board meeting for this morning. I will be at your place in twenty minutes."

"Ah… all right then." Jason looked at his watch.

CHAPTER FORTY-THREE

10 A.M.

Jason and Olivia walked into the boardroom and faced the six suspicious sets of eyes that sat around the wide oak table. They remained poker-faced as they shuffled papers and took their positions.

Olivia instantly took control, like she had done this a thousand times, and started the meeting.

"I'm Olivia Chadwick and I have been looking after Jason's affairs since Clifford Barnes passed. I have been away on leave and have returned to the knowledge that Jason was removed from his position as chair and also moved, or might I say, demoted to another position within Miller Corporation. Is this information correct?"

Everyone was silent.

Then Ben spoke. "That is correct," he said, looking around, wondering why this meeting was called. "Jason could have told you this himself, Olivia, so there was no need to waste everyone's time—our time is expensive," he said smugly.

She paused and looked straight at Ben coolly. "Ben, is it?"

"Yes, I'm Ben Crothers, the CEO." he said, showing his power.

"Right, thanks Ben. No, I haven't requested a meeting to waste anyone's time… and I do realize how expensive you are." she smiled. "Therefore, I will get right to it." She looked straight at him blankly before continuing. "I would like to bring to your attention that the call to remove Jason from his chair position goes against the terms of his agreement. Was this considered before you removed Jason?"

"What terms?" Ben said curiously with an edge of concern.

"The terms stated within his contract," she responded shrewdly.

"I don't know of any terms." Ben looked surprised and also worried.

Olivia quickly moved around the table and handed out copies of Jason's contract to each board member. "Please note the date on the first page where it states Term of Agreement Commencement Date. It is the date of the inception of Miller Corporation."

Jason watched Ben as his eyes were nearly popping out of their sockets as he read.

Olivia paused and looked around and waited to ensure everyone saw the date on their copy. "Can you please turn to page four, paragraph three? I can read the next few pages for you and explain each term in detail, but that will take time—and we certainly wouldn't want to waste that, would we?" She looked at Ben. "Therefore, the drive-through version is that in the event that Jason is terminated, displaced or demoted, he is entitled to a payout of 485 million dollars."

It was as if Ben's jaw hit the floor. "A-ah…" Ben stammered.

"Yes, Ben?" Olivia asked, goading him.

But Ben couldn't respond.

"Um, okay then, this is a surprise," Bruce stated, rattled.

"Ah, well, that is a sizable sum." Ed blurted, blinking as he reread the figure on the contract.

"Well. Um… obviously, if Miller Corp were to pay this to Jason… then I'm afraid that Miller Corp would be… no longer." Mal fumbled.

"I see." Olivia paused for a moment. "However, I would have assumed that you would have thought this through before you removed Jason and demoted him?"

"We… ah, well, we did not know that this agreement was in place." Bruce responded, embarrassed.

"Known or unknown, you have still broken the terms of the agreement. Miller Corporation being financially harmed is no longer Jason's concern."

Jason watched Olivia play them like a fiddle. He sat in silence with his deadpan expression, but inwardly smiled and rejoiced at her tenacity and utter brashness.

"DENNIS," MALCOLM SAID AS HE PULLED UP A CHAIR BESIDE HIS BED. "I'VE referred you to Dr. Chancellor. He is a psychiatrist and I think he'll be good for you to talk to."

"I don't need no psychiatric help," he said gruffly, and crossed his arms defensively.

"Sorry, Dennis… but you do. You're not coping." Malcolm motioned towards Dennis's head injuries. "So, I would advise you to embrace this opportunity for help, because if you don't, it will only get worse."

"PLEASE TURN TO PAGE NINE." OLIVIA SAID, THEN WAITED WHILE EACH OF the members turned to the page before continuing. "I suggest you read through this completely in your own time. I would encourage you to seek legal counsel, but I assure you it's watertight." She smiled confidently. "Again, for expediency, I would like to draw your attention to the terms in paragraph B through D."

She paused a moment before she read. "Miller Corporation shall pay to you—being Jason—," she looked around the room to make it plainly clear who she was talking about, "any deferred compensation, including, but not limited to deferred bonuses, allocated or credited to you or your account as of the date of termination, displacement or demotion."

She continued, "Paragraph C states that Miller Corporation shall pay to you all legal fees and expenses incurred by you as a result of such termination, displacement or demotion. Paragraph D discusses Miller Corporation stock options and paragraph E states, that the payments provided for in paragraphs B, C, and D above, shall be made no later than the 7th day following the date of the change." She took a moment and looked around the room.

Nothing but silence. A tiny pin could have dropped and the faint *tink* would have been heard.

No one spoke… no one was game to.

Malcolm had left the room, and Dennis sat in silence. His mind wandered off again to the times he had with Suzannah… until the voice cut through the calm of his mind.

Die, Dennis!

Dennis put his hands over his head and wept. He felt tortured and trapped, unable to escape his tormentor. A quick thought flashed through his brain… *death is the solution.* He glanced around for any pills or sedatives accidentally left behind. There were none.

He was at a loss. A profound, deep despair crashed over him like a thick muddy avalanche. There was no escape from his torture, and he could only see one way out… and that was to do what the voice had commanded him to do…

Die!

Olivia eventually spoke. "So, I presume that there has been no payment arranged or forthcoming, within the seven-day period from the date of the change. Therefore, we will also seek compensation each day thereof from the date that Jason's position changed, which was, I believe… nearly nine weeks ago. But I will request the exact date." She smiled as she looked around at the shocked faces.

Jason sat in awe at how Olivia worked the room. No one had said anything. What could they say? She had them, and there was nothing they could do.

Mal spoke first and broke the ice-cold air that had frozen the room. "Ah, Olivia… I think you know and, well I know Jason recognizes… that this company just doesn't have the means to provide such a payout as this." Mal looked over at Jason for some acknowledgment, but Jason sat in silence. He hadn't said a word since they walked into the room. "Um, I guess what I'm saying is… that if we put this agreement into action and compensate Jason, then Miller Corp will go into receivership."

"I understand, but the terms of Jason's contract were broken... let alone the anguish that he has suffered from the humiliation. So, what do you suggest?"

"That we reinstate Jason and forget that this ever happened." Mal blurted.

Jason instantly wanted to leap around the room for joy. His stomach started doing little flips of excitement. However, outwardly, he remained cool.

Olivia looked around the room waiting for others to respond, and when they didn't, she spoke, "I will need to discuss this in private with Jason, as he may still want to go through with exercising the terms as stated in his agreement. Please excuse us."

Jason and Olivia rose with deliberate serious expressions, and then walked down the hall into Jason's tiny office. As soon as they shut the door, they started whispering with elation.

"Olivia, you were awesome!" Jason said. "Can you believe this? They will be in there scrambling."

They both started giggling excitedly, like little children.

"I know. It's fantastic!" she beamed. "Did you see their faces? Priceless!" she laughed. "I wish I was a fly on the wall *right now*."

They whispered and tittered excitedly, taking their time to keep the board members waiting in suspense.

"This is utter bull!" Ben fumed. "That is an outrageous sum. How could we have missed this? Who knew about this?" He slammed his fist on the table, glaring around the room wanting answers... but no one responded.

"I don't think anyone knew Ben," Bruce said plainly as he put his head in his hands and rubbed with frustration.

"Well, someone must have known... Mal? Come on, you've been here the longest."

"I didn't know Ben, otherwise I would have said something when you first suggested pushing him out."

"Look Ben, no one knew, okay." Bruce stated angrily. "There's been a full board change since Miller Corp was formed. So..." he paused, "I don't know," he said, exasperated and upset.

"Well, he must have known then," Ben spat.

"I'm not sure Jason did, Ben. He's never mentioned it before." Mal stated.

"Well, there is no choice." Fiona stated, "Jason has to gain his position back. There is no other way," she said, inwardly rejoicing at the thought.

Miriam remained in silence, not uttering a word.

"NO! We can't have this. There has to be a way." Ben demanded.

"Are you serious?" Ed stated incredulously. "Have you lost your mind, Ben?" He scoffed and shook his head.

"It's a ridiculous amount of money, a sum that could never be paid without folding the company." Mal said, surprised at Ben's questioning.

Ben suddenly stood up and completely lost it. "Look, if we allow Jason back into that role, we will lose our jobs…" he paced, rubbing his head. "I… ME… will not have a job." Ben poked himself in the chest as his face paled at the realization of what was about to happen.

"And if we don't Ben, there will no longer be a company. We will lose our jobs, anyway." Ed retorted.

"Even so, Ben, it's better for Miller Corp to stay functioning." Mal stated.

Ben leaped across the room and pointed his finger in Mal's face. "Oh yeah, *you*… that's right, *you're* Jason's advocate, yes *you'll* be fine... You and Fiona will get to keep your positions, that's why you don't care," he said hotly. "You're probably rejoicing at the thought." He sneered.

Bruce sat and watched in dread as Ben stormed around the room, angrily firing off accusations and losing his temper with individuals.

"Ben, calm down," Ed raised his voice. "No one is saying that anyone will lose their jobs, so stop acting like a fool."

"FOOL? FOOL?" Ben retorted. "That's great Ed, good to see you're confident. We will see who is left standing by the end of today, shall we?" he paced.

"Sit down, Ben and get a grip on yourself." Bruce demanded.

Ben looked at Bruce, the only one that he respected in the room, and slowly sat back down.

"There is no choice," Bruce said plainly. "We will have to hope that Jason takes back his position."

CHAPTER FORTY-FOUR

OLIVIA AND JASON RE-ENTERED THE ROOM, AND OLIVIA ADDRESSED THE members.

"Jason and I have discussed the terms at length and he feels it is in the best interest of Miller Corporation to remain operating and not be placed into financial harm. His concern is, and always has been, keeping the business operating in the manner that he deems appropriate. Therefore, if the board agrees, then Jason will accept the reinstatement as the Chair." She waited for a moment. "Those in agreement, please raise your hands."

Everyone except Ben raised their hands.

"Good," Jason spoke for the first time, and Olivia let him have the floor.

DENNIS LAY IN HIS HOPELESSNESS AND CLASPED HIS HANDS OVER HIS HEAD in desperation, squeezing tight to straighten out his thoughts and drown out the voice.

Look at the floor, said the voice.

His eyes dropped, and swiftly a pair of dressing scissors slid out from under the bedside table by an unseen hand.

Do it! The voice hissed louder.

Dennis leaned down, straining to grasp the scissors.

Do it Dennis—end it! Die! Die! Die! The voice chanted with excitement.

He lurched sideways and in one motion clasped hold of the scissors handle.

Die, die, die! Dennis—die, die, die! It continued to chant persistently.

JASON CLEARED HIS THROAT. "RIGHT, SO NOW THAT WE HAVE EVERYTHING back to normal," he looked around to every face within the room. "I will not waste any more time. I still stand by my intentions of changing Miller Corporation's paradigm by removing the termination services, so I want to make myself clear that this will be the future." He paused, driving the point further. "Therefore, I need people who will stand by me, and not undermine me." He looked straight at Ben, who glared blankly at him. "I want a show of hands of who is with me."

Out of the six board members in the room, there were four that raised their hands. Jason expected nothing else.

Ben and Bruce sat defiantly in their seats, eyes directly glaring at Jason, then at those who had raised their hands.

"Okay, well, that makes it clear then, doesn't it?" Jason stated. "Therefore, those who do not wish to support me, I ask that you pack up your belongings from my building and leave." Jason then turned to those who raised their hands. "Thank you, we will endeavor to change our paradigm and see this through." Jason stood up and began to leave.

Ben bounded across the room and grabbed Jason around the collar. "You can't do this, Jason. I have stood by you and built this company."

Jason reacted quickly, grabbing Ben's arm and hurling it downward, releasing his grip. "You haven't stood by me. Others, maybe…" he looked around at the members still seated. "But you haven't stood by me. You made your choice and showed me your true colors."

"This is a mistake, Jason. You cannot do this. You will ruin this company… you need me."

"Then it's mine to ruin. Get out, Ben. Get your things out of *my* office. I do not want to see you set foot in here ever again." Jason raised his voice with venom. It was taking everything in his strength not to thump him.

Ben looked around, humiliated by the eyes staring back at him. "This is not over, Miller," he spat, then turned and marched over to his armchair, reefed his suit jacket from the back of it and stormed out.

. . .

DENNIS HELD THE SCISSORS IN HIS HAND, IMPASSIVELY STARING AT THEM.
His thoughts were in turmoil.

Do it. Do it, now. You will be free from all of this.

Dennis looked over towards the doorway to ensure no one was nearby
and watching.

*Cut deep, Dennis. This is your chance. You will have freedom and peace at last.
You will see Suzannah.*

At that thought, Dennis felt sure of his decision to end it. He flipped
the scissors open and clasped tightly to an open blade. He felt for the
external jugular vein and held the scissor blade ready, pushing hard
against his neck. With one quick thrust, he could cut swiftly and bleed out
in a matter of minutes, and no one would see it until it was too late.

Yessssss, do it.... do it now, quickly. You will be finally free.

Dennis shifted his arm in a move to cut—

What if you won't be free, Dennis? What if you're worse off? The kind voice
that he had heard once before spoke loudly and clearly, shattering all
other voices in his mind.

He stopped. Freezing still. The sharp scissor blade still pressing hard
against his skin as his epidermis began to slit open and bleed. He listened.
There was nothing but silence, no familiar taunting voice…

Nothing!

But those words interrupted him as his mind cleared and remembered
Jason's account. He hesitated for a moment and then glanced sideways at
the brown Bible sitting on the table next to him.

Psalm 40:1-3, he heard the soft kind voice say.

Dennis lowered the scissors and placed them on the bedside table.
He picked up the Bible and found the verse. It read:

I waited patiently for the Lord;
   he turned to me and heard my cry.
He lifted me out of the slimy pit,
   out of the mud and mire;
he set my feet on a rock

and gave me a firm place to stand.
He put a new song in my mouth,
    a hymn of praise to our God.
Many will see and fear the Lord
    and put their trust in him.

Dennis continued to read, calmly soaking in the rest of the Psalm. An unnatural peace flowed over him, enveloping him in a warmth that he had never felt before.

He sat quietly, not realizing that a large majestic angel stood right beside him, protecting him from his attacker.

CHAPTER FORTY-FIVE

"Oh, wow! I wish I could have seen their faces!" Ryan said as he, Chance, Olivia, and Jason ate their dinner at Ambrosio's in celebration.

"It was awesome." Jason declared. "You could have heard a pin drop when Olivia delivered the news. They didn't say a word initially—"

"And Ben couldn't talk at all," Olivia giggled. "He could only stammer… Ah, ah."

They all laughed at the thought.

"And Jason, you *really* did not know?" Chance asked, surprised.

"I didn't," Jason exclaimed. "It sounds odd, but when I set up the company, Clifford did everything for me and I just signed any documents he placed in front of me. I was so fixated on getting the first few clinics started. I trusted him implicitly."

"I couldn't believe it when I stumbled across that old agreement," Olivia professed. "It was like…" she paused and stared upwards with emotion. "I was holding the world's most precious gem in my hands. I think I even cried," she laughed.

"A golden parachute…" Jason smiled. "Who would have thought."

"That's right." Olivia glanced at Jason with a beaming grin. "I tell you —Clifford was one smart cookie. He must have seen this eventually coming and wanted to protect you. Thank goodness he had the foresight to make it so difficult for Jason to be removed. It's such an outlandish amount of money—that price would break most companies."

"Incredible!" Jason shook his head, still in disbelief, but extremely relieved.

"Yep… God never seems to work to our plans, does he Jason?" Ryan winked, then raised his glass, "Here's to Clifford, for his fore-thinking, and to Olivia for her determination… but mostly… here's to God, for His plans, His favor… and His everlasting love."

They raised their glasses together and laughed with sheer relief and joy.

DENNIS REMAINED IN HIS BED, PONDERING AND CLUTCHING THE BIBLE tightly against his chest. His eyes gradually felt heavy, and he drifted off to sleep. The large angel stood firm, standing over him and guarding him faithfully throughout the night.

IN THE DIMLY LIT BAR, WHERE THE SMOKE FURLED AND HAZED THE ROOM, Ben and Bruce sat in a booth tucked away in the back corner.

"He can't do this. I will move heaven and earth to stop him. I will call every investor myself and deter them if I have to." Ben vowed angrily.

"Ben, I don't think there is a thing we can do. We are out… it's done."

"It's not over," he snapped. "I will not lie down and let him do this. I'll fight him to the end if it's the last thing I ever do…"

"Then it may be the last thing you do…" he said dryly, and took a sip of his whiskey. "Ben… we're done, just let it go." Bruce scolded.

"I'm not done, Bruce… I'm telling you I'm not finished with Miller. He will get his own," he said fiercely as he took another sip of his scotch.

CHAPTER FORTY-SIX

MONDAY.

JASON, IN HIS EXCITEMENT, HAD ALREADY MOVED BACK INTO HIS OFFICE over the weekend. He sat in his chair, sipped his takeaway coffee, and opened the New York Telegram. The headline on the second page read.

CEO AND BOARD MEMBER OUSTED FROM MILLER EMPIRE

"You wouldn't think I was such big news." Jason commented as he continued to read the news item.

Another headline below the news clip appeared depicting women being outraged that his clinics were changing.

WOMEN'S PRO-CHOICE RIGHTS HINDERED!

Jason sighed as he read on, then flipped the page. The next headline was.

MANNER CASE: DRIVER CHARGED WITH MANSLAUGHTER OVER UNBORN TWINS.

He read the news article until his intercom beeped and he hit the button. "Hi, Marg."

"Jase, I have a reporter from the New York Telegram who would like to have an interview with you."

"Put them through."

"I'm putting you through now Josie, thanks for waiting." Marg stated.

"Jason Miller speaking."

"Hello Dr. Miller, it's Josie Stein from the New York Telegram."

"Hi Josie."

"I would like to ask you a few questions to go into tomorrow's paper, if you don't mind?"

"Yes, go ahead."

"I guess what's on everyone's mind is why the sudden change towards conducting abortion services at your the clinics?"

"Well, you're probably aware that I had a near fatal accident. Anything like that will make you reassess *everything* in life... and that's exactly what I did."

"Yes, but why change from abortions to pushing for adoptions? That's a big reassessment, don't you think?"

"I guess it is in most people's eyes, but I felt that I needed to change."

"Yes, Dr. Miller, but it's not a minor change. It's a complete flip."

"I agree it is a complete turnaround, but that's what I want. Besides, it's not unheard of. Dr. Bernard Nathanson was an abortionist who helped legalize abortion in the 70s and served as a director and advisor on the biggest pro-choice organization in the country. But he reconsidered only a few years later and became pro-life because of his revelation of seeing the babies on ultrasound, which was breakthrough technology then. I'm sure you are familiar with the film called 'The Silent Scream'?"

She paused as this caught her off guard, and she changed her tact. "But you yourself have said in the past it's not a baby until it is born."

"I was wrong!"

"So... you're now saying that you believe it is a baby *before* it is born?"

"Let me ask you a question. When the sperm penetrates the egg, it forms the zygote, which is unique from its mother. The zygote has its own DNA and will mature through distinct developmental stages. So, is it human? Is it alive?"

"Ah—well, it *has* to be human—it's not a different species, is it? And

246

yes, I guess you can say it is alive. But it's only a mass of cells and nothing more."

"I used to think so, too." Jason paused. "If you look at the developing baby, it's clearly not a blob of cells. You can distinctly see the forming features of a human, and the heart beats as early as 5 weeks. But that statement is an attempt to dehumanize the baby. My staff and I used it all the time, so the woman didn't feel an attachment to the fetus or fear that she was killing her baby… and leave the clinic. We also never showed women the ultrasound because they would see the unmistakable likeness of a human developing, confirming it wasn't just a mass of cells."

Jason took a quick breath. "But if you want an academic confirmation, there are several scientific measures that determine life, and the zygote satisfies all the conditions required to establish biological life. Therefore, you're right… scientifically, it is unquestionably alive at the point of conception. But a mass of cells by themselves does not make up a living organism. An organism has to be a body of cells that work together in a coordinated manner to mature through developmental stages. This synchronized behavior is the trademark of a living organism, and we define humans as living organisms. So, science backs up both statements… being that at conception, it is living and it is an organism."

"Okay, well, I can't argue with science, but I still think your argument is flawed. It's still not *really* a baby."

"Okay, so when do you think he becomes a baby?"

"At birth."

"Yeah, and I would have agreed with you before my accident. So why at birth?"

"Because this is when it is a fully functioning human, independent of its mother."

"Is he really fully independent when he is born?"

"Well, okay, obviously the baby is reliant on the mother for care until a certain age."

"And why is that?"

"Because the baby needs time to grow and become independent."

"Are you saying it's age-based? That it's about time?"

"Yes, I guess I am."

"Well, I agree things take time to develop. So based on what you just said, wouldn't it be fair to say that an embryo is a human that just needs time to develop?"

"I think it depends on the size doesn't it? At that point it's just a tiny blob."

"Are you now saying that smaller humans have fewer rights? So, by your size definition, females are generally smaller than males, so males should have more rights?"

"That's not what I'm saying."

"What about a toddler then, they are small, so it must be fine to kill them?"

"That's ridiculous! What I'm saying that it is still in the embryonic stage and it doesn't matter because it's so small."

"Actually, it matters. You only have to ask any doctor what advice they give to a woman who is pregnant, regardless of what stage. They advise women to be careful about taking pain killers, getting a radiograph or eating certain foods. Also, you can't deny the big push by campaigns dedicated to educating women regarding consuming drugs and alcohol during pregnancy. Why would they even bother if the clump of cells were not a living, developing human being? Why would people even care? Isn't that a contradiction to what you're saying?"

"Okay, Dr. Miller—my genuine concern is all those women who rely on your clinics for help. What are they to do?"

"I would hope that they make better choices—use contraception or look at adoption."

"I think that's a very archaic way of putting it," she scoffed. "Not everyone can take contraception and it's not 100 percent foolproof, anyway."

"You are right, but there are many women who choose not to use contraception. In my clinics, about 50 percent of abortions stem from not using any contraception or from irregular contraceptive use. There was an independent study conducted a few years ago. They found if there was the provision of free contraception, it would prevent up to 75 percent of unwanted pregnancies—hence abortion rates would lower. So, what is that saying Josie, is it lack of education, lack of money, laziness, or lack of responsibility?"

"Well, I still think that's an antiquated view. We are in a modern society, where women are equal and have rights. A right to do what they want with their *own* bodies."

"So do unborn children. They also have a right to their own body. In your view, is the baby a part of the mother or a separate entity?"

"It's a part of the mother and attached to her body."

"I agree. He's attached. But he isn't a part of the mother's body, is he? He's not an extra arm, leg, or a kidney?"

"Well, when you put it that way, then no."

So, we've already established that he is human, haven't we?

"Yes."

"And that he isn't a body part, is he, but his own unique person?"

"Okay, it isn't a body part, but it's taking up residence and it should be a woman's right to do what she wants to her own body."

"I'm not saying that the woman can't do what she wants to her *own* body. But we just established that the child is not a part of the woman's body, didn't we? It's not the woman's body that's torn apart and killed in an abortion—it's the child's, which has his own body, separate from the mother, and therefore his own rights as well."

"I think you're just arguing semantics here."

"Am I? I see that your newspaper is happy to report on the Manner court case. So, what's the difference? Is it because the mother didn't choose on her terms to terminate these twin babies? If what you say is true and you don't believe that these are children yet, then why is this man being charged for vehicular homicide over two clumps of cells? That's not semantics!"

"That's not the point we are talking about. I'm asking if you have thought about all those women and their rights you're taking away."

"I'm not taking any rights away. I'm providing *more* choices. Have you thought about it that way? Besides, both the Constitution and the Universal Declaration of Human Rights say that 'Everyone has the right to life, liberty and security of person'. So doesn't that mean that *all* humans have rights?"

"Yes, it does, but—"

"And we've already established that the preborn are human. So, aren't they covered by this constitution as well?"

"I'm talking about *women's* rights here. The right to do what *they* want and not suffer from an unwanted pregnancy."

"Okay then, if your primary concern is women's rights, have you researched female infanticide? If you do, you'll find that worldwide we abort more females than males. So where are the women's rights there?"

"You're not understanding where I'm coming from. I'm not talking about other countries. I'm concerned with ours and—"

"I'm not talking about other countries, either. At least 50 percent of abortions here are females, but don't be so naïve to think that there isn't sex selective abortion here as well. So, if your focus is on women's rights, then you're discriminating against women *before* they are born. Aren't you taking away *their* right to live?"

"I just don't see it that way. It's a woman's right to have freedom."

"I agree women have rights to freedom, just like any other person. But how does abortion bring freedom? Doesn't it actually oppress women?"

"How so?"

"It allows society to not address the genuine issues and take the easier way out. In fact, it's taking away women's rights to keep their child. If we didn't have abortion, then wouldn't the State have to build more programs and resources at supporting mothers and their children?"

"I haven't really thought about it that way."

"What's cheaper, Josie, an abortion or funding programs to support women and their children?"

"Obviously the former."

"Agree! So, in effect, it's not liberating women at all, is it? Society is actually neglecting women's rights and needs, and discriminating against them for *being* pregnant."

"Wow! Good point. However, I still advocate that it's my body, my choice, Dr. Miller."

"Josie, you can chant that mantra all you like. However, is it really always your choice?"

"Yes!"

"Really? A recent study found that over 65 percent of post abortive women said they felt coerced into an abortion. Their partner, parents, or someone else pressured them. In fact, it would surprise you at how many men actually make the appointment for the women at my clinics. So how does that fit with the 'my body, my choice' mantra?"

"I know many women who wanted their abortion and are proud of it."

"I do too, but based on what we've just discussed, wouldn't you agree they are still taking away a human's right to life, proud of it or not? Does this mean that equal rights don't really exist?"

"Now we are getting into politics."

"Are we? I'm just applying the sanctity of life ethic to everyone, including the preborn."

"Well, what about if the woman is facing hardship? Surely that is a valid reason."

"Look, I totally agree, facing hardship whilst pregnant would be a very tough situation to be in. But couldn't that happen at any point?"

"What do you mean?"

"Well, what if this hardship came when the child was two-years-old? Does that mean that it's okay to kill the child then, because you're in difficulty?"

"Of course not. That's murder."

"So again, you're basing it on the *age* of the child, aren't you, because we've already established that the baby's life starts at conception?"

"Ah… well—I guess when you look at it like that. But by taking away these services for women, you're impeding their ability to achieve their goals, careers or climb the corporate ladder… or have a *planned* family when they are ready. You're taking away *their* rights and creating a hindrance in their life."

"I never said the mother has to keep the child—cause Josie, is nine months really such a sacrifice compared to the mother's lifespan of 80 years? Is it really too much to let the baby live and have a full life of its own?"

"It can still hinder her career or education."

"Why should a woman feel that there is a need to kill her child to achieve her goals, dreams or career aspirations? There are plenty of women who are mothers and in prominent positions. Having a baby hasn't hindered their career at all. Isn't that the epitome of feminism, to do *all* those things?"

"Ideally, yes, you could look it that way, but that's not reality, is it?"

"But this is where *society* has it all wrong. We should create more programs for adoption, strengthen our foster care system, provide greater support to single mothers, offer affordable or even free government-funded childcare. Provide flexible employment agreements and be more accommodating in our schools and universities with class hours so women can continue with their education whilst they are pregnant or caring for their child. That's the *real* problem here. It's not that they *got pregnant*, it's that society does not have enough programs and support to help them. Actually, the public funds that are currently provided to the abortion industry to take lives should be redirected to the creation of support programs to take care of lives."

Jason took a sharp breath. "We should have a framework in place so that women stop seeing children as a threat and that their only option— their only way out—is abortion. Instead, we should welcome these children, these little Americans, Australians, Canadians, Europeans—wherever they are… and not dismember and kill them."

"That sounds very idealistic, but I agree, we need more support programs, Dr. Miller, but that is another topic we could cover another time — So where do you stand if a woman presents with a life-threatening pregnancy? Will your clinics still treat her in these cases?"

"We won't perform any abortions, Josie, and truly life-threatening pregnancies are sent to the nearest emergency center. But if you're referring to cases like an ectopic pregnancy, removal of a cancerous uterus, high blood pressure or other various illnesses that can compromise the pregnancy, then doctors will still do their best to save and deliver the child, as it's two lives at stake. Also noting that these babies can survive from 21 weeks with medical care. If it's impossible to save the child, then this becomes an unintended consequence of the medical treatment and is not classed as an abortion, it's a preterm delivery. But let me ask you, if we can save the mother without aborting the child, then which should we choose?"

"I guess the choice would be not to abort the baby, but that's still determined on how acute the mother is."

"I agree. It comes down to how critical the mother is to how we treat this situation. Just curious, but do you know how long an abortion takes on a baby that is 21 weeks or older?"

"No, I haven't researched that aspect."

"Maybe that's something you should look into. Most commonly, it takes two to three days, sometimes longer if there are complications. To ensure the baby is not born alive, a needle of Digoxin is injected directly into the baby's skull or heart to kill it. The baby does not die immediately, but sometime over the course of 24 hours. After the injection is administered, the cervix is dilated using laminaria over the next two to three days. The woman returns to the clinic to check the dilation and to ensure that the baby has died. If the baby is still alive, then another lethal injection is administered. The woman has to wait for sufficient dilation so she can go into labor to give birth to her demised baby, or a D&E is conducted to remove the baby."

Jason took a quick breath. "Instead of using Digoxin, another way is by injecting a poisonous saline solution into the womb and the baby ingests the liquid. It takes the child over an hour to die as the corrosive solution burns both the internals and also the skin of the child. It's common for the mother to feel the baby fighting… Last, and it's banned in some states, is what is called an intact dilation and extraction, or in popular terms, a partial birth abortion. Dilation occurs over the days prior and the live baby is partially born in a breach position. The entire body of the baby, bar the head, is delivered, but before the baby's head is clear of the birth canal, an instrument is pushed into the back of the skull to collapse it and cause death," he paused, "Josie… ALL of these options are gruesome and traumatic."

Jason heard her sigh. "Oh… I wasn't aware of the details of those procedures." She fumbled.

"I'm not sugar coating it—I'm just telling you the truth, which most people are unaware of… and unfortunately, this industry wants to hide or gloss over. In fact, we would never imagine doing these barbaric acts to a human outside the womb, so how does this make it right that we allow it whilst inside?"

Josie was silent momentarily and didn't respond.

Jason took a quick breath. "Late-term abortions are high risk and have many complications. The mother can hemorrhage, have uterine lacerations, perforations, or even die—it's an extremely traumatic experience. In fact, if the woman's health is that critical, then it seems strange to conduct such a lengthy process that could harm or even kill her. So, Josie, now that you understand these procedures, let me ask you this. If having the baby was so life threatening, wouldn't it be best for the mother to be admitted into hospital for a C-section, which only takes about an hour?"

"Ah, yes, well… I see your point there." She took a breath, recomposed herself, and continued with the interview. "But what about aborting for the emotional health of the mother? It's not a mystery that your clinics used these reasons to abort, is it?"

"No, I'm not denying that we conducted many abortions based on the psychological health of the mother. But let me ask you this question—is abortion a natural process to stop a pregnancy?"

"No, it's not natural."

"I'm glad we agree on this," Jason chuckled, "So if it's not a natural process, then how do you think this will further affect the woman's emotional state, if her life truly is at risk from being pregnant?"

"I'd say probably relieved, to have the abortion and be able to go back to normal."

"That's what I believed, too. I ignored all the studies because I wanted to make a profit. That is what most people will say and think too, but in fact, there is no going back to normal and it can put the woman at greater risk psychologically. Studies suggest that post-abortive women have 35 percent higher rates of depression and anxiety and have over 150 percent more suicidal behavioral tendencies compared to those who haven't terminated their pregnancy. So how is that helping a woman's mental health and setting her up for stability in later years?"

"Well, what about a child that is deformed… or handicapped? Surely the mother has a right to terminate in these circumstances? I know your clinics, and you yourself, Dr. Miller, have recommended terminations based on these instances."

Jason paused, then took a slight breath, "You know Josie, I did… and I regret…" Jason stopped. "Look, doctors aren't perfect and sometimes the diagnoses of a defect in a fetus can be wrong." He paused. "But unfortunately, society is finding it easier and more acceptable to dispose of those with disabilities. Would you kill your brother if he lost his leg, arm or even a few fingers… or got brain damage from an accident?"

"That's not even the same."

"Isn't it? We have gone from caring for our weak to terminating them before they have a chance to live and impact our lives, and before we've had a chance to learn from them. Besides, having a disability does not make someone less human or less perfect… or less loved. By taking this away, aren't we removing the uniqueness that makes up the fabric of our society? Besides, are you perfect, Josie?"

She laughed, "I'd like to think so, but no, I'm far from perfect."

"So why are we striving for perfectionism? Isn't aborting these babies leaning dangerously towards eugenics?"

"Well… No, I think it's trying to mitigate a child from having a tragic life."

"I think you're wrong. We are aborting those with undesirable traits or defects and, therefore, we are chasing the perfect child. And sadly, I was the biggest proponent of this."

Josie was quiet.

So Jason continued, "But, regarding your comment about stopping a tragic life, aren't hardships a part of life? So, it still doesn't mean we should kill them beforehand, because we actually cannot determine if their life will be terrible. There are countless people with disabilities who are living amazing lives. In fact, I read recently in a medical journal that only four percent of parents regret having their child with Down syndrome. The rest advised that their lives have been greatly enhanced. Josie, have you ever watched the Paralympic games and been in awe at what people can overcome and achieve? In fact, you could say that these people are superhuman because of what they have conquered and that we could learn so much from their strength and resilience."

Jason sighed. "Honestly, I've lost count of how many fetuses my clinics terminated for a defect that could have been fixed surgically—like a cleft palate, spina bifida, missing ear… or a heart defect. Just go to the CDC website and read the testimonies of families living with these disabilities. They aren't miserable, they love their children. Besides, there have been countless people who went against doctor's advice to abort and ended up with a perfectly healthy child. The doctor made a mistake in the diagnosis."

Jason took a deep breath. "Incidentally, Josie, do you know how many people are waiting to adopt children with or without special needs?"

"Ah, I haven't researched that. I assume there's a lengthy list because of fertility issues?"

"You're right, approximately 2 million families are waiting. So why are we aborting just under 1 million babies a year when we could give each of these babies a home where they are loved and desperately *wanted*?"

Josie just ignored the question. "So, what about the ones that can't be rectified, or have genetic disorders like… Edward syndrome?"

"Didn't a lady with Edward syndrome celebrate her 40th in Oklahoma years ago? So there have been people who have lived a full and happy life with these issues. But if the baby is unlikely to survive after birth, it's still not a valid reason to terminate. Allowing the baby to be delivered naturally is still the better choice. Josie... I acknowledge this is one of the hardest decisions a parent has to make. I've been in situations where I've delivered bad news and witnessed the devastation from my advice to end the pregnancy, so I don't discount the weight of these decisions. But, although it won't take away the emotional pain, evidence has shown that completing the pregnancy and spending time with the baby, be it only a short time, creating a memory box... conducting a funeral is more therapeutic. It can help the grieving process and result in fewer psychological problems for the mother later on because this life still counted—it meant something... and there is no guilt from deciding to end that child's life earlier. Again, we need to change society's views and increase support services for parents in these instances."

"Okay..." she quickly changed the subject. "Well, have you thought about how it will push women into going for unsafe and illegal abortions?"

"So, what you're saying is... that it's okay to condone murder if people are doing it, anyway? If that's your argument, then should we legalize illicit drugs—just to make it safer?"

"That's absurd, that's not what I'm saying, I'm—"

"I agree women will get unsafe abortions. They are doing it right now, anyway. Changing my clinics still will not alter that."

"But thousands of women could die."

"Oh Josie, come on. There were 39 reported deaths in the US in 1972 from illegal abortions. You can go on the internet to find out that the statistics were fabricated and blown out of proportion to support the case for legalization in 1973. In fact, Bernard Nathanson admitted the numbers of 5000 to 10,000 were unfounded and simply used as a shock factor to push for the legalization. Go to the CDC website and look at the abortion-related death table. You'll find that from 1972 to 1990, there were more deaths from legal abortions than illegal. But it's nowhere near the thousands you're stating."

"I will research that more in depth, however, you haven't really answered my question."

"Yes, women do die from illegal abortions, most of which are in developing countries. Yet still, statistics show that abortion deaths sit around 8 percent in these countries, but out of that percent, 92 percent are dying from other pregnancy-related complications. But if you look further into the stats, why are countries like Guyana, who have legalized abortion, have a maternal mortality ratio of 665, when Chile, where abortion is illegal, has a lower ratio of 13. So really, I think that sex education, contraception, professional medical advice and care is the answer to these issues, and could dramatically reduce or prevent a lot of these deaths."

"So, you still agree that it will make women get illegal abortions?"

"I don't disagree, but that is human nature—you cannot stop people from doing illegal things. For instance, there are over 400,000 murders per year worldwide. So, like I said, what are you going to do, make it legal? I just don't see how me changing the way I do business will create such hysteria and make women seek illegal abortions."

"If you take away your facilities, won't it put more pressure on the system and potentially push women to seek out alternative abortion solutions, so those statistics are bound to increase?"

"Well, let me put it this way. The recorded abortion stats in the US were around 200,000 in 1970. Once it became legalized across various states, it grew to around 1.4 million by 1990. So, statistics went up because it became legal… It's like anything—make it legal and more people will do it. You just have to look at Amsterdam and legalized drug use. Or take Ireland, for example. Until 2013, abortion was illegal, and they had one of the lowest mortality rates in the world. But the concern is, when abortion becomes legal, and governments pay or subsidize the procedures and society deem it as an acceptable way to manage a perceived problem… then, of course, more women will elect to have abortions."

"But Dr. Miller, are you now saying that we should change the abortion law?"

"Look, I'm not entering the banning abortion debate in this conversation, Josie. If people really want an abortion, they will have one no matter the costs." He paused. "My aim is to change *my* clinics and also influence people's views, and… yes, hopefully, change opinion enough for people to *want* to change the laws and make abortion history."

He took a breath. "This country is so divided over the abortion argument—half want it to remain legal, half do not. Now I think if people viewed the pregnancy as a *baby*—a living human child who has a right to live out their life of 80-odd years—they would look at it differently, and they would want to ban these procedures and make it illegal. Besides, when you abort a child, you do not know how he or she, or their generations, could have impacted the world. Did you know, Josie, that since Row V. Wade, we have aborted over 63 million little Americans? So we've actually murdered 18 percent of our total population. In fact, the number of babies we've murdered exceeds the total sum of brave soldiers killed in *all* our wars. Soldiers that fought for our—unborn included—freedom. How can we, as a nation, think this is okay?"

"Ah—I knew it was a lot, but I didn't know it was those figures."

"Well, think about yourself, Josie—what if your mother aborted you? You wouldn't be here talking to me, standing up for what you believe in, writing your news columns and changing people's views? So really, what right does any of us have to take another's life? The fact is Josie, that there are still complications that occur from abortions or taking the abortion pill. Woman still die and have major complications from legal abortions too, so there is never a *safe abortion*. Over 22 women have died and thousands have been hospitalized from taking the abortion pill—which, mind you, is an extremely painful and traumatic process that the medical industry fail to tell the women before handing it over… just go search testimonies of how it has affected women physically and psychologically. But, shamelessly, even our website used to state that it was extremely safe with no ill effects," he sighed, "I simply no longer wish to conduct these services, and that's what I'm saying here."

"All right, Dr. Miller, but you've failed to account for women who have unwanted pregnancies through rape or incest. If your clinics change, then these women alone will suffer."

"That's a very important issue, but it's still not the fault of the child, is it? That's not the problem here—it's the fact that they *were* raped. So, it's actually again… a *social* issue and has nothing to do with the fact they became pregnant. So, we need to educate people that they shouldn't rape, strengthen laws and penalties to deter those crimes, and support these women. That's the *real* issue here! You have to understand, Josie, that it's not the *way* the baby was conceived, but that the baby *was* conceived. It's not the fault of the child and the rapist should be the one that's punished… not the child. Let me ask you, do you think that a crime that your father committed should be passed onto you as a death penalty?"

"Ha! Of course not… but that's not what I'm saying. The father *should* be punished for his crime, but the woman shouldn't be forced to go through with the trauma of the pregnancy."

"I agree. The father should be punished. But we are killing the child, giving them the death penalty for a crime that they didn't commit. Look… rape is an absolute violation of a woman. It is a traumatic and an abhorrent act of violence. But having an abortion does not *un-rape* a woman. Having an abortion is just putting more violence and suffering on top of an already violent and distressing situation. Also, Josie, less than one percent of pregnancies result from rape. So, you cannot make *that* the main reason here. Out of that small percent, only 15 to 25 percent of rape pregnancies are terminated. So, by using today's annual abortion statistics, that equates to between 1000 to 2000 women per year. The other 5000 choose life for the child… so what does that tell you about women choosing to abort because of rape?"

"But Dr. Miller, it still comes down to the fact that I have a right to *choose* what's right for me… if I don't want the pregnancy, it's *my body*, and… I shouldn't choose what's right for another woman. Every woman should be able to make that choice for herself."

"And I totally agree with your rights, Josie—until you impede on another person's rights… being the unborn person, an individual human life inside of you. That's where your rights stop."

"I still don't agree with your viewpoint… and probably never will."

"Okay, so what if my viewpoint is wrong, what's the worst that can happen?"

"You hinder women's rights."

"Exactly… but what if I'm right? Where does that put you?"

"I guess I would be supporting an atrocity then." She paused for a few seconds, pondering.

"Can I ask why you're pro-choice?"

"My aunty died of an illegal abortion, well before I was born. I felt that I never wanted that to happen to anyone."

"Yeah, that's a tragedy, I'm sorry that your family went through that."

"Yes, it's such a pity that abortion wasn't legal back then, she would be still alive."

"Or it's a pity there wasn't more support for your aunty, so she could have delivered the child and they'd both be still alive."

"That's all speculative."

"It is, but it's still a safer alternative than the one she chose."

"I'm honestly shocked that I'm hearing this from you, Dr. Miller. You have always been a stout advocate for pro-choice and you have completely done a double take. So, are you saying that you're now a fully fledged pro-lifer? Is this a religious conversion?"

"Call it what you want. It doesn't really matter what people think. They will disagree no matter what I say. Half the nation hates me right now because my clinics performed abortions, so it will just mean that it will change to the other side now hating me because I'm stopping those procedures. Lucky, I have a thick skin. And yes, Josie, my accident gave me a different perspective on our eternal existence. I now believe in God, and that He created us, and that life begins at conception. That we are planned, and every life counts. But please understand that I'm not out to punish women. My focus is on *my* clinics and not wanting them to perform termination services, because I believe every child has a right to life. That is the message I am portraying."

"All right, Dr. Miller, you've put up some valid arguments. I may not entirely agree with all of them, but I thank you for your time today," she said graciously.

"Thank you, Josie, for talking with me. Enjoy your day." He said before hanging up.

Jason sighed. *Let's see how that turns out tomorrow,* he thought.

CHAPTER FORTY-SEVEN

Jason returned from lunch to find Miriam waiting in his office. "Hi Miriam, did we have a meeting?" he smiled warmly, surprised to see her.

"No Jason, I need to talk to you about something," she said with concern.

"Okay."

"Look," she shifted awkwardly, "I haven't been honest with you," she paused. "So, I'll just come out with it." She shifted again. "Ben coerced me into voting for the no confidence motion."

Jason leaned back in his chair, settling in, ready to listen to the sordid tale. He waited for her to continue.

"The thing is… that… *ahem*," she cleared her throat. "The thing is that Jeremy didn't get the scholarship we had hoped for medical school."

Jason squinted and remained silent, waiting for this story to unfold.

"… And, well… well… Ben somehow knew about this and… well, he offered to assist."

Jason raised his eyebrows, but remained silent for her to continue.

"And, *ahem*… well, you see… we can't afford his tuition… without getting a second mortgage and so… well… Ben… he offered to help." She looked at him squarely, "and well he—"

"How much?" Jason stated, blank-faced.

"140,000."

Jason sat in silence, pushed his head back into the headrest of his chair, breathed deeply, and contemplated. The disappointment was obvious and seeped from his face. They had sold him out for a 140 grand. He had been betrayed with deception and fraud, and it stung to hear it.

"I… I… I'm so sorry Jason," she shook her head with her own disgust. "And I'm here to give the money back and also… to give you this." She handed him an envelope and Jason knew it was her resignation. "I don't expect you to forgive me, nor understand." She looked down. "I was undecided on the decision anyway and wanted the best for my son, so the temptation was too great and I stupidly took it." Her eyes welled with tears. "It's the biggest mistake I have ever made, and I am so ashamed and disgusted at what I did." She looked away and dabbed her eyes with a tissue.

Jason didn't know what to say—he remained silent—disappointment etched into his face.

"I hope that telling you and returning the money will be enough. I also hope that you do not call the authorities." She looked concerned and pale, her voice quivering.

Jason couldn't speak. He felt deceived by a trusted member of his corporation and he felt the anger, disgust, and frustration rising to the surface like deep molten lava. Suddenly, he felt all the hurt and embarrassment that they had caused him rushing at him like a tidal wave—overwhelming him. He was about to stand up and unleash his fury upon her, and tell her to get out and leave, when immediately a soft clear voice like fine-spun silk pierced through his rage, abruptly interrupting him.

But I forgave you… didn't I, Jason?

He stopped, catching himself before any harsh words came out. Those soft words resonated throughout his heart and soul like a wrecking ball crashing through a concrete wall, blasting all the rage and hurt into fragments. He knew that his eternity meant more than any of this, and he knew instantly what he had to do.

Jason remained in his seat in silence for a minute. His eyes softened, his anger subsided, and the shroud dropped from his eyes for him to see Miriam like he had never before. He took pity on the broken middle-aged woman sobbing in front of him. After a long while, he spoke. "It doesn't matter, Miriam. I forgive you."

She lifted her face to look at him, her eyes and cheeks were streaked with black teared mascara, her red face looked at him with confusion. "Y-you what?" she whispered.

"I hold nothing against you... I forgive you."

She looked at him incredulously, unable to fathom what he had just said. "But I betrayed you," she whispered, barely audible. Her face screwing up at the horror of those words... and her own actions.

"It doesn't matter anymore, it's okay." He said as he pushed the envelope on the desk back towards her.

She looked at him in confusion. "W-what are you saying Jason, that you—"

"I'm saying, Miriam, that it doesn't matter. That I want you to stay on the board."

"I-I don't know what to say, how can you just—"

"There's nothing more to say. We never have to speak of this again. I will tell no one Miriam... I forgive you!"

DENNIS WAS BACK IN HIS CELL, TIDYING UP THE MESS THAT HE HAD created before they took him to the infirmary. Satisfied, he gathered his clothes and headed off towards the shower block before dinner.

Six inmates casually walked out of the showers into the change area. They each had a towel hanging around their head and were drying their hair vigorously when Dennis arrived in the room.

One inmate glanced at the others, and they quickly all swarmed around Dennis. With one swift move, Dennis felt the blade go in deep. He buckled forwards as the inmate made the final upward drive with the weapon.

"Benny said, we don't want nutters like you in here. Got it?" he said venomously, then removed the knife as they all quickly scurried away down the corridor with the towels still covering their heads to disguise.

Dennis lay on the floor in a pool of thick crimson blood. The bright red liquid gradually trickled across the tiles, zigzagging as it flowed along the grout lines. He lay motionless on the cold, wet floor.

Tuesday.

"Wow, Jason!" Marg grinned. "You're all over the New York Telegram this morning… I've put a copy on your desk. Nice work, Dr. Miller." She winked.

Jason strode quickly to his office. This was the moment that he had been dreading and he was eager to see the hounding and mockery that he believed he would receive from the interview. He picked up the paper and found the news article from Josie on the first page.

Dr. Miller, a man of conviction.
by Josie Stein

Jason read the article slowly, taking in every word.

Dr. Miller's decision to change his clinics will impact local communities…

… women's rights hindered!...

Dr. Miller did not shy away from the hard questions…

Jason read the column and found that Josie had presented a balanced view, not skewing his responses as he had feared. *She was an excellent reporter;* he thought. Jason read the last summation with a surprise.

I've always believed it is the woman's right because it's what I've grown up with, surrounded by photos of my mother protesting and pushing for legalized abortion in the late 60s. But something's changed after listening to Dr. Miller's thoughts… my opinion is wavering. Maybe it's my views that are wrong, maybe there is some truth in his stance, maybe we should not be so stubborn in what our own rights are… but consider the rights of the child.

I'm certainly not going to rush out and join the pro-life protestors, but after carefully listening to the other viewpoint… I feel I may reassess my hard-core stance on pro-choice.

Jason closed the newspaper and put his head on his desk in relief. "Thank you, Lord," he said with such appreciation.

His cell rang. It was Ryan.

"Oh, man… Jason!" Ryan said. "That was such an awesome news article. Well done, buddy!"

"Yeah, I know—it really surprised me. I thought she would annihilate me." He chuckled.

"Well, she didn't. It was well written."

"It could have gone either way, so I'm glad it went well. I have been sweating about it all night."

"Things are definitely looking up."

"Yes, it's very different from the past 11 months, but I still have a way to go yet."

"Yeah, but it's moving, and that's the key thing. Hey, you up for dinner?"

"Sure am!"

"I'll bring Chance too. Oh, do you want to invite Olivia?"

"Sure, I'll see what she is up to. I know she's been busy, so she may not be interested. But I'm definitely in. Ambrosio's, 7 p.m.?"

"Nope, not that flash, buddy. Let's keep it simple and go to Denny's," Ryan chuckled.

"Sure, I'll see you then."

As Jason finished the call on his cell, his desk phone intercom buzzed.

"Ben is on the line wanting to know when he will receive his severance pay," Marg stated.

Jason sighed and rubbed his face. "Put him through. Thanks Marg."

"Putting you through now, Ben."

"Ben." Jason said, emotionless.

"Jason!" Ben returned the same level of affection. "I've figured I'm owed just over 833K in my severance pay, plus the bonuses that I will have coming pro rata."

"So, it will be 833K less the 140K you stole from me and gave to Miriam, will it?"

Ben was deathly silent.

"Yes Ben, she told me… and she has returned the money."

"So, did you fire her?"

"No."

"Seems one-sided, don't you think? You fire me, yet keep her?"

"Yes, I've kept her on. I have forgiven her for what she did… I'm still working on forgiving you."

"So, you would really trust her over me? Someone who has been loyal to you for the past seven years, helping you grow your business?"

Jason scoffed. "Loyal? Come on, Ben. You're only as loyal as long as the paychecks keep coming. The state Miriam was in showed that she will never betray me again. Therefore, it makes her more of an ally than an adversary. You, on the other hand, are like a viper waiting to strike at any chance you can get. You've proven you're not trustworthy, even more so with the stunt you pulled with the bribery. I would have called the police if it wasn't for ruining Miriam." Jason paused and took a breath. "You'll get your 833K Ben… but not a cent more."

Jason hung up the phone. "God, I choose to forgive him. I choose to forgive him. Please help me to forgive him," he whispered in desperation.

CHAPTER FORTY-EIGHT

Jason, Chance, Ryan, and Olivia were at Denny's restaurant eating burgers.

"That article in the paper was fantastic!" Chance stated.

"Yeah, it turned out really well," said Jason. "I didn't think Josie would take that viewpoint, so it surprised me when she did."

"That summation was gold." Ryan smiled. "It sounded like you really had her rethinking the whole pro-choice stand. It was great!"

"Thanks buddy," Jason smiled as he ate his fries.

"So, now that you have confessed to the world that you are a believer in Christ… and now that they can't label you insane and kick you out of Miller Corp… when are you going to write that book?" Ryan asked.

"Ah," Jason wiped the side of his mouth with a napkin. "Yes, well, I have been thinking about it. I just haven't put pen to paper."

"You mean, a laptop?" Chance scoffed.

"Yeah, but I'm a useless typist. I take ages."

"Well, you can't write on paper and then get it typed. It will take twice as long." Chance stated.

"And no one can translate a doctor's writing anyway," Ryan mocked in between bites.

"I know!" Jason laughed. "But… I thought I could just buy some software that would type when I spoke… you know, there's plenty of that tech stuff out there," Jason responded before taking another bite of his burger.

"I can type it for you." Olivia stated. "I'm about 53 words per minute," she said as she ate her fries.

They all looked up from their meals and stared at Olivia.

"What?" she laughed. "You don't believe me?"

"Yeah, it's not that." Ryan grinned. "I just don't picture you as a speed typist."

Olivia snorted. "Hey, I'm pretty good… I did a touch-typing course at the Youth Center, so I could do all my assignments quickly."

"I don't expect you to do that, Olivia. I know how busy you are with your firm—"

"It's fine," she waved him off. "I'd be happy to. I'm not working all the time. I've got weekends."

"Well, only if you want to. I wouldn't expect you to do this for me, you've already done more than enough."

"All good, we can start this Saturday if you like?"

"NO!" they all chimed in, then laughed together.

"It's our wedding," Chance said kindly.

"Oh, that's right, sorry." Olivia said, slightly embarrassed that she had forgotten.

"That's fine," Jason stated. "We can do it the Saturday after," he smiled.

"You want another Coke, Jase?" Ryan asked.

"Sure, happy to take in more sugar. I'll jog it off later tonight." He grinned.

THE NEXT MORNING, BEN SAT IN A LEATHER CHAIR OPPOSITE HIS accountant, Charles.

Charles looked up blankly from the paperwork on his desk and calmly stated, "So, looking at your financials, Ben, you need to sell your assets."

"Is there any other way?"

"Not unless you can get a high-paying job within the next month. You have no available cash."

"Gees!" Ben rubbed his hand though his hair, then got up out of the chair and started pacing anxiously. "If I downsize the house, will it get me out of trouble then?" he asked with concern.

"Not exactly. Prices in housing have dipped substantially and the fact that you got into a bidding war and paid nearly 600,000 more than the property was worth, doesn't help. You won't get your money back. I think you would be lucky to get 75 percent back in the current market."

Ben kept pacing. "It is a prime location, and the market was hot. That's why I went for it."

"Well, I told you not to get into a fight over that property. Anyway, it will not help your cause now."

"What if I sell the lot—cars, everything? Where will it get me then?"

"If you can sell the house quickly, and all your shares and assets," Charles did some quick figures on his laptop. "You will still be short 3.8 million."

"Gees," Ben raised his voice. "Surely there's a way? Maybe I should just get someone who *knows* what they're doing and can help me." He started getting nasty.

"Fine, Ben, but you need to pay them. You already owe me 35K and I'll probably never see that." Charles smirked.

"Okay, okay," Ben backed down, "I'm sorry, I'm just frustrated..." Ben thought for a moment while he paced, "So, what are my options?"

"File for bankruptcy."

"I can't, that will—"

"It's your only option, Ben—to keep the creditors off your back. You need to get in first."

"But that will hinder my future. I won't be able to borrow or set up a—"

"Unfortunately, you don't have a choice. It's the only way."

———

JASON ARRIVED AT THE PENITENTIARY VISITOR'S RECEPTION AREA.

"Jason Miller to see Dennis Talbot."

The receptionist smiled, tapped the keys on her keyboard, and then looked at Jason with concern. "Dennis is not here. They have transported him to the State hospital."

"Didn't he just get out of the infirmary?"

"He did, Mr. Miller, but there was an incident when he returned and he is now at NYS Hospital."

"Oh gees. Is he all right?"

She looked at her computer screen. "It says that he is in critical condition at present."

"What happened?"

"I'm sorry, sir, but I cannot give out that information. Are you a relative?"

"A friend." Jason said, as he ran his hand through his hair with concern. "Can I visit him?"

"No visitors allowed."

"Can you at least let me know how he's going? I'm a doctor."

"You're welcome to call the hospital, Dr. Miller. They may provide you with limited information about his condition, but I can't allow visitors until I get approval."

"I understand." He sighed. "Thank you for your help."

"You're welcome, Dr. Miller."

Jason walked back out of the correctional center and got into his car. He drove a few miles down the road before he put a call into the hospital.

"NYS Hospital, how may I direct your call?"

"Can I speak with Dr. Peter Chambers, please?"

"Whom may I say is calling?"

"Dr. Jason Miller."

"One moment, please."

Jason waited and listened to the soothing music on the telephone line.

"Jase… buddy, how have you been?" the familiar voice of Peter Chambers responded.

"Hey Pete, I'm well. And you?"

"Great! Busy, but great." He laughed. "So, I take it that this isn't a social call, we're not doing a golf day?"

"Sorry Pete, it's not. I was wondering if you could give me information on a patient you have. Correctional services brought him in. His name is Dennis Talbot."

"Sure, hang on. I'll search the system."

Jason could hear Peter's computer keys tapping.

"Mm, okay. Nasty one."

"What happened?"

"He presented in cardiac arrest, caused by pulmonary laceration between the sixth and seventh intercostal space, piercing the LLL, resulting in a large pneumothorax and…" he took a breath as he read the information on the screen, "has hemothorax in the pleural cavity…and blood loss from the intercostal bleeding."

"What caused it?"

"Stabbing."

"Is he stable?"

"At present, but it says that he is still critical."

"Okay, thanks Pete. Listen, can I call you later tonight to get an update?"

"Sure, I'm on until 11.30. Call me just before then if you like… Is he a friend of yours?"

"Kinda. Thanks Pete, I'll talk to you tonight."

"OH, MAN! REALLY? HE GOT KNIFED?" RYAN SAID, SHAKING HIS HEAD IN disbelief as he spoke to Jason on his cell.

"Yeah, it's not good. He's not out of the woods yet, either." Jason responded uneasily.

"So, what does that mean for him?"

"Well, if he gets through this, he'll stay in hospital for a few weeks on medication and will need to do regular breathing exercises for his lungs. But, if there isn't much damage to the heart from his heart attack, he should recover reasonably well."

"That's sad. Just when you made some progress."

"Yeah, we need to pray that he will pull through Ryan, he's not out of danger yet… and I know where he is headed if he doesn't make it."

DENNIS LAY MOTIONLESS ON HIS HOSPITAL BED, WITH THE TUBE IN HIS SIDE draining the fluid, and the respirator clicking and whirring as it oxygenated his lungs. He was unconscious and unaware of his surroundings. The trauma from the attack caused a cardiac arrest, and it was several minutes before they discovered Dennis lying unconscious on the floor in a mass of blood.

As the machine breathed for him, Dennis dreamed deeply. He dreamed of many things, but one dream was clearer than all. It was of Suzannah.

"Dennis, I have missed you so much." She said as she cupped his head in her hands and kissed him gently on the lips.

He didn't answer, but looked at his wife in awe, staring at her beauty. She was just like he remembered.

"Come sit over here," she beckoned him as she sat on a picnic seat in their favorite park. "I want to talk to you." she smiled.

Dennis sat close. He turned towards her and stared. He couldn't take his eyes off her beauty. She seemed different—she emitted peace and seemed to glow. She looked up at him and he gently tilted her chin and kissed her on the lips. He smiled as the familiar feeling of being with her washed over him. "I've missed you so much... I love you Suzannah."

"I love you too, Dennis." She responded and kissed him back. They embraced in a long and meaningful squeeze. "I need to talk to you," she smiled and took his hand, then looked into his eyes. "I want you to forgive me... for what I did to you... for what I did to us."

He stared at her completely confused, his thoughts racing. *Was he dreaming, or was this reality? Was she alive, and they were in their favorite park? Or was he imagining this?* He said nothing, but stared back blankly.

"What I did to us, to you... and to our child was wrong. There is no excuse for it and if I had my chance again, I wouldn't do it."

Dennis's dream quickly rewound back to images of the arguments, the screaming matches, the silent treatment and last, the sheer pain and anguish of her death, followed by the long listless days that he had endured without her. He stared at her with tears in his eyes. "Why... why did you do it?"

"I'm so sorry, Dennis," she said with a tear streaking down her cheek. "I'm so, so sorry!"

Dennis said nothing. The feeling of being near her again, but the confusion that it wasn't real, just gave him more pain.

"I need to tell you that when I jumped, I realized it was a mistake. I cried out to God to save me, and he did, Dennis... he did." She looked at him seriously. "Jesus saved me, Dennis, and I am now in Heaven. If I hadn't asked for forgiveness before I died, then I would have ended up in Hell," she said plainly. "Dennis, I am in Heaven with our daughter… the one I took from you… our daughter Rosie." She said as she looked sideways and then held out her hand.

Rosie stepped forward out of a hazy mist, and Dennis saw his daughter for the very first time.

CHAPTER FORTY-NINE

DENNIS SLOWLY STOOD UP AND TOOK A FEW STEPS TOWARDS ROSIE. He looked at her through blurred eyes as he gently bent down and kneeled before her. "Rosie," he whispered. "I'm-I'm… your daddy," he choked.

Rosie beamed a beautiful smile and suddenly pitched forward and embraced him lovingly.

Dennis wrapped his arms around her and buried his face into her soft, blonde curly hair and wept. He held her tightly as wave after wave of raw emotion flowed over him.

"I love you, Daddy," Rosie said innocently and earnestly, as if somehow this little girl knew exactly what Dennis needed to hear.

"I love you too, Rosie… I love you so much, sweetie." He said as he clung on to her.

Suzannah smiled as she sat and watched. She knew this time was precious and was needed… for Dennis.

Dennis sat on the grass and Rosie sat beside him and huddled into him, looking at him lovingly.

Suzannah joined them. "Dennis, I know what you did… I know you tried to kill Jason and I know you are paying for that decision right now. What I did was wrong, but there was no need to hurt Jason because it was *my* choice and *my* actions. It's nothing to do with him, and what you did was unacceptable. I have to tell you this because you need to repent and ask Jesus to forgive you for your sins. You need to follow Him, otherwise you will end up in a place of torment."

Dennis stared at Suzannah blankly, confusion muddling his mind. *Is this a dream, or is this conversation real?* The images swiftly changed in his mind and he was back in his house, sitting at the dining table reading the daily newspaper. The dream then jumped to him listening to Suzannah talking on the phone to her parents, and then randomly changed to him mowing the lawn in his backyard. Rapidly, Suzannah's voice cut through the erratic images of his hallucination.

"Dennis, are you listening to me? You need to repent and ask Jesus into your life. When you die, I want you to spend eternity with us—but you won't Dennis, if you don't repent," she said, her face desperate and serious.

Rosie innocently looked up at Dennis. Her perfect green eyes seemed to penetrate right into his soul.

And then Dennis felt an overwhelming fear glide over him. Swiftly, the dream changed. He saw a dark mist swirling like a mass of bees forming in the trees nearby, edging slowly toward them—alive, swarming, and exuding evil.

The mist lurched towards him as if its dark arms were raking at him, trying to drag him in. He felt a strong, overwhelming malevolent presence as it encased him and wrapped its tendrils forcefully around him.

"Dennis? DENNIS?" Suzannah panicked.

The ground started to shake and break apart beneath him. Chunks of earth shifted sideways, cracking and opening up into a cavernous black hole.

He began to fall.

"DENNIS!" Suzannah shrieked as she reached out her hand, stretching towards him.

He tumbled downwards, twisting and churning, grasping and grappling to seize hold of something. He could smell the raw open earth—he felt the malicious darkness locking onto his leg and pulling him further and further down into the blackness.

The cardiac monitor attached to Dennis's chest in the hospital abruptly beeped erratically and an alarm on the machine sounded. Two nurses came running into the room, looking at the rapid, irregular heartbeat on the screen.

"He's in VF." One nurse shouted as she hit the emergency button on the wall. She frantically removed Dennis's breathing tube. "Start CPR," she said to a male nurse as she quickly readied the AED machine.

Dennis felt himself falling into a yawning black void. His panic and fear deepened as he felt the evil closing in on him. The piercing grip of claws on his leg intensified, locking on tighter as he was being drawn downwards. He screamed in a frenzied panic, desperately scraping at the sides of the endless hole, grappling for something to cling onto. His fingernails tore off as he fought against whatever was dragging him downwards. The calm dream had become a violent nightmare.

The female nurse quickly placed on the electrode pads onto Dennis's chest. "Stand clear!" She cautioned.

The male nurse quickly moved back.

The female nurse hit the 'shock' button, and Dennis's body lurched under the jolt of the current. They watched as the line on the machine spiked and then became erratic again, still showing that Dennis was in ventricular fibrillation. The male nurse jumped in and immediately started resuscitation for two minutes.

"1, 2, 3, 4, 5…" the male nurse counted the CPR cycle.

"Still VF!" the female nurse stated. "Stand clear!" Again, she pressed the button and Dennis's body arched under the shock wave. The emergency doctor and resuscitation team raced into the room as the male nurse continued to administer CPR.

" We've delivered two shocks." The female nurse stated.

"Get the epinephrine ready." The doctor said and watched on as the male nurse continued CPR. "Still in VF! Epinephrine!" he demanded and then injected the drug into Dennis's arm. They continued to alternate between the AED, epinephrine, and resuscitation… but Dennis's heart beat remained rapid.

"Get me amiodarone 300 mg," the doctor shouted.

Dennis continued to fall. The darkness and fear had become so intense he thought his stomach would turn inside out. The grip on his leg was excruciatingly tight as he felt claws biting into his flesh, piercing through his skin and into his muscle. He felt fear like he had never experienced before.

His thoughts raced with confusion. *Am I still dreaming? Is this a nightmare, or is this real?*

He continued to scream in terror as he was being dragged further and further down, falling into a thick shroud of evil blackness.

CHAPTER FIFTY

"Peter?" Jason said, surprised as he answered his cell.

"Your friend is in VF."

"Oh no!"

"They're working him right now. It's not looking good!"

"Which room?"

"J16."

"Okay, thanks." He hung up, then dialed Ryan. "Dennis is in trouble. He may not make it."

"Are you going there?"

"I'm on my way now."

"I'll pray!"

The team of emergency staff worked frantically to get Dennis's heart beating normally again.

"Time?" the doctor asked.

"13 minutes," a nurse responded.

Dennis felt the fall slowing, and the presence of evil intensify. He again desperately reached for something to grab onto, but there was nothing. He still felt the gripping pain of something on his leg, dragging him downward. His hysteria exploded as he felt things reaching out for him, scratching and touching him as he progressed further and further into the void.

Ryan called Chance and then Pastor Trent, asking them to pray for Dennis.

Jason drove unnervingly fast, covering the 40-minute drive to the hospital in only 27 minutes. He screeched to a halt in a doctor's car park, slammed the door and ran.

"Give him another shock," the doctor ordered.
Again, Dennis's body arched under the current.
The line on the monitor spiked twice, then became erratic again.
"CPR," the doctor shouted.
Then suddenly the monitor line jumped,

once…

twice…

and then…

Flatlined_____.

Dennis's fall abruptly stopped, and it felt as though he was standing on a solid stone. The surrounding darkness was thick, enveloping him and crawling over him like a mass of black lice.
"Dennissssss!" a familiar voice hissed right into his ear.
He jumped sideways.
"Bahahaha," it laughed. "You've arrived at your place… of peace," it mocked as the darkness seemed to pull back and the face coming out of the blackness was his hideous tormentor.

The doctor immediately took over the CPR on Dennis. "Come on, come on…" he whispered as he rhythmically pumped Dennis's chest.

The face and head were that of a reptile with snake-like features. Its many teeth were like long thin syringes surpassing its lower jaw, ready to inject poison. The eyes were reptilian, glowing a bright green with the occasional flicking third eyelid across its lens. Its neck was long but its body, although covered in rough black scales, took a similar form to a large-muscled man.

"Welcome Dennisssssss," it hissed. "You finally made it." it taunted as it wrapped its giant claws around Dennis's neck.

Dennis screeched a blood-curdling scream. "HELP MEEEE!".

RYAN CONTINUED TO PRAY, AND AS HE DID, UNSEEN ANGELS STARTED falling from the sky like a celestial kaleidoscope across the firmament.

DENNIS SCREAMED WITH HYSTERIA, FRANTICALLY TRYING TO REMOVE HIS attacker.

"Dennissssss, we have been together for a long time now. This is where you belong… with me… forever," it hissed into his ear.

"NOOOOOOOO! SUZANNAH! he screamed.

"Hahaha, Susannah isn't here," it grinned, with yellowing mucus dripping from its jaw. "You're not leaving Dennissssss. This is now your home," it laughed.

The flatline on the monitor immediately spiked and bleeped.

"We've got a beat," the doctor said as he kept working on Dennis.

"HELP ME, HELP ME, GOD HELP MEEEEE!" Dennis screamed and fought as the demon lurched forward and bit viciously into his neck, the long spiking teeth penetrating and ripping into his muscle and bone. As he felt the poison inject into his veins, the chilling liquid and excruciating pain jolted his body.

The monitor bleeped again…

… and then again, sporadically.

"Give him 150 amiodarone." the doctor barked.

"We've maxed the dosage." A nurse responded.

"JUST GIVE IT TO HIM!" he yelled as he continued to do CPR.

The nurse administered more drug into the intravenous line.

"Defib," the doctor demanded.

"Stand back." The nurse hit the 'shock' button.

"Come on, this is it man… come on… don't die on me now." the doctor pleaded.

The power shocked Dennis's fibrillating heart once again, and his chest lifted off the table with an intense force.

Dennis felt a jolt, like a lightning bolt had hit him.

At once, a burnishing, bright light lit up the cavernous black hole and he could see the evil mass that had surrounded him. He heard the piercing screams as the light hit the deformed, evil black creatures, sending them scurrying away for cover.

He felt a gentle hand upon his shoulder and heard the familiar kind voice say, "It's not your time."

With force, he was swiftly pulled upwards, gaining momentum at a rapid pace. He looked at the large angel gripping hold of his arm as they ascended. As he glanced back down, he saw the intense darkness that had encased him fill back in and disappear quickly behind him.

JASON RAN TO THE HOSPITAL ENTRY AND HIT THE ELEVATOR BUTTON. IT seemed like an eternity before the doors opened.

AS DENNIS BURST FREE FROM THE CAVERNOUS BLACK HOLE, HE desperately tried to scream, but he couldn't. His mind raced with acute panic. *DON'T LET ME DIE. DON'T LET ME DIE.*

The cardiac monitor beeped rhythmically, and the doctor watched the monitor intently. Dennis's heart had started to beat normally again, but the rhythm was increasing rapidly.

Dennis came out struggling and thrashing. His eyes popped wide open in terror as he screamed. "DON'T LET ME DIE. JESUS, JESUS, JESUS… JESUS… HELP ME!"

The team tried to calm Dennis as he flung about on the bed, knocking over the IV stand.

"CALM DOWN, CALM DOWN DENNIS!" the doctor yelled. "YOU'RE ALIVE!" he clasped Dennis's shoulders, holding him down, and stared into his eyes to gain recognition.

Dennis froze and gazed at the doctor. His horror-filled eyes conveyed the utmost terror as he momentarily halted in his panic and gazed deep into the doctor's eyes for a guarantee he was alive.

His dread subsided as he realized he was safe. But swiftly, his emotions overtook him, tears flooding his eyes as he broke down and sobbed uncontrollably.

Jason ran to the room and halted, staring at Dennis and the medical staff that surrounded him. They were busy preparing the oxygen mask and settling him.

Dennis saw Jason in the doorway and burst into tears again. "Jason," he said with relief, as he reached out towards him. "I have to talk to you." he choked.

CHAPTER FIFTY-ONE

Jason sat alongside Dennis's bed. The guard at the door didn't seem to mind or care that Jason had spent the last 30 minutes with him while Dennis told Jason about his nightmare.

"I need you to forgive me Jason, for what I did to you." he cried with tears streaming, "I'm so, so sorry. Please forgive me." Dennis's breathing became rapid.

"I already did, Dennis. You're fine now... you're alive, okay? Now take slow breaths. The oxygen will help."

Dennis pushed the mask tightly against his face and took a few breaths to calm himself before he talked again. "I think it was real... they said that I actually died." His whole body started shaking with emotion.

"I believe you." Jason nodded reassuringly. "Now calm yourself and breathe slowly." he said concerned.

"I mean... that... that thing." He said, screwing up his face. "It was there... it's the same voice that I've been hearing for so long."

"So... you've been hearing that same voice?"

"Yes, it has been relentless. It doesn't leave me alone. Day and night, it harasses me. It was the voice that kept telling me to kill you." He then inhaled deeply into the mask and winced at the pain from his injuries.

"Hey, I can't let you in. Who are you?" the guard demanded.

"Ah, I'm Ryan Carter... Dr. Jason Miller called me." Ryan said.

The guard entered the room. "Is he with you?" he asked Jason.

"Yes!"

The guard turned and motioned to Ryan to enter, then leaned back over to Jason. "Look, I don't want any trouble. This is against regulations, so keep it down... and keep *him* calm," he pointed to Dennis.

Ryan pulled up a chair beside the bed.

"Dennis, this is Ryan—the guy I told you about."

"Hi." Ryan said.

Dennis nodded towards him nervously, and then suddenly he felt a wash of fear and sweat rush over him.

You didn't think you could get away from me that easily—did you, Dennissss? it was the voice.

"No!" Dennis clasped his hands over his ears and looked at them frantically. "Please make it stop."

"What? What is it, Dennis?" Jason asked.

"It's... it's back!" he said with fear, recalling the image of the reptilian face. He started to sob with dismay, his breathing increasing rapidly again.

Jason glanced at Ryan nervously.

"Dennis, I don't know what you're hearing, but there is only one way to be free of this torment." Ryan said, taking control.

Tell them to leave, tell them to shut up. They're lying. You'll never be free—you deserve this. The voice demanded.

"Shut up!" Dennis said, squinting and clasping his head and breathing oxygen fast. "It's telling you to shut up, saying that... that you're lying."

The guard peered around the corner suspiciously for a moment.

"Dennis, listen to me." Ryan stated. "Don't listen to what that demon is saying. We are not lying. You need Jesus."

Dennis looked at Ryan and froze, trying to process what he had just said. *Demon?* He thought. *Is that what it is?* "D-demon?" he finally asked.

"Yes, that thing you're hearing... is a demon," Ryan responded.

Dennis looked at Jason for reassurance.

"He's right," Jason stated. "You need to repent and ask Jesus to be Lord of your life, just like Suzannah told you to."

Tell them to leave now! The voice snapped.

Dennis clasped his head tighter. "I-I will do anything to be free of this and to never return to that place."

Noooooo, don't listen to them. The voice hissed in panic.

"Shut up!" Dennis blurted, wrapping his arms around his head. "Please hurry, help me," he pleaded to Ryan and Jason.

NO! I WILL KILL YOU DENNISSSSS. YOU BELONG TO ME! The voice screamed into his psyche.

"Repeat these words," Ryan said. "Jesus, I believe you died on the cross for my sins and rose to life, and that through you I can have everlasting life. I am a sinner, and I ask for your forgiveness for all that I have done. I repent of my sins and choose to turn away from my old ways and follow you… to obey you and declare that you are my Lord and Savior."

Dennis repeated those words and as he did, the peace fell upon him like light feathery snowflakes. He couldn't see it, but he felt it—as the blackness that encased his hardened heart cracked and splintered into tiny shards, disintegrating. The large angel that was beside him watched as the beam of light shone on him and through him and his heart became shining and brand new.

"In the name of Jesus," Ryan said, "I command you, demon, to release Dennis's mind, and leave."

The demon's claws immediately clicked and popped free.

"NOOOO!" it hissed and spat as it was forced to release its grip on Dennis's mind. It fell backwards and looked up, frightened at the guardian angels that had dropped into the room.

"NO! DON'T TOUCH ME! I'LL GO, I'LL GO NOW! DON'T BANISH ME!" it screamed out in panic as it faced the myriad of shining heavenly beings.

"I'll gladly finish him," the large angel said, as he stepped forward and plunged his blazing sword into the demon's abdomen. The sword arced, sizzled and flashed as the demon screamed out in agony, its tongue flicking desperately as it bent over from the blazing angelic weapon.

Dennis heard the tormented cry of his assailant and knew that he was free. The silence and relief coated him like a warm, soft blanket. He lay and closed his eyes, feeling peace for the first time… in a very long while.

CHAPTER FIFTY-TWO

THE REST OF THE WEEK PASSED BY QUICKLY. JASON AND MARG WORKED together closely with the hired change agents. The plans were in motion to transform each center into providing more services and instantly cease terminations. Protestors still rallied outside each center, but now for different reasons. The protestors were pro-choice and upset at the decision to cease abortions.

Jason had conducted a video conference for all staff, illustrating the transition. Some employees quit, while others were excited to embrace the new future.

Amid Jason's busy schedule, he and Ryan had visited Dennis both Thursday and Friday in the hospital. They read the Bible together, and Dennis's demeanor and face had transformed. He looked and acted completely different, and for the first time in a very long time, he had felt hope.

———

JASON WAS SO RELIEVED TO MAKE IT THROUGH THE WEEK, BUT ALSO excited that Friday had rolled around and he could enjoy Ryan's buck's night. He jumped in his BMW, pulled out from the office underground carpark and dialed Ryan.

"Hey bud," Ryan answered.

"You good?"

"Sure am. I've got the hot food in the oven, Dad's manning the drinks station and the guys should start arriving in about half an hour."

"Great, I probably won't get there for another hour. I've got to go home and sort out a few things."

"No worries. I'll ensure the guys don't eat all the food." Ryan laughed.

"See you soon."

Jason pulled into his drive and rushed up the stairs towards his front door. He thought he glimpsed someone dive around the side of his house. *What now?* he thought in irritation. He ran around the side path leading towards the back of his house and gingerly looked around. "Who's there?" he called.

Nothing but silence. He continued around the back of his house into the yard, searching for an intruder hiding. He saw nothing.

"Hey Jason," Mr. Evens, his neighbor peeked over the fence at him. "What are you hollering about?"

"Oh, hi Mr. Evens, how are you?"

"Good, good."

"Hey, did you see anyone in my yard?"

"No, when?"

"Just now."

"No, I didn't… but that's a worry." Mr. Evens looked around with concern.

Jason didn't want to burden the eighty-nine-year-old, so he said, "Don't worry. I've had a big week and it may just have been my imagination." He laughed.

"I get that a lot," he chuckled. "All right, you have a pleasant night then." He waved and walked back into his house.

"You too!" Jason smiled, then stood surveying his yard. He knew he had seen someone, so he walked around the other side of his house. Still nothing. He figured that if there was an intruder, he was long gone by now.

I'll install security cameras outside, he thought.

JASON STOOD NERVOUSLY AS A GROOMSMAN UP THE FRONT OF THE CHURCH alongside Ryan. He didn't know why he was nervous… he just was. They all looked amazing in their deep navy-blue tuxedos, and the crisp white shirts contrasted nicely against their black lapels. Each of them wore a white rose pinned to their lapel, along with white handkerchiefs in their side pockets. All but Ryan wore the straight black ties, he donned a black bow tie.

They murmured amongst themselves as they waited for the music to start and the bride to enter.

As Chance walked down the aisle, Ryan felt as though his breath had been swept away. His heart was about to burst with joy and his stomach felt like there were a thousand butterflies trying to escape. The smile on his face could not describe the pride and excitement that he had been feeling for this day. This was the day he was to marry his best friend, his love, the one that God had chosen for him before the origin of time.

Chance slowly moved rhythmically with the music, taking small steps down the aisle towards Ryan, her bouquet of cream and white roses held low in front. Her white dress was modern yet modest, the scalloped lace off-the-shoulder neckline showed her toned and tanned shoulders, yet created a graceful, demure elegance. The lace overlay covered the entire dress and her back. The fitted-waist design turned into a tulle skirt with a small train to create a timeless and romantic dress.

Her soft curled brown hair with caramel highlights, hung long on her shoulders with loose twists pulling the top half of her hair back. Her laced white veil fell gently and perfectly over her face.

Ryan was mesmerized. He didn't even notice the bridesmaids move into position, but could only focus on Chance.

They stood together looking into each other's eyes whilst Pastor Trent asked them to say their vows, and they did with loving words. When it was over, they both strode down the aisle hand in hand with beaming smiles.

The reception was at a quaint restaurant. It was only when they were all seated that Jason noticed Olivia sitting at one of the guest tables.

Ryan leaned over to Jason. "We had some last-minute cancelations and Chance had wanted to invite Olivia. I forgot to tell you—I hope you don't mind."

"Not at all. I can see Chance and Olivia striking a good friendship. I think it's great."

Olivia looked at Jason and waved. Jason nodded with a smile and then continued on with his groomsman duties.

They all watched as Ryan and Chance moved onto the dance floor for their wedding waltz. Five minutes later, the groomsmen and bridesmaids joined them in the dance.

Afterwards, Jason walked over to Olivia and asked if she would like to dance. She accepted with a smile.

"You look like you have done this several times," Olivia stated as they gently glided around the floor.

"I've attended a lot of weddings—just never my own." He smiled.

"How's the clinic change going?"

"Great… it feels fantastic to be finally moving forward," he said, as they maneuvered around and dodged other couples on the floor.

"I've got the new paperwork drawn up if you want to call into my office during the week."

"Sure, or can you bring them when you come over on Saturday?"

"Oh yes. I didn't think, I'll bring them then." She smiled.

The music stopped. It was time for the cake, so they both went back to their seats.

The night flew and soon the crowd stood watching as Ryan and Chance's limousine drove off, heading into the night.

"They will love the Maldives," Olivia sighed with a little envy.

"Yeah." Jason said reminiscently as he remembered holidaying there.

"Well, I better get going," Olivia said.

"Do you need a lift?"

"No, I drove. I'm parked over there."

"No worries. Well, if I don't speak to you during the week, I'll see you next Saturday for the big book writing session." He grinned, "I'm really not sure how it will go though, I'm not a writer."

"It will be fine," she laughed as she turned and walked to her car.

CHAPTER FIFTY-THREE

ONE WEEK LATER

"SO, HOW DO YOU WANT TO DO THIS?" JASON ASKED AS OLIVIA PLACED her laptop on his dining table.

"Um," she thought for a moment. "Just talk and I will type. It won't matter if you ramble, we can fix it later."

"Okay. Do you want a drink?"

"Sure. Lemonade, if you have it?"

Jason went to the refrigerator and retrieved a can of lemonade and a glass of ice, poured it for her, and placed it on the table.

He sat down beside her. "All right… so where should I start? I've never done this before," he shifted nervously.

"Just start from the beginning… I don't know, maybe start at the moment that you first remember. The feelings you had, what you saw… maybe start off with what your first words or thoughts were. I guess your account of what happened from your perspective and not in the third person. It doesn't have to be perfect — this is only the first draft."

"So, I'll just start off with exactly what I said… and what I experienced, then?"

"Perfect!" She smiled.

"Okay. The first thing I remember saying is… Oh God, I can't breathe. God, God I can't breathe. Help me… somebody…"

It was mid-afternoon, and Ben was sporting a massive hangover. Still fuming from being fired, and now having to file for bankruptcy, he had hit it hard last night.

The blonde woman beside him stirred, and Ben looked over at her, surprised, not recalling last night's events. It was a complete haze.

Great! he thought. *How do I get her out of my house?*

She rolled over onto her back, took a deep breath that ended with a snort, then progressed into a dull rhythmic snore.

Ben rolled his eyes and sighed. He laid quietly, but could feel the rage inside growing, the humiliation of being fired. The news reports about it had his head swimming with hateful thoughts about Jason. He secretly thundered inside and wanted revenge for what Jason had done to him. His mind was spinning on what his future would hold. He bounced from anger to deep despair at the prospect of losing everything that he had worked hard for.

"Wow! That's intense," Olivia said, shaking her head in wonderment. "To go through what you did… I mean, I know you told me previously, but obviously not in such detail… So, we probably have six chapters already. I think we are off to a great start."

"Yeah, I think so. Did you want to get an early dinner? Maybe eat out or—get takeout?"

"Let's eat out, we've been in here all day," she said as she got up and stretched. "We've done over ten thousand words."

"Is that good? I mean it sounds a lot… and it feels like I've talked all day."

"You have," she laughed. "It's a great start. I found a blog that said that you should aim for over 80K in total. At this rate, we could knock this over in about two months if we're lucky." She beamed, happy with herself.

"Right, so after we write this, then what?"

"We polish it, and then we find an agent. I think it will be easy because of who you are… and also because your story is unique, you may even end up having a few publishers to choose from."

"Okay, sounds like a big deal."

"It IS a big deal." She chuckled. "Your experience will impact so many people and tell the world why you feel so strongly against abortion —and more importantly, show how God feels about it. I think it will be huge."

"You think?"

"Definitely… I can feel it."

BEN HAD FINALLY GOTTEN RID OF THE WOMAN. HE HAD SHAKEN HER AWAKE and made a lame excuse that he promised to go see his grandma. She believed it, got dressed and left in a cab. Relieved, he called Bruce.

"How's your head?" Bruce answered.

"Sore."

"Do you remember anything from last night? You hit the scotch pretty hard."

"I don't, but I found a blonde in my bed."

Bruce laughed. "Wow, you must have been out of it."

"You got time to meet up again tonight? I need to talk to you."

"No, but how about tomorrow?"

Ben sighed. "Sure."

"Besides, I don't think you would be up to going anywhere by the sounds of it."

"Nah, I'm pretty trashed."

"Go back to bed and sleep it off."

"MORNING, MARG," JASON SAID AS HE STRODE INTO THE OFFICE AND handed Marg a takeaway cappuccino.

"Thanks Jase. How was your weekend?"

"It was great! So much better knowing that I can come here and run my company again." He grinned.

"I'll bet. On that… I've put the completed plans and additional equipment needs for each center on your desk. Also, the sales agent rang and we've sold most of the termination equipment from each of the centers."

"Good work. How's Chandler going with overseeing the renovations?"

"He said that they're underway and on track for completion within the next two weeks."

"Perfect! Looks like everything is going to plan. Thanks Marg." He said as he walked down the hall to his office with a bounce in his stride, feeling joy welling inside with every step.

Jason turned on his laptop and opened the mail sitting on his desk. He read each letter, but one made his face instantly drain and pale.

"You should have died. You don't deserve to live... You will pay."

That was it, in bold black typed print. Jason's thoughts spun. He studied the letter, looking for anything to show where it had come from. There was nothing but a plain envelope with his name on the front.

He shifted uncomfortably in his chair, then resigned to the fact that it was just more hate mail that he received so often. He binned it and checked his emails.

"I can get you a job as a physician at Woodside Medical." Bruce stated.

"What will it pay?" Ben asked.

"220K."

"What about the CEO position at A&K?"

"That will not happen. I'm sorry."

"Gees, Bruce. I can't live on that."

"Ben, wake up to yourself. A $220K salary is more than the majority earn and second, no one will touch you because of what happened at Miller. No one will trust you to run their company. Be grateful I can land you a position anywhere right now."

Ben swore. "Bruce," he pointed his finger nastily. "You were the one to suggest the bribe and to push him out."

"I merely hinted at it. I didn't say do it... that was your choice." He smirked.

"Oh yeah, how the worm turns! Hey, I thought you had my back."

"I do, Ben... I do. Now calm down." Bruce tried to diffuse the situation. "I've got you that position over at Woodside, okay? Things will be fine. Just keep your head down and work hard. You will get through this."

Ben sighed in frustration and ran his hand through his hair. "Yeah okay. Thanks, Bruce. When do they want me there?"

"You start Wednesday."

JASON HAD PUT THE THREAT NOTE OUT OF HIS MIND. HE HAD VISITED Dennis in the hospital and was now at home in his living room, reading his Bible. He sat with his eyes closed for a moment and thought about the verse he had just read in Jeremiah 29:11, "For I know the plans I have for you," declares the Lord, "plans to prosper you and not to harm you, plans to give you hope and a future."

"Thank you, Lord," he whispered gratefully, tears welling in his eyes at the relief that he was finally doing what God had asked him to do nearly a year ago now.

Ryan was right, he thought. *It was God's perfect timing. It was His plan.*

He continued to sit in silence, thinking of the changes and the impact that it would make when a clear voice resonated in his heart. *I love you, Jason. I am so proud of you, my son.*

Those words washed over his soul like a deep, cleansing wave. He could feel the love and warmth engulf him. Those words he so longed to hear as a child, the love that he yearned to feel was gently wrapping its strong arms around him, clothing him with a soothing tenderness. For the first time in his whole life… he felt loved.

CHAPTER FIFTY-FOUR

Saturday

"Are you ready for another big day?" Olivia smiled as she set up her laptop.

"Sure am!" Jason said as he placed a glass of lemonade with ice in front of her. "What was the last thing I said?"

"Mmm," Olivia looked at the last sentence. "It was when Tolman told you that these are all the children you had murdered."

"Oh, yeah… that was like a punch in the stomach. It was terrible." Jason sat down, remembering every aspect. He had found that as he recounted his story to Olivia, it was as if he was there again, reliving every detail. "It was pretty bad," he sighed and looked at Olivia with emotion.

"Jason, I can't understand what you went through. It was tough! But this account is worth telling. People need to know that there is a Hell and a Heaven and that their eternity is at stake. They also need to know that abortion is wrong." She gulped. "Just listening to you has made me realize I can't take what Jesus did for me lightly. I admit… I kind of envy you. You've experienced such an amazing gift, something that you will never forget."

"I'm grateful too, but I'm more grateful that God gave me a second chance at life. I would still be in Hell if he hadn't."

Olivia's eyes sprung wide, and she gasped. "That's it! Second Chance —that's what you should call it," she said, beaming excitedly.

"Yeah, because it is," Jason grinned. "I've been given a second chance at life."

"BRUCE, THE JOB'S A CROC. I HATE IT." BEN SAID ANGRILY OVER THE phone.

"What? You've been there three days. Come on Ben, get a grip."

"It's pathetic! The staff are pathetic, the patients are pathetic, it doesn't pay enough and—"

"Listen here you," he growled, "I stuck my neck out for you… you ungrateful little twerp. Now you buckle up and fly straight. You be thankful that you've got that damn job, you hear me?" Bruce said furiously. "I don't have time for this, Ben. I'm happy to talk, but don't call me whining and complaining," he stated, then hung up.

"SO, HOW HAVE WE DONE?" JASON ASKED.

"We have 20,000 words. That's fantastic!" Olivia beamed.

"Yeah, you're right, that is good. Only sixty thousand to go," he rolled his eyes.

"I know it sounds a lot, but I bet you didn't think we had done ten thousand today?"

"Well, all I know is that it feels like I haven't stopped talking and you haven't stopped typing, only for a quick lunch break. It's been constant."

"A few more weekends like this and we will have it done."

"So… it's eight thirty—did you want to get a bite to eat?"

"Definitely, I'm famished."

"I hope you're okay doing this for me—I mean… you don't have to, Olivia."

"Actually, I am really enjoying it. It's fun!"

"Okay good. As I would hate to think you feel forced into this."

"Not at all."

"Ambrosio's?"

"Why not?" She grinned.

"I should still be the CEO," Ben fumed as he sat alone in a bar. "Another!" he said to the bartender and watched on as he poured him another shot. Ben picked it straight up and threw it down his throat. "Another!" he said again and watched the barman pour yet another shot of whisky.

"This isn't over, Miller. I swear you will pay for what you have done," he grumbled to himself. "… Another!"

"Hello, Dr. Miller," the waiter greeted. "Can I get you both something to drink?" he smiled.

"Can we please have a bottle of mineral water?"

"Certainly," he said, then walked off to get their drinks.

"It's been a big day. Sorry, 9 p.m. is probably a little late to be having dinner."

"Not at all. Sometimes I get so busy with work that I forget to eat at all." Olivia laughed. "It's been a great day. I've enjoyed hearing the details of your experience."

"It's been good… and also bad to relive it. I think retelling it just solidifies that it really happened, that I wasn't just imagining it. I mean, it's been twelve months now."

"I guess it seems so distant, and you question if it really happened."

"Exactly... but I *know* it happened! —Thank you, Ronnie," Jason said to the waiter as he poured the water.

"Are you ready to order, sir?" Ronnie asked.

"Yes. Olivia would like the duck with a side of vegetables, and I'll have the lamb."

"Good choice!" Ronnie nodded, then walked off.

"This is such a nice way to end our day." Olivia smiled and took a sip of her water.

"It is. Hopefully, it shouldn't take up too many more of your Saturdays."

"I don't mind, it's been nice. I would have been out shopping with friends otherwise. Least I'm saving money," she giggled.

"That's a relief then."

"So, your parents passed when you were young?"

"They did. Car accident."

"That must have been hard!"

"It was. But you didn't have a golden upbringing yourself."

"No, I didn't. I always looked at other kids whose parents doted on them. It felt like I was always the outcast. It hurt to see them with their seemingly perfect family, when I kept getting moved on."

"I understand that lack of love feeling. I had to move to my aunt's place, and she is a frosty person… I knew she loved me in her own special way, but she never showed it. I felt like I was an inconvenience and she was doing it out of obligation to my mother."

"I never knew my parents. I heard that my mother had me as a teen and then handed me to the State, so I bounced around in foster care, until I finally found the youth center."

"That's tough!"

"It was," Olivia sighed. "I think the worst is not feeling like you belong, that you haven't got a permanent home, or that you're even loved. You're on edge all the time—you can't relax or be yourself because it's never really your home and they could kick you out at any moment. I had one family go on holidays without me. They packed up my stuff and took me over to a respite house and just left me there. I was only seven years old, but I remember how it made me feel like it was yesterday. They never came back to pick me up, so they placed me with another family."

"I'm so sorry to hear that."

She nodded. "Unfortunately, that happened a few times, and it is only some of what I've been through… I then resorted to running away all the time." She took another sip of water and became serious. "Jason, you have shared so much with me, things that were deep, so I feel that I'd like to share something with you." She paused and took a breath.

Jason put down his glass and listened attentively.

"When I was fifteen, before I went to the youth center, I found out I was pregnant. I had been drinking, smoking and…" she paused. "sleeping around—just to find some kind of acceptance and love. When I discovered my pregnancy, I was so distraught, not knowing what to do as I didn't have any money… or anyone to turn to. But at around ten weeks I found out that I could get an abortion for free. So, I went to a clinic, and went ahead with the procedure. I honestly can't say that I felt anything afterwards… simply relief, because I knew that I couldn't bring up a child on the streets… I felt then that I had no choice and it was the right thing to do. But once I got to the youth center about twelve months later, I saw things differently."

"Wow Olivia. I would have never imagined you in that situation. It must have been so frightening."

"It was—my life was an absolute mess," she shook her head sadly.

"It must have been terrible being so young without support." Jason consoled, "but you said you saw things differently when you got to the center?"

"Yes, there were two girls that were pregnant when I arrived. One was keeping her baby, and the other was placing hers for adoption. At the time, it didn't really affect me. But occasionally the thought crossed my mind that I too could have found help, like at the center, and I could have at least placed the baby for adoption. I saw that these girls' lives weren't ruined by being pregnant. I realized then that I would have been okay and it actually would have been comforting knowing that the baby was alive— that maybe one day I could meet him or her. But I pushed those feelings down and got on with my life and never thought of it much at all. However, it caught up with me later."

"Oh?"

"Yeah, it was when I had been working for a year as a practicing lawyer in my early thirties that things changed. I began feeling depressed. Feelings of self-loathing, guilt, and sorrow would wash over me about what I had done. I kept thinking about the baby, what it would look like, how old it would be—was it a boy or a girl. I couldn't look at babies or young children without having a gnawing knot of remorse wash over me. Sometimes I would suddenly burst into tears as I kept having this overwhelming regret of deciding to have the abortion and thinking about what I could have done differently. When previously, I hadn't really thought much of it."

"Did anything trigger it?"

"No, there weren't any actual events—it just suddenly started. I realize now I was actually suffering from Post Abortion Syndrome," she paused. "I remember one day just sitting in church and feeling such shame, thinking *how* could God possibly love me after what I had done.

That surely, He couldn't forgive *this* sin," she emphasized with her hands. "What made it worse was my friend and her husband were desperately trying to have a baby, undergoing fertility treatments, and I couldn't bring myself to tell her I had an abortion all those years ago. I was too ashamed to tell anyone, and afraid that people would find out."

"That would have been difficult."

"It was… and it took me down a very dark path. I withdrew from friends, I stopped going to church regularly, I started drinking heavily, and had thoughts of suicide. My thoughts were constantly telling me I wasn't worthy to be forgiven, and God could never love someone who murdered their own child. I would have nightmares, reliving the abortion, or hearing a baby crying, and when I awoke, I felt somewhat numb but also a pain so intense, like my heart was physically being torn apart. I had this nagging guilt following me around like a vulture that wouldn't go away."

She breathed. "Now… after hearing your story, it's become quite obvious to me. It's exactly like you described seeing that demon pouring that black stain on us. That... that guilt and shame of what we have done." She paused. "And with all this going on, I was so frightened that someone from church would find out about my sin… and I would be condemned, hated and judged… so I stayed away and withdrew."

She took a sip of water, then continued. "I would also relive the feelings of that day—it would play over in my mind. The comments from the protesters outside the clinic. They called me a murderer, they said that God will judge me and that I would burn in Hell for killing my baby. It horrified me. I was so traumatized just getting into the clinic. What they were shouting just crushed me, but I couldn't see any way out of my situation. Ironically, this made me angry that they judged me, and I remember sitting in the waiting room feeling resentful toward those people outside who knew nothing about me and what I was going through. I don't know… I look back on it now and wonder if that is the best method to get the message across... it's so… I don't know… judgmental, loud and hate-fueled. I mean, is that really showing the love of Christ?"

"I know what you mean, they're—"

"Of course you do," Olivia realized who she was talking to and shook her head. "Sorry, go on."

"Well, some protestors outside our clinics would shout hateful words to our staff, tell them they are murderers and are committing a crime. We have a separate gated parking entry for each of our clinics for the safety of our employees because we had four staff members attacked several years ago. Thankfully, the injuries were not too serious, but the venom portrayed was shocking. We've had arson attacks and had our clinics vandalized and burgled. We've had staff members stalked both physically and online and have had threats made against them. I cannot count how many threats I've had. Hate letters, confrontations—you name it, it's been done."

"Well, um—you *were* murdered." She smirked.

"Yeah," Jason realized and chuckled. "What am I saying?" He paused, reflecting, "You know, if I hadn't had my Hell experience, I would have never known Christ. The hate I have been exposed to from some people outside my clinics is completely the opposite to what Christ is, and it turned me off all religion… not that I was interested anyway, mind you. However, I'm not saying all protestors are like that, and I have seen an enormous shift over the past few years."

"How so?"

"I've noticed more protestors acting peacefully, and respectfully talking with the women or our staff. They also have banners saying that they will adopt the baby or help financially. Theres definitely been an increase in this peaceful style of protesting outside my clinics. For example, I have a clinic in Rochester and the protesters there were non-violent. It wasn't hate-fueled and didn't involve yelling abuse at the staff or women. One time I was at that clinic going through some paperwork, sitting in the office with the window open, just listening. I heard them tell both the men and women as they walked in that God loves them, that there is financial support and help for the mother and baby, whilst pregnant and after the birth, and also alternatives to abortion. They stood outside and quoted scripture, sometimes singing worship songs, praying, but still telling them the truth about abortion... but it was done calmly. I actually remember stopping what I was doing to listen."

He paused, pondering. "Anyway, that clinic had more women cancel their abortions on the spot than any of my others. I've seen it happen—they'd be in the reception area listening to them outside, then just get up and walk out… or not even make it inside the clinic in the first place, they'd change their mind. We also kept stats and found that we had more cancellations with this style of demonstration. So protesting outside clinics definitely works—it used to aggravate me as it affected our revenue. Funny how things can change," he smiled.

"I think that's the way it should be—do it in love and not yell insults at the women. I truly believe if someone had spoken nicely to me and told me there was help like that, then I probably wouldn't have gone through with mine. Also, you know… there's that saying, that you can catch more flies with honey than with vinegar."

"Yes, true!" he smiled. "Women need support, not only when they are pregnant but also after, and that is what I'm trying to achieve by altering my clinics. I think if I can help change the way society feels about unwanted pregnancies, then we may just see some dramatic changes in the future."

"I couldn't agree more. We all make mistakes, we all have regrets, but if society has programs or, or… I don't know… just more places to go to for help, then I think we would see fewer women having abortions just because they feel that it's their only option. It will open up new opportunities for women—opportunities that will make them feel *good* about their decision, not end up with regret at some point in their lives… like I did."

"Sorry Olivia, we got side-tracked. So, what happened with you?"

"Well, my work suffered. I lost a case that I should have easily won. It was bad!" She paused. "However, luckily a senior attorney helped me appeal, and we ended up winning… but it shattered my confidence and put me in an awkward position with the firm," she said remorsefully. "Anyway, I eventually worked up the courage to tell Sister Marguerite about how I was feeling. I was so ashamed as I hadn't told a soul before, but she was so gracious and just loved me through it. She walked with me on the journey, and showed me that God forgives me—but she also explained that I needed to forgive myself for what I had done. She gave me the verse where God says He forgives our sins as far as the east is from the west."

"It's amazing how many times I've heard that scripture." Jason smiled, thankfully.

"Yeah, but it still took me a while to *really* get it. Anyway, she told me that if God has already forgiven me, then why should I hold on to the guilt and shame? I should let it go, as I'm only hurting myself. She gave me the verse from Romans 8:1 to memorize. 'There is therefore now no condemnation for those who are in Christ Jesus.' I repeated it… I think…

at least fifty times a day. And another one, from 2 Corinthians 5:17 'if anyone is in Christ, he is a new creation; old things have passed away; behold, all things have become new.' I hung onto those two Scriptures so tightly, and every time that vulture of guilt and condemnation circled—I said them aloud."

"So, it worked?"

"It did, but she also sent me to a Christian prayer counseling center, which also assisted significantly. They helped me deal with my past and set me free from the things in my life that I didn't realize were holding me back. They didn't condemn me but showed me kindness and love, which was exactly what I needed. I heard someone say once," she smiled, "that you can catch the fish, but it still needs to be cleaned. I think churches seem to focus on getting people saved, which is exactly what we're called to do. But they are often lacking in educating people on how to get free from their issues... like past mistakes, spiritual bondages, generational curses and guilt in their life—to enable them to walk freely with God. Like the fresh-caught fish, they are not cleaned, but try to continue on in their Christianity like... I don't know, the walking wounded. And that's exactly what I was—a wounded Christian trying to look and live life right, but inside I was still a mess. But by accepting God's forgiveness and forgiving myself, along with the Scriptures, prayer and counseling, these were the keys to setting me free from the guilt and pain that I had carried all those years. It took away the power of the enemy to condemn me."

"So how do you feel now?"

"It's hard to describe... it's like I have the vivid memory of it—I'm definitely not proud of what I have done... I don't think that will ever go away... but the sharpness of the pain and guilt have gone away. I can talk freely about it, help others, and not have that gnawing and stabbing pain because I know deeply that I am forgiven."

"That's awesome, Olivia."

"Yes, but it could have ended badly if I didn't seek help. I'm so glad that I reached out, and since then I've seen specific programs to help post-abortive women which is really encouraging."

"Mm okay, maybe that's something I can add to the clinics."

"I think that would be fantastic, so many women are suffering, burying their hurt so deep as they do not know how to overcome this... Interestingly, through this journey, I've found that many women will often support the pro-choice movement because they are looking to reinforce to themselves that their decision was right. It's like if they feel accepted by others who have done the same, then the guilt will fade. But honestly… deep down, I think every woman knows that it isn't right, no one can kill their baby and still be fine."

She paused. "I also read a study on those who've had an abortion, and they have an increased risk of mental health problems later in their life… which explains me."

"You seem open to talk about your experience, though."

"I choose *whom* I tell my story to." She smiled and shifted slightly in her chair. "I think you have to be wise in who you tell. There are still so-called 'Christians' that will judge and condemn you. But… I've found those who don't… they're going through their own stuff and they understand. They are the true Christians, the ones that don't make you feel guilty or frown upon you for your mistakes. I guess it comes back to removing the log out of your own eye before trying to remove the speck from your brother's," she sighed. "Besides… I have to admit, I *really* struggle with the fact that some Christians think abortion is fine, or even side with or vote for politicians who stand for it. It just saddens me so much that God's people would support it directly… or indirectly through electing people who represent those policies and laws. We shouldn't agree with politicians who are for those policies, but side with those who are against them."

She took a quick breath. "And… I will be bold enough to say, that I believe God will hold people accountable for their vote. It comes down to a vote for good or evil, not a political party. It doesn't matter if you don't like the candidate's personality, or that you've always voted for one particular party all of your life, it's about their policies, and I think this nation has lost that perspective. I'm not the only one who is saying this either, by the way — but if I had cast my vote for a political party that supports abortion, or that has strategies to continue to fund centers that conduct abortions, then I would be on my knees before God asking for forgiveness for my part in voting them in, and then doing everything in my power to help change that policy." She sighed, frustrated. "What we should do is unite and stand against it, so these laws change." She paused and smiled, "I saw another heartbeat bill get passed the other day."

"I saw that too. That's a step in the right direction."

"Anyway, I even know a few Christians that have gone to your clinics. That's what really pains me, those who say they are followers of Jesus, but still believe that abortion is okay... or okay under certain conditions. There's simply no gray, and as a Christian you cannot agree with it."

"Mm I know! We have a religion selection on the forms and there were many Christians, along with other denominations, that came through my clinics. I always thought it strange because a lot of the protestors claimed to be Christians. I simply put it down to double standards, you know?"

"Yes, the 'it's wrong, but not when it happens to me' mentality."

"Yeah, which... I don't understand, knowing what I know now."

"But I also believe the Church needs to step up and help those who find themselves in an unwanted pregnancy situation."

"I thought they would be supportive—you know, love and embrace everyone?"

"Ha! You have a lot to learn about human nature and religion, Jason. Unfortunately, that's not always the case. At that time, I felt I couldn't tell anyone in the church about my abortion. Since then, another congregation member and I have changed our church's culture around this topic and become known as someone people can come to. Our church now assures these women that this sin doesn't disqualify them from the love of God, nor does it make them less worthy in the church. Anyway, we've now helped thirty women in our church make the right decision not to have an abortion, they've either kept their baby or let someone adopt."

"That's great!"

"I know! It's fantastic that I can use my experience and help stop someone else from making the same mistake. Our church now openly talks about the righteous stance on sex before marriage and abortion. But instead of judging and pouring out the wrath of God on those who make mistakes, our church will now embrace and support them through it."

"So, will this view permeate into other churches?"

"I really hope so... because the church, being the body of Christ, is supposed to be a place where people can turn for help. I've noted that preachers seem to be comfortable teaching on other subjects like drugs or pornography, or simply focussing on feeding the poor, but they are too afraid to tackle the topic of abortion from the pulpit because it's so polarizing and they don't want to offend. They go silent!" She sighed. "But if they presented it lovingly, we would see changes in the congregation's view and maybe they would gain the knowledge and courage to stand against it."

Jason nodded thoughtfully.

"I also really feel that social attitudes and values would change if women could see that they have the privilege to be the custodians of a new life. That it is a gift that they can carry children and not a burden. God has blessed us with this amazing ability and we should embrace it, not devalue it."

"Well, my encounter has certainly changed my opinion, and I'll do everything in my power to help facilitate this change of perspective."

"Did you ever doubt your views before your NDE?"

"Not once! I believed termination was truly a choice for the mother, right up to birth." He sighed, reflecting. "I look back now and see how hardened and callous I was. I felt absolutely nothing when performing an abortion or running one of the largest abortion chains in the nation. Honestly, I thought my clinics were helping women eliminate a problem, with the added benefit of making a lot of money. But all I really cared about was the money—not the babies I was slaughtering. Just the money!"

He stopped briefly and took a sip of mineral water. "Olivia, what I did, I can never reverse—I know I deserve to be in Hell. But God saved me and I will do everything to undo what I have created."

Olivia nodded in agreement. "Like me Jason, you have been forgiven by our gracious God."

Jason nodded, "I sure have!"

Olivia sat momentarily, reflecting, "When I was getting counseling, I was sitting in bed one night, just reading my Bible, when I started thinking about my baby. I was pondering the gender. No sooner had that thought entered, I heard God's whisper, *I named him Daniel*." Olivia choked a little, her eyes filled with tears.

"Hey." Jason gently put his hand on hers.

"It's fine," she smiled. "These are tears of gratefulness. Gratefulness that God loves his children so much, that even if they don't get to live a life on earth, He will take them, love them and give them a name of their own… But he also gave me a few minutes with my son."

"Wow!"

"Yeah, it was special. One night I was asleep, dreaming… but I know it was real." she affirmed. "My son, Daniel, came up to me, kissed me on the cheek, and told me he loves me and that he forgives me for what I did. It was brief… but it was healing."

Jason was silent, in awe of Olivia's honesty.

"Look, I don't condemn anyone else who has had an abortion. I've certainly made my own mistakes. Who hasn't?" she smirked. "But I want to see it change. I don't want more children killed, or more women scarred for the decision that they made… or see Satan have a claim to torment and heap guilt and shame upon those who have sinned. To—to drive them to become mentally or emotionally unstable, like I was. I wish I could tell every woman that there is no sin too great that God cannot forgive and all they need to do is reach out to Him."

She took a short breath. "But I will be totally honest with you, Jason. When I saw your name in my appointment book, I decided I would not see you. I knew who you were and what you did. I was going to ask Clair to cancel your appointment, but again… God whispered, telling me to wait and hear you out."

Jason shook his head. "I understand, and wouldn't have blamed you for not seeing me."

"Yeah, I know. I could have ignored that prompting and canceled, and have never known your wonderful testimony and transformation." She smiled and changed the subject. "So, you never wanted to have a family yourself?"

"No, I decided I wouldn't about ten years ago, as I am too focused on my career. You?"

"I'm the same… I think it's because I felt they gave me a chance with the scholarship. I just wanted to excel and make the most of it… The depression phase didn't help either. But I've never really focused on marriage or children anyway… I'm 44 now and I don't see that chang-ing." She laughed.

"Sounds like me," he smiled.

Olivia looked at her watch. "Oh my, it's 11.45. I didn't realize it was that late. I'm sorry, Jason."

"That's fine. I didn't note the time either."

"Well, thanks for the dinner. I think we achieved a lot today."

"We did. I feel like I haven't stopped talking," he smiled. "How about I call you a cab?" he motioned to the waiter.

CHAPTER FIFTY-FIVE

"It was paradise," Chance exclaimed excitedly in the café. "I've never seen such clear blue water, and white sand. Oh, and the coral and fish, they were spectacular—I couldn't get over the colors."

"Yeah, we spent most days kayaking or snorkeling around the reefs. It was so relaxing." Ryan stated.

"I can't believe that I read two books." Chance said. "I haven't read an entire book in twelve months and I've finished two. Oh, how's yours going, Jason?"

"It's getting there," Jason looked over at Olivia.

"It's going really well." Olivia reassured.

"That's great. I cannot wait to read it. I want an ARC like you promised." Ryan demanded.

"Yeah, I know," Jason smiled, "but I've got to get a publisher first."

"Jason has already had a response from three agencies." Olivia beamed excitedly.

"Already?" Chance said, amazed.

"I thought, why wait? Just submit a synopsis to a few agents and see where it gets him. And they jumped on it." Olivia said.

"That's awesome. So, how soon?" Ryan asked.

"I'd say within the next few months we will have it ready for submission." Olivia said excitedly.

"That's great news. It's a testimony that everyone needs to hear," Chance said. "And I'm glad God brought you back to share it."

"Me too." Jason sighed gratefully.

DENNIS LAY IN THE HOSPITAL BED. IT HAD BEEN OVER FOUR WEEKS SINCE his admittance. His recovery was going well, and he was to return to the penitentiary infirmary. He had spent his time reading the Bible. The words came alive as he read fervently through the verses. It was a relief to be free of the tormenting voice that berated him relentlessly day and night. He had found peace at last.

"Okay Talbot, you ready?" the prison guard said as he walked into his room and held out the chain cuffs.

"Yes, sir," Dennis said as he stood up and held out his arms, allowing the cuffs on for his transport. Apprehension about his return suddenly washed over him.

"DAVENPORT'S STATS CAME IN THIS MORNING," MARG SAID TO JASON IN his office. "I know it's only been one week for this clinic, but it's looking good." She said as she handed Jason the report. "Although protesting is still happening from pro-choice."

Jason quickly scanned the figures. "Yeah… these are not too bad for the first week." He looked at her and smiled, feeling encouraged.

"I think it's great, everything going smoothly… for once." She laughed.

"I'll say, let's hope it remains this way."

DENNIS HAD ARRIVED BACK AT THE PRISON, INTO THE INFIRMARY, WHERE Malcolm happily greeted him.

"Hey, Dennis. You're looking much better." He smiled.

"I am. I feel terrific!"

"That's fantastic news." Malcolm stated, surprised. "Well, we need to keep you in here another few days before you go back to your cell," he said, then paused and looked at Dennis's face. "You look different," he squinted. "Did something happen?"

"Yes, I met Jesus!" he grinned.

"Now that's the news I've been waiting to hear." Malcolm smiled and put his hand on Dennis's shoulder. "Welcome to the family, buddy."

MARG STUCK HER HEAD AROUND THE DOOR OF JASON'S OFFICE. "ANNIE Sandler just called. We got our first adoption sign-up," she said excitedly, hardly able to stand still with delight.

"Really?" Jason's emotion welled up inside. He couldn't contain the joy. "We have to celebrate. Call the others in and we will pop some of that non-alcoholic champagne." he said eagerly.

Marg ran off to tell the other staff in the building to meet in the boardroom.

Jason sat at his desk and took a moment; tears tumbling down his cheeks as he whispered, "Thank you, Jesus, for this opportunity to accomplish your purpose. For letting me make things right." His heart was bursting with joy. "Thank you for the child we have saved today. I will work hard to defend more, and I promise to serve you the rest of my days." He wiped his face and composed himself before he walked into the boardroom.

Marg handed him the bottle. She already had the empty glasses lined up on the table.

"Well everyone, this is the reason we've worked so hard, to save lives and not take them. Today marks a day of celebration, because we received our first adoption commitment."

Everyone burst into cheers and started clapping with excitement.

Jason continued. "Congratulations everyone, I couldn't have done it without you." Jason undid the cork, and it burst upwards with a pop and fizz.

Marg quickly helped Jason pour the liquid bubbles into each glass and handed them to every team member.

Jason continued, "This is exactly why we are doing this, to change the way people think of babies. So, let's raise our glasses and remember this day as the first day that we *saved* a life."

The glasses clinked, and people laughed with joy and excitement.

Jason looked around, smiling at the others celebrating, and as he did, he felt the tender touch of an unseen hand upon his shoulder.

"Well done!" he heard a gentle voice say.

"Fantastic news, Jase!" Ryan exclaimed. "This is part of a massive movement in our society."

"I know. It feels like a lifetime waiting for this moment. To finally start doing what God told me to do. You should have seen the team—they were so excited. I felt so proud today… and I honestly couldn't ever say that before."

"Wow! You certainly are a different man than twelve months ago." Ryan stated.

"Congratulations!" Chance said.

"To a future of welcoming babies." Olivia lifted her glass.

"Let there be many more." Jason smiled as the four of them raised their glasses.

CHAPTER FIFTY-SIX

"Okay Dennis, you're all clear. It's time for you to go back to the main population." Malcolm stated.

Dennis got up and collect his things, but his apprehension showed and Malcolm noticed it at once. "Remember what we talked about. Pray daily. Jesus will be your protector." he said.

"Yeah," Dennis sighed, "but you know *exactly* what it's like in there."

"I do, and I will be praying for you. I think you'll be surprised… it may not be as bad as you think."

"Will you visit me?"

"For sure! I'd rather meet you socially instead of you coming in here for treatment all the time."

They both laughed and, as Dennis was being escorted out by the guards, he turned. "Thanks, Malcolm, for all that you—"

But Malcolm was gone.

Dennis hesitated and looked at the guards, then stepped over towards the counter to talk to the medic behind it. "I just wanted to say one more thing to Malcolm. Can you call him back, please?"

"To who?"

"To Malcolm, the other medic."

"We don't have a Malcolm working here, Dennis. Never have!" The medic looked at him strangely.

CHAPTER FIFTY-SEVEN

DENNIS WALKED INTO HIS CELL AFTER FIVE WEEKS OF BEING AWAY. HE stood in the middle and looked around at the bleak stark walls that were his daunting future. The recent events had been both traumatic and surreal, and it left him feeling overwhelmed at the prospect of facing another 14 years inside. He closed his eyes briefly and heard a soft gentle voice whisper, *Isaiah 43:18-19.*

He scrambled to open his Bible and quickly flipped to the verse and read.

'Forget the former things; do not dwell on the past. See, I am doing a new thing! Now it springs up; do you not perceive it? I am making a way in the wilderness and streams in the wasteland.'

Dennis sat on the edge of his bed, both encouraged and relieved. "Thank you, Jesus!"

BEN STOOD BLANK-FACED AND HIS GUT CHURNED AS HE WATCHED HIS maroon Maserati Gran Turismo and black Ferrari 599 GTO being loaded onto the back of a flatbed truck. Yesterday, the removalist took all his house possessions. It was a bleak outlook. They left him helpless to recover any assets. Inwardly, he seethed and his rage grew at the reason behind his downfall. He picked up the bottle of scotch and walked back into his empty house.

THE BUZZER SOUNDED, AND THE ELECTRONIC METAL DOORS WRENCHED open with a clank. Dennis whispered a quick prayer to subdue his anxiousness before he stepped outside his cell. He reached the exercise yard and walked gingerly around the perimeter, trying not to make eye contact with other inmates.

"Hey, Talbot!"

Dennis looked up ahead. It was Benny and his gang. His stomach lurched and flipped with nervousness, and a wave of nausea unexpectantly hit him. He quickly reached out and grabbed onto the wire mesh fence to steady himself.

I am with you Dennis. I will give you the words to speak… Trust! He heard the gentle voice say.

He took a few breaths, and his nausea quickly subsided. Taking courage, he looked up, smiled and sauntered towards the 13 inmates. "Good to see you, Benny," he smiled genuinely, a sudden rush of boldness overtaking him.

"Didn't think we would see you again." Benny smirked.

Dennis didn't respond.

"You may have lived through this one Talbot, but you won't the next." Benny threatened.

Dennis stood firm, unafraid, and then took a deep breath of courage. "I forgive you, Benny, for the part you played. In fact, I forgive *all* of you." he said as he looked at the others standing around. "Thank you all for what you did to me. You don't know how much I appreciate it."

Benny and the others looked around at each other, confused.

Dennis continued. "If it wasn't for you, I would be going to Hell," he paused. "I died Benny." He looked squarely at him. "And I went to Hell! But through the grace of God, they brought me back to life and now Jesus is my Lord and Savior. I owe it all to you. Thank you, because I know I will go to Heaven now!" he said, and continued on his walk around the yard.

Benny and the others remained dumbfounded.

"Jesus!" Benny scoffed and looked at the others. "What a weirdo."

… But inwardly he felt something twinge.

Six weeks later

"We are nearly there, Jase," Olivia said excitedly. "We just have to go over it once more before we give it to Bailey. He is the best choice."

"Yeah, it just feels right that he takes it on."

"I think so." She smiled. "I cannot wait to see it published—it will blow minds."

"I hope so, because that's what people need."

You guys up for lunch today? A text came through from Ryan.

"Do you want to have lunch with Ryan and Chance? I mean, that's if you think we will have this done by then?"

"Yes, it should only take another few hours and then I'll email it to Bailey. Maybe a late lunch. Say 1.30?"

"Sounds good."

"Hey bud!" Ryan said as he hugged Jason. "Is it done?"

"Yep!" Jason said with relief as he sat down.

"It will be awesome," Olivia said enthusiastically. "Bailey from B & C Agency is fantastic. He is so excited about it."

"How long did he say?" Chance asked.

"He's already got a few publishers lined up, and he feels it may be six months, or even earlier."

"Wow, I thought it took years before a book hits the stores." Ryan said.

"I did too, but Bailey said that he has some publishing houses that focus on a few books at a time, and they match the bigger publishers regarding marketing pull."

"I have learned so much about publishing." Jason laughed and shook his head.

"So, you will have all this free time on weekends now," Chance smiled.

"Yeah, I guess," Olivia looked at Jason. "I *must* go shopping with the girls." She laughed.

"And I need to catch up on my golf games." Jason smiled.

DENNIS FELT EYES ON HIM, WATCHING FROM A DISTANCE AS HE SAT IN THE library. He briefly glanced to catch who it was, and it was Benny. He quickly dropped his head back down to read, but felt uneasy. He stole another glance, but Benny had left. Letting out a sigh of relief, he wondered why he was being watched so intently. The thought made him nervous.

I am your refuge and strength, a gentle voice said.

Dennis whispered, "Thank you, Jesus!" and the apprehension left.

"YOU'RE AN IDIOT, BEN," BRUCE RETORTED. "YOU THREW AWAY A GOOD job—now what are you going to do?"

"It was pathetic, anyway," Ben spat.

Bruce leaned back into the café booth and looked at the man who had changed so much over the past few months. He had shifted from a well-dressed, enthusiastic and confident CEO to an unshaven, bedraggled drunken mess. "What's happened to you?"

"What do you think?" he said sarcastically. "A dead-end job, no house —I now live with my mother… what do you think has happened, Bruce?" his anger showing.

"You can get through this Ben—just clean yourself up, get another job and you will be fine."

"What's the point? I've lost everything because of Miller. He's gotten everything he wanted, he's made the changes, and the business is going well. He just kicked me to the curb like I was nothing."

"Hang on! We were the ones that kicked *him* to the curb first, so why would he keep you as CEO? He's not stupid."

"He could have let me back in. He didn't have to fire us and humiliate me like he did."

"Gees Ben, you are not making any sense." Bruce shook his head. "Why would he keep you on? You betrayed him."

"*We* betrayed him."

"Yeah, we did." Bruce said, "Looking back now, I think I probably wouldn't have done it the way I did."

"You're kidding me. Now you have regrets?"

"Yes, I do." Bruce snapped. "It was wrong to remove him the way we did. We could have supported him and it would have been a better outcome... I see that now."

"He was going to *ruin it*, that's why we did what we did Bruce. Don't you forget that."

"But he hasn't—look, it's all great in hindsight. We can't change the past, so you just need to pull yourself together and start again."

"The only thing I regret is that I let Miller humiliate me and ruin my career and reputation. If I had my chance again, I would have made sure he didn't come out of that hospital."

"Don't be stupid. You don't know what you're saying, Ben." Bruce spat angrily.

"I'm serious! If I'd known what would happen, I would have made damn sure they put Miller into a wooden box and not walk out of that hospital room... I mean it."

Bruce just stared at Ben for a moment, pondering. He slowly picked up his cell phone from the table and stood up. "I think we're done," he said, "Goodbye, Ben." Then threw cash on the table and walked out.

———

THAT NIGHT, BEN LAY RESTLESS IN A SINGLE BED AT HIS MOTHER'S SMALL apartment. His mind was racing and raging, his anger becoming heightened, and thoughts of past events swirling furiously throughout his mind.

He needs to pay. He heard a strange voice say.

"Yes... he does," he agreed.

CHAPTER FIFTY-EIGHT

IT HAD BEEN SEVERAL WEEKS SINCE JASON'S MANUSCRIPT WAS DELIVERED to the agency. Jason had been focusing all his energy on his clinics to ensure that the changes were successful. He hadn't spoken to Olivia much, or even seen her, until she called for him to come into her office to sign some documents.

He sat patiently opposite, staring at her as she concentrated on the legal papers on her desk. His thoughts meandered as he sat quietly, gazing at her face. It was like he was instantly seeing her with fresh eyes.

Abruptly, with an overwhelming flush of emotion, his words burst out uncontrollably before he realized what he was saying. "You're so beautiful, Olivia."

Olivia smirked. "Okay... and you've suddenly noticed this... when?" She didn't look up, but continued to read the documents.

"Ah, well... I knew you were beautiful when I met you," he backtracked. "But, um... I guess I'm seeing you differently now." He grimaced, shocked at his own words and at what he was feeling.

"Right," she smiled. "Okay, Dr. Miller. Sign here, here and here," she pushed the papers across her desk towards him.

"Do you want to come over to my place for dinner tonight?" he picked up the pen and signed.

Olivia looked at him skeptically for a moment before she answered. "I guess," she hesitated. "Where's this going?"

"I-I don't know," he said thoughtfully as he stared back at her, confused at his own emotions.

"I'll be there at seven."

————

"I'VE PUT MAIL ON YOUR DESK, JASE," MARG SAID AS JASON BREEZED past.

"Okay, thanks," he said without stopping, concerned at the new emotions he was feeling.

Jason placed his laptop onto his desk and looked at the three letters and one parcel.

He opened two of the letters—just standard mail. But when he picked up the third, he hesitated. It looked familiar. He pulled out the letter inside and felt dismayed when he read the bold type font:

You will die for what you've done!

That was it, nothing else. He screwed up the letter and threw it in the trash.

"Idiots!" Irritated, he grabbed his laptop and left early for the afternoon. "I'm heading home, Marg."

"Good for you, Jase. You deserve an early mark."

"If there's anything urgent, please let me know."

"No worries, enjoy your evening."

"Thanks, I'll see you tomorrow."

BEN PACED ABOUT IN HIS SMALL BEDROOM. AS HE GRABBED THE BOTTLE OF Xanax, his hand was unsteady. He shook out two tablets and swigged the bottle of Bacardi to drink them down. He momentarily lost his balance and crashed into the wall.

"Ben, will you come out here?" His mum thumped on his door angrily.

Ben cracked the door ajar and gingerly peered out.

"Gees, Ben, it smells like a brewery in there. Enough is enough! You need to clean up and get a job. I didn't put you through medical school for you to end up a forty-year-old bum." She said, then stormed off.

Jason did this to you. The now familiar voice spoke into his psyche. *He ruined you!*

"Yes, he did!"

What are you going to do about it?

Ben's thoughts ran wild with anger.

"HEY, TALBOT!"

Dennis looked up. It was Benny—he had just stepped out of the shower. He and his gang had left him alone since his return, and he wasn't sure why.

"I wanna talk to you."

"Sure, Benny," he felt apprehensive as the large muscle-bound man covered in tattoos made his way over to him, with nothing but a towel wrapped around his waist.

"I wanna ask you a few questions—about your newfound religion."

"Okay—ah now? Or do you want to get dressed first and talk later?"

"Later!" he said, then turned and walked away.

Dennis didn't realize that he was holding his breath until he let it out with a sigh of relief.

Trust! The voice in his heart reassured.

JASON WAS AT HOME, QUICKLY PUTTING THE SHOPPING AWAY BEFORE HE made himself a coffee for reassuring comfort. As he sat quietly in the lounge, he felt in turmoil with the feelings that had rapidly overcome him. It was never his intention to feel this way, and he felt frustrated. He sat confused, with mixed emotions at his new feelings for Olivia. "This wasn't my plan," he whispered apprehensively.

No, but it was mine! He heard the voice in his heart that had become so familiar now.

"But I don't understand… I just want to focus on doing my purpose… and nothing more."

I will give you the desires of your heart.

"But I don't desire this. I never have."

Don't you?

Jason sat in silence and pondered that response. It was as though God had switched a light bulb on and it was shining directly on his deepest emotions. He felt a renewal of something that had been buried deep for a long time bubble and surface within him. A cavernous stirring so great that it frightened him to allow it to come to life and break down the solid stone walls that had kept his emotions inaccessible for so long.

Don't be afraid, Jason. I am doing a new thing.

He sat still as he allowed this new feeling, this new emotion arise and surge, swelling inside his chest like an effervescent overflow of magma bursting through to the surface. The sudden feeling of joy rose within him, then a wave of love flowed through him. He could feel as though he'd never been able to before. It heightened every sense. The joy and then the utmost love washed over him as he uncovered something that he had never realized before... ever.

"I love her," he whispered.

I know!

CHAPTER FIFTY-NINE

DENNIS SAT BY HIMSELF IN THE DINING HALL AND PICKED THROUGH THE assortment of food on his dinner tray.

"Hey!" Benny said as he sat down opposite him at the table.

Dennis looked around and noticed that none of his gang members were coming over to sit with them.

"I told them I wanted to talk with you alone," Benny said, noticing Dennis's curiosity about why he was unaccompanied. "Listen, I'll just get to the point. I never liked you, even more so when you started carrying on like a nut. But you've changed recently, man. I don't know what it is… but you even *look* different."

He paused, looked around, and leaned in closer. "When you said something about Jesus, the week you got back, I payed little attention and just laughed it off. But I've been watching you, and I see you got something there—something different. I wanna know what that something is."

"Okay," Dennis shrugged. "What do you want to know?"

"I wanna know what you got, that's what. I didn't come over here to have a candlelit dinner with you, Talbot… So, what is it? What's the difference I see in you?"

Dennis cleared his throat nervously. "Well, like I said, I asked Jesus to forgive me for my sins and become the Lord of my life. It changed me.

My mental state changed, and all the depression and anxiety left. It was like I was made brand new... instantly."

"Really?" Benny looked at him eagerly. "So... just like that?"

"Yes."

"So, how do I get a piece of that?"

Dennis smiled. "It's easy! I'll show you." He pulled a small Bible out of his pocket and opened it.

JASON TRIED TO KEEP HIS COOL AS HE WAS PREPARING FOR OLIVIA TO arrive, but it was difficult. He couldn't contain the joy and love that he felt, along with the excitement that was bursting within him. He felt like a young schoolboy.

The doorbell rang. He checked himself in the foyer mirror and nervously composed himself before he opened the door to find Olivia waiting. "Hi," he beamed with joy.

"Hi," she smiled suspiciously. "You look happy."

"I am. Come in."

The smell of roast beef and vegetables filled her senses as she sat at the granite stone kitchen bench. "Mm, smells delicious."

"I hope so. I got it from the butcher down the road, he's always great. It's just the cook that can ruin it." He said as he fumbled around nervously in the cupboards.

"Are you all right? You seem, I don't know—nervous?" she quizzed.

He stopped what he was doing and looked at her. "I'm great... just great." He said as he poured mineral water into the glasses.

"Okay," she said. "So, how's everything been going? I didn't have time to ask you about the clinics today."

"Great. Everything is just great!"

"That's... really... great!" She laughed. "Jason, what is up with you tonight? You're not yourself. What's going on?"

"Nothing, well, everything—but nothing really. I'm just happy and feeling, well... great!"

Olivia rolled her eyes. "You are not making sense. But anyway, I'll help you serve up—I am famished!"

. . .

Dennis showed Benny the verse in John 3:16. "Here, it says," he pointed as he read aloud, "For God so loved the world that he gave his one and only Son, that whoever believes in him shall not perish but have eternal life." He paused. "That's what I have now. I have eternal life because I declared and believe that Jesus died for my sins… and this one," he quickly opened to a pre-marked page in Acts 2:38. "Peter replied, "Repent and be baptized, every one of you, in the name of Jesus Christ for the forgiveness of your sins. And you will receive the gift of the Holy Spirit."

"You see Benny, God loves us no matter what we have done, no matter what crime we committed or why we are here. He will forgive us… if we come to him earnestly and repent and change our ways."

Benny sat listening intently, absorbing everything like a dry thirsty sponge.

The other members of Benny's gang moved toward them curiously, drawing closer to hear what Dennis was saying.

Jason and Olivia ate their meals, laughing and reminiscing about the past eleven months that they had known each other, and telling each other different stories and experiences in their lives. They packed away the dishes in the dishwasher and headed for the lounge with a dessert and hot chocolate.

"So, I wanted to talk to you," Jason paused. "Well, about what I said to you today, at your office."

"Mmmm,"

"Well, it's just that… it's only now that I've realized that…" he cleared his throat. "Well, that I… umm. Well."

She smiled at him.

"That is… well that… I love you."

"Right!" she casually took a sip of her hot chocolate and allowed him to continue.

"Well, I know that this may come as a surprise, especially since I said that I wasn't interested in a relationship with anyone, and that was true… but something changed recently—very recently, in fact."

"Okay…" she took another sip.

"And, well… I know that… Well, Olivia. You are the most amazing woman that I have ever met. You have a heart for God, you're a brilliant and beautiful person. And frankly, these past weeks without seeing you, has left a hole in my life and it's made me realize that I need you. That's why I want to spend the rest of my life with you."

"What are you saying? —Was that a proposal?" she chuckled.

"Well... YES!" he said, surprised at the realization. "I guess it is." Jason hastily dropped to one knee in front of her. "Olivia Chadwick, will you do me the honor of becoming my wife?"

"You're serious, aren't you?"

"I am! So, what do you say?"

She smiled before her answer. "Yes, I will marry you, Jason Miller!" she said sweetly as she cupped his cheek and looked into his eyes. She leaned forward and gently pressed her lips against his with a tender sweep.

His heart skipped a beat as their lips met.

She gradually pulled back and looked affectionately into his steel-blue eyes. "I love you too, Jason! I have for quite a while."

They surrounded Dennis. Thirteen enormously muscled and tattooed hard-core criminals, all huddling close to hear more of God's Word. He could feel the Holy Spirit empowering him to speak.

"There is no other way, but only one way to God." He read from his Bible, looking around intently at each of them. "Jesus says in John 14:6, 'I am the way and the truth and the life. No one comes to the Father except through me.' So, you need to repent of your sin and acknowledge Him as your Lord and Savior and you will be forgiven and made new. 2 Corinthians 5:17 says, 'Therefore, if anyone is in Christ, the new creation has come: The old has gone, the new is here!' That's exactly what's happened to me, that's why I have changed. I am a new creation in Christ."

"When did you know?" Jason asked as they sat in the lounge close together.

"It was around the third week that we were writing your novel. It just hit me. I remember looking at you as you were talking when the realization fell. I'd never felt like that about anyone before, and I remember I had to ask you to repeat the last ten minutes, as I had typed nothing."

Jason laughed. "I remember that—I just thought you were tired of listening to me."

"Never!" she smiled. "It was then that I realized what a wonderful man you were with characteristics I admired. It was that very moment I realized I loved you."

"But you said nothing!"

"No, because I knew if it was right and from God, that I wouldn't have to do anything, that he would make it happen. So, when did you know?"

"This afternoon," he grimaced.

Olivia laughed. "Oh, okay then, you're much slower." She giggled. "You took me off guard with your remark at my office today. I thought something was up." She grinned. "But I could see that you were still working it out."

"It wasn't planned. It was like God took the blindfold off and I realized what was in front of me… and that I did not want to let that go… ever."

"Well, I'm glad He did. Oh, also Jase… you are extremely good-looking." She giggled.

"Even with my eyebrow scar from the accident?"

"It makes you look tough and gives you that handsome, rugged look." She laughed.

"Okay then," he laughed. "Hey," he said excitedly, "let's just cut to the chase and not wait around. Let's do this in the next few weeks."

"Hang on… you have to give a girl some prep time," she laughed. "At least give me four weeks?"

"Agreed." He smiled, then kissed her gently again. "I cannot believe that I'm doing this. I would have never thought." He said as he put his arm around her shoulder and pulled her in close.

By the end of the dinner shift, Dennis had 13 hardened criminals on bended knee as he led them through a prayer of repentance, repeating Ryan's words from memory.

Black-encased hearts cracked and disintegrated as a release of emotions and tears gently rolled down their toughened cheeks. Unseen chains suddenly broke and fell to the floor, releasing each captive. Angels started descending and standing firm, guarding their newly assigned saint.

The rejoicing and praises of creation flowed upwards like gentle floating colorful ribbons, and the heavens sang out in glory as 13 souls in the jailhouse had been set free.

CHAPTER SIXTY

"About time, buddy!" Ryan exclaimed as he embraced Jason. "I was wondering when it would hit you," he grinned.

"What? So, you knew?" Jason said, surprised.

"Yeah, I knew when I first met her at your place." Ryan laughed.

"What?" Olivia said. "Really?"

Ryan winked and nodded. "I have connections in high places, remember." He grinned.

"Congratulations. I'm so happy for you both." Chance said as she embraced them.

"So, when's the big day?" Ryan asked.

"Four weeks." Olivia stated.

"Fantastic!" Ryan beamed.

"Oh, and Chance—I would love it if you would be one of my bridesmaids," said Olivia.

"YES!" she squealed and hugged Olivia.

Jason looked over at Ryan. "Buddy… I want you to be my best man."

"Done!"

"Okay, well that's sorted then." Jason motioned to the waiter, and he poured some sparkling wine.

"Oh, sorry… none for me." Chance covered her glass with her hand.

"It's non-alcoholic, but… Oooooh," Olivia looked directly at Chance with a glint in her eyes.

Chance nodded with a smile. "Yesssss!" she squeaked enthusiastically. "We confirmed it today."

"Oh wow! This is definitely cause for celebration. Congratulations to you both on your baby." Jason beamed excitedly.

"Thanks Jase," Ryan said and lifted his glass.

DENNIS HAD SPENT MOST OF THE DAY WITH HIS NEWLY FORMED GANG OF baby Christians. Praying, talking, reading Scriptures together and answering as many questions as he could. He sat and looked in awe at their shining faces, and couldn't believe that only yesterday, these guys were the most feared criminals in the jailhouse.

FOUR DAYS LATER

Ryan and Jason met up for a quick morning coffee at their regular café.

"You will not believe this. I got a call from Dennis last night," Jason said, "and he has led the worst gang in the prison to Christ."

"GET OUT! SERIOUSLY?"

"Seriously! It's the gang that stabbed him."

"Whaaaat?" Ryan shook his head in amazement. "That's so cool… man, I love how God works. It just blows me away."

"I know, it's great news. Well, he wants us to come and talk with them. He's starting a Bible study group and wants us to help."

"I'm up for that."

"Thought you would be. He's also asked if Trent could do water and Holy Spirit baptisms." Jason smiled."

"Yes, that would be so good. We can ask him on Sunday… So, you all set?"

"Yep, flights booked and I cannot wait to start the rest of our lives together."

"Excellent! Oh, how are the clinics?"

"They are going really well!"

Jason's cell rang. It was Marg.

"Jase. Josie Stien called, and she wants to do another interview—an update on the clinics." Marg explained.

"Right, when?"

"She said she'd like to talk with you this morning, so she can make tomorrow's paper."

"Sure, I'll head in now. Thanks," he said before he hung up. "Sorry, Ryan, but I have to run. That reporter wants to do another interview with me."

"That's good!"

"Yeah, I hope so. Reporters always make me nervous."

"Yeah, but she printed an awesome column last time. I think the more publicity around this subject, the better."

"You're right. Well, I better go. I'll call you later." He waved and walked off down the street.

————

"Hi Josie, it's Jason Miller, just returning your call." Jason said in the privacy of his office.

"Thanks for calling me back, Dr. Miller. I wanted to do a quick update on how your clinics are going now that the changes have been underway for some time."

"Sure. Well, it's been exciting. We are averaging at least two adoption commitments per week from each clinic, and the number is increasing weekly with more public awareness of what we do. The changes we have put in place initially caused some community backlash, but that seems to have settled and we are being perceived as beneficial to the community with the expansion in medical services we now provide."

"Okay, that sounds terrific. So now when an expectant woman comes into the clinic, what services are you providing that differ from before?"

"Well, firstly, we no longer offer abortions. We advise that we do not practice terminations, nor will we refer them to a clinic who does."

"Isn't that one-sided? I mean, if a woman comes to you seeking help, then you are denying her if you do not offer a balanced view?"

"There's nothing stopping her from leaving the clinic and looking up the nearest abortion center—if that's what she desires. But we will not discuss a termination in any of my clinics—we only describe the alternatives to abortion."

"Okay, so what do you offer then?"

"First, we determine her needs and if she wants to keep the baby or place it for adoption. We offer counseling, help with applications for financial support, housing and food programs. Also, we work with the local day-care centers to help secure a position when the baby is born if needed and also connect with crisis centers when needed. Further to this, we offer services to those who are seeking to adopt."

"So, your entire focus is on adoptions?"

"Our focus is on an outcome that will let the baby live. We encourage each expecting mother to give the child a life—be it with them, a family member or with another loving family—and we help facilitate that as much as we can."

"So, it's working? Your message is gaining momentum?"

"Yes, it is. Besides what we do at the centers on a local perspective, we also have our own regional representatives that go into the communities to educate about the opportunities available to expecting mothers. They also speak at the schools to educate the younger generation about the alternatives to abortion."

"Really? That's unique."

"Yes. Also, a part of their role is to speak to local council members and government agencies to get backing for changing the way we support the mothers and view children."

"How so?"

"Our aim is to change society's culture to give more flexibility to mothers—in the workplace, in education, providing more funding options for day-care and helping with housing and meals. We also have our own buses that travel around offering free pregnancy tests and ultrasounds. We find that when an expectant mother sees the ultrasound, sees the heart beating, they realize that it's a baby. Our recent stats show that 99 percent want to give their baby a life."

"Wow, sounds like the full package."

"Well, we are doing as much as we can to change the way people view babies—along with providing as much support as possible when they enter this world. Each woman that continues with the pregnancy, be it keeping or placing their baby for adoption, we assign a care worker to support them throughout their journey. This continues after the child is born, as we believe that it's not just about preventing the abortion, it is about caring for both mother and child after the birth and ensuring that they continue to be supported both financially and emotionally."

"You must have doubled your staff?"

"Not quite. We partner with various organizations for their help. We engage them to provide post abortion therapy programs at each of our centers, to help those who are mentally and emotionally suffering from their past decision. We are receiving positive feedback from those who have completed the program."

"Oh? Is it just women going through this program?"

"At the moment, but we are currently working towards a program for men. I think we often forget that men are affected by abortion as well."

"Well, it sure sounds like this change is having an impact. So the big question is, has this affected your bottom line? Are Miller Corp shareholders screaming blood?"

"It's still early days yet. I can say that initially we took a bit of a hit in the pocket, but with the additional medical services that we now have, we are on track to turn a larger profit this year than we have in the past. So, to answer your question, Josie—the shareholders are extremely happy with the changes."

"Well, that's good news. I really wasn't sure how it would pan out for the corporation."

"Yes, I'm really pleased with the outcome."

"Oh, and one more question… on a personal note, if I may?"

"Ah… I guess."

"I hear that a renowned bachelor has finally been taken off the market… is that correct?"

"Well, I haven't heard that term used before—but yes, I am getting married."

"Congratulations! I'm sure a lot of women will be jealous!"

"You're probably exaggerating that, I think."

"You'd be surprised, Dr. Miller, you'd be surprised. Anyway, great interview! Thanks for your time. I'm looking forward to printing this update."

"Thank you, Josie. Take care."

CHAPTER SIXTY-ONE

Wedding day!

Ryan watched as Chance was the first to walk down the aisle, followed by two of Olivia's other bridesmaids. He winked at her as she took her place on the opposite side of him. She grinned at him with excitement.

Jason stood steady and confident in his navy-blue suit, light blue tie, and even lighter blue shirt. Each blue hue setting off his electric steel-blue eyes and handsome features. He quickly sucked in his breath as Olivia appeared standing under the arched doorway of the old stone church. He had thought she was beautiful before, but nothing could have prepared him for today, and he stood mesmerized.

Her ivory and petal A-line gown fitted her exquisitely. The drop waste and sheer lace bodice complemented her slim figure and gave her a refined elegance. Her long, silky dark curls softly fell over her shoulders.

Their eyes met, and she smiled, then stepped forward down the aisle with Sister Marguerite proudly clinging to her arm. They both glided together in time with the music and then smoothly landed before Jason.

"Who gives this woman in marriage?" The priest asked.

"I do," Sister Marguerite smiled, then turned to take her seat in the front row.

The priest started the ceremony and asked for their vows. They had both written their own.

"Olivia, I never searched for love or even expected it, but without realizing you suddenly became the one I wanted to spend the rest of my life with… you became my perfect surprise. I stand before you and promise that I will share your dreams… your goals. I will remain faithful to you forever and, above all, I will honor God. So, in the presence of our Lord Jesus, I give you my heart, my commitment, and without any doubt… I choose you. I give you everything I am… forever."

The priest then motioned to Olivia.

"Jason. It was always you. Who would have thought God's perfect story would weave us together when our paths were so far apart. I am grateful to our Lord for allowing me to find love… in you. So, today I make a promise in the presence of God to love, cherish, and always hold you in the highest regard. I promise to remain faithful to you in both good times and bad, when our love is easy, and when it is an effort…. and I promise only to love you twice," she smiled, "that is now… and forever."

"And now it's time for the rings." The priest smiled and motioned to Jason.

"I, Jason William Miller, give this ring to you as a token of my love and devotion. With this ring, I marry you; with this ring I give you my heart." Jason then gently slipped the gold diamond studded wedding band onto Olivia's finger.

"I, Olivia Maree Chadwick, pledge my love to you. I give you this ring as a sign of our covenant. With all that I am, and all that I have, I commit my life to loving you." She slipped the gold band on Jason's finger.

"It's with greatest honor that I now pronounce you husband and wife!" The priest smiled at Jason. "You may kiss the bride."

Jason leaned forward. Their lips touched warmly, for the first time as husband and wife. They had sealed their promise.

Everyone cheered, and the music played.

It was only a small gathering of friends… and one relative, Jason's aunt. Telegrams of congratulations from friends overseas were read at the reception, and one from Dennis and the inmates.

"You finally get to dance at your own wedding, Mr. Miller." Olivia grinned as they moved around the dance floor to their bridal waltz.

"And this time, you are the bride and not the bridesmaid... Mrs. Miller," he smiled.

"Oh, how I love that name," she sighed.

He tenderly kissed her cheek, and she cuddled into his strong shoulder.

"This time tomorrow night, we will be dining on the Eiffel Tower." Jason murmured.

"Mmm, I can't wait." Her eyes glinted.

"Dr. and Mrs. Miller!" Ryan grinned as he and Chance swept past. "Such a fantastic-looking couple."

"Why, thank you." Olivia replied in her poshest voice. "You make a handsome couple yourselves." She laughed as they danced onwards.

As the cake came out, Jason and Olivia laughed and both looked over at Chance and Ryan.

"We couldn't resist." Ryan beamed and shrugged.

The cake topper was the spitting image of them both, dressed in their wedding outfits, but as a doctor and a lawyer. Olivia blew them a thankyou kiss before they both held the knife and cut the cake.

As the night closed, Olivia and Jason said their farewells, and Ryan and Chance enthusiastically embraced them both.

"I'm so happy for you, bud. Have a fantastic trip." Ryan said to Jason with emotion.

"Thanks for all you've done Ryan... I really mean that." Jason responded.

"I can't wait to see you both when you get back." Chance said with tears of joy.

They climbed into the limousine, and Ryan shut the door and watched them drive away.

"Mmm, Paris! Now that would be lovely this time of year." Chance said whimsically.

"One day, my love…" Ryan embraced her, then dipped her for a kiss. "I will take you to Paree," he said in a French accent.

Chance laughed.

BEN SAT ALONE IN HIS BEDROOM, TAKING THE OCCASIONAL SWIG FROM HIS vodka bottle whilst watching a late-night movie. He was drunk and high on the medication that he had prescribed himself earlier in the day under an alias. His state dulled and his eyes grew heavy.

You're a failure. Look at what you have become... a useless nothing. The voice started again.

"Gees, shut the heck up, will you? Leave me alone." He took another sip and held the newspaper article again. "Married today, were you Miller? That won't last. You'll be looking for the next woman in no time." He scoffed and took another drink. "I should be the one celebrating life, not you."

He did this to you. He's the one that should pay.

"Yes, you're right. He should be the one to damn pay," his voice raised higher, and he threw his bottle to the floor.

Thump, thump, thump—the wall sounded. "Ben, I am warning you… I will not continue to put up with this in my house!" his mother screamed from the adjacent bedroom.

CHAPTER SIXTY-TWO

THREE MONTHS LATER.

"YOU WILL NOT BELIEVE THIS, JASE!"

"What?" Jason looked up from reading the paper on the lounge as Olivia showed him the pregnancy test. "Seriously? But I thought you said you didn't think…? This is amazing!" He jumped up and embraced her excitedly.

"I know, it's a miracle. Can you believe we will be parents?"

"No, but I can't wait." Exhilaration was all over his face. "Let's call Ryan and Chance."

LATER THAT NIGHT, JASON WENT OUT FOR HIS NIGHTLY JOG. HIS HEAD WAS spinning with thoughts of becoming a father, and he felt excitement about the future.

As he rounded the corner, he thought he heard another jogger's footsteps in the distance behind him. He quickened the pace, feeling a little unnerved as he rarely saw other joggers on his late-night runs. He could still hear the steps, so he slowed and glanced around to see the other jogger dressed in black quickly veer off across the other side of the road and hasten his pace away from him. Jason watched suspiciously as the other jogger disappeared into the distance.

He put in a sprint to get back home.

NEXT AFTERNOON

"Congratulations, buddy!" Ryan said as he embraced Jason in the café.

"Yeah, we are so excited." Jason responded.

"How many weeks?"

"The test came back at eleven weeks already."

"Whaaat? A Paris baby?"

"Yep. Looks like our honeymoon formed more than just awesome memories."

"Wow. How is she?"

"Thrilled. Liv thought she couldn't have children because of her age, so we decided we would adopt. She didn't notice because of her hormones being so crazy, so it didn't tweak that she could even be pregnant."

"God can do anything, buddy. Sometimes we only see things the way we think they should be. We forget that nothing is impossible for Him, and often He will bring about what we never imagined."

"I know. When I think about what God has done for me… He brought you into my life. If he hadn't, I would be dead… and in Hell, and I would have never changed the clinics…. or met Liv… or be having our own child." he beamed. "He put you in my life to help, support me and teach me His ways. I know this sounds soppy, but buddy… I am so happy that we met."

"Me too. This entire experience has been life changing. Raising a dead person, WOW!" Ryan shook his head. "Now that alone was mind-blowing. But watching you grow and change has been the absolute best. And now you, Liv… and a baby—that is just the icing on the cake."

"It sure is!"

———

As Jason drove away from the café, he noticed the familiar black car. A car that had been following him on occasions for the past few months. He put his foot down and then screeched to a halt at the red traffic lights. The car came up slowly behind him but kept its distance. He couldn't recognize the driver hidden by a cap and dark sunglasses. He quickly hit the gas and went through the red light, leaving the black car behind.

"Bruce, I need to talk with you."

"I told you never to call me again, Ben—we're done."

"No, you don't understand, I just want to—"

"Ben! I said we're done. I don't want to hear from you… EVER!" He hung up.

Ben heard the click and seethed. "He'll get his."

Yesss, he will! The voice agreed.

"Shut up! Leave me alone. I don't need you."

You DO need me.

"I don't need anyone. Just leave me."

"Who are you talking to?" Ben's mother said in his bedroom doorway.

"No one, it's just the television."

"Doesn't sound like it, Ben." She sighed, annoyed. "Have you looked in the paper for a job this week?"

"There's nothing that would suit my qualifications."

She exhaled with frustration and walked away.

The sun glinted over the whitewash as the waves crashed onto the shore. Another beautiful day was dawning, and Jason relaxed, having his coffee on the kitchen bench before he set off for work.

"Jason," Olivia said, concerned, as she came through the front door after her morning walk. "There is something written on the GT."

"What?—Written?"

Olivia grimaced. "Yeah. Someone has scratched something horrible into the paintwork."

"What? Oh, no!" Jason rushed outside and looked at the letters *DIE!* etched into the bonnet of his Porsche. He stood for a moment, both flabbergasted and crushed, and then drifted intensely around his car, checking the rest of the body for more scratches.

"Who would do this?" Olivia stood in front of the car.

"I-I don't know." Jason shook his head in dismay. "Maybe… but I don't know—"

"Maybe what?"

"Maybe the same person who's been sending me the notes."

"What notes?"

Jason waved it off so not to worry her. "It's nothing."

"This isn't nothing, Jason," she pointed to the car. "This is a very strong message. What are you not telling me?"

"I haven't told you, as I didn't think it was important. I get threats all the time, it's normal."

"You still get threats?" she looked at him incredulously.

"Not threats, just typed notes. You know—it's normal—"

"Ah HELLO! It's not normal! Have you told the police?"

"I've been through this a dozen times before Olivia, there is nothing they can do." He said, frustrated, continuing to look over his car. "It's a part of the job. I've always gotten them… but they stopped for a while when I changed the clinics."

"How did they get in then?" she looked around. "The security gates are closed."

Jason looked about to see if there was any breech in the steel fence. "I don't know," he stood, dismayed.

"I'm calling the police, Jason—we need to treat this seriously… and we need to get those security cameras!" Olivia said as she stormed off into the house.

———

"JASON," MARG SAID, CONCERNED. "I OPENED SOME OF YOUR MAIL THIS morning, and… well, I know we sometimes get hate mail… but this one seems, well… more serious." She handed Jason the letter.

You think you can get away with ruining people's lives? Well, you're WRONG!

Your days are numbered, Miller. I am going to kill you!

Jason sucked in his breath, holding it for a moment. He knew this had become more serious over the past few months.

"I think you should notify the police, Jase—this one seems more… sinister."

"I've spoken with them already this morning about an incident at home… and about the other notes I've received. They can't do anything."

"Other notes? Have you received more like these?"

"About ten others now. I just bin them."

"Oh Jase, this is serious. You need to call the police again… who do you think it would be?"

"How many people do you think hate me?" Jason shrugged. "A hundred? A thousand? I wouldn't be able to count."

"Stop taking this lightly," she said, annoyed for his safety. "Do you think it's now a pro-choice person?"

"Gees, who knows? I can't seem to keep up with the 'who hates Jason Miller this week?'"

"Just call the police Jase," she sighed.

"Okay… I will." His cell buzzed as he walked to his office. It was Ryan. "Hey, buddy."

"We're heading to the hospital now. Chance is in labor."

"Okay, do you need anything?"

"No, we're good. Our obstetrician is on her way now—so we're fine." He paused. "I guess I'll call you with the good news."

"I can't wait. Ring me as soon as you can and I'll go get Liv—she'll be so excited."

"Okay, talk then."

Jason hung up then dialed Olivia. "They're headed to the hospital now."

"Oh, okay. Do they need us to bring anything to them?"

"No, they're fine. I'll be home soon and we can sit and wait for the phone call."

———

LATER THAT NIGHT, JASON'S CELL RANG.

"It's a girl Jase, and she is so beautiful... well, as beautiful as a wrinkly newborn can be," Ryan laughed. "But watching the birth, I can't explain it," he choked. "It was so amazing... God is so amazing!"

CHAPTER SIXTY-THREE

THREE MONTHS LATER

"I'M STANDING OUT THE FRONT RIGHT NOW, AND IT'S IN THE WINDOW. IT looks so cool. I really love the cover design—it looks creepy with the demon in the background." Ryan said excitedly on his cell.

"Yeah, I know—I saw it this morning. They said that it would be on the shelves today." Jason said.

"Well, it's selling! I'm watching people pick it up and buy it. When are you book signing?"

"Tonight, for an hour."

"We might swing by."

"That'd be nice. I need some moral support... What if no one shows?"

"Hardly—not by the crowd that's gathered here now."

"Do you want to get dinner after?"

"Sounds good."

"Okay, I'll see you tonight."

"THERE WERE 150 PEOPLE THAT CAME THROUGH THE BOOKSTORE IN THE hour I was there. I think I have writers' cramp," Jason laughed. "I never thought it would be so popular."

"Congratulations, buddy." Ryan gave him a pat on the back. "It was bound to be a hit, Jase. I mean, what a story—people will talk about it for a very long time. It will be a game-changer for some. I saw it on the news this afternoon, too."

"I saw it too," said Chance. "There's a lot of hype around it."

"And sceptics." Jason said. "I've already seen some negative reviews."

"Yeah… but there are always sceptics." Olivia stated and rubbed his back reassuringly. "Not everyone will believe what happened to you."

"I don't get people writing negative reviews," Chance stated, annoyed and defensive. "I mean, what if one word or one sentence in the book is *exactly* what someone else needs to hear, but that critical review stopped them from buying the book?"

"Yeah, I agree!" said Ryan. "I'll write a good review, but if I didn't like it, then I won't do a review at all. I figure that my opinion differs from someone else's anyway, so who am I to judge and deter anyone else from reading it. Anyway Jase, some don't want to believe what you've written either."

"Why wouldn't they?" Jason asked.

"Because if there is a God, then there's accountability… and a Hell." Chance said as she picked up baby Lilly from the basket and held her on her lap. "Without a God, people can do whatever they want and not feel guilty."

"Yeah, you're right. I did what I wanted." Jason sighed. "But I'm relieved that it's now published and people can read it… and hopefully be changed through it."

"You did exactly what God wanted you to do, Jase." Ryan patted him on the back. "You changed the clinics and wrote your story. That's an enormous accomplishment."

Jason smiled with a sense of relief that he had made it this far. "I have to admit, it hasn't been an easy journey… You know, it's nearly two years since my accident?"

"I know, I thought about it the other day—that it's only a few weeks away from the anniversary date that I found you squashed in your Beemer."

"I still can't believe it some days." Jason pondered. "It feels so surreal that God has absolutely changed my life around. I was a self-absorbed, money-loving, lonely, driven-control freak—although I didn't know it then," he chuckled. "And now I have so much." Jason's eyes sparkled as he looked at Olivia and his close friends around him. "I would have never thought it could be so wonderful." He paused. "Also today marked the 350th baby signed for adoption since our clinics changed."

"Wow! That is brilliant," Ryan beamed. "You've not only saved lives but are changing our society's views on abortion."

"I know, I'm so proud of what we do now, and so are all the staff." He said as he looked at Lilly. "We are saving babies… just like this little gem."

"She's grown." Olivia commented and touched Lilly's cheek.

"I know… and fast. How are you feeling?" Chance asked.

"Enormous," Olivia laughed. "And looking forward to this one arriving." She patted her tummy.

"I know exactly how you feel. When I was just over eight months, I had shortness of breath and terrible cramping in my legs—it's so uncomfortable."

"Yes! It's awful, and the heartburn too… but look what you get at the end of it all." She smiled and took Lilly's tiny hand. "So worth it!"

"Well, we better get back home and put Lilly to bed. I tell you this parenthood thing is such a lifestyle change. Everything evolves around Lilly at the moment." Ryan said with a smile. "But I wouldn't change a thing." He grinned.

"Me neither… I can't wait." Jason smiled at Olivia.

CHAPTER SIXTY-FOUR

10 P.M. ON A TUESDAY.

"My waters have broken—where are you?" Olivia said with an element of panic in her voice.

"I'm so sorry. I got held up at the meeting. Have you got contractions?"

"Yes, they've just started." She winced.

"Look, it will be over an hour by the time I drive back home and we get to the hospital. So, I will call the ambulance to come and get you right now. I have to get the car from the parking garage, so I will meet you at the hospital soon. Okay?"

"Okay… I love you, Jase."

"I love you too." Jason smiled, then hung up. His excitement overtook him at the thought of becoming a father. "Wow!" he said, shaking his head in awe.

He quickly dialed the hospital for an ambulance. Then, once confirmed, he took off running, taking a shortcut to the parking garage through a myriad of alleyways between the streets. The dim lighting cast shadows that bounced off the brick buildings as he sprinted through the backstreets.

As he rounded the corner in a back lane, he heard footsteps echoing fast behind him. His hair stood on end as he reeled around to see Ben coming up swiftly behind him. He relaxed a little, relieved to know it wasn't a stranger. But as Ben came closer, he noticed he looked disheveled —his hair was a mess, he was dirty and unshaven.

Ben stopped, and they both stared at each other in the dimly lit alley.

"Ben?" Jason puffed curiously, bending over with his hands on his knees as he caught his breath. "What are you doing here? It's been ages…"

"You—you've ruined everything." Ben said with venom. "You've taken away everything."

"What? Look, not now, okay," Jason shook his head in frustration. "I've got to go. Olivia—"

"Shut up—I don't want to hear it. I've listened to you for too long."

"Ben, you're not making sense… I haven't seen you for nearly—are you drunk?"

"ENOUGH!" Ben yelled, the echo rebounding off the tall brick buildings. "I've heard ENOUGH!" he screamed, his eyes becoming wide with anger.

"Ben, why are you here? I really have to go. We can talk lat—Are you high?" Jason stared at him, noticing his frantic eyes. "What's with you?"

"SHUT UP, JUST SHUT UP!" he screeched as he reached into his jacket and pulled out a revolver.

"WOAH! Ben, now hang on." Jason held his hands out in front and stepped backwards.

Ben stood with the gun pointed directly at Jason, his arm shaking nervously.

"Ben, calm down, this is crazy… don't do anything you'll regret."

"I won't regret this." He spat with venom.

"You're not thinking rationally—you'll go to jail if you do anything stupid."

"I don't care, it'll be worth it. I want you dead, Miller."

Yesss, do it. Ben heard the voice as he continued to hold the gun directly towards Jason.

"Ben. Listen to me—we can work this out, just you and me… over dinner if you like… somewhere." Jason tried to calm him.

"NO! Shut up! You're not listening to me. You've ruined EVERY-THING. MY WHOLE LIFE IS RUINED!" He shouted.

"Ben, stop! Think rationally… we can work it out, we can go some-where right now, just—." Jason stepped towards Ben slightly.

"STOP! Don't come any closer. *I will kill you, Jason.* I've been dreaming of this exact moment."

Pull the trigger, the voice said.

Ben shook his head. "Shut up! Shut up! I've got this. I don't need you to tell me what to do."

Jason stood stunned. He could see that Ben was delusional—he was speaking to something unseen, and his eyes were wild and crazy. "Listen to me, Ben… this is not smart, okay? You won't get away with this. There's no need to do this—we can work it out. Just put the gun down and we can talk it through."

"No, it's done—we can't work it out. I've lost everything." Ben started to choke and cry.

Do it! The voice said.

"I told you to SHUT UP!" Ben screamed, and started slapping his head with his free hand.

Jason stood with trepidation. "Look Ben, I know we've had our differ-ences, but—"

"Differences? You're kidding, right? You just ripped everything out from under me. YOU DESTROYED MY LIFE, MILLER." He waved the gun angrily towards him. "Do you even get that? No one will touch me now! I can't even start my own practice because of you."

"Ben, calm down," Jason said, motioning with his hands. "We can fix this. I can help you, whatever you need, money—I can—"

"Help me? Help me?" he said sarcastically, leaning towards Jason. "You weren't there when I needed help, when I lost my house, my cars, my life… everything. I didn't see you come to my rescue then… so why the hell would you come now… eh?" he sneered. "You only ever think of yourself, Miller, and no one else."

"Ben, that's not true. I've changed, you don't under—"

"Shut up!" he snapped. "I will not listen to you anymore, you're no different."

Kill him! The voice reverberated throughout Ben's mind.

"ENOUGH! Let me handle it, STOP ORDERING ME AROUND! I'll do it in a minute — will you SHUT UP NOW!"

Jason froze at the sight of Ben yelling to himself, momentarily mesmerized at his frenzied start-stop screaming. Then he quickly took his chance and launched himself towards Ben's legs. He heard Ben's knee crack as he drove in hard and tackled him to the ground. Ben screamed in pain as Jason laid on him, fighting and reaching forward to get the gun from his hand. They rolled towards the right, smashing into garbage cans, scattering the rubbish across the dark laneway. Ben pulled the first punch with his free hand and it connected squarely with Jason's jaw, rolling him off Ben sideways.

"I've been wanting to do that for ages," Ben sneered.

Jason sprung back onto Ben before he could get up, sat on his chest and punched him four times in the face before Ben could aim the gun towards him again. Jason lunged for the gun, and Ben lost his grip. It flew backwards over his head, clattering and sliding across the concrete only five feet away. Jason jumped up and made a leap for the gun. Ben came from behind and tackled Jason to the ground and Jason's chin connected with the concrete pavement hard, knocking the wind out from him.

They rolled, tossed and grappled over the ground, punching each other as the moist air dampened their bloodied, dirty and sweat-ridden clothes.

Ben rolled and grasped the gun again. Jason kicked Ben's arm to dislodge it, but Ben grabbed Jason's leg, which tumbled him over backwards. Ben lunged at Jason as he was getting back up off the ground, jumping on top of him, pushing hard on his chest, and forcing him back down onto his back. Both their hands were pressing hard against each other's, both gripping the gun, each not wanting to lose this battle... each not wanting to lose their life.

Ben leaned his whole bodyweight on top of his hands, overpowering Jason's strength. Jason's hold on the gun started to slip and gradually... Ben tilted and maneuvered the barrel to point towards Jason's chest.

Do it now! Ben heard the voice say.

Click.

BANG!

The echo rang out through the alleyway.

CHAPTER SIXTY-FIVE

"HER CONTRACTIONS ARE ONLY THREE MINUTES APART," THE PARAMEDIC said as he wheeled Olivia over to a nurse in the hospital.

"Great work, Ted. Thank you! We'll take it from here." A nurse said before she focused on Olivia, "What's your name, honey?"

"Olivia Miller."

"Okay Olivia, is this your first baby?"

"Yes."

"Do you have next of kin, sweetie?"

"Yes, my husband Jason—he shouldn't be too far away."

"Okay hon, we will get you into a room. How do you feel?"

"Scared."

"Okay," the nurse chuckled, "I get that—we all feel scared at this point," she smiled, "but pain wise... how do you feel?"

"All right for now... I guess."

"Okay, did you discuss with your obstetrician regarding any drugs?"

"Yes, I told her I wanted as much as she can give me."

The nurse let out a laugh. "Good girl, so what's her name?"

"I've called her already, and she's on her way—Aaaaarrrrggghhhhhh.. Oh, oh, oh, that hurts, oh my, oh, it hurts," Olivia cried out, clutching and buckling over in pain.

"Okay, hon, breathe through it—you're doing just fine. It will pass."

· · ·

BEN SLOWLY GOT UP, RELEASING HIS HOLD AGAINST JASON'S CHEST.

Jason could feel the intense, searing pain throbbing throughout his upper body. He contorted in pain as he put his hand on his chest and felt the warm liquid.

Jason looked down, taking short swift gasps, watching as the blood pumped and seeped out through his blue shirt. He looked up at Ben, but now saw that Ben wasn't alone. There was a being standing right next to him. A demon.

He could feel his conscious fading quickly, he could hear the blood pumping louder and louder in his ears and the pain engulfing him.

As he was slipping from this realm, he saw another demon move nearby, grinning at him. He felt no fear. He looked back at Ben in his hazed state and gasped. "We could have worked this out. I never meant to harm you, I'm so sorr—" Jason stopped as he saw the faint light in the distance rapidly becoming stronger. He heard the rhythm of rushing wings reverberate louder and louder.

He beamed a massive smile as he saw a familiar friend.

"Aduri." He whispered…

and then fell silent.

"OLIVIA, YOU NEED TO PUSH OKAY, BUT WHEN I TELL YOU TO—YOU GOT it?" the doctor stated.

"Yes," Olivia panted. "Can I… please… now?"

"Not yet, hold on. Just wait okay, not long now."

"Where's Jason, where's my husband?"

"I don't know, but this baby will not wait for him."

"OH GOD, WHAT HAVE I DONE?" THE REALIZATION HIT BEN AS THE adrenaline subsided, and he was looking at a dead man on the ground in front of him. The panic accelerated. He held his head in his hands as he spun around in terror, looking for a place to stash the gun and run.

"STOP RIGHT THERE! POLICE!"

He saw the four officers aiming their weapons directly at him, walking toward him, poised and slow.

"Put the gun down or we will shoot." One officer warned.

Ben started to comply, then hesitated.

The officer saw his indecision. "Don't do anything stupid. We *will* shoot!"

Ben thought for a moment, then slowly bent down, making motions to put the gun on the ground. Suddenly, he twisted the barrel back upward and under his chin.

It happened in a split second... the click of the trigger...

the *CRACK* of the gun.

He immediately dropped to the ground—his twisted frame lay in a pool of his own crimson blood.

"Not long now Olivia." The Doctor stated. "Just a few more pushes and you're there. Okay... get ready to push down again. Ready? Push!"

Ben felt himself come out of his body like a suction. He looked back and saw the officers hovering over his limp corpse, checking for vitals, avoiding the mass of blood that was slowly pooling around his body. He watched and waited, both astonished and ashamed.

He examined his arms and torso in both confusion and amazement of his new form, and stared at the two bodies lying lifeless in the alley.

The shrilling sound of sirens coming closer took his attention momentarily until he felt the piercing of claws cutting into his flesh. He screamed as he reeled around to face the most hideous of beings.

"Well done! You finally listened to me." It said, grinning a row of sharp fangs.

Ben screamed!

The large black demon laughed and bit hard into his face, ripping off half his cheek and jawbone. It clutched him tightly, dragging him away from his body that was laying contorted and bloodied on the concrete alleyway.

IN THE EARLY HOURS OF THE MORNING, A BABY LET OUT A CRY IN THE theater.

"It's a girl!" The doctor smiled as she placed the newborn onto Olivia's stomach.

"Oh," she cried, overwhelmed. "She's beautiful!" she gasped as she held her with pure joy.

CHAPTER SIXTY-SIX

Jason was rocketing through the atmosphere with Aduri beside him, giving occasional glances and smiling reassuringly. The feeling was exhilarating, and Jason knew exactly where he was going...

Home!

"Excuse me, Olivia." Her doctor came into the hospital room, followed by a female police officer. The baby was already in a basinet beside her bed.

"Is he here? I've left several messages on his cell." Olivia responded eagerly, excited to show Jason their new baby daughter.

"Olivia," the doctor cleared her throat awkwardly. "I-I have some terrible news." She grimaced. She really didn't want to deliver this message.

"What? Tell me!" Olivia's tears already forming in her eyes.

"It's Jason." She paused briefly. "I'm afraid there was an altercation on the street and..." she hesitated. "Well... Jason was shot... and I'm afraid he didn't make it. I-I'm so, so sorry Olivia—" she placed her hand on hers and swallowed. "… he passed away at the scene." She finished, with a tear slipping down her cheek.

"I'm so sorry, ma'am." The officer said softly and placed her hand gently on Olivia's shoulder. "I will need to return and ask some questions later… when you're feeling up to it," her eyes revealing her condolences. She nodded at the doctor before she left.

The doctor pulled up a chair alongside Olivia and remained holding her hand. "I'm so sorry, Olivia." she whispered.

The intense pain pierced like a dagger through Olivia's heart. She buckled under the shear agony. She gasped as uncontrollable sobs rose from the depths of her being. The tears flowed like unstoppable torrents, and her heart ached and burned with a cavernous anguish. The man that she had loved for only a short time had been taken from her.

She gently picked up her baby, held her close to her chest, and profoundly sobbed.

As Aduri and Jason alighted onto the lush green field, Jason's excitement and relief was overwhelming. All the fear, worry, pain and sorrow washed away as he took his first step onto Heaven's vibrant green grounds. He fell face down in both awe and thankfulness.

As he buried his face deep into the grass, he could hear it giggling and tickling his face. The exhilaration and joy bubbled up inside him so much that he laughed uncontrollably.

Aduri chuckled, watching as Jason rolled onto his back, looking skyward, laughing as the warmth of God's light beamed on his face.

He had made it home!

CHAPTER SIXTY-SEVEN

THE TICKING OF A CLOCK AND THE NIGHT STAFF'S MUFFLED TALKING IN the distance were the only sounds resounding through Olivia's hospital room. She sat in quiet solace, watching her baby sleep beside her. She felt like her heart had been torn from her and it left her with a gaping, throbbing, aching void.

I am with you! She felt the reassuring, still small voice.

But the sharp pang of her loss overwhelmed her. She slid down under the covers and buried her face deep into the soft downy pillow and sobbed.

ADURI LET JASON HAVE HIS MOMENT AND THEN MOTIONED FOR HIM TO stand.

Jason quickly sprung to his feet and looked in the direction that Aduri faced. He saw the familiar ball of light coming his way. "Tolman." Jason grinned with excitement.

As the sphere of light came closer, it morphed into the magnificent white and silver lion ambling toward them.

"Jason, my friend... you have returned." Tolman said eagerly.

"Tolman!" Jason beamed. "I'm so happy to see you again."

"We are too." Tolman grinned, his pearl iridescent canines glistening.

He stepped close to Jason and touched him on the shoulder with his gigantic white paw. "Congratulations, my friend. You have done well! Heaven is very proud of you."

Jason looked stunned as he immediately noticed the many angels standing around applauding. They all looked upon him proudly as their shining faces nodded with joy and acceptance.

All of a sudden, he felt something pounce on the back of his legs, making him stumble forward.

"Hey, buddy," Jason grinned knowingly as he turned around. "It's so good to see you!"

Ardie took off madly running around, barking and yelping with excitement in seeing his master return.

Tolman laughed. "The King would like to see you now."

"Oh?" Jason became nervous. He had read the Bible daily and listened to His promptings… but to meet Jesus in person… now that was another thing. *How would he feel?* he thought. *Would he bow, stand, fall down in front of Him and worship?* His thoughts were running wild with anticipation.

"Don't be anxious… He is very pleased with you. Let's go!"

Jason looked out towards the direction that Tolman turned and saw a magnificent gate made from an enormous single pearl. He quickly remembered this described as one of the 12 gates.

The pearl gateway shone and shimmered, reflecting different colors in the light that emanated throughout Heaven, and engraved on its entry was the name *Joseph*.

As he walked through, he looked in awe at the great angel that smiled welcomely. His emotions fluttered with excitement as he stepped through to Heaven's kingdom and he instantly fell to his knees.

"Thank you, Lord, I have made it home," he rejoiced with both relief and elation.

Immediately, as he spoke, he saw his words float like colorful cords mixed with diamonds and other precious gems, gliding and furling outwards.

These spoken words started a chain reaction. Other people and angels instantly started praising and worshiping the King, and as he watched, their praises mingled and became like a colorful, sparkling aurora throughout the grounds. It was spectacular!

He looked over at Tolman and saw him lift his mighty head in praise.

His white and silver mane gently shifted like fine strands of silk floating in a breeze with the sway of his body.

Jason was silent in reverence, as all of Heaven was singing in unison. He joined them again, praising his Lord wholeheartedly.

———

Jason was lost in his rapture, and what seemed like minutes had turned into hours, until—unexpectedly—it stopped, and the people and angels dispersed.

Tolman nodded towards Jason and smiled, "Come!"

As Jason and Tolman meandered along a glorious, glistening gemstone pathway, he saw more flowers, fields, and mountains. He could see a magnificent temple in the distance and as they came closer, the gemstone path became pure gold.

They passed a beautiful still pond where he could see multicolored fish singing and moving in harmony with their songs. As they continued towards the temple, Jason became more nervous and felt himself weakening.

Tolman noticed and veered off to the side of the path towards a blossoming tree and picked a purple, yellow and red-colored fruit. It looked like a ball of shimmering glass, constantly changing colors and hues. He handed it to Jason.

"Eat. It will strengthen you." Tolman stated.

As Jason bit into the soft flesh, the most amazing sensation occurred throughout his body. The taste was exquisite, like a fuse of honeycomb, chocolate and strawberries. He could feel a tingling sensation start from his tongue and move down to his toes. He abruptly felt a surge of strength throughout his body.

"Wow! That is amazing. Can I have another?"

Tolman smiled, walked over, picked another and handed it to Jason. He eagerly ate it, feeling the burst of strength increasing.

"Come, we must keep going." Tolman smiled as he turned towards the temple.

. . .

In the early hours of the morning, Ryan and Chance hurried into Olivia's room.

"Oh Liv," Chance said as she rushed over and hugged her in tears.

Olivia bawled as her friend held her. "Why? We have just started our life together. Why did God let him die?"

Ryan put his hand on hers to comfort her. Tears flowed freely from the three of them. They spoke no words... for there were none to say.

As Jason and Tolman continued to walk towards the temple, Jason tuned in to the calming, rhythmic, soft padding noise of Tolman's paws and the clicking of his silver claws on the golden path.

He looked around, taking in the amazing surrounds, watching other people sitting under trees, eating the fruit, swimming and diving in the water, and casually walking or sitting reading books.

This is magnificent, Jason thought... *and this is home.*

As they neared the temple, Jason looked in awe as they walked through the massive gates. They continued past the large stone pillars, and then he noticed a figure about 40 feet away talking to someone. He knew in his soul that it was the King. His heart skipped a beat as he looked at Jesus for the very first time.

CHAPTER SIXTY-EIGHT

"How are you doing, Olivia? Do you want to take something?" A doctor on duty came in to check on her.

"No, I don't want a sedation if that's what you mean," she paused. "But… could I please see him?"

"Do you think that's wise… right now?"

"Yes, I want to see him. To see for myself. I still—well, I can't believe it."

"Okay, if you feel that's what you need to do."

"Yes, I do… I really need to," she sobbed.

"Alright, I will arrange it for you."

"Olivia!" Sister Marguerite came rushing to her bedside.

"Oh, Sister Marguerite." A new well of tears started gushing as she held on tightly to her surrogate mother. "It's so unfair—unfair!" she exclaimed in anguish, her head buried deep into Sister Marguerite's shoulder.

"I know, honey… I know!" Sister Marguerite soothed as she held her close.

. . .

Jason saw Jesus in the distance wearing a white flowing, shimmering garment. It looked as though it was dripping with diamonds. He had medium length hair and a neat, short, clean-cut beard. He looked like a regular person, but Jason could feel the intense love, peace and power emanating from his King.

Jason stopped. He felt his body growing weak again and his knees trembling as Jesus walked closer towards them. He could see Jesus' welcoming smile radiating the love that he had for him.

Ryan, Chance, Olivia, and Sister Marguerite stood behind the glass frame of the viewing room in the morgue and looked at the lifeless body of Doctor Jason Miller. Placed on the gurney, his pale, cold skin marred his handsome features.

Olivia wept. Deep gasps started to erupt and explode from the pit of her stomach as she buckled over and put both hands to her mouth. "Can I please go in and see him?" she muffled to the attendant.

The attendant opened the door, and they all went in and stood around Jason's motionless body.

Olivia placed her hand on Jason's. "Oh Jase, why?... I love you so much. We're supposed to spend the rest of our days together," she said, as fresh tears fell. "I don't want you to leave me. I need you here." She cried out desperately. Then abruptly she paused, took a deep breath to gain courage, and wiped away a tear. "We have a baby girl," she smiled proudly. "But I can't be without you." She burst into tears again.

Ryan gently put his arm around her, and Sister Marguerite squeezed her hand tightly. They stood in solace as Olivia continued to speak her heart to Jason's lifeless body and pour out her grief.

The King stood in front of Jason. His eyes were powerful and bore right into the core of Jason's soul, and without notice, Jason fell to his knees in worship. The glory and the power of Jesus were so overwhelming that he could not stand. He felt euphoric to be in His presence and laughed with joy and relief as he kneeled, looking upward before his Lord.

Tolman also took this moment and bowed down low in reverence.

Jesus smiled and reached out with his hand to take Jason's, helping him stand to his feet.

"Jason!" His voice smooth like silk, but with power and strength. "Well done, good and faithful servant." Jesus smiled. "You have fulfilled what I called you to do." He stated with a beaming grin.

At the power of His voice, the words penetrated throughout Jason's being, and he trembled and nearly fell to his knees again. Jesus laughed and hung onto his hand to steady him.

"My Lord, I am so honored to be here. Thank you! Thank you so much for giving me a second chance and thank you for what you did for me, for all of us, the sacrifice that you made."

"My pleasure… and I would do it all again if I had to."

As Jason looked upon Jesus's face and the love that radiated from him, he knew this to be true.

"I'm proud of you, Jason—what you have achieved, the message you have spread—it is exactly what I wanted you to do. You have fulfilled your purpose well."

"Thank you…" Jason felt overwhelmed, and also embarrassed, for who was he to be thanked by the King? "But I couldn't have done it without you."

"Through me all things are possible. However, a person's will can impede my desires. But your yearning Jason was to finish your race… and for that I will reward you." Jesus smiled.

Jason couldn't believe it. Here he was standing before the King of Kings and Lord of Lords—Jesus—and He was thanking him. Overwhelmed, he dropped to his knees again and bowed in gratitude. "I am absolutely nothing compared to you," his words barely audible.

"Jason, you are my beloved, with whom I am well pleased. Arise and walk with me for I have great things to show you." Jesus extended his hand to help Jason to his feet again. And as he did, he saw the deep scars from the nails that were driven into his flesh on his crucifixion. Before Jason's thoughts had formed, Jesus spoke.

"These are a reminder of what was done, the payment for sin and death." He smiled, then started walking towards the gates.

Jason stood unmovable, mesmerized by his Lord.

Jesus stopped and looked back. "Are you coming?" he grinned.

Jason hurried after him and stepped in beside him and Tolman slowly meandered behind at a slight distance.

OLIVIA REMAINED BESIDE JASON'S COLD, PALE BODY. SHE HAD POURED OUT her heart. Her sorrows and fears of a future without him. She stood in silence, but the turmoil and heart-wrenching sorrow were staggering. Her pain was tangible. Her heart ached and longed to hold her husband again, and the tears fell like diamonds leaving long shimmering streaks down her cheeks.

Unseen beside her stood two large angels. One had a wing wrapped around her tenderly. Both had a hand on her shoulder as they comforted her in her grief.

"I WANT TO SHOW YOU A FEW THINGS." JESUS SAID AS HE WALKED ALONG another golden path around the temple grounds. He pointed proudly to the snow on the peaks. "There is my father's storehouse of snow."

Jason looked towards the peaks and saw the white and silver glimmers. The verse from Job 38 suddenly came to his mind. He could see the writing instantly passing through his brain. 'Have you entered the storehouses of the snow or seen the storehouses of the hail…' he looked upon the snow caps in awe as he continued to follow Jesus towards a large door on the side of the temple.

Jesus opened it and beckoned Jason to enter.

As Jason walked in, he stopped short in wonder at the enormity of the space. There were thousands of books—rows and rows of them on the shelves, and a few encased in clear crystal glass boxes sitting on their own tables.

As Jason looked around, he saw three large golden books in the middle of the room sitting on pillars. There, beside the books, were three massive golden angels that stood at least 15 feet tall. Their enormous, magnificent feathered wings shimmered and shone various hues of gold, and in front of them were two smaller golden angels that were three feet tall. The smaller did not have any wings but held large golden pens. They were busily writing in two of the books whilst the larger winged angels stood and watched closely.

Jesus walked over to the book in the middle and nodded politely towards a smaller angel. The angel turned to a specific page in the book.

"This is the Book of Life, Jason. Look!" Jesus motioned for Jason to come and see.

Jason walked over, staring at the angels before him. He then peered at the writing on the page. At first, he couldn't understand it, as it was written in characters. But then swiftly the characters reformed and he could comprehend the words. He saw his name written.

Jason William Miller.

He was awestruck. "I'm in the book." He looked at Jesus, relieved.

"Yes!" Jesus smiled.

Jason re-read his name again. The letters stood out as if they were three-dimensional, shining brightly and rising upward for him to see. He scanned the page, but only could make out his own name. Quickly, he saw three names disappear. He glanced at the angel and it expressed sadness as it spoke.

"The Lord God says in Revelation 3:5, 'The one who is victorious will, like them, be dressed in white. I will never blot out the name of that person from the Book of Life, but will acknowledge that name before my Father and his angels.' "

Jason instantly remembered what Ryan had told him about people losing their salvation. Again, he felt honor and relief to be standing in Heaven.

Jesus thanked the smaller angel, then faced Jason. "I promised that I would never leave them… but I never said that they could not leave me."

Jesus then stepped to the left in front of another book and motioned to the small angel to open it. The angel did as requested, and Jesus motioned to Jason to look.

Again, the characters transformed into words that he could understand. He started to read, and it was an account of his life, his very own story. He read in amazement the very words he had spoken, thoughts and motives on every single day of his life. The book was a record of *absolutely* everything.

Jason continued to read. He read about his childhood, his teenage years—every single word that he had spoken, or thought, was written. He looked at the angel as it spoke.

"The Lord God says in Revelation 20:12, 'And I saw the dead, great and small, standing before the throne, and books were opened. Another book was opened, which is the book of life. The dead were judged according to what they had done as recorded in the books.'" As the angel spoke, a rumbling sound began, and the temple shook. The angel continued. "The Lord God says, in Matthew 12:36, 'But I tell you that everyone will have to give account on the day of judgment for every empty word they have spoken.'"

Jason looked concerned.

Jesus placed his hand on Jason's shoulder to reassure him, "Those who are mine, their sins are forgotten and they will remain with me, but their words, thoughts and motives have been recorded. On that Day, these will be put through fire, tested and assessed."

Jason stepped back and looked at Jesus. He noticed he had surprisingly gone solemn. "I am not looking forward to the day that I have to sit in judgment and tell those who are not mine to depart from me... forever."

CHAPTER SIXTY-NINE

Olivia was back in her room. Her newborn was in the nursery and she was in solitude. She prayed a meek and despondent prayer.

"God, I don't understand," she sighed. "But... I will still follow and love you all the days of my life." Her tears fell, trickling down her cheeks, sparkling like small gems.

An angel placed a hand on her shoulder in comfort.

"Please God, please help me get through this," she sobbed. Her heart felt like it had shattered into a million pieces, her body ached, her head was heavy, and her emotions drained. She buried her face back into the pillow and wept herself to sleep.

Late that night, Ryan and Chance sat at home on the lounge sipping hot chocolate. They spoke no words. Their hearts were solemn as they sat in silence, struggling with their own thoughts of sorrow, disappointment, and confusion. They had lost their friend, and their hearts ached boundlessly.

Jason peered at the third large golden book positioned at the end.

"That one is the Bible." Jesus said proudly.

Jason walked over towards it and lay his hand gently upon it in reverence. He closed his eyes as he felt it pulsating through his core—it was alive and active.

Jesus smiled. "Come, I have more to show you."

Jason followed Him through the room, and Jesus pointed to a large shelf full of books. Some looked like clear glass with only a very faint outline, some were solid gray and then there were others glowing a solid white.

As he looked, he saw the books change before his eyes from clear to gray, then some from gray to solid, glowing white with gold writing for the author and title. They were gradually changing and appearing sporadically all over the shelf.

"These are my Father's children's books. They are His inspired books that you are seeing being written and published right now on earth. The ones that are merely outlines are His ideas that are just forming in the person's mind. The solid gray ones are those that are being written, and the glowing white are the ones that are complete, published and being read. These books help further my Kingdom and help people grow in knowing me. Look over there." Jesus pointed.

Jason looked to where Jesus showed him, and he saw the row of crystal boxes he noticed when he first entered the room. Each box contained one to several books.

"These books are the ones anointed by God. His children have listened to His heart and have written books so powerful that he protects them day and night."

Jason watched and saw the lid of one crystal box open. Then a book inside opened and a flurry of tiny blue birds and purple butterfly-type creatures fluttered out, each with symbols imprinted on them. They formed a swirl and disappeared out a window. The book closed, and so did the crystal lid.

Jason stood in astonishment, and before he spoke, Jesus answered.

"What you just saw are the anointed words heading to earth to touch the souls who read that book."

As Jason looked at the row of crystal boxes, he saw one standing out and glowing brighter; it was vibrating lively and beckoning to him.

Jason walked over towards it. As he stood over it, the crystal became clearer so he could read the golden writing on the single book inside.

Jason looked over at Jesus with a beaming smile. "That's mine."

Jesus smiled back. "You have touched so many lives already with this book, Jason. Thank you for taking the time and giving your testimony—it has bought truth into the world, impacted souls and advanced my Kingdom."

As Jesus was speaking, the crystal lid opened, then the book, and then a flurry of yellow and gold birds and butterfly creatures swirled around like a mini-whirlwind before heading out of the library window. Jason's heart felt as if it would burst, knowing that he had pleased God.

Jason continued to watch with amazement as crystal lids opened randomly and colorful creatures swirled outward and disappeared.

OLIVIA ATE HER BREAKFAST IN SILENCE. HER NEWBORN BABY GIRL LAY IN A basinet beside her bed, fast asleep. The toast, eggs, and juice seemed taste-less as she forced herself to eat. She wasn't hungry, but the nurse had directed her to eat for the sake of her health. She chewed and swallowed motionlessly… routinely. The numbness was overwhelming. The repetitive thoughts of Jason and the life that they had planned together continued to play in her mind. The grief was crushing as she stared listlessly into space.

A male attendant entered the room.

"Mrs. Miller, I'm sorry to do this so soon… but we have to move the… ah," he fumbled. "Dr. Miller."

She snapped out of her vacant stare. "What do you mean, move him?"

"I'm sorry, ma'am, but we need to move him to the city morgue. The coroner would like to examine him today, and I need your consent to conduct the autopsy and release him to the city morgue."

"Oh… that is soon." She sat processing it for a few seconds, not wanting Jason to be so far away from her… even though he was, she thought.

The attendant could see Olivia's distress. "Um, do you want me to leave the documents with you? I can come back if you like?"

"No… I understand," she managed with courage, tears forming in her eyes as she took the pen and signed the paperwork.

"Thank you, ma'am… and ah… I'm so sorry about your loss," he said genuinely.

"Yeah…" she said distantly. "Me too," and gave him the pen.

He hurried out of the room.

She startled as the phone beside her rang, snapping her out of her empty thoughts. The baby gently stirred but kept sleeping.

"Hello," she said listlessly.

"Liv, it's Chance. I was checking in to see how you are."

"I'm okay… I didn't sleep much last night." She said robotically and vaguely.

"Can we come over this morning?"

"Sure."

"We will see you around 10am."

"Okay, bye," she said apathetically, then hung up.

"Oh Ryan," Chance looked at her husband with tears welling. "She sounds terrible."

Ryan pulled her in close and hugged her. "I know." He soothed, as his own heart was breaking.

CHAPTER SEVENTY

JESUS WATCHED JASON'S AWESTRUCK FACE AS HE STOOD IN THE LIBRARY looking around.

"I have something else I would like to show you." Jesus motioned and as they walked towards another door, Jason turned and took a long look at the massive room once again.

The small angels were back busily writing in the books and three large angels slowly nodded in acknowledgement to him and smiled.

Jesus walked through a large silver door into a dimly lit room with large, velvety, shimmering pearl colored theater chairs. He gestured for Jason to sit. When they both had settled in, a three-dimensional vision appeared in front of them.

In the vision, there were hundreds of children smiling, crawling, and wandering around laughing with joy.

A little one-year-old boy walked towards Jason, reached out, and took his hand. He looked directly into Jason's eyes and, without speaking, the child's thoughts projected into his mind. "Thank you, Jason," the little boy smiled, then turned and merged back into the crowd of other children.

Another child, a tiny little girl, came up to him and kissed him on the cheek. He heard her thoughts. "My name is Fay. Thank you for my life. I'm going to be a Sunday school teacher and influence an entire community for Jesus."

Another little boy came up and hugged him. "Thank you, Jason, for helping me live. My name is Bill and I will be a successful dairy farmer and finance the Kingdom."

Then, another child tottered towards him and touched his cheek softly. "My name is Paul. I will foster many children and teach them about Jesus."

This lasted for ten minutes. Children of all cultures and colors reached out to him and spoke into his mind.

Jason's eyes pooled, the tears softly trailed down his cheeks, for he knew in his heart who these children were.

"Yes Jason," Jesus smiled. "These are the ones... the souls saved by the changes you have made across the nation... the ones that would have been terminated. This is what's happening on earth. Those children are alive and real—they are asleep, dreaming of you and this event right now." Jesus beamed excitedly.

Jason could feel how proud He was of him. He peered back at the vision with all the children smiling at him and realized how different this experience was two years prior. He let out a sigh of satisfaction and smiled back at his King, who had tears of joy in his eyes.

"WE'VE GOT THE RELEASE PAPERS FOR DR. MILLER," THE MALE attendant said as he strode into the mortuary cool room.

"That's great, Sam," a female mortuary assistant said as she was busy filling out more documents. "I can't believe the night we've had—it's been crazy. We had 23 bodies admitted last night, and with already having 11 in here, I can't fit any more in... Nobody else better die today," she said, trying to lighten her stress.

"Gees, what was it... a murder spree last night?"

She laughed, "Na, not that dramatic. It was a bus accident on 4th and 7th."

"Well, here is the paperwork for Dr. Miller. I'll get the remaining bodies' release signatures for you."

"Thanks, Sam—you're a gem." She smiled as she walked over to the cooler and pulled open the drawer that housed Jason's body.

"I'm sorry Dr. Miller that I have to move you this soon," she said as she pulled on the rack and his body came out. "I don't think this one will be hard for the coroner—an obvious gunshot wound to your chest," she said as she studied Jason's wound, "Your poor wife," she sighed, "now all alone to bring up that baby girl," she mumbled as she prepped Jason's body for the move. "You turned out to be a good man, Dr. Miller."

OLIVIA WATCHED AS A GIGANTIC BUNCH OF FLOWERS CAME THROUGH HER door carried by Ryan, with Chance following behind with a pink wrapped present. She tried to smile, but the sadness she felt had marred the joyful celebration.

"Good morning, beautiful." Chance said as she leaned over and kissed Olivia on her cheek.

Ryan did the same. "How are you feeling?"

"Not great," she responded with sad eyes.

"I know," Chance responded.

"I'll get a vase to put these in." Ryan wandered off towards the nurse's station.

Chance pulled up a chair beside Olivia and looked over at the baby asleep in the crib. "She is so gorgeous, Liv."

"I know." She looked over and touched her tiny hand and smiled.

"Have you named her yet?"

"No, it doesn't feel right without Jase," her eyes pooled. "We talked about naming the baby Faith if it was a girl... but—" she choked with tears. "It doesn't feel like it fits now."

"Don't worry. It will come to you." Chance gently held her hand.

Ryan came back and pulled up a chair beside the baby. "She is so cute," he smiled, trying to push past the sorrow that he felt to remain strong. His cell suddenly buzzed. "It's Dennis!" He stood and walked out of the room.

Olivia spoke softly, "I had to sign paperwork for the coroner this morning. They have to move him to the city morgue..." she sniffled, "I know it's strange, but I don't want him moved, it's as though whilst he is in this hospital, somehow it feels like he is still with me." She cried. "I just want to wake up from this nightmare. This should be our time to celebrate." She cracked, her face etched with pain as she sobbed again. Chance held her tight as they both cried together, soothing each other's grief.

"Dennis!" Ryan said as he answered his phone in the hospital's hallway.

"I just heard the news—the warden called me into his office this morning to tell me. Gees, I can't believe it."

"I know, me neither... it's tragic."

"How's Olivia doing?"

"Not good, but I wouldn't expect anything different."

Ryan could hear Dennis sigh. "I still don't get it, you know—such a great guy. Why now?"

"I don't know... I don't understand it either."

"Can't you pray for him, like you did the first time?"

Ryan sighed. "I wish my faith was strong now, but I feel so distraught myself... you know... I've lost my best friend and—" he choked, "it feels hard to even utter a prayer right now."

"Yeah... I know. It's cut me."

Ryan paused in reflection before he spoke again. "I saw him in the morgue yesterday. It was horrible to see him like that. It just reinforced that he is really gone."

"I know exactly how you feel. I've had to deal with the grief of losing someone close." Dennis paused. "But I didn't know God back then. So, I will not let this deter me." He felt a fire rising inside him. "I will pray for a miracle, Ryan. I'll rally the guys here anyway and we will pray for the miraculous to happen."

"Thanks, Dennis."

JESUS GOT UP FROM HIS CHAIR. "LET'S WALK OUTSIDE."

Jason followed through another door and saw Tolman waiting under a large tree with an ornate stone bench seat underneath. As he stepped outside, he again marveled at the grounds. They were extraordinary—the colors of the flowers and the trees were spectacular.

Jesus strolled towards the bench and sat down. He motioned for Jason to do the same.

. . .

Sister Marguerite entered the room and gave both Olivia and Chance a warm hug. "How are you today, my child?" She placed her hand on Olivia's.

Olivia's eyes met hers, and without words, the tears tumbled. The three of them sat in silence together and cried.

Dennis quickly ran to the exercise pen and went up to each of the guys in the study group telling them to come to the main hall.

Ryan walked back to Olivia's hospital room.

"How is he?" Olivia asked.

"Shocked, upset… like all of us." They sat in silence for a few seconds. Ryan shifted awkwardly and then spoke. "He wants to pray for Jason to… ah… come back to life… like he did the first time." He shifted nervously again in his seat, not knowing how Olivia would react to that suggestion.

"Well, why not? It worked the first time." Olivia responded with an unexpected hope.

Chance noticed the optimism in Olivia's eyes and looked over at Ryan.

"Okay, then let's do it." Ryan said boldly.

"Oh, but do we have to be there with him?" Olivia asked.

"I don't think so," Sister Marguerite said. "The power of God will work anywhere, honey." She squeezed Olivia's hand.

"Okay, let's begin then." Chance said eagerly.

Ryan started off. "Dear Father, you did a miracle before with Jason, we ask you do it again…" they each took turns and continued to pray.

Their fervent prayers went unseen by human eyes, but in the spiritual realm they were like colorful ribbons, floating upward into the outer dimensions, and as always…

God was listening.

CHAPTER SEVENTY-ONE

"JASON, WHEN YOU WERE IN THE OUTER REALM LAST TIME, YOU WANTED TO enter Heaven, remember?" Jesus asked.

"Yes, I didn't want to go back... I *never* want to leave this place," he stated adamantly.

"Well, we didn't give you a choice, then. Your orders were to return and I'm so glad you did because look at the impact it's had."

Jason pondered at the statement. *If it wasn't for God's plan to intervene, and Ryan's faithful prayer, he would still be tormented in Hell.* He shivered at how close he had come to spending his eternity there.

Jesus knew his thoughts. "You're right. If it wasn't for my plan to restore your life, along with Ryan's obedience to the Holy Spirit's prompting, you would still be there. And, if you hadn't repented, you would have returned there. So, we actually gave you a choice. Tolman showed you the gravity of what you had done... but you still had a choice... to ignore or to repent. You chose wisely." Jesus smiled warmly and put his hand on his shoulder.

Jason sat silently, reliving the moments of the first time he met Tolman.

"Do you know that you have a daughter?" Jesus beamed widely.

"No! Oh, wow! I didn't... is she... I mean, are they all right?" Jason had been in such awe of where he was that he hadn't given any thought to where he had come from.

"Yes, they are both healthy—but Olivia is heartbroken that you are not there with her to enjoy the moment."

"Oh," Jason suddenly became somber. "Will they be okay?"

"They will. Olivia is strong in her faith, and she has good friends to support her. She will pick up the pieces and continue with her life… in time."

Jason sat in silence with divergent feelings. He felt joy and relief to be here but now also conflicted that he had left Olivia and his baby girl back home.

"OKAY GUYS, I'VE GOT SOME REAL SAD NEWS… SOMEONE MURDERED OUR buddy Jason last night." Dennis announced to the prayer group.

"What? How?" Benny responded with grief on his face. Others gasped.

"A guy that he fired shot him." Dennis stated.

"Oh man, not Jase… what about his wife?" someone else asked.

"Olivia is in hospital. She just delivered their baby girl."

The 53 men in the group were stunned and silent.

Dennis continued. "Now, as you all know, God did it before, so I'm gonna ask Him to do it again. I think we should pray for Jason to have his life restored."

"Yeah, now we're talkin. I'm in." Benny stated excitedly.

"Awesome, let's do it." Dennis said, and the group all gave a clap and cheered.

CHANCE PRAYED. "GOD, I THANK YOU FOR YOUR RESURRECTION POWER. We pray you raise Jason from the dead now in the name of Jesus."

JASON SAT ON THE BENCH, AND JESUS MOTIONED TO TOLMAN. TOLMAN unfolded his giant feathered wings, and an image appeared. It was Olivia and his newborn daughter in the hospital room.

·   ·   ·

DENNIS PRAYED. "JESUS, WE THANK YOU FOR THE BLOOD THAT YOU SHED for us on the cross. That you conquered death and the grave, and we ask right now that your healing power comes over Jason's body and restores back his earthly life. I ask Lord God that you bring him back to us."

JASON GASPED AT THE VISION BEFORE HIM, AND TEARS OF JOY WELLED IN his eyes. "She is so beautiful!" his heart pounded and he could feel the love emanate for this little soul.

Jesus smiled. "Yes, she is! My Father has created a real cutie," he winked.

Jason chuckled. "He sure has." His heart was bursting.

"HALLELUJAH, JESUS. YOU ARE THE NAME ABOVE ALL NAMES, THE KING OF Kings and the Lord of Lords," Ryan praised. "Father, your word in Matthew 10:8 says for us to go out and heal the sick, raise the dead. So, we come to you, Lord, and ask you to raise Jason back to life. To restore him back to us and his family."

TOLMAN FOLDED HIS WINGS BACK, AND THE VISION WAS OVER.

Jesus faced Jason and his expression became serious. "Jason, I will now give you a choice."

"A choice?"

"Yes, you weren't given one last time. You *had* to return. However, this time I will honor what you have done for me... and this time, I will give you a choice."

"What kind of choice?"

"The choice to stay here with us... or to return to your family."

Jason was aghast. "You mean... I can return if I want to?"

"I will grant you that... if that is your desire."

Jason sat and looked around at his surroundings. The peace and love that he felt was incredible, he had no words to describe. He was home. He was where he belonged with his Creator to worship for eternity. His heart tugged at him as he looked around at the heavenly grounds. The pull to remain here was powerful, and he knew in his heart that he never wanted to leave... that he wanted to stay here...

forever.

CHAPTER SEVENTY-TWO

BENNY PRAYED, "THANK YOU GOD FOR WHAT JASON HAS DONE, HELPING us come to know you. We ask that your Spirit breathes upon him and restores his life, so his baby girl can have a father and Olivia can have a husband."

"I DON'T WANT TO RETURN!" JASON REPLIED ADAMANTLY. "I DON'T WANT to ever leave Heaven. This is my home!" He looked around at the beautiful surrounds, feeling the love and peace enveloping him. The thought of returning to all the pain and suffering on earth made him even more resolute in his decision to stay... but then one final thought slipped into his conscious... "Will they be all right without me?"

"I will look after them, Jason. I promise I will never leave them or forsake them. They will be fine... anyway... their earthly life is just a vapor compared to eternity."

OLIVIA PRAYED. "GOD, PLEASE TELL JASON THAT I LOVE HIM, THAT I understand if he does not want to return to me because he is with you and he is home. But I ask that you tell him one thing—tell him I promise only to love him twice... that is now... and forever."

. . .

Jason was silent, his emotions pondering what Jesus had just said. Something was resonating in his heart… *life is just a vapor.* The words Jesus just spoke repeated in his mind, *Eternity… life is just a vapor compared to eternity.* His mind continued to contemplate. His earthly time in life was nothing compared to the time he would spend in eternity… here.

Suddenly, images appeared in his mind of Olivia and him holding hands, her beautiful smile. Taking their daughter to the zoo and seeing her excitement when she saw a monkey or giraffe for the first time. Birthday parties in the backyard, playing on the swing set, her first ride on a bike or a pony.

Unexpectedly, he had an urge come over him—a yearning rushed through him like a gushing waterfall flowing over him—he didn't want to abandon them or have his daughter miss out on a father, or Olivia not have a husband.

This earthly life was absolutely nothing compared to eternity, he thought. *It was just a vapor… So why wouldn't I return?* He was just about to speak when he heard Olivia's voice break through the realm.

"Tell him I promise only to love him twice… that is now… and forever."

Jason's heart burst with emotion, and his voice filled with urgency. "I *need* to return! I *want* to return—to be with Olivia and raise my little girl. I don't want to miss out on making all those memories. You're right, our life is just a vapor and is absolutely *nothing* compared to eternity — Jesus," he gulped. "I want to be back home with my family and continue to do what you called me to do."

Jesus smiled knowingly. "I knew you would make the right choice."

The mortuary attendant had wheeled Jason's body into another room amongst four other bodies that were awaiting pickup. She was busy filling out documents for each of them.

"Hi, Shirl."

She looked up. "Hey Ralph, how you doin?"

"Yeah, I'm good. Every day above ground is a great day." He chuckled.

"I'll say," she smiled. "Who you here for?"

"Um," he flipped a page on his clipboard, "I'm here to pick up a…" he scanned his paperwork. "Dr. Jason Miller."

"Yep, got him prepped. I just need to check his file and I'll hand him over to you."

DENNIS AND THE OTHERS CONTINUED TO PRAY. "LORD, PLEASE RETURN our brother's life. For the sake of his family, we request you bring him back."

JASON SAW ADURI TEN FEET AWAY, WAITING PATIENTLY.

"I'll sure miss this place." Jason said with a feeling of loss in his voice.

"I will always be with you, and you will return. Besides, you have made the right choice—there is so much more you can achieve by going back, so many more souls that your testimony will touch and save." Jesus winked.

Suddenly, Jason could see a vision inside the library. It was of the crystal box that held his first book. Already, an outline of another book had formed, and Jason knew exactly what he would write.

"I'm glad you have chosen to return." Jesus smiled.

"RALPH, CAN YOU PLEASE SIGN THESE WHILE I CHECK THE Pronouncement of Death form?" Shirl handed Ralph the release papers and he signed to accept Jason's body for transport.

Shirl rechecked the form to ensure it was complete and signed off by the physician. "Okay, they look like they're in order. I think you're good to take him."

CHAPTER SEVENTY-THREE

"I'm ready." Jason stated with eagerness, then quickly had a thought. "Except... this time, could I please have my body *completely* healed... that was terrible last time."

Jesus chuckled. "Yes, I know *exactly* how you felt." He smiled. "Of course... your body will be fully restored."

"I hope to see you soon, my friend," Tolman said and laid his massive white paw on his shoulder. "Well, actually not too soon—I hope."

They all laughed.

Ardie came bounding up to Jason, as if he knew his friend was leaving... again.

"It's okay, bud. I will return and next time we will never be apart." He bent down and hugged his old companion.

"One more thing Jason," Jesus said. "Tell my people that I am coming soon. Tell them to be prepared, because it's sooner than they think."

"I will!"

"Are you ready?" Jesus asked.

"I think so."

"Goodbye, Jason," Tolman nodded, his opalescent canines glistened as he smiled warmly.

"Remember... I will never leave you, Jason. Keep fulfilling your purpose." Jesus' eyes shone with love as Aduri stepped forward to take Jason by his hand.

RYAN, CHANCE, OLIVIA, AND SISTER MARGUERITE WERE SINGING WORSHIP songs in the room. The hospital staff peered in occasionally, some rolling their eyes and walking away, others watching curiously, feeling peace surrounding them.

RALPH WHEELED JASON'S BODY OUT OF THE COOLER ROOM AND DOWN THE hallway towards the exit. Shirl was casually walking beside him, then stopped with a wave of realization.

"Oh, shoot! Ralph, hang on. I forgot the autopsy consent papers," Shirl said as she ran back down the hallway.

JASON FELT THE RUSH AGAIN AS HE HELD ADURI'S HAND. HE LOOKED AT Jesus, Tolman and Ardie standing quietly as they lifted off at a gentle pace. Then Aduri looked into Jason's eyes with a gleam of mischief and spoke. "You want a ride you'll never forget?"

Jason's eyes widened at hearing Aduri speak for the first time. "Heck, yeah." He beamed with excitement.

Aduri took off at a speed Jason had not felt before, he started looping into a vertical roll, twisting and somersaulting, and Jason felt like he was pulling constant negative Gs.

Aduri took Jason on a quick detour to see other sites of the universe, a display of cosmic beauty of nebulas, clusters and formations, of luminous clouds of gas that appeared like rolling hills and mountains. Jason gasped at the beauty and colors—arrays of purple, red, bright white, yellow, orange and blue hues. He looked across at the myriad of stellar activity that felt vibrant and alive, as though they were bursting with joy and singing praises to their Creator.

. . .

Dennis and the group were lifting their voices in praise and worship. The songs drifted upward towards the heavens like rays of multi-colored streamers twisting and furling into the skies.

Angels started dropping in amongst them, glorious beings of light walking around, singing and touching each person in the main hall.

"Sorry, Ralph," Shirl said as she handed him the autopsy consent form. "I don't know where my head is sometimes. It's been a terrible morning with all these bodies to process."

"No worries," Ralph said as they both continued to walk down the hallway, pushing Jason's body on the gurney.

Aduri glanced at Jason and he knew then that they had turned towards earth. They burst through the thermosphere and into the colorful display of the auroras.

Jason could feel changes in the temperature as he descended through the atmospheric layers. He could see the earth and all the countries as if it was a map of the globe, observing Australia, Asia, Russia and the snow-covered land of the Arctic come into clear view.

"I'm not sure if it will work Ryan, maybe it's too late... or maybe God doesn't want him to return... or he doesn't want to come back." Olivia said in tears, her hope waning and desperation showing.

"Keep the faith, Olivia. Let's keep trying. It took over two hours last time. Let's not give up hope." Ryan said, as he could feel the power of the Holy Spirit with them.

Aduri suddenly snapped his wings wide and slowed their descent.

Jason could see the gray roof of the hospital below.

"What time are you on till?" Ralph asked as he wheeled the gurney down the corridor.

"6 p.m. then I'm taking the kids out to dinner. You?"

"This is my last drop off, then me and the missus are heading north for a few days."

"Sounds great," Shirl sighed. "I'd love to get away for a while."

"What do you reckon, boys? Keep singing?" Dennis asked.

"Yeah, let's keep going. The atmosphere is amazing." Benny responded, relishing the peace that enveloped the room.

Aduri looked over at Jason, and he knew it was time. Aduri gently let go of Jason's hand, gave him a wink and once again, Jason felt the experience of free falling.

"I'll get the doors," Shirl said as she hit the large green button to release the bulky double security doors and push them open.

Ralph maneuvered the gurney through the doors.

Olivia praised. "I thank you for your power, Lord God. You can do all things. You can raise the dead to life."

Everyone could feel a mighty presence of God in the room.

LIKE A SHOCK WAVE, JASON FELT HIMSELF ENTER HIS BODY.

"SWEET MOTHER!" SHIRL SCREAMED AS SHE JUMPED BACKWARDS. "RALPH! RALPH!" she pointed at the white body bag containing Jason, her finger and hand trembling, "Did you see that? Did you see that?"

"See what?" Ralph looked to where she was pointing and then around the area in confusion.

"He's moving—I seen him moving!" She stood back wide-eyed with fright, both hands now covering her mouth in fear.

"Come on, Shirl, you've been doing this way too long... HOLY JUMPIN' SMOKES!" Ralph yelled in fright as he jumped backwards in fear.

JASON FELT HIMSELF BACK IN HIS BODY. HE COULD FEEL AND HEAR THE blood pumping through his veins. His heart was pounding loudly but calmly in his ears. He was alive, and he was back in his earthly home.

As Jason moved, he felt the plastic against his face and body, and he could hear someone sobbing in fear right beside him.

"OH MY! Oh my! Oh my!" Shirl was holding her hands to her mouth, shaking and crying.

Ralph was too shocked to say anything and just stared at the moving bag on the gurney.

Jason spoke, "Ah... can someone please unzip me?"

CHAPTER SEVENTY-FOUR

SUDDENLY, THERE WAS A FLURRY OF ACTIVITY AT THE NURSE'S STATION. With hushed whispers and medics running wildly down the hospital corridor. Ryan stopped mid prayer and watched the commotion. He went back to praying, thinking it was a medical emergency.

JASON WAS NOW SITTING UP ON THE GURNEY AND A PHYSICIAN HE KNEW was examining him—taking his blood pressure, listening to his heart, checking his ears and eyes. Jason sat quietly as he let the doctor go through the motions.

"WOW! Jason, you are a miracle," the physician said as he looked at Jason's chest. "Look, you don't even have the open wound anymore, just a small scar from the bullet entry point."

Jason looked down, remembering Jesus' words about a reminder. He knew He'd left it there on purpose. He touched the scar and smiled to himself knowingly.

"Hallelujah Jesus, hallelujah." Shirl said with her arms waving in praise and tears streaking down her cheeks.

"I thought you didn't believe?" Ralph commented.

"I do now, honey… I do now."

. . .

DENNIS AND THE PRAYER GROUP WERE STILL SINGING PRAISES. THE WARDEN and other prison staff members looked on, some sitting, some standing, but all were basking in the peace and love that surrounded them.

A CROWD OF HOSPITAL STAFF HAD NOW FORMED AROUND JASON IN THE corridor next to the morgue.

"Well, for someone who's was pronounced dead, I think you're doing just fine." The physician smiled widely. "I just don't know how I will document this one." He shook his head, "Jase… you're like a cat with nine lives." He grinned happily.

The hospital staff all started cheering and clapping with joy.

SISTER MARGUERITE, OLIVIA, RYAN AND CHANCE STOPPED MID PRAISE when they could hear a commotion, the sound of people laughing and shouting growing louder down the corridor towards their room. They quietened, straining to hear what was going on, when immediately the crowd became hushed, whispering as they slowly walked towards Olivia's room.

AN OVERWHELMING PRESENCE WAS FELT IN THE PRISON AS DENNIS AND THE group continued to praise and worship. Some other prisoners watched, wept and repented, dropping to their knees, asking the Lord into their hearts. The warden sat back in a chair and placed his head in his hands and asked God for forgiveness.

"HELLO, BEAUTIFUL!" JASON SAID TENDERLY, AS HE STEPPED INTO OLIVIA's room.

There was a buzz in the atmosphere as a crowd of hospital staff gathered around as excited, silent onlookers.

Olivia placed her hand on her cheeks. "Oh, my," she squeaked. "Thank you, God," she said as she rushed into his arms.

Jason squeezed her tight, breathing her in as she sobbed with joy and relief.

Jason glanced and saw Aduri standing in the room's corner.

"I just couldn't miss this one," Aduri said with a cheeky grin.

Jason smiled and then embraced Ryan, Chance, and Sister Marguerite.

"Welcome back, buddy. I bet you've got another book to write." Ryan beamed with tears pouring in overwhelming amazement.

Jason grinned but said nothing—his emotions overcame him. He looked over towards the crib and walked towards it. He leaned over, picked up, and held his baby girl for the very first time.

Olivia whispered through her tears of joy. "I haven't named her yet— I couldn't. Faith just didn't suit her."

"No, it doesn't... she's definitely a Grace... God's Grace." He smiled.

Aduri's eyes met with Jason's. He tipped his head and gave him a brilliant smile... unfurled his magnificent white wings... and headed home.

CHAPTER SEVENTY-FIVE

27 YEARS LATER

JASON SAT IN HIS FAVORITE CHAIR ON THE PORCH OF HIS OLD TIMBER LAKE house, looking outward across the smooth still water. The evening sun was dropping and throwing rays of orange and white hues across the sky, then reflecting upon the water like a mirror. He could hear the occasional clutter of dishes being washed and dried in the kitchen and the sporadic laughter from the adults and children housed within. It was peaceful.

"Grandpa?" Billy, his six-year-old grandson, said as the old screen door squeaked open.

"Hey, champ! Come sit with me." Jason patted the seat next to him.

"Grandpa, will you tell me the story of the time you went to Hell and saw the demons?"

"Oh Billy, you know what happened last time. We got a roasting from your Ma and Grandma because of all those nightmares you had. Remember?"

"I know, but I'm much older now… and besides, I'm not scared. I will never go there because Jesus is *always* with me."

EPILOGUE

Ryan and Chance still live in the city. They have four children and one grandchild. Ryan continues to work with the youth and has helped create several other youth centers throughout the country. Ryan also kept his promise to Chance and took her to Paris to celebrate their 10-year anniversary.

The State released Dennis on good behavior after serving only eight years of his 15-year sentence. He's remarried and has three children with his wife, Fiebe. Dennis works with Benny in running several prison ministries across the State and also serves as the Associate Pastor at City Life Church.

Jason continues to work and write. He has six books published about his life, insights and adventures which have touched and changed the hearts of many. He enjoys spending time with Olivia, Grace and his other five children through adoption, and six grandchildren. His clinics continue to expand throughout the nation, and his determination helped change laws to make abortion history. His centers prevented 8.3 million abortions and have now placed over 12.7 million babies into loving homes.

And he hasn't seen Aduri again…

Yet!

PLEASE REVIEW

I hope you enjoyed reading Second Chance as much as I enjoyed writing it. If you liked it, please take a moment to post a review and tell a few friends to help other readers discover it. Reviews are vital for any author... especially new ones. Even just a line or two can make a big difference.

So please review Second Chance.

Also... it's very exciting when I get notified that a new review has arrived —I love reading them and each review has encouraged me greatly. So thank you to those who have taken the time already, as it has spurred me on to keep writing.

There are more books coming... so Follow Me at Amazon and be notified when they are released.

FORGIVEN

This story may have touched your heart in some way, or be stirring thoughts within you. You may be wondering where you would spend eternity if you died right now, or you may be suffering from remorse because of something you've done in the past.

Then know, like Jason and Olivia, there is no sin so great that God will not forgive, and that all you need to do is reach out to Him and ask for His forgiveness. The Bible says in Isaiah 1:18:

> "Come now, let us settle the matter," says the Lord.
> "Though your sins are like scarlet,
> they shall be as white as snow;
> though they are red as crimson,
> they shall be like wool.

I think this says it all to the measure of God's grace and love for us.

If you are already a believer in Christ, then know you are forgiven, and that you are a testament and an overcomer that can help others.

If you don't believe in Jesus but would like to know Him, then read Acts 2:38 below:

And Peter said to them, "Repent [change your old way of thinking, turn from your sinful ways, accept and follow Jesus as the Messiah] and be baptized, each of you, in the name of Jesus Christ because of the forgiveness of your sins; and you will receive the gift of the Holy Spirit. (AMP)

So, what Peter is saying is:
1. Repent of your sins and trust and believe in Jesus as your savior.
2. Be baptized – get water baptized in the name of Jesus - Acts 22:16.
3. Receive the Holy Spirit – Ask God for the Holy Spirit to come and fill you.

Prayer:
Lord Jesus, I confess I am a sinner and I ask for your forgiveness. I believe you are the Son of the living God, that you died for me on the cross, that you bore all my sins and then was raised to life again. I repent of my sins and ask that you cleanse me now from all my sin and fill me with Your Spirit. I trust you to be Lord of my life, and I ask that you help me change and be obedient to Your Will for my life. In Jesus' name, Amen.

Like Ryan explained in chapter 18, this is both an abiding lifestyle and a heart change, deliberately choosing God's ways and not our own. Matt 16:24 says:

Then Jesus said to His disciples, "If anyone wishes to follow Me [as My disciple], he must deny himself [set aside selfish interests], and take up his cross [expressing a willingness to endure whatever may come] and follow Me [believing in Me, conforming to My example in living and, if need be, suffering or perhaps dying because of faith in Me]. (AMP)

If you have decided to follow Christ, then welcome to the family. Spend time reading the Bible, and find a good church family to help you grow in Christ.

Kym

BE A DIFFERENCE MAKER

What can you do to help change society's views on abortion?

Get involved!

There are so many Pro-Life organizations and individuals working hard to change society's views and laws on abortion. Find your nearest one, contact them to see how you can help, pray for them, or support them by volunteering or donating financially.

A great site to visit is CHOICE42.com, a worldwide Christian, anti-abortion organization that's passionate about educating people, and equipping them to make a stand against the inhumanity of abortion. They also provide support to pregnant women, encouraging them to choose life for their babies, along with assisting those who are regretting their past choices.

For those who want to get out of the abortion industry, And Then There Were None (abortionworker.com) is an organization established by Abby Johnson to help those in the abortion industry quit their jobs and find new careers outside of this trade. They've helped over 600 people leave and you can read many of their courageous stories on this website.

Note that although I share the above links with permission from the owners, it does not mean that this is an endorsement for this novel.

Also, if you're in a position of leadership in the church, then teach your congregation the seriousness of this subject. Deliver the message with love… but don't be silent.

Your involvement can make a difference… and save a life.

ABOUT THE AUTHOR

Kym Streat discovered her passion for writing only a few years ago, and with encouragement from her husband, she decided to take a leap of faith and complete her first novel, *The Lie*. From there, the next on the list was to finish *Second Chance*.

Her vision is to create a positive influence through her writing and deliver strong messages of hope, truth and endurance, along with providing stories that are interesting and sometimes challenging.

Kym works in the engineering field during the day, and during the night she escapes all the bureaucracy and formalities and creates her own tranquil world through her writing.

ACKNOWLEDGMENTS

Thank you, Jesus, for giving me the chance to live…. and to write. I'm truly blessed to know you, and for that I am extremely grateful. We get to spend eternity together and it's going to be awesome!

Andrew, thank you! You're the best husband, friend, and encourager. I'm so thankful for your love and confidence in my abilities, especially when I doubt myself and falter. You pick me up and tell me to keep going.

Thank you, Mum, Dad, and Minky for your support. Your love, prayers, and encouragement have helped finish this one… only a few more to go ;).

Nat, my good friend and editor. Thank you so much. You are truly a gem who shines brightly.

And thank you to my furry best friends, the spoodles, Bailey and Clover, whom stay with me late at night while my keyboard taps away… and listen attentively to the beat of the backspace key.

ALSO BY KYM STREAT

THE LIE

ARE YOU READY... OR WILL YOU FALL?

A Christian Spiritual Warfare Suspense Novel.

An unseen conspiracy. A supernatural battle to keep it concealed. The Man who unveils the truth behind the lie... Are you ready or will you fall?

AVAILABLE NOW ONLINE!

www.ingramcontent.com/pod-product-compliance
Lightning Source LLC
Chambersburg PA
CBHW020248120726
47904CB00001B/122